McCormick

sometimes the smallest towns hold the biggest secrets

Raymond R. MANN

"McCormick"

Sometimes the smallest towns hold the biggest secrets

By

Raymond R. Mann

This book is dedicated to my Grand Mother, Evelynn Jean Metzelburg—You inspired me daily to be a better man, and I miss you.

To Jeannie—Even though I'm older, I've always looked up to you.

To Kim—My time at the "Bluff House" made this book possible. Thank you.

To Heidi—Thank you for getting me on track.

Table of Contents

McCormick – Part One

Chapter One: Saturday, August 11, 1956

McCormick, South Carolina, is like most small towns in the south, hot and muggy. It's 8:30 p.m., and Marilynn Franklin dropped two ice cubes into a glass and then added vodka—her favorite drink any time of the year. She made her way past her husband's study, Pastor John Franklin of the McCormick Baptist Church. The ice in her glass clicked as she walked, and John said, "Marilynn is that another glass of lemonade? I sure could use a glass myself. It's a hot one that's for sure."

Marilynn made her way to the screen door that led to a wraparound porch that led to the sidewalk of Oak Street, just a few blocks from the church in which her husband preached the word of God to as many that would listen. The house was part of the arrangement as pastor, but Marilynn didn't care much for the house. It was too big for just two adults and two children. The entire third floor was empty, and the church wouldn't allow the family to rent the rooms.

Lisa Marie, fifteen going on twenty-five, had inherited her luscious body and flowing auburn hair from her paternal grandmother for sure. Marilynn stood at the screen door looking out at her daughter flirting with the Joseph boys, the twins, Mike and Steven, and then Tom, the handsome, rugged boy of about twenty-three, maybe twenty-four. Marilynn noticed he liked to stare at Lisa Marie, and occasionally Tom would adjust his genitals through his Levi jeans.

Marilynn yelled out, "Lisa Marie! Come in, we've got church in the morning."

Lisa Marie looked up at her mother and then back at the boys while twirling her long, auburn hair.

Lisa asked, "So, you're saying we're going to get in this old car, make our way to McCormick Lake, and just swim, nothing more?"

Lisa was no stranger to what the boys wanted; she had given herself to a boy just a few weeks earlier. He was visiting from Texas or Oklahoma; regardless, he was handsome, older than she by a few years, and she enjoyed herself several times during his two weeks in McCormick. Mike and Tom looked at each other. Tom had a look of excitement while Mike wasn't too keen on the idea of taking a fifteen-year-old girl to swimming. Steven, or Lump as he was affectionately called, just looked around, taking peeks at Lisa Marie's breasts while fondling himself through his highwaters.

Tom replied, "Yes, that's what we're saying."

Mike said, "Listen, Lisa Marie, you don't have to go; it's not a big deal."

Lisa Marie looked at Lump and asked, "What's he doing?"

Tom replied, "Oh, he stole a bag of marbles from my dad's hardware store and doesn't want anyone to see them, so he's playing with them in his pocket. He does it all the time."

Lisa smiled at Lump, and Lump smiled back and looked up to the sky mumbling.

"Well, I won't tell anyone, Steven," Lisa Marie said. Calling him, Steven really caused a stir in Lump as he began to twist side to side humming.

Tom replied, "Daddy took them from him and put them right

10

back on the shelf. It's a game they play. Lump may seem stupid to most, but inside that head is a real genius, right Lump?" Tom tussles Lump's hair, and it agitates him and he grunts.

Lisa looked up at her mom who is now standing on the porch about forty feet away. She's nursing that glass, and it's apparent she's losing her patience with Lisa Marie.

Lisa Marie replied, "I don't have a swimsuit, and if I go in to get one, my mother won't let me leave."

Tom answered quickly, "You don't need a swimsuit. It will be dark soon, and no one will see you anyway."

Lisa Marie bites her lower lip. "Okay, let's go. Hurry, get in the car!"

The four quickly get into the old Ford and take off toward McCormick Lake. Marilynn runs toward the speeding car and slaps her hand on the fender, yelling, "Lisa Marie, you get back here now!"

In a bit of anger with a hint of being drunk, Marilynn falls to the concrete, breaking the glass. She began to cry as she stared at the wet spot made by the vodka and ice. The screen door swings open as John Sr. and John Jr. make their way to Marilynn.

"Marilynn, what happened? Where is Lisa Marie?" John asked as he reached down to help his wife to her feet.

"She left with the Joseph boys in that old car for God knows where!" cried Marilynn.

By now the scene had gained some popularity as neighbors had come out to see what the commotion was about. John whispered to his wife, "Come on dear, let's get you inside. I'll take Junior and we'll go looking for Lisa Marie, okay?"

Chapter Two: August 1976, San Francisco State University

As new students made their way to the dorms, Robert Franklin stood in front of his father and mother. Marilynn had tears welling up and John Sr. put his right hand on Robert's left shoulder.

"Son, I'm not sure why you needed to come across the United States to attend college, but we support you, and your mother and I want you to experience the world. Just know that if you ever want to come home…"

Robert interrupted, "Dad, Mom, I know this is a big stretch for you both, but I need this. I have dreams of doing great things, seeing the world, and staying in McCormick wouldn't allow me the opportunities."

John and Marilynn look at each other and smile.

"Robert, your father wanted you to have this." Marilynn reached into her purse and brought out an envelope and handed it to Robert.

"There's $2,500 to help you get started."

"Mom! I can't accept this!" as he tries to hand the money back.

John spoke up, "Son, it's important for you to spend the first few months concentrating on your studies and not worrying about a job."

Robert looked at his parents and began to tear up. Mom joined in, but Dad, he's hiding it pretty well. Robert wrapped his arms around his parents and reminded them how grateful he is, and that he will write as much as he can, and that he loved them.

"Robert, your mother and I better get on the road. We have a few stops on the way home, and the Grand Canyon is one of those stops," John said.

"Gosh, I wish I were going with you."

Marilynn piped up, "Wait, I brought a camera and thought we could get a group picture! Excuse me, young lady!?"

A petite brunette turned to Marilynn.

"Me?"

"Hi, would you mind taking a picture? We live a long way from here, and it would be nice to capture this moment."

"Sure!"

Marilynn stood between her husband and son as the young lady raised the camera. She stopped. "I'm sorry, have we met?" she said, looking right at Robert.

Robert looked at his parents, "No, sorry, I just got here."

"His name is Robert," Marilynn added.

The young lady tilted her head. "Yes, Robert, we had a class together last fall."

Now everyone is confused as Robert replied, "I'm sorry, miss, but I literally just got here. This is my first semester."

"Okay, well, you look like someone I knew. My name is Sara, without an *H*."

Before Robert could reply, John replied, "Well, Sara, without the *H,* maybe you could keep an eye out for our boy; he's never left McCormick County!"

"Dad, please stop, your embarrassing me."

"Where's that?" asked Sara.

John replied, "South Carolina."

Sara looked at the family and shrugged her shoulders, raised the camera, and took a couple of pictures for good measure. She handed the camera to Marilynn and walked away, her bell-bottom pants slapping with each step.

Marilynn watched her walk away and said, "Nice enough girl, but her fashion sense is a bit odd, don't you think?"

No one spoke as Marilynn placed the camera back in her purse and both John and Marilynn hug Robert one more time, and then they turned and headed toward the Buick Estate Wagon, which rode like a dream but drank gas like a camel drinks water, but this car didn't store anything in a hump.

Robert watched as the big car backed out, made a slight turn, and off they went. Marilynn waved out the window, and Robert waved back. He picked up his two suitcases, turned, and made his way toward his dorm.

"Residence Hall!" Robert said out loud.

Just then, a man smacked Robert on the back. "Yes, that's right, Residence Hall!"

This startled Robert, and he dropped one of the suitcases. He turned and looked down to see an Asian man of no more than 5'3", maybe 5'5". This would be his first encounter with anyone other than Caucasians and Blacks. Robert gathered his suitcase once again.

"I'm Jin Chao, resident manager, but please call me Jimmy!"

Robert shuffled the suitcase from his right arm to under his left arm and extended. "I'm Robert Franklin."

"Yes, Robert Franklin, from McCormick, South Carolina, named for Cyrus McCormick, the inventor who founded International Harvester," Jimmy replied.

"Wow, that's…" Before Robert could finish, Jimmy was already talking and told Robert the rules, where his room was, and how to get to student dining. Jimmy just walked away waving his right hand in the air.

Robert made his way to the stairwell at the end of the hall as Jimmy instructed and made his way to the second floor, room 202. Robert opened the door to the corridor and found that the room before him was room 238, which meant his room was at the other end from where he started from and he could have taken the stairs just behind where he and Jimmy spoke minutes ago. Robert shook his head and headed down the long hallway and found room 202. The door was already open, and the room was filled with people. Robert just stood there and stared at everyone, and only then, a man around his age broke through the crowd with right hand extended.

"Hi, I'm Jake Richards, you must be Bobby Franklin?" the man said.

Robert set his bags down and extended his hand. "Hi, it's Robert…"

Jake did some sort of "whatever" expression, put his right arm on Robert's shoulder, and yelled out, "Everyone, please if you will, this is my roommate, Bobby!"

Robert leaned into Jake's right ear. "It's Robert."

"Sure, whatever you say, man," replied Jake.

Then, like a synchronized swim team, everyone yelled,

"Hello Bobby!"

Robert raised his right arm waist high and waved.

A woman pushed her way to Jake and Robert. "Hey, Sara without an *H*—right?" Robert said.

Sara looked at Robert a long while then smacked him in the face.

"So, Robert, why would you lie to your parents and act as if you didn't know me? So, was I just a one-night stand or, in your case, an abusive near-rape encounter!?" Sara said into Robert's right ear.

Robert turned back and stared at Sara with a puzzled look and replied, "Sara, I honestly have no idea what you're talking about. I literally just got here today—the first time I have ever been here—I promise you that. You must have me confused with someone else." Robert had a bit of tremor in his voice, but before Sara could respond, Robert was pulled into a group of fellow students and then more chanting.

Robert looked over his shoulder as he's being dragged away and watched as Sara turned and walked out of the room. Another man yelled into Roberts' ear, "Hey man, don't worry about her; she's known for getting around if you know what I mean."

Robert looked at the man with a puzzled look. After all, he had no idea what some of this meant, especially when it came to girls. Being the son of a preacher can make dating almost impossible, especially since his sister Lisa Marie gave his parents so much grief growing up, and then her death in 1968 really didn't help, so Robert lived a somewhat sheltered life.

The room began to empty after what seemed to be days of

loudness, and people were just sitting, standing, or laying around not doing a whole lot. Robert made his way over to his side of the room and placed both suitcases onto the bed and then opened them. He moved to the end of the bed and to the wardrobe where his clothing would soon hang, and his other items will be placed in drawers or shelved. Just behind him is a washroom as the dorm has communal showers. The restroom allowed for just enough space for his shaving and dental needs.

"Hey, Bobby! Tell me about where you're from?"

Robert looked in the mirror and under his breath reminded Jake, "My name is Robert."

Robert turned around and made his way toward the chair at the desk on his side of the room. He pulled the chair out, and it filled the room with a scraping sound on the tile floor.

"Jake, please, my name is Robert, not Bob, not Bobby, okay?"

Jake threw a hand up as if to discount Robert's request.

"Ok, gosh, don't get your underwear in a bunch! So, tell me about where you're from?"

Robert leaned forward in the chair with his elbows on his legs.

"Well, McCormick is a small town about two hours northwest of Charleston, South Carolina, which is off the Atlantic Ocean, or about 2,700 miles east of where we are. The town was named after..."

Jake interrupted, "What did kids your age do for fun? I mean, the ocean seems fine, but did you ever make the trip?"

Robert leaned back in his chair, "My father took my family

there when I was maybe five or six, I guess. I don't remember it really."

Jake flopped back on his bed, causing the aged springs to creak, and within seconds Jake was snoring, so Robert stood and made his way to the window. Staring out into the lush greenery, he saw Sara standing there, just looking up at him. She raised her right hand as if to wave and suddenly gave Robert the finger. Robert dropped his arm to avoid waving back, turned, and walked away from the window shrugging his shoulders.

As the day began to close, Robert decided to head out for some dinner. He grabbed his jean jacket and walked out into the hallway. He looked both ways and then made his way to the stairway, which was blocked with a sign: "Stairwell Closed For Repair." Robert smiled and said, "Well, Jimmy isn't so bad after all."

Robert walked the long hallway, made it down the stairs skipping steps, and was out the door and into the chilled California air. The salty smell made him smile as he began to navigate the campus looking for food.

Chapter Three: April 1968, Washington DC

As protestors gathered to protest the war in Vietnam, a young Lisa Marie Franklin lay in what some would consider a self-induced coma, but she was truly exhausted, and all she really wanted was some rest and a break from the world. She was coming up on her twenty-seventh birthday in a few months. Her dreams were vivid and colorful, which was a direct result of heroin, the drug of choice among adults her age.

A young man of Lisa Marie's age rolled to his side, reached over to her, and brushed her hair away from her face. He then leaned in to kiss her, but Lisa Marie suddenly woke.

"Hey, man, what are you doing!?" she yelled as she sat up rubbing her arm where she injected her last cocktail.

The man sat up too, put both hands facing away from him onto the floor, and leaned onto them. She had a surprised look as if she had no idea who he was, and really Lisa Marie didn't know this man. They met last night, found a place to crash, shot some dope, and since she was naked from the waist down as was he, they must have made love.

"Lynn, right?" the man asked.

Lisa Marie lifted her head, and with her left hand, she moved her long auburn hair away from her face.

"Yeah, Lynn," she replied. She coughed from phlegm build-up and stood. She looked around for her jeans, socks, and shoes and gathered up her belongings and stumbled to a bathroom.

The house they were in was enormous, and the two were apparently on the second floor. The hallways were large with wood flooring, and there were many doors. Each door she opened was much like the room she left. People sleeping, some naked, some not, but it was clear this was primarily a flop house.

She opened a door that went into a bright bathroom; it was as if she walked into heaven. The room was clean and smelled of lemon. She turned and locked the door. She walked to the bathtub and ran the water until it was hot enough to plug the drain. The plug hung from a small chain that was laid over the spout. She then sat on the toilet waiting for the water to heat up. She stood, turned, and flushed the toilet by pulling a chain that hung from the tank above her. She undressed, found a washcloth and soap, and then slid into the hot bath. The warmth felt terrific, and when the water was high enough, she used her right foot and turned the water off. She bathed, went under the water to soak her hair, and then relaxed as the heat seemed to take away the pain while the steam opened her pores.

Suddenly a knock at the bathroom door.

"Hey, man, who's in there?" a voice asked.

Lisa Marie quickly sat up, which resulted in some water leaving the tub and splashing to the floor. "Ah, give me a minute. I'll be out in a minute!"

She reached to the front of the tub, pulled the drain plug, hung it as it had been, and stood. She reached for the towel and quickly wrapped it around herself. She stepped out of the tub onto the cold tile floor and dried herself vigorously. Again, there was a knock at the door.

Lisa replied with aggravation, "I said give me a minute!"

She dressed without a bra or panties, pulled her belt tight, sat on the toilet again, and put on her socks and shoes. She took her undergarments and shoved them in her purse, walked to the door, and opened it. Three young ladies were staring at her. All three were naked, and it didn't seem to bother them. One girl said, "It's about time. We want to clean up too!"

Lisa Marie pushed her way through the small group and headed toward a large winding staircase. She was about to make the big turn when a voice from above yelled out, "Say, Lynn, where are you going? I thought we liked each other!"

Lisa looked up to see the man she spent the evening with wrapped in a blanket all scruffy and looking lost, staring at her. Lisa Marie kept her pace and made it to the front door and out to the sidewalk.

"Excuse me, sir, what time is it?" Lisa Marie asked a passerby.

The man stopped, pushed his coat sleeve up, and looked right at Lisa Marie's breasts, which were showing through the thin shirt under her floral-patched jean jacket. Lisa Marie caught his gaze and quickly closed her coat and promptly walked away out of pure embarrassment.

The man yelled out, "Don't you want the time, young lady?" He then shook his head and walked away.

Lisa Marie had always drawn attention to herself as she developed larger breasts than women of her size. Being 5'3" with measurements of 36-24-36 made her the talk of all the boys, especially growing up in a small town called McCormick, South Carolina.

The cold spring air caused Lisa Marie to hug herself as she

made her way to Union Station at 50 Massachusetts Avenue, NE, Washington, DC. She had memorized the address from a few days prior—a talent she had acquired growing up listening to her father's sermons every Sunday. Lisa Marie had three feelings come over at once: hunger, needing a fix, and loss. She approached a diner and decided she should eat. The turnstile door leading into the diner required Lisa Marie to use both hands, which left her vulnerable because the coat she had been wearing was too small to button, so her breasts would be exposed so to speak because of the tight shirt underneath. She was in the diner now, and to her surprise, the place was almost empty.

"Hello, miss," a voice said.

Lisa Marie looked down the counter to see a frail old woman standing behind it and behind her was the window to the kitchen where plates of food would be passed through. A man of about fifty-five had his arms crossed resting on the sill and his chin atop his arms. He noticed Lisa Marie right away, and a creepy smile came across his face as he lifted his head to expose his one tooth in that smile.

"Sit anywhere you'd like," said the elderly woman.

Lisa Marie made her way to the end of the diner and out of sight of the pervert in the kitchen. She slid into the booth and stared out the window.

"So, what'll you have?" asked the old woman.

Lisa Marie snapped out of her trance and looked at the woman, "I'd like coffee, two eggs over easy, and rye toast, dry. Oh, and a couple strips of bacon, extra crispy."

The woman wrote down Lisa Marie's order and turned away.

"Ma'am! Do you have grits?" asked Lisa Marie.

Without missing a beat, the woman said, "No, this is Yankee country, and I don't mean baseball." She followed her comment with a laugh that sounded more like static from an old radio, which probably meant she smoked.

Lisa brushed her off and lifted her purse from her side and placed it on the table. She opened it and pulled out a Greyhound bus ticket. She looked at the clock above the kitchen window, glanced at her ticket, did some math in her head, and then relaxed a little. Thumbing through her pocketbook, she found her fix for later, and there was just over $3,000 in the money slot, money she had taken from the church offerings where her father was the head pastor. She knew deep down inside she had done wrong; however, making this trip was far too important, and she needed it, for not knowing was too much to bear.

Chapter Four: August 1976, San Francisco

Jake Richards woke Sunday afternoon, looked over, and saw Robert sitting at his desk reading.

"Hey dude, what time is it?"

Robert paused from his book, looked at his Timex wristwatch, and recited, "It's 13:56."

Jake rolled up onto his elbows with a puzzled look on his face, "What's 13:56?"

Robert paused from his book again, turned, and looked at Jake. "It's military time, which means it's actually—Robert looked at his watch again—1:58 now."

Jake flopped back to the pillow, closed his eyes, and said, "Great! I'm rooming with Sergeant Bobby Franklin!" He then forced himself to a seated position with elbows on his knees and looked up at Robert.

"So, Sarge, did you eat yet?"

Robert marked his page with a bookmark, closed the book, and stood it between his alarm clock and a rock he brought with him from home. He turned to Jake, smiled, and said, "No, as a matter of fact, I haven't."

Jake looked to his left, reached out for his pants and a crusty shirt that was drooped over his desk chair, stood, and slowly dressed. The night before was a bit too much for him, for he had been out of practice. Drinking and partying at home didn't often happen since Jake's parents were somewhat strict and worried about their reputation, so they kept Jake and his siblings under wraps. When Jake returned to school, of course, he wanted to remain cool, which meant partying until wee hours of the morning, and since it was Sunday, he would have time to recoup before class started tomorrow.

Jake put on his shoes, walked over to the bathroom, relieved his bladder without closing the door, which judging by Robert's face, annoyed him. Jake zipped up, turned around, and noticed Robert was looking at him.

"Hey man, I hope you don't have some weird ideas about me!" Jake barked out.

Robert stood and walked toward Jake. "No, Jake, I just found it odd that you didn't close the door before you let loose like that. Your bladder must be the size of a gallon jug!"

Jake laughed and said, "Yeah, right, sorry about that, Sarge," and then he slapped Robert on the back and gave him a little nudge toward the door. Robert looked at his shoulder and thought, gross, he didn't wash his hands. "Do you have a car?" Jake asked.

"No, my parents brought me here, remember?"

Jake stopped, reached into his pocket, pulled out keys, and said, "No worries, my dad gave me a car to drive," and then he started twirling the keys on the index finger of his right hand. The two men made their way down the hallway to the stairwell and out into the August air. The weather here was much different from McCormick.

Robert looked into the sun and said, "Does it ever get hot here?"

Jake laughed, "What, this isn't hot enough for you? It must be at least seventy-four degrees."

Robert looked at Jake, who was still laughing at his question, and said, "We left McCormick on Saturday, August seventeenth at 09:00, and it was already eighty-five degrees, and the humidity was as thick as soup."

Jake stopped suddenly and said, "Are you saying it was already eighty-five degrees and the sun hadn't been up that long? Good God man, what was normal?"

Robert thought about the question and replied, "Well, summertime was always hot and humid. We'd see temps well into the nineties or even one-hundred plus."

They made their way to the student parking lot. Jake still couldn't fathom temperatures that high. They walked up to Jake's car and Robert stood and stared at it. He had never seen anything like it.

"Jake, what is this?"

Jake unlocked his door, slid inside, and reached over to unlock the passenger door. Robert opened the door and about fell into the seat.

"Easy there, old man," said Jake.

Robert was bewildered, to say the least.

Jake put the key in the ignition, pressed the clutch to the floor, and brought the little car to life. It purred like a kitten as Robert looked all around the interior; the black leather went well with the green exterior. It was unlike anything he had ever seen before and was far more exciting than the old Buick he spent the last week in.

"Bobby my friend, this is a 1967 Porsche 911 Targa...blah, blah, blah. This is a car my parents gave me for a twentieth birthday, which was last year. I hate the car, it's too small, and pretentious, but it handles well and gets me to and from. It's essentially a Volkswagen, but much cooler."

Jake slammed the car in reverse and it made a small but quick grinding sound. He let out the clutch and they were off in a flash. Robert thought to himself. He was right; the vehicle did handle very well.

"Jake, what does a vehicle like this cost?"

Jake shrugged in his seat. "I'm not sure. I thought I heard around $6,200 or so."

Robert was astonished but kept his thoughts to himself. His father may have made that amount in a year, maybe a little bit less. A pastor in a small Baptist church in middle South Carolina wasn't driving a Porsche, no way. The Buick belonged to the church as well as the home Robert shared with his family. Robert stared out his window as the city seemed to fly by.

"Sarge, do you like Chinese food?"

Robert turned from the scenery, "I've never had Chinese food."

Jake kept his eyes on the road and began to laugh. The green Porsche whipped into a parking lot and screeched to a stop. Robert moved into the dash and then slammed back against his seat. He then reached up and massaged the back of his neck. Jake slapped Robert on the right knee.

"Come on, my brother, you're going to love this food. It's the best I've had near the school. Don't worry, you can use a fork while learning chopsticks."

Both men exited the little car and entered Hunan's Palace.

The young Asian woman at the hostess stand greeted Jake with a bow followed by a hug. The exchange had a lot of flirting between the two, and Jake turned to Robert. "Chin Lea, this is my friend Bobby. He and I share a dorm room."

Robert extended his right hand, and Chin Lea bowed, which caused Robert to pull back. He did his best to duplicate Chin Lea's bow as Jake put his arm around Robert's shoulder.

"Come on, let's go eat," Jake said as he pushed Robert to follow Chin Lea to their table.

The restaurant was dimly lit and very quiet. The sound of some sort of music came from a radio shelved just above the kitchen door. Robert looked around at the décor, which definitely screamed Asia, and he admired how clean the place was, which reminded him a lot of the diner back home. Lucile's on Main had the best biscuits and gravy anywhere. The menu was enormous, and since Robert had never eaten Chinese food, he had no idea what to order.

"Say, Jake, what do you recommend?"

Jake looked up at Robert, smiled, "Get the General Tso's Chicken…you can't go wrong."

Robert looked over the menu with hopes of finding the dish Jake had suggested. He saw chicken and a few other words that didn't make sense, but he thought what the heck, you only live once. Chin Lea came to the table holding a small pad of paper and a pencil ready to write.

Chapter Five: April 1968, Washington, DC

Lisa Marie stared out the window while waiting for her meal and began to daydream. She recalled a better time in her life, a time when she was fifteen, and all the boys in McCormick noticed her significant maturity from the year before. Lisa Marie then looked down at her breasts. She looked up again just as the old woman walked up to the booth.

"Here you are, young lady. Two eggs scrambled, white toast with butter, sausage links, and a glass of orange juice."

Lisa Marie looked at the plate, and before she could correct the order, the woman just walked away. Lisa Marie sat back as she put both hands on the bench seat and looked at the plate again and then to the woman, who was now standing at the counter with the cook. Yes, he was looking right at Lisa Marie. He had a toothpick between his lips and must have been flicking it with his tongue and smiling at her. The sight of the cook made Lisa Marie wince as she drew her coat closer and began to eat.

The food wasn't bad and she thought the orange juice would do her good instead of the coffee. She finished her meal, drank the orange juice, wiped her mouth with a paper napkin, and sat back into the booth. She felt an urge coming on and knew she needed to hold off until she was out of DC and on the road north.

Lisa Marie looked at the table and saw the bill and didn't recall the woman leaving it. She raised the paper and read her order—two over easy, rye dry, crispy bacon. She looked at the woman and then the cook. He made the change for sure, and the woman didn't catch it. Lisa Marie slid out of the booth, paying attention to her coat to ensure the pervert didn't find a glimpse, and made her way to the register. With her left arm across her chest, she handed the woman the bill with her right hand. The woman looked at it over her glasses.

"That will be $2.05!"

Lisa Marie handed the woman a five-dollar bill and five pennies.

The woman seemed annoyed with the pennies as the register rang open. She dropped the coins and placed the five in the second slot from the right, lifted a small spring weight, and removed three one-dollar-bills and handed them to Lisa Marie. Lisa Marie looked at the woman and then turned back to see the cook now leaning on the counter and bearing all his upper body weight on his left hand. He was apparently looking at Lisa Marie's ass and realized she saw him, and he quickly stood up straight and looked in another direction.

Lisa Marie shoved the money in her purse, turned, and walked out the door with no signs of tipping the woman. After all, she brought her the wrong order, and Lisa Marie felt she was rude.

The spring air, although chilly, felt good against her skin as she made her way to the bus station. She glanced back at the diner and saw the cook and the old woman peeking from behind the opened door. Her first thought was to flip the bird, but what would that do? So, she turned back and chuckled to herself. The sidewalk seemed empty, but it was a Sunday, and most of the city was probably in church. Union Station looked the same as it did on Friday when she bought her ticket. She looked at the departure board and looked for Petoskey, Michigan. It was departing from Door L at 10:05 a.m. She scanned the lobby for the door and a clock, which wasn't hard to find, it was just above the departure board, so she laughed and said, "9:46, just in time."

Lisa Marie made her way to Door L and found a man standing there checking tickets. She reached into her purse, pulled out her ticket, and waited behind two other people doing the same. Except the woman couldn't find her ticket, and her husband looked back at Lisa Marie and said, "Hi, sorry, go ahead."

"Thank you!"

The woman looked up from her purse and took in Lisa Marie's beauty, which was followed by an elbow to her husband's stomach. The man gulped and stepped back from his wife and said, "Hey, what did I do?"

The ticket taker put his left hand out for Lisa Marie's ticket, which she handed to him. "Nice place, Petoskey…been there a few times, right on Lake Michigan. First time there?"

Lisa Marie looked at the man, smiled, and said, "Yes, first time."

"Visiting relatives?"

"Yes, something like that."

The man placed her ticket on a clipboard, stamped it, and then handed it back. He smiled and said, "There will be a few stops along the way, but you should be there about this time tomorrow, barring any bad weather."

Lisa Marie took the ticket, smiled, and said, "Thank you, have a nice day."

The ticket taker reached up to his hat and tipped it toward Lisa Marie. He smiled, looked away, and said to the couple now behind her, "Ma'am, did you find your ticket?"

31

Lisa Marie glanced back at the couple and noticed the husband looking at her as his wife feverishly dug through her purse. There were many busses all lined up and running, which made it loud and the stink from the diesel engines made her pinch her nose to help block the smell. She made the few steps into the bus, which was about half full. Scanning for a seat, she noticed the right side all the way to the back at a window was open. Lisa Marie brought her purse to her chest as she walked the bus aisle and plopped into the seat. She looked out the window; breathed heavily onto the glass, which caused it to fog; and then drew a smiley face. She turned her attention to the front of the bus and began daydreaming once again, and before too long she was asleep.

The sound of the engine racing and the airbrake release woke her, as the driver announced their departure and closed the bus door. Lisa Marie looked around again but didn't see the couple, so she assumed maybe the woman lost her ticket or they were on a different route. Lisa Marie counted twenty-seven people including her, and there were now thirty-two, so that meant the seat next to her was empty. She turned sideways, brought her feet onto the seat bottom next to her, and she leaned back, closed her eyes, and soon she was sleeping again.

Chapter Six: August 22, 1976, San Francisco

Jake unwrapped his chopsticks and Robert did the same, and he began to study them. Jake spoke up. "So, do you have brothers and sisters?"

Robert took his attention from the chopsticks. He looked at Jake and replied, "Yes, I do. My sister is Lisa Marie, and she's about fifteen years older than I, and then my brother John Jr. is about seven years older. John Jr. came home from Vietnam in May of this year, and my sister, Lisa Marie, died April 26, 1970."

Jake looked at Robert, "Man, I'm sorry about your sister. What happened? I mean, if I'm being too forward I'm sorry."

"She died of a drug overdose at home, in her room. My father found her and everyone firgured she had been dead a couple of days."

"Wow! Man, that sucks. I'm so sorry."

Jake reached over to Robert's chopsticks and positioned them in Robert's hand. He then picked up his chopsticks and gave a quick tutorial on how to use them without saying anything.

"I have three sisters, all younger than me, but not as much of an age gap as you and your siblings. My parents worked it out so that we are all about two years apart. You know, you might like my sister Hannah. She's eighteen and kinda dorky like you," Jake said.

Robert laughed and continued to attempt his chopsticks.

Then Jake asked. "Tell me about your parents."

Robert broke his concentration and looked up at Jake. He

33

then sat back in the booth, which caused the vinyl to squeak, and thus made Robert lean forward quickly, and said.

"Well, my parents met in the late 1930s while my father was at Bob Jones University in Greenville, South Carolina. My mother was a waitress fresh out of high school, and from what I've been told, she was undecided in her career path, but when my parents met, as my father would say, "It was love at first sight"—and they married soon after. In 1941 my sister Lisa Marie was born."

Robert's voice started to crack a bit after mentioning his sister's name, and he cleared his throat and wiped a tear that formed under his left eye. Jake leaned back and placed his chopsticks on a small plate in front of him.

"Robert, are you okay?"

Robert looked down at the table and went quiet. He stayed that way for a few minutes and then the food arrived.

"Excuse me," said the waitress, not Chin Lea. It was an American woman of about twenty, her hair was long and black, her eyes were a piercing blue, and she was a knockout. Robert was taken aback by her and Jake didn't seem to notice—maybe he didn't like the black hair or perhaps he was too tired to care. Robert leaned back as the woman placed the plate of food in front of him.

"Thank you," Robert said.

The woman then placed Jake's plate down, and Jake didn't even look at her or thank her.

"Will that be all?" the waitress asked.

Robert looked at Jake who was still looking down and then

looked at the woman and said, "Thank you, I guess we're all set."

The woman smiled at Robert and winced at Jake. She walked away and disappeared into the kitchen.

"Jake, you were a bit rude to that woman,"

Jake looked up at Robert and gave a quick smile, "Yeah, she hates me. We've gone out a few times, and then I blew her off."

Robert glanced at the woman as she came from the kitchen. They locked eyes and she smiled, as did he. Jake was using his chopsticks as if this would be his last meal, and Robert was giving the sticks a good attempt, but Jake would be done and ready to leave before Robert made it halfway through his meal.

"You know, this is really good. I mean really good. What was it called again?"

Jake coughed, stopped eating, and replied, "General Tso's Chicken. I knew you'd like it."

Just as Robert was about to bring another small portion to his mouth, the waitress came over. "Here, you're going to starve to death at this rate." She handed Robert a fork. Jake laughed but didn't make eye contact with her, but Robert looked up at her, smiled again, and reached for the fork.

"Is it that obvious?"

She smiled at him and released the utensil as he took it. She turned away and ducked back into the kitchen. Robert looked at Jake who was by now leaning back in the booth holding his belly.

"Wow, I'm full!"

Robert made good work of the meal now that he had the right tool to do so. He shoveled down the food and repeated Jake's gesture.

"So, Jake, what's her story?"

Jake leaned forward and asked, "Who?"

Robert leaned, "The waitress, she's beautiful."

Robert felt flushed because he soon realized the waitress was standing at the table. Robert looked up at her, and she too was

Chapter Seven: April 1968, Toledo, Ohio

The bus came to a stop, and the brakes set sounding like a giant ricochet. Lisa Marie sat up, stretched, and looked across from where she was lying to see a man of about forty gazing at her. She looked down and knew why. Her stretch had opened the coat, and this gave the man an eyeful. She quickly pulled the jacket together and turned, facing the front of the bus. The man got up and made his way to the front of the bus only looking back at Lisa Marie once, no expression on his face, just a blank stare.

"Okay folks, this is Toledo, Ohio. I know a few are leaving us, and we may have a few join us, so take the next thirty minutes to grab a snack and use the facilities, oh, and I leave on time!"

The bus door opened and passengers stood and shuffled out one by one. Lisa Marie leaned forward for a moment and thought about the need to do the dope, but decided to wait, the stop was short, and the terminal was bustling, much more so than DC. She looked up and saw the driver standing as if he was waiting for her to exit. Lisa Marie stood, grabbed her purse, and made her way to the front of the bus.

"Sir, how much longer until I reach Petoskey, Michigan?"

The driver lifted his hat, scratched his forehead, and thought. "Well, we have a couple more stops in Michigan, and so we should be in Petoskey around 1:30 a.m."

Lisa Marie could feel the itch of needing the heroin but fought it hard. "Okay, thank you. Oh, what's in Toledo?" she asked.

The driver lit up, "This is the home of the Jeep, or what once was Willy's Overland. I drove a Jeep in the war. Fine vehicle, never got it stuck once."

"Yes, the Jeep, my brother drove a Jeep in the war," Lisa Marie said.

The driver did a rearward lean and said, "Your brother was in WWII?"

Lisa Marie smiled, "No sir, sorry. My brother John Jr. was in Vietnam."

The driver shrugged and replied, "That wasn't a real war, my dear. I was D-day, plus two, now that was a real war. Okay, you've got less than thirty minutes to take care of any personal needs." The driver motioned for Lisa Marie to exit the bus.

Lisa Marie exited to the concrete and shivered. Toledo was colder than DC, and the air had a smell that she couldn't make out, but it was a combination of oil and God knows what. As she made her way to the door into the terminal, she made a mental note, Door 7. She looked down from above the door and saw the man that was across from her on the bus standing just to the right of the door looking right at her with a blank, yet odd stare. She looked away and entered the terminal scanning for a ladies' room.

She entered the ladies' room,; she went to the very last stall, went in, closed the door, locked it, and began to shiver as she undid the buttons of her jeans. She sat placing her purse on her lap and then reached in to remove her pocketbook. She opened a small pocket and with her index finger and thumb reached in and removed the small wrapper that held her drug of choice. She looked at it, placed it back, and began to urinate. She stood, slung her purse over her left shoulder, buttoned her jeans, exited

38

the stall, and went to the sink. She looked toward the door and noticed a lot of light changes coming from the gap—door to floor—it was as if someone was pacing just outside.

She washed her hands and dried them on the cloth towel that hung from a box on the wall. It read, "Pull Down For Clean Section." She did so and marveled at how the dispenser worked, which meant a person could always dry their hands with a clean cloth. She turned toward the door, looked at the gap, and saw that it had a steady section of light as well as dark spots. This meant someone was standing just outside the door. Lisa Marie waited for a moment and then smacked the door, which caused whoever was out there to walk away quickly, leaving a steady flow of light coming from under the door. Lisa Marie opened the restroom door, and off to her right, she noticed the man from the bus, the man she had seen again at the door coming into the terminal.

Passengers were headed to their respective busses as did Lisa Marie. She stepped onto the bus and looked around, hoping to have the same seat from earlier, and she did. The bus had lost several passengers at this stop, including the strange man.

"Okay, everyone, let's take a seat. This bus leaves in less than one minute. We will stop briefly in Ann Arbor, Michigan, and then Alma, Michigan, for another thirty-minute stop, and then Gaylord, Michigan, and then Petoskey, where I'll grab some sleep before heading out again."

Lisa Marie felt that urge but closed her eyes and resisted. The brakes released and the buses engine revived and it began to move backward. Lisa Marie repeated her seating situation by laying across the seats at the back and used her purse as a pillow.

The bus jerked and swayed as the driver maneuvered out of the station and onto the highway, and within a few minutes, the bus was steady, and the engine had dropped to a peaceful drone.

She fell asleep and began to recount a time in her life. The man from earlier was in that dream, but he was considerably younger, and yet, Lisa Marie remained her current age. Soon her dream became scary, and she was being dragged into the water, her clothes were now gone. She was naked while three men had their way with her, one after the other, and this seemed to go on for an eternity. Suddenly she awoke, tears were dried to her face, and a woman's voice said, "Miss, are you okay?"

Lisa Marie sat up quickly to find an elderly woman partially seated with her. This caused Lisa Marie to draw her legs inward and to swing around the woman and place her feet onto the bus floor.

"Hi, yes, I'm fine. Where are we?" asked Lisa Marie as she scanned the bus and the outside through the bus windows.

"We're in Detroit, and you must have been having a nightmare. You were clawing and fighting at something. Are you sure you're okay?" the woman asked.

Lisa Marie ran her fingers through her long hair, rubbed her face, smiled, and said, "Yes, I'm fine, thank you. Why Detroit?"

The woman stood, shrugged her shoulders, and put her hand out. Lisa Marie accepted, stood, and pulled her pant legs down as they had bunched up. The two of them exited the bus, and Lisa Marie thanked the woman again. She walked into the terminal and toward a restroom.

The urge came over her as she sat in the stall. She removed

the heroin from her purse, looked at it, and return it to her pocketbook. She took another look at it and then dropped it in the toilet. She stood, buttoned her jeans, turned, and flushed the toilet. She watched the little wrapper swirl with the water and then disappear. She stood, staring at the rippling water as the bowl filled, and thought she made a good choice, yet at the same time felt she had made a bad decision. She turned, opened the stall door, and made her way to the sink. She washed her hands and face and ran her wet fingers through her hair. She cranked the towel dispenser, which was paper this time, and a rough paper at that. She dried her face and hands, grabbed her purse from the counter with her left hand, and tossed the paper in the trash with her right hand. She grabbed the door handle, opened, and walked out into the terminal.

She stood, frozen. This time she didn't look for the door number and stared at the busses through the large windows. Suddenly number 0722 flashed before her on ribbed aluminum. She went to the first door and walked out into the cold night air, looked down the row of busses, and saw her bus, number 0722. Thank God, she thought. The last passenger stepped onto the bus, and the driver was at the side closing the luggage compartment below.

"Hey, Missy! I thought I had you until Petoskey. Hurry up and get on board," the driver said with a smile.

"Thank you, sir,"

She stepped up, grabbed a rail handle, and turned to the left. She looked down the aisle and noticed a young couple had found her seat and were loving on each other. The elderly woman waved and said, "Come here, sit with me, child. I could use the company."

Lisa Marie smiled and took four short steps and sat next to the woman. The woman looked at Lisa Marie, smiled, and said, 'Hi, I'm Elizabeth Carroll."

Lisa extended the courtesy and said, "It's nice to meet you, Ms. Carroll. I'm Lisa Marie Franklin."

The woman waved her hand. "Please, call me Beth. My husband has been for more than fifty years."

Lisa Marie liked her. She smiled and said, "Ok

Chapter Eight: Tuesday, December 25, 1962,
Near Detroit, MI

Detroit was known for being the home of automotive, and people came from far and wide hoping to land a job at Ford, or even General Motors, but Tom Joseph wasn't in Detroit to work in a factory. He was driving a truck hauling stolen cigarettes and alcohol. It was a risky career, but the money was great, and he was well-liked by his bosses in Chicago because he just wanted to drive, nothing more. He had no interest in women or drinking, or gambling, just driving. His route was the same: leave Chicago, drive to Detroit, then to Pittsburgh, and then back to Chicago—always with a full trailer. Occasionally he'd have to give local and state police some items from the truck, or a little cash to let him do what he did, but it was a life he enjoyed, and it was far better than the small-town life and working for his dad at the McCormick Hardware.

Tommy, as he was called, pulled into a greasy spoon, the name given for truck stops because the food was just that, greasy. Tommy stunk from driving for days on end. He pulled his 1962 Mack F-model—a cab over engine truck with a sleeper—up to a fuel pump, got out, and removed the fuel cap. He looked up at the attendant and waved, and she waved back. He removed the nozzle from the pump and placed it into the fuel tank neck and squeezed the handle, which sprayed diesel fuel into the tank. He was proud of this truck; it was brand new, just shy of a month old. The dark green paint really stood out from other trucks, and the shiny trailer with the name "Giovani Brothers," Chicago, IL, stenciled on the side gave him the upper hand everywhere he went. He was respected among other drivers.

Tommy stood there holding the handle while the tank filled. He whistled a tune and looked around. Being that it was Christmas, not many drivers were out, and he began to think of home. Suddenly fuel leaked down the side of the tank and Tommy jerked back and released the nozzle. He looked around to ensure no one saw him and returned the nozzle to the pump by moving the lever back to the start position and then placing the nozzle, which was connected to a hose, into the slot. He made sure it was locked in place by wiggling the handle. Satisfied, Tommy looked at the pump. Forty-six gallons, which meant he was four gallons from empty. He took some paper towels from a dispenser and wiped the tank's filler cap and around the cap, which seemed a bit useless since the truck was covered in snow and ice and salt, but it was a matter of pride for him. Tommy made his way into the station to use the men's room, and to pay for his fuel. Before he entered, he kicked the concrete wall to knock the snow from his boots. He opened the door, stepped in, and shivered while rubbing his hands together.

"Hello, Tiffany! Merry Christmas!" Tommy said and waved as he headed for the men's room. As he was about to open the door, he fell forward since the door was being opened from the other side.

"Tommy!" a burly man of about forty-five said. He was enormous, standing about 6'5" and at least 300 pounds. Tommy knew him from the route; he drove for the O'Connor Brothers out of New York, but they moved mainly alcohol and sardines. Not sure why sardines were so hard to get, but Tommy never asked questions.

"Hello Mike, Merry Christmas."

Mike smiled and pushed Tommy back about three feet, which didn't require a lot since Tommy was 5'9" and 155 pounds with all his clothes and boots on.

Mike asked, "So, have you given much thought about our proposition?"

Tommy looked to the floor at a puddle that started below his feet, or maybe it had been there from Mike. Anyway, he looked up.

"You know Mike, I really appreciate the offer, but I'm pretty happy where I am, and I like my route."

Tommy proceeded forward, and Mike pushed him back and said, "I see you have a new Mack, which engine does she has?"

Tommy looked up at Mike, "It's the Cummins 315 horsepower. Now if you'll excuse me, I really need to use the restroom." Tommy spun around Mike and pushed open the door. Mike turned and stopped the door and said, "It's okay, Tommy. I'll see you again real soon. The O'Connor Brothers always get what they want!"

Tommy looked over his shoulder as the door closed and made his way to the urinal to relieve himself. He began to shiver, maybe it was the cold or maybe it was adrenaline. Mike and others from the O'Connor Brothers have been pressuring him to join them for months, but again, Tommy was happy where he was, and that new Mack made it worth the harassment. He shook, zipped, and made his way to the sink. Hot water in his hands, he put his head to the basin and splashed the water in his face and then scrubbed a bit before soaping his hands and rinsing them. He reached for the towel just as the door opened and two men walked in. He watched their reflections in the mirror as he dried his hands.

"Say, is that your Mack out there?" one of the men asked.

"Yes sir, it is."

The man responded, "Nice rig." He opened a stall door, and both men went inside and closed the door. Tommy tossed the paper towel in the trash and hurried out the door. He made his way to the dairy cooler, reached in, and grabbed a quart of chocolate milk. He found his way to the counter and saw his favorite on a shelf. The Hostess Ho Hos always made him smile, and since Moon Pies weren't very popular in the northern states, the Ho Hos were his second choice. He laid the items on the counter and reached into his back pocket for his billfold.

"Hi, Tommy!" said Tiffany with a big smile.

"Hello again Tiffany. So, what do I owe you?"

Tiffany tapped away at the register. "That'll be $26.09."

Tommy dug into his pocket for the change before opening his wallet. He pulled out a handful of coins and a ball of lint. Using the index finger from his right hand, he moved around the coins looking for four pennies and a nickel. He handed her the nine cents and shoved the rest of the coins back in his pocket. Then he opened his wallet, took out a twenty and a ten, and handed them to Tiffany.

"Here you are."

Tiffany took the bills and with the change she tapped the register again and it made a jingle noise and the drawer came open. She placed the bills in their respective slots, divided the coins, and placed them accordingly. She lifted the spring-loaded arm above the dollar bills and pulled out a stack, counted out four, placed the remaining bills in the slot, and slammed the drawer shut. She turned and handed Tommy his change.

"Do you need a receipt?"

Tommy looked at her and said, "No, I'm good. Thank you."

Tiffany smiled and said, "Tommy, why is it that you never flirt with me, or ask me out, or even pay me a compliment? The other drivers always have something to say." Then she turned her waist showing her butt for Tommy to see. She then leaned forward placing her hands on the counter, elbows in, pressing her breasts together giving Tommy clear vision of her enormous cleavage.

Tommy looked her over, smiled, and said, "Tiffany, you are amazing for sure, but I guess I have too much respect for you. When I see a beautiful woman, I ask myself, "Could I bring her home to meet my momma?"

Tiffany smiled and replied, "Well, would Momma approve?"

Tommy looked at her and said, "No, I'm sorry, you're too loose." He turned and walked toward the door.

Tiffany yelled, "Screw you Tommy!"

"Merry Christmas Tiffany!"

Tiffany's anger switched right back to her flirting when the two men from the restroom walked up.

"Hello gentlemen, how are you?" She flashed her butt once again.

The men laughed and replied, "Sorry honey, we don't go that way."

The men paid for their gasoline and the few items they

gathered while walking to the counter and walked out of the station hand and hand laughing. Tiffany slammed the register closed, looked around, leaned against the counter, and began filing her nails. She laughed to herself and looked up at the clock. "Wow, I still have another four hours to go," she said. She then returned to her manicure.

Chapter Nine: August 22, 1976

Robert leaned in and asked Jake, "So, what happened with the waitress?"

Jake looked at Robert and replied, "You must really like her. To be honest, she's not my type, too conservative, you know, no sex before marriage, meet the parents after two dates. I'm a bit too outgoing for that."

Robert leaned back and looked around the restaurant. He leaned in again, "What's her name?"

Jake leaned back in the booth and replied rather loudly, "Tina!" This embarrassed Robert to the point he reached out to put his hand over Jake's mouth, but Jake moved to the side and turned away from Robert and again he said, "Tina!" Robert was now furious and red in the face.

"Yes," a small voice said.

Robert looked up to see Chin Lea and Jake laughed. "Sorry Chin Lea, my friend Robert seems to have taken a liking to Tina and I wanted her to come over so that I could introduce them."

Chin Lea looked at Robert who was as red as the seatbacks and replied, "Oh, I see, one second. Tina come here please."

Tina came to the booth and looked right at Robert. She too was red. "Tina, this is Robert, and he'd like to meet you." Robert looked at her and extended his right hand as did she. They shook hands and Robert said, "Hi Tina, it's a pleasure to meet you."

Tina looked at Jake and then at Robert, "Yes, it's nice to meet you as well."

The awkwardness began to dissipate, and Tina with Chin

Lea walked away from the men. They giggled and went into the kitchen.

Jake was doing his best to hold back laughter, but soon he burst into a low belly laugh while slapping his hand on the table. Robert went from being angry laughed and then said, "Wow, that was the hardest thing I think I've ever done. Tina is so beautiful."

Jake looked at Robert, and with a straight face asked, "Are you still a virgin?"

Robert felt flush again and replied, "Well, I, you know, there was this time when—"

Jake put his hand up. "Stop, you're embarrassing yourself. It's okay to be a virgin at nineteen." Then Jake began to laugh, which embarrassed Robert again.

Robert looked at Jake. "I'm a bit conservative too and hope to save myself for marriage."

Jake stopped snickering and looked at Robert and said, "Okay, I get it; sorry, man."

The two men slid out of the booth and made their way to the register to pay. Tina greeted Robert with a smile and barely glanced at Jake. "Will this be together or separate?"

Jake quickly replied, "Please let me get this." He reached into his back pocket, removed his wallet, and then produced a credit card. He handed the card to Tina and she reached beneath the register and brought out the machine that processed the charge by placing the card into a specific spot. She then laid a piece of paper over the card and slid a handle across the card and paper, making a crunch—crunch sound from both directions.

She removed the paper, which were three sheets with the middle sheet being carbon paper. She wrote in $8.63, looked at Jake, and he said, "Oh, add two dollars for the tip." Tina looked at Jake again and he said, "Okay, make it three dollars."

Robert thought the tip was very generous for sure and smiled at Tina who smiled back. He liked her. She handed Jake his credit card, the papers, and a pen. "Please sign here."

Jake took the card, laid the papers on the counter, signed where told, and with both hands handed back the pen and papers. Tina tore off the bottom copy and handed it to Jake and said, "Thank you."

She turned her attention to Robert and said, "It was really nice to meet you; maybe we'll see each other around campus."

Robert looked right at Tina, smiled, "Yes, that would be great. Maybe we could have dinner sometime?" He then realized his thoughts came out in words and clammed up. He looked at Tina and the two began to laugh.

Jake put his right hand on Robert's left shoulder and said. "Come on lover boy, let's go." Robert turned quickly and knocked over the toothpick dispenser, but luckily, they stayed on the counter and maybe a fraction came out of the holder. He fumbled them back together with both hands, which made it worse.

Tina put her hand on his, they looked at each other, and she said, "Don't worry, Robert, I'll take care of it."

Robert pulled his hands back and then placed them at his sides. "Okay, sorry."

Jake and Robert exited the restaurant and out to the bright sun, which caused Robert to put his right hand above his eyebrows to be used as a visor. Of course, Jake already had on his sunglasses and wasn't bothered by the mid-day sun.

"What would you like to do now?" asked Jake.

Robert opened his door and climbed inside the Porsche. Jake got in, closed his door, reached over his left shoulder, and pulled his seat belt to the locked position. "You didn't answer me," Jake said to Robert.

"Sorry, my mind was still inside the restaurant. I'm a bit tired still from the ride out here, and the food has made me even more sleepy. Maybe you could take me back to the dorm, so I can take a nap."

Jake replied, "Suit yourself. I've got a friend to see. It's been weeks, and I miss her." The car started again with a quick turn of the key, crunched into reverse, and moved effortlessly out of the parking spot and onto the street. Soon the two were back at campus and at the front of the dorm. Jimmy was out front tending to the plants and turned to notice the car. He winced and went back to the plants.

"Well, thank you. That was very nice. Several firsts for me."

Jake looked at Robert and asked, "What were the firsts?"

Robert looked out the windshield, "Riding in a Porsche and Chinese food. So again, thank you." He then removed his seat belt and reached for the door handle.

"No worries, we'll make you into a party animal soon enough,"

Robert opened the car door and twisted in the seat. He planted his feet on the concrete and stood. He closed the door and walked toward the building as Jake raced off.

Jimmy stopped what he was doing and asked, "McCormick! Did you attend here last year?"

Robert asked, "Are you talking to me? I'm Robert."

Jimmy laughed, "To me, you are McCormick—where you come from!"

Robert laughed and said, "Okay, and no, I didn't attend here last year. I have been asked that already. I must look like someone that did."

Jimmy waved him off, and Robert walked inside. He made his way down the long hallway to the stairs leading to the second floor and made his way up and then back down the long hallway to his room. The door was open about six inches, so Robert looked above to ensure it was the right room. Room 202. He opened the door and said, "Hello, who's in here?"

The bathroom door opened, and Sara without an *H* stepped out, drying her hands. She finished, turned, and tossed the hand towel onto the sink. Robert's thought was twofold, why is she in here and why she didn't hang the towel?

Sara walked up to Robert and grabbing his shirt; she bunched up the fabric in both hands, pulled Robert down to her, and kissed him. It was a deep kiss filled with anger and passion. Robert wasn't sure what to do, so he just stood there, no response, and looked to his right and not at Sara. Sara stopped, pushed him back, and said, "You know, maybe you're right; you didn't attend here last year. The guy that forced me down and kissed me had a fire inside him, anger if you will, and you act like a choir boy. Are you gay?"

Robert looked down at his wrinkled shirt, wiped his mouth that Sara covered with lipstick, and replied, "Why don't you believe me? I have never been here before. I have never met you, and no, I'm not gay!"

Sara noted Robert's sincerity. She turned and walked out the door. Robert followed her, stepped just outside the door, and called out, "Sara, will you please talk to me?"

Sara kept pace. She raised her right hand and gave Robert the finger. Robert threw his hands in the air, brought them down, and slapped his thighs. He turned back into the room; closed the door gently, resting his head on the cold metal of the door frame; and said, "What is going on here?"

He turned and looked at his desk, which was disheveled. Most likely Sara without an *H* had done it. Robert straightened his desktop, stood the books, closed the drawers, and flopped to his bed, which made the springs creak and squeak. Placing his hands behind his head, he intertwined his fingers and closed his eyes.

Chapter Ten: April 1968

"Lisa Marie where are you from?" asked Beth Carroll.

Lisa Marie looked up from her hands, which were on top of her purse, and noticed her fingernails were looking a bit rough. She realized her habit caused her to chew her nails when the need for heroin came. She balled her hands into fists and looked at Beth and replied, "I'm from a small town in South Carolina about eighty miles west of Columbia."

Beth lit up and said, "I just came from Greenville, South Carolina, visiting some friends."

Lisa Marie looked at her hands again, "I have been to Greenville, nice town, much bigger than where I'm from. Where do you live now?"

Beth replied, "I live in Ann Arbor, our next stop. My husband is a professor at the University of Michigan. He's going to retire soon, I hope." Beth then looked out the window into the dark. Lisa Marie saw Beth's reflection in the window, and it appeared she was starting to cry. Without looking at Lisa Marie, Beth Carroll placed her left hand on Lisa Marie's right knee and said. "Well, child, try to get some rest."

Lisa Marie situated herself in the seat and laid her head into the seatback and closed her eyes. Within seconds, she was dreaming, but this time it was of two boys playing in a yard, and she played with them. She ran with them and wrestled with them, and occasionally she would hug and kiss them. The three laid in a field of tall grass and Lisa Marie would point to the heavens and explain things to them. She looked healthy and bright, and more alive than ever before. The boys were laughing as she would tickle them; it was pure joy.

The setting brakes of the bus woke Lisa Marie as the interior lights came on. She looked at Beth who was fast asleep. Lisa Marie gently placed her right hand on Beth's left shoulder and slowly shook her and said, "Beth, we're here, Ann Arbor."

Beth woke, looked around, and smiled. The two women stood and shuffled to the front of the bus. The driver stopped Lisa Marie. "Ma'am, this is a ten-minute stop."

Lisa Marie looked at the driver and then smiled before saying, "Yes, sir, ten minutes."

Lisa Marie stepped off the bus and turned around to aid Beth off the bus. A man of Beth's age walked up and said, "Hello, Beth, how was your trip?"

Beth grinned, walked up to the man, hugged him, and replied, "It was fine. I met this nice young lady. Her name is Lisa Marie."

The man extended his right hand, and Lisa Marie did the same. They shook hands and he introduced himself. "Hello Lisa Marie, I'm Professor Robert Carroll Sr. and this is my son, Robert Jr." The man looked around, but the boy was inside the terminal where it was warm. "Oh, there he is," Robert Sr. said.

Lisa Marie looked at the boy and smiled, and he smiled back. "Handsome young man," Lisa Marie replied.

Beth said, "Thank you, he's our pride and joy."

Lisa Marie looked at Robert and Beth and thought they must be in their late fifties or early sixties, and to have a boy that age, he must have been adopted, or maybe they had a daughter that died, and they are now his legal guardians. It didn't really matter. They were happy, and the boy looked well enough.

Beth came up to Lisa Marie and hugged her, which caught her off guard. She quickly hugged back. Beth said, "It was nice traveling with you. I hope wherever you're going you make it there safe."

Just then the driver walked up and handed Mr. Carroll his wife's suitcase, tilted his hat, and whispered to Lisa Marie, "You have five minutes."

Lisa Marie looked at him, waved off the family, and went into the terminal as the Carroll' boy was coming out. She found herself staring right at him as if she knew him, but he had his head down as he pushed through the door, and his ball cap kept his face almost hidden. The boy disappeared into the night and Lisa Marie ran to the ladies' room, used the facilities, washed her hands, and without drying them ran back to the bus and got on. She noticed the back row was now empty and the bus was essentially hers. She made her way to the favored seats, flopped down, smiled, and started chewing her nails but quickly stopped after looking at how far she had gnawed at them.

The brakes released, the interior lights went out, and the bus moved backward in a back and forth motion causing Lisa Marie to do the same. The bus stopped, the engine revived, and off they went, maneuvering around the large lot and onto a side street and then to the highway. It was about 10:00 p.m. and Lisa Marie recalled the driver saying a bit after 01:00 a.m. they'd be in Petoskey. Her stomach began to growl, and butterflies formed, which brought on the need for heroin. Lisa Marie closed her eyes and tried to sleep.

Chapter Eleven: Saturday, July 4, 1959, Brooklyn, New York

Police sirens filled the city streets as gunfire was masked with the sounds of fireworks. Growing up on the mean streets of New Jersey, Mike Jameson, a rookie with the NYPD, was ready for anything the city had to offer; however, he didn't expect to be on his seventh homicide in less than two days, and this crime scene was different. He knew the two boys that now lie dead on the sidewalk in front of him. He had just played stick ball with them the night before. Timmy and Pauley lived in the same building as did he in Queens. What brought them to Brooklyn weighed heavily on Michael as he knelt over them lifting the fabric of their shirts with his pen.

"Hey rookie? What do you think you're doing? You're a beat cop, not a detective, get away from my crime scene!" a man barked.

Michael stood, "Yes sir, detective, sorry. I knew these two."

The detective wiped the sweat from his forehead and replied, "Sorry kid. Did you know them well?"

Michael, still looking at his friends, shook his head yes, turned, and walked away.

The detective stopped Michael and placed his right hand on Michael's left shoulder and said, "Hey kid, I knew your father, and if you're anything like he was, you'll be a detective real soon, and you can work to catch the scum of the earth. But until then, you must keep your wits about you, or this job will eat you up!"

Michael looked at the detective and replied, "Thank you, sir, I'll do my best."

Michael walked to the squad car and rested against the Ford's big fender. He looked around at all the people, and as he studied each face, he can't help but wonder why the world is the way it is. He's just an Irish kid hoping to make a difference and to last on the force longer than his father did before him.

"Hey kid, you okay?" a voice asked. Michael looked to his right to see Sergeant Anthony Marely walking toward him.

"Yeah, Sarge, I'm okay. I just played stick ball with those two less than twenty-four hours ago. What the hell were they doing here, in Brooklyn?"

Anthony Marely is now standing right in front of Michael. He took his NYPD-issued hat off, wiped his forehead with a handkerchief, and put his hat back on. He folded the handkerchief and put it in the left rear pocket of his uniform pants and replied, "Were those two in a gang, or did they use marijuana? This seems to be the place to buy that stuff, and it's becoming more prevalent each day."

Michael looked over at his dead friends and then at Sergeant Marely and replied, "I have no idea what those two knuckleheads were into. I just know they were good kids and never bothered nobody."

Anthony Marely looked at the two bodies, scanned the growing crowd, and said, "Well, we'd better get out of here and back to the streets. It's going to get busier the darker it got, and we need to have a presence, you know?" He then turned and made his way to the driver's side of the big Ford. Michael pushed away from the car, turned, opened the passenger door, and climbed in. He closed the door hanging his right arm out the window with hopes the breeze while moving might cool him off a bit.

The two remained silent for some time as they patrolled the mean streets of a true melting pot of varying nationalities. Michael was the third generation to join the NYPD; his father and his father's father walked the streets for many years. The first time Michael saw his father in a uniform, he knew right then he too would be a cop.

The night was eventful as people celebrated the nation's birthday. They made a few arrests, mainly for battery. The heat of summer kept everyone on edge, and tonight being a Saturday, and the biggest celebration of the year, you can bet a lot was going to happen.

Sergeant Marely said, "Hey kid, I'm really sorry about your dad. He was a good man, and a good cop. We all respected him very much. That cancer is a bad thing."

Michael turned to his left and saw the sincerity on the face of Sergeant Marely, "Thank you. He was a good man, and the best father. I hope I can live up to his standards."

Chapter Twelve: Sunday, August 12, 1956, 03:24

John Franklin Sr. opened the screen door as John Jr. brushed by him and walked into the house. Marilynn came from the dining room, looked at the two, and sat on the floor. John Sr. put his hand on John Jr.'s head and said, "Go ahead son, it's late, go get some rest. We have to be up in a couple of hours."

John Jr. looked at his father, "We tried, Daddy, we tried." He then turned and made his way to the staircase that led to his room.

John Sr. walked into the living room, sat on the couch, leaned his head back, and began to speak. "Marilynn, we drove all over the county looking for that girl and no sign of her anywhere. Sheriff Tiltman even joined in the search. We stopped by the Josephs' home and the boys and the car had been home for hours. They swore that Lisa Marie told them to stop just before old Brewer Road and Highway 28. She got out and they just left her there and went home. Mike Joseph said she had something she needed to do."

Marilynn looked up at her husband and replied, "What could a fifteen-year-old girl have to do, really, Johnathon!"

John Sr. leaned forward, "I have no idea what a fifteen-year-old girl would need to do on a Saturday night, in August!" He stood and went to the kitchen, opened a cabinet, and pulled out a bottle of vodka. He then reached for a glass that was drying on the counter next to the sink and filled the glass half full. He went to the freezer, pulled out two ice cubes from a bowl, and dropped them into the glass. He turned to his wife, walked to her, and then handed her the glass and said, "Here, this should make up for what you lost earlier on the sidewalk."

Marilynn looked up at him and in a fit of anger she slapped the glass from John Sr.'s hand, causing it to fall to the floor losing its contents. Just then the screen door opened, and Lisa Marie stepped in. She was covered in dirt and blood, and most of her clothes were missing. She looked at her parents who were frozen. She fell to the floor like a dirty dish rag.

John Sr. ran to her, followed by Marilynn. He picked up his daughter and ran her into the living room and onto the couch. The home was a total panic, which caused John Jr. to bound down the steps. John Jr. ran to his sister's side and stood there helpless, staring at his sister's exposed body covered in blood. The sight caused him to fall to the floor and cry.

John Sr. went to the front door and closed it and then he ran up the stairs to the bathroom. He soaked washcloths with cold water, grabbed towels, and ran back down the stairs to his daughter. Marilynn was hysterical and screaming. It was as if the world went into slow motion. The family surrounded Lisa Marie, and everyone was crying, yet she remained motionless, staring at the ceiling.

Marilynn cried out, "Lisa Marie, please say something!"

Lisa Marie looked at her mother and tears began to fill her eyes.

Chapter Thirteen: Thursday, December 25, 1986, Los Angeles, CA

The FBI Field Office in Los Angeles, California was essentially quiet; however, there were a few agents working, including Supervisory Special Agent Robert Franklin. His desk was considered managed chaos. Articles, papers with handwritten notes, field reports, and photos were stacked chronologically in front of him. Robert sat, pushed back from his desk, leaned his elbows on his thighs, and the phone pressed against his left ear with his left shoulder, air tapping an ink pen with his right hand.

"Hi honey. Look, I'm sorry about today, and I hope to make it up to you this weekend." He's talking to his fiancée Tina Kettering, a girl he met while at San Francisco State University nearly ten years ago.

Tina is leaning on a counter where she worked as a nurse in a small hospital in Freemont, California. She replied, "I know, Robert. I guess I thought this Christmas would be better than last. You worked then too."

"Yes, that was a bad Christmas. Winter in Montana is brutal. How do those people do it? But like my boss always said, crime doesn't stop during the holidays." Robert sat up, leaned back, and laid his head backward over the seatback. He saw two LAPD officers talking to his newest agent and they're all looking at him. "Love, I have to go. Somethings come up. I love you. Merry Christmas." Robert hung up the phone and stood, adjusting his tie and grabbed his suit coat from the back of the chair.

Tina can't respond before the click of Robert's phone. She hung up and replied to herself, "I love you too, Robert." She turned, picked up a chart from the counter, and flipped through the pages. She made a mental note and walked away.

Robert walked up to the officers with right hand extended and said, "Gentlemen, Supervisory Special Agent Robert Franklin in charge. What can we do for you?"

The uniformed officer shook Robert's hand. "Hello, I'm Sergeant Tom Jacobs and this is Lieutenant Richard Garcia."

Richard Garcia extended his right hand to Robert. "It's nice to meet you."

Garcia asked, "Do you have somewhere we can talk, maybe a conference room?"

Robert raised his left arm shoulder height, turned, and said, "Certainly, right this way. Oh, coffee?"

Both officers looked at each other and replied, "Sure!"

Robert looked at Special Agent Randy Miller and said, "Please bring coffee to Conference Room 3B. Thank you."

Randy Miller replied enthusiastically, "Yes sir, right away!"

The three men enter the room and Robert closed the door, only to have Miller open it with one hand while balancing a tray with a coffee carafe, cream and sugar dispensers, and four cups. "That was quick. Here, let me take that," Robert said to Miller. Robert placed the tray on the table and Miller took over, waiting on the men.

Garcia looked at Robert. "We've had numerous tips..."

Miller interjected, "Cream, sugar?"

Garcia sat back in his chair. "No, black for me, thank you."

Jacobs replied, "I'll have cream and sugar, thank you."

Robert looked at Miller and smiled and then looked at Garcia, "You were saying, Lieutenant?"

Garcia accepted the cup of coffee with both hands, nodded, and replied, "We've received tips of a warehouse not far from here that may have dead bodies, and we believe they could be from your guy."

Robert sat up straight and replied, "My guy, you mean the Pearl Necklace Killer?"

Garcia took a sip of his coffee and wiped his mouth.

Jacobs replied, "Yes, that guy."

Robert looked at Miller who is looking right at Jacobs. Robert is silent for a moment and replied, "What do we need to get in the place? Do we have a warrant?"

Garcia looked at him, reached into his sport coat, and produced a folded 8 ½" X 11" document and replied, "The ink on the signature is still wet."

Robert looked at his Paneria wristwatch—a graduation gift from his college roommate Jake Richards—and it read 19:22. He looked again at Miller and said, "Well kid, I guess you're on your own tonight. I'm going to head out with these two officers and execute a warrant."

Garcia said, "We have several other officers meeting us there shortly. We are about thirty minutes from the location on a normal day, and since it's Christmas, we should be there much quicker."

They all stood and exited the conference room. Robert said, "Let me grab my keys and overcoat."

Chapter Fourteen: April 1968, Petoskey, MI

The driver turned right, and Highway 131 became Highway 31. The bus rolled on for a few minutes and turned right into a small parking lot. The driver set the brakes, which brought Lisa Marie to a seated position, and she twisted her head side to side while rubbing her neck. The interior lights come on and she put her right-hand palm outward in front of her face to shield her from the glare.

"Okay everyone, this is our last stop for the night, and if Petoskey is your destination, I'll be outside the bus ready to hand out luggage," said the driver.

Lisa Marie stood, shook a little, and shuffled to the front of the bus and down the steps and into the April air of northern Michigan. It was easily ten, maybe fifteen degrees cooler than a few hours earlier. She shivered, and the driver came to her. "Young lady, that chill you feel is coming from Lake Michigan, which is right over there." He pointed northwest. Lisa Marie glanced over, but saw nothing except dark, a few lights, and maybe the moonlight shimmering off the water, or even ice since there was still snow on the ground, something Lisa Marie had never seen in person being from the south.

She looked at the driver and asked. "Sir, do you know if this town has an all-night diner or maybe a hotel close by?"

The driver looked at his watch, which read 1:16, and replied, "Well, give me a few minutes and I'll walk you to a hotel that has a bar that may be open late, and since we are in the off season, they may have rooms to let."

A few cars come and go picking up presumed loved ones and

the driver locked the bus. Lisa Marie and he walked into town. After a few blocks they're standing in front of an old hotel with a "Vacancy" sign hanging.

Lisa Marie looked around, looked at the driver, and said, "Well, thank you again, sir." She extended her hand as does he, but his grip is tight as if he doesn't want her to go.

He asked, "Would you like to have a drink with me?"

Lisa Marie smiled and pulled her hand back, "No, thank you, I'd like to get a room, take a hot bath, and go to bed."

The driver smiled. "A hot bath, that sounds really nice."

Lisa Marie walked away appalled.

"Hey, you can't blame me for trying, little lady!"

The entrance to the hotel was closed and a sign on the door read, "For a room, see bartender in the Boar's Head Room." Lisa Marie looked to her right and saw a wooden sign shaped like an arrow pointing downward to the bar. She took the few steps down, opened the door, and walked in. She saw the bus driver sitting at the bar and he's talking to the bartender, a man of about sixty. The room was filled with smoke and there were another five men nursing drinks. The whole room stopped, and all eyes were on Lisa Marie. Her coat is open and giving the men plenty to think about, especially with the current temperature. She looked at herself, drew herself inward, and closed her coat around her breasts the best she could.

The bartender excused himself from the driver's conversation and walked toward Lisa Marie. Grinning from ear to ear, the bartender asked, "What's a hot little fox like you doing in a place like this?"

Lisa Marie cringed and replied, "Sir, I just want a room for a few days, please."

The bartender looked at her and still smiling, "Sure thing, little mamma, we can do that. Do you want a room bayside or street side?"

"The cheapest room will be fine, thank you."

The bartender turned, walked to the register, rung it open, and removed several brass keys. As he thumbed through them, he looked at Lisa Marie and then he scanned her from head to toe. His greasy smile and the fact that all the men are still eyeing her made her nervous.

He held up a key and smiled. He replaced the other keys, grabbed a clipboard, and walked to Lisa Marie. "Okay, here you go. Your room will be street side, and all I need is for you to fill out this card. Will that be cash or charge card?"

Lisa Marie looked at the card and then back at the bartender and replied, "Cash, and for five days."

The man put his right hand on his chin, looked up to the ceiling, and mumbled, "So, fifteen dollars times five is?"

Lisa Marie saw the struggle and replied, "Seventy-five dollars, right?"

The bartender stopped the strain and said, "Yeah, seventy-five dollars!" His tone seemed irritated as he took the cash and clipboard and handed Lisa Marie the key.

Lisa Marie then asked, "Sir, how do I get to my room? The main door is locked."

He turned and barked back, "To the end of the bar, last door on the left. Take the stairs to the third floor, room 3!"

Lisa Marie walked past the bar and the bus driver, and to the last door on the left. She entered the stairwell and began her climb to the third floor. The stairs were old and worn, but she felt safe enough. She opened the door to her floor and looked left. She saw just four doors, three on the right side of the hall and one on the left side. She recalled the driver pointing to the bay and based on her current orientation, she must be in the only room on the left, which when she approached the door it was clearly see the number "3" in tarnished brass right there in front of her, just inches above her head.

She rattled the key into the lock, made a turn to the left, and the door sprung open. She stepped in, looked to her right, and pressed the top button of the old light switch. A lamp lit up on a table situated next to a chair. The room was quaint and there was a bow window where the shades were drawn a quarter of the way down, allowing the light from the post just outside the hotel to cast an upward shadow of the windows onto the ceiling.

Lisa Marie walked to the windows, lifted a shade, and looked out to the street below. There he was, the bus driver standing there looking up at her. She could see the ember of his cigarette as he drew in. He smiled at her, waved, turned, and walked away. She drew the shades and began to undress while walking toward the bathroom. The light flickered on and she went to the tub and turned the faucets until she felt the desired temperature, and then used the rubber plug to stop the water from draining. After several minutes, she turned out the light and lowered herself into the hot water. She dipped the washcloth, folded it in thirds, and laid it across her closed eyes. She then put both arms along the rim of the claw-foot tub.

Chapter Fifteen: Wednesday, December 26, 1962, Sterling Heights, MI

Tommy Joseph woke to the sounds of knocking on the side of his sleeper. The Mack was comfortable and ran well, which kept him nice and warm through the night.

"Tommy! Are you awake?" a man's voice asked.

Tommy came to a seated position by hanging his feet off the edge of the bunk. He rubbed his eyes, tussled his hair, and reached for his boots. He replied, "Jimmy? Is that you?"

The man outside the truck replied, "Yeah, it's me...nice truck by the way."

"Thanks, I'll be out in a sec!" while doing up his laces. He stood bent slightly at the waist, grabbed his coat from the back of the passenger's seat, and put it on. He went to the driver's seat and rolled down the window and said, "Hey Jimmy, how are you? Merry Christmas!"

Jimmy Looked up at Tommy and replied, "Yeah, Merry Christmas to you, too! So, I've got one going to New York!"

Tommy looked at his dash, located the ignition key, and shut the truck down. The diesel rattled and shook to a stop. He opened the door and swung to his right, putting his left leg out onto the first step, and then in a fluid motion, he was out and on the ground in front of Jimmy.

In a surprised voice, Tommy asked Jimmy, "Why is Anthony sending me to New York? That's O'Connor turf. I mean, don't get me wrong, but Big Mike and I had a conversation several hours ago and he didn't seem so happy that I wouldn't join them, and now Anthony wants me in the lion's den. What gives?"

Jimmy looked at the ground while moving snow around with his boot. He looked up at Tommy and replied "Listen man, I have no idea, but I do know this, the load you're bringing back here—"

Tommy put his hand up, "What do you mean, back here? This isn't normal, Jimmy! I run Chicago, Detroit, Pittsburgh, and back to Chicago. I never stop in Detroit with a load going west!"

Jimmy put his right hand on Tommy's left shoulder and replied, "Look kid, all I know is that Anthony asked for you specifically, so who am I to say either way…you know? Besides, Anthony wants you to do a couple short runs locally, and head to New York Sunday, pick up the load, and have it back here Monday."

Tommy ran his fingers through his hair and looked down at the snow-covered ground. He looked at Jimmy and then asked, "What's in the trailer from New York to Detroit?"

"I didn't ask, but I guess it's a pretty big deal. Anthony handpicked you for this job, so don't mess it up, okay?"

Tommy extended his right hand and replied, "No worries, Jimmy. I'll take care of it, but for now, what am I running today?"

Jimmy lifted a clipboard, thumbed through a couple pages, and shook his head.

Chapter Sixteen: April 1968, Petoskey, MI

Lisa Marie woke shivering. She had fallen asleep in the tub, which had since turned cold. She stood, reached for a towel, and then there was a knock at the door. She quickly stepped out of the tub, wrapped herself tightly, and stepped to the door. She said, "Yes, may I help you?"

"Yes, ma'am, just wanted to be sure you got tucked in okay?" It was the bartender and his voice made her skin crawl.

Lisa Marie placed her right hand on the door and replied, "Yes, I'm fine, thank you."

"Alright then, enjoy your stay." Lisa Marie placed her ear against the door and could hear his breathing. She remained motionless, and then after what seemed an eternity, the man walked away.

The next morning, Lisa Marie awoke and looked at the Seth Thomas clock on the table next to the bed; it was 10:20. She rolled to her back and looked at the ceiling. She knew she couldn't fight the urge any longer and her need for today was a good high, but would this small town on Lake Michigan be able to supply her need? She guessed she'd have to wait.

She crawled from under the goose-down comforter and made her way into the bathroom. She went to the radiator and felt to see if her undergarments and socks had dried; they had and then some. She lifted her panties and they were as stiff as cardboard and had retained the shape of where they lay the entire night. She laughed to herself as she shook them out, as well as her bra. She put them on, pulled on her jeans, buttoned her shirt, and sat on the floor to tie her shoes. After that she went to the window to open a shade, which got away from her and recoiled quickly and fluttered at the top, which caused her to jump back.

The sun was shining, and the air looked cold, so the second item of her day would be to buy a long coat and maybe some mittens, but first she needed food. She put on her jean jacket, grabbed her purse and the room key, and made her way to the main floor. In the daylight the hallway of the third floor was well lit from the sun coming through a window at the end. She noticed an opening just a few feet from her door. It was the stairs going to the first floor, and as she made her way down them, she could hear voices, mostly women chatting. Lisa Marie rounded the corner into what would be the hotel's lobby. The women stopped talking and looked at her.

An elderly woman wearing a name tag that read "Karen" made her way toward Lisa Marie and said, "Hello, you must be staying in room 3. I'm Karen, welcome. If you're hungry, there's a small buffet in the dining area, and since we are light on guests, there will be plenty of food."

Lisa Marie looked into Karen's eyes and saw sincerity. A woman that most likely has many grandchildren and loved them all the same. Lisa Marie replied, "Thank you very much, Karen. Yes, I am hungry." She extended her right hand and Karen took it and then led Lisa Marie to the dining room.

Karen asked, "So, you will be here the whole week. What brought you all the way up here from South Carolina?"

"Well, I'm looking for an old friend. He once lived in Texas and we lost touch over the years, and I recently learned he lived here with his aunt. You may know her, Kathryn McCray?"

Lisa Marie sat at a table that gave a glimpse of the splendors of Lake Michigan.

Karen lit up and replied, "Yes, of course. Kathryn is a dear friend. As a matter of fact, she was here earlier this morning!"

Lisa Marie reached into a front breast pocket and pulled out a piece of paper and replied, "Oh, that is great news. Does she still live at 600 Rose Street?"

Karen replied, "Yes, you can't miss the house. It's the biggest on the street. So, if you look out there." Lisa Marie turned in her chair and looked to where Karen is pointing. Karen continued, "Out there is Bay Street. Take that east to Williams Street and turn left. Williams will dead end at Rose and the big house is essentially right there. Believe me, you won't miss it."

Lisa Marie turned back to the table and replied, "Thank you, Karen. One last thing. Is there a store where I could acquire a long coat and maybe some mittens?"

Karen brought her right hand to her chin and replied, "Well, where do you plan to go from Petoskey? I ask because I could lend you a coat and mittens while you are here, and if you are going back to South Carolina, you probably won't need the articles any longer."

Lisa Marie smiled and replied, "Thank you, that's a good point, but my travels will take me across America to San Francisco and I would rather have the coat just in case."

Karen shook her head and replied, "Ah yes, that makes sense. So, when you leave out of here instead of going east on Bay Street, go west on Bay then south on Howard to Mitchell Street. You will see JC Penney on the corner; you can't miss it. Once you finish there, go east on Mitchell Street to Williams

Street and then to Rose Street and again, biggest house in town."

Lisa Marie took all the information from Karen, processed it, and then stood and said, "Thank you very much. If you don't mind, I'd like to eat. I'm really hungry."

Karen lightly clapped her hands and responded, "Oh yes, by all means, help yourself." As she motioned toward the buffet, she asked, "Would you like coffee?"

"Yes, please. Cream and sugar, thank you."

Karen disappeared into a room, presumably the kitchen, as Lisa Marie made her way to the buffet. She took a plate from the end of the table and made her way down the line of eggs, potatoes, bacon, sausages, and fruits. She neatly stacked her plate and returns to the table. As she sat, she noticed a man in the lobby looking right at her. He waved and walked away. She thought it was odd but brushed it off. A few seconds later, Karen returns with a tray and on that tray is a small kettle, a bowl of sugar, and a cup of cream.

"Here you are young lady; enjoy your meal. I'll place the bill right here. Once you're finished, just see me at the desk to pay. Thank you."

Lisa Marie added cream and sugar to her coffee and sat back in her chair to look at her feast. She took the rolled napkin from the table, opened it, took out the silverware, and placed the napkin on her lap. She began to eat slowly, savoring the food and sipping her coffee from time to time.

Chapter Seventeen: December 25, 1986, Los Angeles, CA

Robert Franklin, Sergeant Jacobs, and Lieutenant Garcia were in the hallway awaiting the elevator car. Robert looked at his watch and it's now 19:52.

Robert looked at Garcia and asked, "Why haven't you come to us any sooner?"

Garcia looked at Jacobs and Jacobs looked to the floor. Garcia responded, "Well, we thought this perp was just another sideshow clown until tips started coming in, and each tip led us right to his place of residence. It's an old warehouse that was converted into lofts a few years ago, but only one unit sold and the other three were leased out by some corporation and never used. We've learned this guy brought the women in, but they never leave, and without probable cause…"

"Wait, you're saying without probable cause. Cause for what?"

Jacobs interjected, "The women were never reported missing, most likely prostitutes, so without a missing persons complaint, what do we do? However, just two days ago, we got word that a young woman had gone missing from a gas station near the loft."

The elevator dinged, and the door opened. Robert motioned the two men inside.

Garcia asked, "What's up with the elevators in this building? They take forever. I had assumed you feds would have elevators that would—"

"Yes, we know they're slow and a service call has been

76

made. So, this girl, was she too a prostitute?"

"No, an aspiring actress waiting tables at a diner across from the station where she was filling up. The attendant called us, and we did our diligence and we finally convinced a judge to grant a warrant, and here we are."

The elevator jerked a few times, kept going, and then eventually stopped at the ground floor. The door slowly opened, and the men stepped out.

"Robert pointed to his black Impala and said, "I'm right here if you'd like to take my car."

Garcia handed Jacobs the keys to his unmarked and tells him to meet them at the site.

Garcia and Robert got into the car and within seconds the car came to life, squealed in reverse, and onto the street with tires smoking headed toward the loft.

"So, how long you been a fed?"

Robert looked at him and replied, "I graduated from SFSU in 1980 where I majored in psychology and minored in criminal justice. Went straight to Quantico and a little over twenty weeks later I was stationed here in Los Angeles."

Garcia nodded, "Are you from California?"

Robert laughed, "No—"

"Sorry, turn here!" Garcia said quickly.

"I'm from South Carolina."

"Where are you from, Lieutenant?"

"Isn't it obvious, last name Garcia, we're in LA? Born and raised here. My parents are from Mexico. So, I'm first generation

Latino in the USA. I've been on the force since August of 1965, just a few days before the Watts riots. That brought me up to speed quickly."

Robert looked at Garcia, "Wow, I'd say so. That was essentially a one-day deal that did a lot of damage to a community, right?"

"Yes, it was a day of pure hell. Turn here, it's right over there, see that squad car?"

Robert ducked down slightly and peered through the windshield. He made a few maneuvers through the lot and parked next to the other cars.

Garcia remarked, "Wow, we got here faster than your elevators!"

Robert laughed and put the Impala in park, causing a rocking motion, and the two men exit. Within seconds Jacobs pulled up and parked. The three men, and four other police officers, convened in front of the loft's would-be front entrance.

Garcia put on his commander hat and said, "Okay Mick, open the door! Rogers, you and Moe lead in and spread out and we'll follow. Johnson, you stay here and keep watch for anyone returning!"

The building wasn't that big, and it appeared the only way in was through two metal doors—very odd for a building where people lived, Robert thought. The lot had only the police vehicles and it was relatively dark, and on the other side of those doors was an unknown.

Garcia said, "Let's get busy, gentlemen."

Robert looked at Mick and thought he could have opened

the door with his mass alone, he must have been 6'5" and 280 pounds, obviously ex-military, or maybe he liked wearing his hair in a flat top.

Mick swung the sledge and literally knocked the door off its hinges.

Garcia looked at Robert's face, "Yeah I know, that's why we bring him."

Robert nodded slowly at Garcia. One man after another entered the building yelling, "LAPD search warrant; LAPD search warrant!" Dust and bent metal and debris were all that was left of the entrance.

The men walked through the first level, which is essentially studded walls and some leaning drywall. It was as if the work started and just stopped and all that remained was some wood, sheet rock, and heavy dust. There was electrical, for there were a few temporary lights hanging throughout the space. At the other end of the building were stairs, and with flashlights drawn, the men made their way to the second floor. Robert recalled his days of living in the dorm where he had to walk to the very end of the building to climb stairs that led to a hallway, only to come back to the front of the building, and that was essentially what had happened. Certainly, the goal was to have stairs in the middle of the main hallway. After all, the stairs they had just climbed were roughed in and seemed temporary. The only difference from the first floor to the second floor was one apartment had been finished.

The men made it to the door and Mick did what he does best and removed the door from the hinges with a single blow of a ten-pound sledgehammer. The men entered the unit and found that it was spotless, not a thing out of place, well, except for the front door which had been shoved halfway through a closet.

Garcia yelled out, "LAPD search warrant!"

The entire space must have been two-thousand square feet and wide open, just a few walls that went up about eight feet and not the full twelve feet exposing the wood beams above. The HVAC ducts hung from the ceiling about nine feet above the floor. It was a neat space. To the north there were three doors leading to what should be rooms.

The men looked at each other and Garcia motioned for Mick to take the door on the left, Jacobs to take the middle door, and Moe to the door on the right. The men readied themselves at their respective doors and on Garcia's count, the doors blasted open. Mick hit the floor like a big bag of flour since these doors were hollow wood, and he went through his door leaving it latched and hinged. Jacobs and Moe were able to stop and stay planted. Mick found what would be considered the bedroom. Jacobs was in the bathroom and Moe found the HVAC and laundry room. The bathroom was again, spotless, sterile if you will. The HVAC room was empty, not even clothes in the washer or dryer, and the dryer lint trap was clear of any lint. Robert and Garcia helped Mick to his feet, no easy task for sure.

Robert brushed some dust from Mick's right shoulder and replied, "Mick, are you okay?"

Mick looked at Robert and shook his head as if to say yes.

Garcia began opening empty drawers, one at a time, only to slam the shut-in anger. The closet was empty too.

Garcia looked around and said, "Well, he must have known

we were coming!"

Robert sat on the bed and looked at the dresser, but his eyes drew him to the floor, just behind the dresser. It was gold! It stood out against the concrete floor and black furniture. He stood, walked over to the item, and noticed it was a necklace that had fallen behind the dresser. He said, "Hey Mick, do you mind moving this dresser to the left?"

Mick walked over and with a giant right hand, he palmed the dresser and slid it out and about a foot from where Robert knelt. Robert reached into his coat pocket and pulled out a pen. Rogers walked up and handed him an evidence bag. Robert looked up and him and said, "Thank you." Rogers nodded.

Using his pen, Robert lifted the necklace and placed it in the provided bag. Rogers removed his radio from his belt. "Johnson, you copy?"

Seconds later. "Yeah, go ahead."

"Anything going on out there?" asked Rogers.

Johnson replied, "A Mercedes convertible stopped at the corner longer than it should have and then sped off."

Garcia grabbed the radio from Rogers. "Tim, did you get a plate number, anything?"

"No sir, it's too dark, but it was a Mercedes, one of those SL models, black, maybe dark blue, not sure. The streetlight above that intersection is out."

Garcia pressed the radio into Rogers' stomach. "Here, take this!"

The men convened in the living area and Robert said, "I will get this back to my office and run for prints, should have something late tomorrow."

Garcia waved him off and walked toward the exit. The men follow suit.

In a semicircle near the cars, Garcia reached into his right coat pocket and brought out a pack of Camel cigarettes and lit one. He took a long drag, pointed his head skyward, and exhaled. Between the cool air and the smoke, it was obvious he was irritated. He scratched his forehead, looked at Johnson and then at Robert, and said, "Well sir, I'm sorry we wasted your time this afternoon, but hopefully you'll be able to pull something from that necklace."

Robert replied, "From what I can tell, it looked like the same style found with the six deceased women."

Jacobs interrupted, "I thought it was five?"

Robert looked at Jacobs. "It was five, but this time last year I was sent to Montana to investigate a murder that fit the five from before. We know he's not just the West Coast. Seattle, Portland twice within a month, and the two here in LA."

Garcia replied, "Well, I guess we'd better get back to work. Thank you for coming out on such short notice." He then extended his right arm and the two men shook hands, as does Jacobs. The other cops give waved as they make way to their vehicles.

"Garcia…"

Garcia turned to Robert, "Yeah?"

Robert then asked, "Is that the diner and gas station right there?" and pointed to a diner about seventy-five yards to his right.

Garcia looked at where Robert is pointing and replied, "Yes, that's the one. The kid that called it—one second..." Garcia reached into his coat pocket and brought out a small notepad. He walked to the front of his car and leaned over just enough to use the headlight as he thumbs through the pages. He stopped, straightened up, and walked back to Robert. "His name is Mark James. He was a bit on the cocky side when we spoke, typical know-it-all punk."

Robert looked at Garcia, "Look, I know this is more of an LAPD thing, but since I'm here, I will go talk to the kid. Have a great night. Oh, and Merry Christmas."

Garcia raised his right hand and waved the notepad as he walked away, "You too, Agent Franklin, you too. If you learn anything, please give me a call." He got into his car, dropped the transmission into drive, and squealed off.

Robert stood there looking at the gas station, the diner, and back at the loft. Mick and Moe were securing the entrance that Mick destroyed minutes ago.

Roberts climbed into the Impala but doesn't start the car. He got out and walked toward the station. The air has chilled a bit, so he flipped up the collar of his overcoat and shoved his hands into the pockets.

Chapter Eighteen: April 1968, Petoskey, MI

Lisa Marie took the last of her coffee, wiped her mouth with the cloth napkin, reached for the bill, and brought it into reading distance. She stood and grabbed her purse from the seat to her right and walked to the front desk. She laid the bill on the counter and retrieved her pocketbook from her purse. Karen came into view and waved and said, "Well, I guess you have an admirer and your meal is taken care of."

Lisa Marie looked puzzled and replied, "Really, who might that be?"

Karen laughed, "Not sure, but they left money and a note that said: 'This is for the lady eating breakfast.'"

Lisa Marie put her pocketbook away, "Okay, I guess, thank you."

"Do you remember how to get to JC Penney?"

Lisa Marie looked at her, shook her head yes, and walked out the front door and onto Bay Street. The sun is bright, yet it's cold, very cold as she shivered. The temperature change from inside to outside was a bit much for a girl from South Carolina and her teeth began to chatter. She fast-walked heading west onto Bay and then south on Howard to Mitchell Street. Petoskey, she thought, was a quaint little town, clean and very quiet.

She stopped at the corner of Howard and Mitchell, looked to her left, and across the street was the JC Penney Karen had told her about. She looked both ways and made her way across and to the entrance. She stopped quickly as a woman with two-small children came rushing out the door. The mother seemed to have her hands full, so Lisa Marie held the door open as they hurried past her. The woman looked back and mouthed, "Thank you."

Lisa Marie smiled, twirled, and entered the store. Being from a small town, this store seemed enormous. She stood and looked around and just then a woman asked, "Hello, miss, may I help you find something?"

Lisa Marie caught eyes with a woman of about forty and replied, "Yes please. I'm looking for a long coat and mittens."

The woman looked at Lisa Marie from head to toe and replied, "You know, we may have remaining stock. We will be changing to spring clothing soon, so come with me."

The woman took them to an escalator and up to the second floor, and within seconds they were in the women's clothing section. The woman maneuvered through racks of clothing until she found coats. She looked at Lisa Marie again and said, "Well, you're short in stature; however, you are bustier than most, so here." She moved a few coats aside and brought out a long flannel coat with white wool colors and cuffs. "Try this one and I'll find you some mittens."

Lisa Marie took the coat, which was much heavier than her jean jacket. She laid the coat on the rack and dropped her purse to the floor. She removed her jacket and then laid it too on the rack. She then put on the coat and buttoned it. She already felt warmer and the fit was perfect. It went just past her knees. The woman returned with mittens and Lisa Marie put them on. She turned from side to side looking at each hand and replied, "Thank you, this is perfect!" After removing her wallet from her purse, she took her jean jacket and rolled it up tightly and put it in a bag.

The woman smiled and said, "Great! I can take care of payment over here. Will that be cash or charge?"

"That will be cash." She paid for the items, put her purse inside the bag with her jacket, and made her way out of the store. She stepped outside and looked east down Mitchell Street.

McCormick – Part Two

Chapter Nineteen: Wednesday, December 26, 1962, Sterling Heights, MI

Jimmy was still thumbing through pages on his clipboard and suddenly stopped at a page and said, "Here you go Tommy, you can do some short runs. General Motors has asked for some parts to be delivered from Warren to Flint. You'll do two trips up and back, today, tomorrow, and Friday, and then you're off to New York."

Tommy looked at Jimmy, "Where in Flint?"

"Looks like Buick City and AC Delco."

Tommy shook the paper out since the wind had folded it over. He looked over the documents and saw that Jimmy was correct. "Okay, I'm headed to Warren. I guess I'll see you when I see you."

The men shook hands and Tommy again said, "Merry Christmas Jimmy!"

"You too kid, you too!"

Tommy climbed back into his rig and cranked it over. The Cummins engine roared to life, which always made Tommy smile. He released the brakes and left the lot headed for Warren, Michigan. Traffic was light since a lot of the local businesses are shut down during Christmas and New Year. Tommy made quick time and was at a gate waiting for a security guard to acknowledge him. Finally, after waiting for what seemed like an hour, Tommy exited his truck and went to the guard shack. He looked in the window to see an elderly black man sitting in a chair sleeping. Tommy didn't want to startle the old man, so he knocked gently on the door, and then opened it. The old man sat forward and said, "Hi, can I help you?"

"Yes sir, I have to pick up a load from here and drive it to Flint."

The man slowly stood up holding his lower back and replied, "Oh yes, I remember now. You'll be here a couple days, right?"

"Yes, a couple of days, two loads per day until Friday."

The old man extended his right hand and Tommy took it. "I'm Sully!" replied the old man. "I'll be here every day this week, so we should know each other's names, right?"

"It's a pleasure to meet you Sully. I'm Tommy!"

The old man motioned Tommy toward the door and they both stepped outside. The old man buttoned his coat and pulled a stocking cap from his pocket and put it on. He raised his right arm and with a frail hand he pointed and said, "See over there, it reads 'Shipping and Receiving'; well you aren't going there. Go to the first drive, hang a right, and go behind building J. There will be men waiting to guide you where you should be, okay?"

Tommy looked at Sully and responded, "Thank you, Sully. You'd better get back inside where it's warm."

"You can believe that. Let me open the gate and you head on in. No need to stop on the way out; just use that air horn and I'll open the gate."

Tommy shook his head and climbed into his truck. Sully entered the shack and hit a button on the wall, and the gate slowly opened. The Mack truck coughed a cloud of black smoke and lurched forward. Tommy followed Sully's directions and within a few minutes he approached building J, and sure enough there were a couple men waving him to enter through a large overhead door. The room is large, like a warehouse, and not well lit, so Tommy turned his high beams on and followed a man walking in front of him. The man stopped, turned around, and waved for Tommy to stop. He then motioned across his throat to say, "cut it," and Tommy did just that. He set the brakes and the big rig shook to a stop.

Tommy rolled down his window as a man approached and said, "Hi, I'm here for a pickup. Nothing on the sheet telling me what I'm getting."

The man stopped Tommy from opening his door and climbed up to the window and said, "No need to get out. We will load the trailer; you just hang tight, kid!"

Tommy shook his head yes and the man jumped to the floor, causing a dust plume.

Tommy looked in his mirrors to see ramps being placed onto his trailer but cannot see much more since the trailer doors were only opened partway. He heard what sounded like a car starting and then the rig started to shake a little as the trailer is being loaded. Tommy leaned back in his seat and closed his eyes, which was short lived. The man from earlier slapped his door causing Tommy to jump.

"Wake up kid; you're all set. Head straight through and hang a left to leave the complex. This load goes to a lot at the northeast corner of Dort Highway and East Atherton Road in Flint. There will be shipping containers lined up and a few men there to unload the cargo. See you back here in a few hours!"

Tommy waved at the man and started the truck, released

the brake, and brought the engine up. He let out the clutch and the truck rolled forward as a large overhead door opened. He looked in his mirrors again as he neared the door and the rear door was closing. He saw a glimpse of what looked to be sports cars. Tommy looked up to ensure his rig will clear the door as he slowly made his way out. He made the left and soon he saw the guard shack, and as instructed, he sounded the air horn. Seconds later the gate rocked back and forth as it slowly opened. He approached the structure, gave a quick tug on the air horn cable, and waved as he drove through. He stopped the truck before the street and pulled out a map. He knew I75 north was his route but needed to get there from his location. He released the brakes and made the left and headed west toward I75 north, and within a few minutes, the truck was on a ramp taking him north. The traffic was very light, and getting to the posted speed, he knew Flint would be about an hour and a half or just under two hours.

Chapter Twenty: December 25, 1986, 20:12, Los Angeles, CA

Robert Franklin walked to the corner where the gas station and diner paralleled each other. He turned back to the loft and then to the gas station. He saw a young man behind the counter with his index finger up his nose past the first knuckle. Robert laughed and walked across the intersection and to the front door of the station. He pulled on the door and the young man removed his finger from his brain and quickly wiped it on his pant leg. It was his left hand, so shaking his right hand would be okay, maybe.

Robert made first contact. "Hi, are you Mark James?"

The kid looked at him and replied, "Who's asking?"

Robert reached into his back pocket and removed his badge holder, "Special Agent Robert Franklin, FBI."

The kid went blank.

"Not long ago, you gave a statement to the LAPD about a girl that works at that diner. Do you recall?"

James looked at the clock and replied, "Look man, I get off in a few minutes and I have things to do."

Robert got within inches of the kid's face and said, "Listen, this girl went missing, and we need to find her, get it?"

He then poked James in the chest, which caused the kid to respond with, "Ouch! That hurt!"

"Wow, I barely touched you. So, fill me in on the girl."

Mark James stepped back and rested against the countertop, "Look, there was this guy; he looked like you in a way. He came in, bought a few items, and asked for thirty dollars on pump three, premium, I think. I recall he used the restroom. So, Mindy, the waitress from the diner, was in here with a bunch of girlfriends. They were laughing about whatever it is girls laughed about when the dude came from the restroom. His fly was open, and the girls made fun of him. Mindy was the instigator. It embarrassed him, and he stormed out and forgot to put gas in his tank." James reached into his front shirt pocket and brought out forty-six dollars. He continued, "He paid with a fifty-dollar bill, but again, no gas, and here's his change."

Robert asked, "Do you recall the car? Was it a convertible, dark blue, maybe black?"

The kid scratched his forehead, "You know, it could have been, but as you can see, pump three is on the other side of pump one and it was dark."

Robert looked at the kid and asked, "You say he looked like me?"

"Yeah man, about your height and build, hair cut about the same. He wore glasses though, nerdy glasses. You know, from maybe the nineteen fifties?"

Robert processed what the kid told him and walked out the door.

Mark James yelled out, "Merry Christmas—jerk!" He then laughed and removed the register drawer, most likely to count the day's earnings.

Robert crossed the small street and stood in front of the diner. The sign read, "Closed—Celebrating the birth of our Lord and Savior." Robert smiled and thought of his dad standing on the pulpit giving those Sunday morning sermons. He made his way back to his Impala, got in, and started the car. He dropped it into drive and squealed off and onto the main street back to his office. It was close to 21:30 by the time he stepped out of the elevator. He opened the door going into his suite and must have woken Randy Miller. He had fallen out of his chair and scrambled to his feet.

"Robert, how did it go?"

Robert sat at an open chair, placed both elbows on his knees, and looked up at Miller, "I watched a monster of a man remove a steel door from its hinges with one swing of a sledgehammer. It was incredible. I had never seen anything like it. He just drew back and wham! The door flew into the building." Robert leaned back and began to laugh.

"Sir, are you okay?"

Robert stood, "Yeah, I'm good. The building was empty. Oh, wait, I almost forgot." Robert reached into his coat pocket and pulled out an evidence bag and handed it to Miller. "We need to get this checked for prints quickly."

Chapter Twenty-One: April 1968, Rose and Clinton Street, Petoskey, MI

Lisa Marie stood and stared at the giant home just thirty feet to her immediate right. She began to shiver, and not from the cold. The new coat was very warm, so maybe nerves. After all, it had been more than twenty years since seeing the man that she gave herself to.

As she approached the door, she looked left and right down the street. She saw the man from earlier at the hotel standing next to what she thought was a Camaro. He flicked a cigarette and then got into the car, started it, and backed into a driveway. He turned outward away from her and down a hill he went.

Her thoughts went back to the house at 600 Rose Street. She climbed the steps to the double front door and knocked, four raps on the door with a steady beat. Moments later she heard a woman's voice say, "I'm coming."

The big door opened and a woman of around sixty stood staring at Lisa Marie. The woman was beautiful, and it was obvious she had money; her jewelry was exquisite and not a hair out of place. "May I help you?" she said.

Lisa Marie cleared her voice and extended her right hand. "Yes, Mrs. McCray, my name is Lisa Marie Franklin and I knew your nephew Mack. He and I met when he was visiting McCormick, South Carolina, where I live."

"Yes, I know who you are. Mack talked about you from time to time during his stay with me and my husband. Please come in."

Lisa Marie wiped her feet and stepped into the foyer, which led to a large open area. In front of her was the most elegant staircase she had ever seen. It went up and to the right and left. Above her was a chandelier that was as big as a Volkswagen Beetle. "You have a lovely home, Mrs. McCray."

Mrs. McCray turned to her, looked around, and said, "Well, it's a bit much, but we like it. May I take your coat?"

Lisa Marie removed her mittens, unbuttoned her coat, removed it, and handed it all to Mrs. McCray.

"I can see now why Mack took a liking to you,"

Lisa Marie looked down at her breasts and then back to her host.

Mrs. McCray led Lisa Marie to a parlor and motioned for her to sit. The room is, in a word, "gawdy" at best. The furniture was very old, and the couch isn't very comfortable and made creaking noises every time Lisa Marie shifted her body.

"Tell me, Lisa Marie. What brought you from South Carolina to Petoskey?"

Lisa Marie shifted in her seat hoping to find that spot where she is comfortable and replied, "Well, I've been hoping to find Mack to, you know, reconnect, to talk I suppose. Once he left McCormick, we did our best to stay in touch, but I understood he moved here around 1958, is that correct?"

Mrs. McCray looked at the entrance to the parlor and naturally so did Lisa Marie, which caused her to jump. There was an elderly man standing there. Mrs. McCray said, "Pardon me, dear, this is Malcom; he helps out around here. Would you care for some tea?"

Lisa Marie looked at Malcom and then replied, "Yes, that would be nice, thank you."

Malcom nodded his head and turned away.

Kathryn said, "You were saying?"

"Is it true he moved here in 1958?"

Mrs. McCray looked at her and said, "Yes, his mother, my sister, had died in late 1957, and his father had drunk himself to death by 1958. Since I was his only living relative, it was best that he come stay with me."

Lisa Marie was puzzled by her response and then asked, "Why would a young man of twenty have to come live with you?"

Kathryn replied with a laugh, "Twenty? He was just sixteen when he came to us."

Lisa Marie, even more puzzled, "When he and I met in August of 1956, he told me he was 19."

Kathryn laughed. "No child, he was born in 1942, which means he was fourteen going to be fifteen later that year. I know he looked older; he got that rugged handsomeness from his father, Kenneth McKinstry, Sr."

"You thought Kenneth was handsome, did you?" Both women looked to the doorway and there stood a man of about sixty-five. He was short and stout.

Mrs. McCray smiled and turned to Lisa Marie and said, "This is my husband James. Honey, this is Lisa Marie Franklin. She's come from South Carolina looking for Kenneth."

"Kenneth?"

Mr. McCray walked to her, extended his right hand, "Ah, yes, the southern belle that Kenneth, or as you know him, Mack, spoke of for so many years. It's a pleasure, young lady."

He looked at Mrs. McCray and said, "It's no wonder Mack liked this woman."

She nodded, "Indeed, she is lovely."

Malcom entered the room with a tray, two cups, a sugar bowl, and a tea pot. He set the tray on a serving table and poured both glasses with hot tea and looked at Lisa Marie and asked, "One or two?"

"I'm sorry, one or two what?"

Mrs. McCray replied, "Sugar cubes, one or two sugar cubes?"

"Oh, yes, two will be fine, thank you."

Malcom added two cubes, stirred the contents, and handed Lisa Marie her cup. He added one cube to Kathryn McCray's cup and repeated the stirring and then handed her the cup. He turned and walked out of the room.

Mr. McCray said, "Thank you, Malcom."

And then Mrs. McCray said. "Yes, thank you."

Mr. McCray looked at his wife and asked, "Have you told her about Kenneth?"

Chapter Twenty-Two: December 26, 1986, Los Angeles, CA

Agent Miller took the evidence and walked away. Robert said, "Miller, check that in, lock it up, and let's get out of here. It's been a long day."

"Yes, sir...long day for sure!"

Robert turned to a phone on the desk in front of him, picked up the receiver, and put it to his ear. He listened to the hum without doing anything and then the hum turned to a loud beep, beep, beep. He hung up the phone, stood, stretched, and waited for Miller. Both men were now at the elevator.

Robert looked at Miller and said, "Merry Christmas."

"Merry Christmas to you as well."

The elevator dinged, the door opened, and Miller stepped inside. Robert hesitated, looked at his watch, and said, "You go ahead, I just thought of something."

"Is there something I can help you with?" as the door closed.

Robert Franklin brought his right hand to his chin as he stared at the floor. He turned and walked to his office and sat at his desk. He reached for the phone, and while the receiver was in his right hand, he pecked at the keypad with his index finger. He brought the phone to his ear and leaned back in the chair. He heard the other end ringing, and after about four, maybe five rings, a woman said, "Robert...is that you?"

Robert leaned forward in his chair and said, "Hello love, how are you?"

Tina Kettering replied, "Robert, are you okay?"

"Yeah, I'm fine. I'm tired and I miss you, that's all. Wanted to hear your voice."

Tina replied, "Oh, I miss you so much. I just got home about thirty minutes ago and took a bath, and now I'm watching a rerun of *The Golden Girls*. Yes, that's going to be me, old and living with other old single women."

"No, I don't think so. You will be old and living with me as my wife."

Tina is silent and then she began to weep. Through her tears she said, "Robert, we've been together for ten years, and you have said that numerous times, but I'm still looking at my left hand and don't see a ring."

Robert's eye welled up with tears as he leaned back and replied, "I know, honey. I'm sorry, but I mean it this time. When I see you in a few days, let's go to a jewelry store and pick out an engagement ring, okay?"

"Do you really mean it? I already have a design in mind, and I have a dress idea. Oh, and who I will ask as my bridesmaid!"

"Wow, I guess you're ready." He laughed and then said, "Listen, I'm going to get some rest. I'm still in my office. Local thought they had a suspect and the location we entered was empty, but I did see a man knock a steel door right off its hinges with one swing of a sledgehammer!"

"Robert, I knew the moment we met I would spend the rest of my life with you. You were so nervous; it was so cute to watch you stumble. Even though Jake was a jerk to me, I'm now grateful to him, and it's nice that we've stayed in touch, don't you think?"

"Yes, Jake is a character, and I too am grateful. Who would have thought he'd marry so soon after we graduated?"

"Okay, get some rest. I'm on tomorrow again, twelve hours. I'm covering for a friend. See you in a few days. I love you, Robert."

"I love you too," and hung up. He turned slightly in his desk chair and opened a drawer and brought out a checkbook. Thumbing through the pages to his last entry he smiled and said, "It's time, Tina. It's time." He put the checkbook away and closed the drawer. He stood and walked out toward the lobby. He stood in front of the elevator without pushing the button and then turned and walked toward a door leading to the stairs. He pushed the door open and bounded down the stairs to the parking garage. He climbed into the government-issued Impala, started it, backed up, and then chirped forward and onto the street. He turned on the map light, looked at his Paneria, and read 01:38. He turned the map light off and continued the drive home.

Chapter Twenty-Three: 1962, Flint, MI, Dort Highway

Tommy saw the lot with the shipping containers, two semitrucks, a van, and three sedans. He gave the air horn a quick pull letting the team know he's arrived. A man got out of the van and walked out to a spot where Tommy assumed he needed to be. The man waved him to stop and then came to the door as Tommy was rolling down the window.

Tommy said to the man, "Hey, how are you?"

"Back up to that green container. I'll be in your mirrors guiding you. When you stop, keep your eyes forward and the window up. Got it?"

"Sure thing." He pulled forward enough to get the truck into position before backing up to the container. A slight grind and the truck's engine stuttered as the truck moved backward. In the mirrors, Tommy saw another man waving him back and within a few seconds the man waved his arms overhead to indicate stop. Tommy set the brakes and looked ahead as instructed. His curiosity got the best of him and he looked at the passenger side mirror and saw the door from his trailer, which begged the question, "Why do they care if I look? I can't see anything anyway."

Tommy took the map from the dash and opened it. He was trying to understand his route into New York. He followed the highway lines, and before he made it to Pennsylvania, there were three quick but obvious raps on the door. He folded the map and tossed it back to the dash. He leaned forward and rolled down his window.

A short, squatty man, maybe Middle Eastern, said, "Okay,

go for more!" Tommy looked at both mirrors and saw men in them. They were all looking toward him and waving him on. Tommy released the brake and drove out of the lot and onto Dort Highway for the trip back to Warren.

It was beginning to snow heavily, and his visibility was essentially ten feet. He backed down the throttle as he entered I75 just in case a motorist didn't see him merging. The truck rolled on as the snow flew, and within a mile or so the snow was gone, and the sun was doing what it could cut through the clouds.

Tommy looked down at the fuel gauge and it read just over three-quarters of a tank. He patted the steering wheel and said, "Good truck," and laughed. He reached for the radio and turned up a song being sung by Dion and he began to sing along. "They call me the wanderer, yeah the wanderer. I roam around, around, around…" A fitting song for a boy from McCormick, South Carolina.

The weather was in his favor as he pulled up to the gate at General Motors and tugged the cord for the air horn just enough to get Sully's attention, but not to scare the old man. The gate began to open, and Sully was at the window waving him through while he talked on the phone, most likely letting the guys know he was back. He does the same drive around the back to building J and waited for the big overhead door to open. He pulled in, stopped, set the brake, shut the truck down, and waited. He moved his shirt sleeve up and looked at his watch. It's just after 2:00 PM, which means he will be back here around 7:00 PM. Just in time for a nice dinner and a good night's sleep.

Tommy reached for the map once again, but this time the

load was quicker, and he soon got the same three raps on the door. The truck started, and he released the brakes as the door before him began to open. He edged forward and soon he was back on the main road toward I75. No change in the weather, which meant smooth driving all the way to Flint.

Chapter Twenty-Four: December 26, 1986, Los Angeles, CA, 06:00

Robert Franklin was lying in bed staring at the ceiling and his alarm sounded. With his left hand, he slapped the clock and the alarm stopped. He rolled up and swiveled his body and placed his feet to the floor. The room was essentially dark aside from some light that came through the gap in the curtains, streetlights mainly. Robert already knew it would be a nice day, at least considering the weather. At times he missed the rainy season of South Carolina. It was a peaceful sound and he always slept better. Los Angeles was noisy with all the traffic and it never rained.

He stood, stretched, and did his daily routine of exercises, a habit he developed his sophomore year while at San Francisco State University. He finished his training, took a long shower, shaved, and then headed into the kitchen where a coffee pot set to a timer had made the apartment smell a bit like heaven. Toast with peanut butter and a hardboiled egg were how he started his day. He poured the rest of the coffee into a thermos, put on a holster, and slid his side arm into place. He grabbed his coffee, a briefcase, an overcoat, and walked out the door.

"Hello Robert, Merry Christmas," said an elderly woman that lived across the hall and was bent over to pick up her morning paper.

"Merry Christmas to you, Ms. Jenkins. How are you?"

Ms. Jenkins stood with some difficulty and replied with a smile, "Oh, I'm fine now. When will you leave that girlfriend and marry me?"

Robert laughed, "Well, Ms. Jenkins, I may just do that."

They both laughed, and Robert said, "You have a wonderful day!" as he walked away.

She waved him off and went back into her apartment. Before Robert exited the building, he set his thermos and briefcase on the floor, put on his overcoat, grabbed both items, and out the door he went. He put the key in the lock of the government-issued Chevrolet Impala, opened the door, and tossed his case to the back seat. He slid in and rested the thermos on the seat next to him. He made a few physical adjustments because his coat had bunched up, restricting the use of his arms. Once settled, he leaned forward, put the key in the ignition, and turned it, and the car came to life. He threw his right arm over the back of the seat and stared out the back window as the car moved in reverse. He turned toward the windshield and put the car into drive. He drove out of the parking lot and onto the street.

The radio was playing a song he's never heard before and the beat was very energizing; he began to tap the steering wheel while he moved his head from side to side the sun was bright and he felt alive. The sky was cloudless, and the color blue was vivid. Within minutes he drove over a slight bump and into the parking garage of his office. He whipped the sedan into a parking spot and screeched to a stop. He reached for the volume knob taking it to the max and continued to listen to the song until it was over, hoping to hear the name and band, but instead the DJ moved right into another song, one he was familiar with. He turned the car off and pressed the unlock button on the door trim panel with his left hand. He opened the door, swiveled sideways, and placed his feet on the concrete. He stepped out, thermos in hand, opened the passenger door, ducked in, and grabbed his briefcase. He slammed the door and then reached in and selected the lock button and closed the driver's door and walked toward the entrance whistling the tune he just heard.

"Good morning boss!" Randy Miller yelled out.

Robert looked to his left and replied, "Good morning, Miller. How was your night?"

"Great, since I still live at home, my mom made a big dinner for Christmas and I was able to bring in a lot of the leftovers." He raised a paper bag to show his haul for the day.

"Say, I heard this new song on the way in, something about happy being happy with you?"

Miller laughed, "You mean 'Stuck With You' by Huey Lewis and the News? Yeah, that song's been on for several months."

Robert looked at Miller with a smile. "Yes, I guess maybe I should listen to the radio more often. Anyway, it's a catchy tune."

Miller tucked his bag under his arm and reached for the door and held it open while Robert walked through.

"Thank you," Robert said.

As they approached the elevator, it was clear that the stairs will be how they get to their offices. "Sorry for the inconvenience. The elevators were being serviced."

Miller stopped and stared and then said, "Wow, after what, seven months they're finally going to fix—"

Robert interrupted, "Fix or make worse?"

The men laughed and headed toward a door leading to the

stairs. Robert then asked, "When you submitted that evidence, did you request a rush?"

"Yes, I wrote in big letters —'RUSH'—as you know there weren't many of us in the office yesterday."

"Oh, yes, I forgot it was Christmas. Well hopefully we'll know something today or tomorrow. Oh, did I mention that one of the cops could have passed for Sasquatch?"

They both laughed as they entered the office area. Several agents were seated and of course the agent in charge was sitting in Robert's office.

Robert looked at Miller and said, "Well, here I go, wish me luck."

Miller saluted and made his way to his desk.

Robert entered his office, set his briefcase and thermos on his desk, and began to remove his overcoat.

Special Agent in Charge Scott Decker said, "You should leave that on; you won't be here long." Robert shrugged the coat back on and said, "Is everything alright?"

Decker stood, walked to the door, and closed it, "Robert, take a seat." His tone was somber and fatherly. Robert's hands began to sweat, and his heart started to race as that lump in the throat you get when something's just not right forms.

Robert looked at Decker, "Ok, spill it. What's going on!"

Decker looked at Robert and then to the floor and said, "Robert, I'm not sure how to say this, but…"

Chapter Twenty-Five: April 1968, Petoskey, MI, McCray Home

Mrs. McCray looked at her husband and replied, "We were getting to that."

Lisa Marie looked back at Mrs. McCray intently. Mrs. McCray continued, "You see, Mack came to live with us after his parents died as I said and was left with $75,000.00, which was to remain in trust until he reached eighteen, which was 1960. He barely graduated high school, took the money, bought a car, and just left. We have no idea where he went; he just vanished. Mr. McCray thought about hiring an investigator to find him, but soon we agreed he chose his path, and who were we to interfere? We did our best for nearly three years, and the loss of his parents was apparently too much for all of us."

Lisa Marie leaned back in her chair, investigated her cup of tea, and then said, "Well, I'm sorry to have wasted your time. I guess I was hopeful to reconnect with Mack. He and I shared a lot during his two weeks in McCormick."

Mr. McCray stood and said, "If it's any consolation, Mack mentioned you a few times; he even asked if we'd take him to see you, but we were just too busy, or the timing just didn't seem right. Who knows why, really, we just didn't. For that, I'm sorry."

Lisa Marie looked at him, smiled, and then stood. She placed the cup and saucer on a tray and walked up to Mr. McCray and hugged him. Mrs. McCray stood and she too hugged Lisa Marie and said, "It sure was nice to meet you. Can we take you anywhere?"

"No, thank you. I'll walk back to the hotel."

They left the parlor and Malcom helped Lisa Marie with her coat. At the big door, Lisa Marie asked, "Is there a chance you have a recent picture of Mack? I mean a photo of him before he left?"

The McCray's looked at each other and Mr. McCray replied, "You know, oddly enough, when he left, he took all photos of himself, and if there were group pictures, he cut himself out of them; something we never understood."

Lisa Marie replied, "Yes, that does seem a bit odd. Well, again, thank you for your time." She opened the door and stepped out onto the stoop and looked toward Williams Street and then west down Rose Street. She decided to go west and make her way back to the hotel.

The temperature had risen slightly, and the sun was warm on her face. She saw a beautiful glimpse of sparkling water and smiled. She began to recall the time she spent with Mack. The talks they had, and the love they made. He seemed so mature for his age, and then she smiled and then laughed and said, "Wow, he was younger than me." She meandered through town until she found a quaint diner and went in for lunch. The place was bustling, and the servers were racing to get food to patrons. A young woman came to her and said, "Sit where you'd like; someone will be right with you."

Lisa Marie smiled, looked around, and saw a two-top table to the left at the window was available and made her way over.

"Hey, South Carolina!" a man yelled from across the diner.

Lisa Marie looked to her right and there he was, the bartender.

He was sitting with a group of men of his age and stature. She ignored him as they all laughed among themselves.

A waitress looked at Lisa Marie from another table and mouthed, "I'll be right with you."

Lisa Marie nodded and began to stare out the window. The man she thinks she saw in Toledo and earlier that day was across the street looking right at her. She shivered in her seat and just then the waitress said, "I know, it's a cold one. What can I get for you?"

Lisa Marie was startled and jumped slightly and said, "Oh my, you startled me."

"I'm sorry, dear."

Lisa Marie laughed and took a quick look at the one-page menu and replied, "It's okay. I'll have the tuna fish sandwich and a Coke, please."

The waitress wrote the order on a small pad and said, "Sure thing, coming right up!" She then turned and walked away. Lisa Marie looked out the window again and the man was gone. She started to think about the fact she hadn't had a fix in almost two days and her arm began to itch. Over her shirt she scratched and then sipped from the glass of water the waitress had set on the table before taking her order.

The lunch crowd was leaving along with the bartender and his friends. They walked by the window and of course stared at Lisa Marie as she ate her sandwich. Lisa Marie began to daydream again; the memories of her rape were coming back, most likely brought on by the lack of heroin and the taunting from the bartender. A tear formed and went down her check.

The waitress said, "Honey, you okay? I know the food isn't the best—"

Lisa Marie interrupted, "No, the sandwich was fine. I must have looked into the sunlight a bit too long."

The waitress looked out the window and saw it was more overcast than sunny and replied, "Okay, can I get you anything else?"

"No thank you. What do I owe you?"

The waitress thumbed through her slips and replied, "Let's see, a tuna sandwich and a Coke; that will be $1.15, please."

Lisa Marie grabbed her purse from the chair next to her, reached in for her pocketbook, and handed the waitress $3.00 and said, "Here, you've been wonderful. Keep the change."

"Wow, thank you very much. Have a wonderful day."

Lisa Marie drank the last of her bottled Coke, wiped her mouth with a napkin, stood, put on her coat, snatched her purse, and out the door she went onto Mitchel Street.

Chapter Twenty-Six: Friday, December 28, 1962, Flint, MI

Tommy was pulling into the same lot on Dort Highway in Flint, Michigan, where the same vehicle and yes, the same men were there to greet him with their warm and friendly demeanor. Tommy had never questioned anything he has delivered and by now it was clear these deliveries were automobiles headed out of the country. After all, they would never use a box trailer and shipping containers for the USA and Canada. This went on all the time. A hot new car that can't be had anywhere but America would be stolen and shipped to places like Saudi Arabia, China, and even Europe. Tommy recalled seeing an article about the new Chevrolet Corvette, a radical change from 1962, and was been dubbed "The Stingray" because of its shark-like lines, a split rear window, and hidden headlights. It's was that it would change the way the world looked at American sports cars.

Tommy waited for the trailer doors to close and to be paid. Three men walked to the driver door and Tommy rolled down the window. The short Middle Eastern man handed an envelope to a taller man who in turn handed it to Tommy. Tommy took the envelope, opened it, and assumed the $2,500.00 he was promised would be there, but it wasn't; it was more.

Tommy said to the men, "Hey, I was told $2,500.00 and there's $3,200.00."

The Middle Eastern man waved his stubby hand, "Yes, thank you for doing a good job. You made this happen ahead of schedule, and for that I rewarded you"

"Thank you, sir. Will that be all?"

The man nodded his head and Tommy waved, rolled up his

window, released the brake, and was on Dort Highway headed for Detroit to fuel his truck and then to New York. He felt that stopping at his favorite truck stop would allow him to say hi to Tiffany again, and hopefully she'd be over their little squabble from Christmas day. Tommy's thoughts took him back to Big Mike's offer and if that would be the end or would he continue to harass him into joining the O'Connor Brothers?

About twenty minutes into the trip, the snow began, and within seconds, Tommy was driving blindly through a total whiteout. He downshifted the truck and brought it to about twenty miles per hour. Luckily for him there weren't as many travelers going southbound. He reached over and turned the radio down to keep his full attention to the road. The snow swirled and a few times the wind gusts rocked the big rig, causing Tommy to panic and grip the wheel at ten and two. His twenty-mile-per-hour pace lasted about forty-five minutes and then it was as if Mother Nature flipped a switch and the sun was out and the roads were clear. He said out loud, "Why would anyone want to live here?"

He made his exit and onto the service street. The truck stop was lit up as usual and there were only a few trucks parked, and thankfully none were O'Connor Brothers, just Kmart and a few unknowns. Tommy quickly put the truck and trailer at a pump, set the brake, and shut the truck down. The cab shook a bit and then silence. Tommy opened the door and made his way to the ground after a few quick moves and a small jump.

He looked inside the station and noticed Tiffany was at the register chatting with a couple of men. He saw her body moving back and forth as she flirted, twirling her hair with her index finger. He went to the pump, pulled the handle, and cranked the start lever downward, and the pump came to life. He removed the fuel cap and placed it on the fuel tank. He dropped the nozzle in the hole and squeezed the handle. The smell of diesel hit his nostrils and he quickly wiped his nose. The air was cold, but the wind was slight, which made it easier to fill the tank. Once full he returned the nozzle to the pump, put the fuel cap on, turned, and went into the station.

Tiffany looked at him and then turned back toward the men that were paying attention to her. Tommy made his way to the restroom, relieved himself, and then washed and dried his hands before heading out to the store area. He went to a cooler and took a bottle of Coke and then to a rack and grabbed a bag of potato chips. It was close to 6:00 p.m. and he could either start his trip to New York now or wait until morning. Either way, his drive would be easy, he thought.

He walked to the register and stood in line. The two men saw him and backed away. One said, "Hey, sorry, we're just talking. Be my guest."

Tommy nodded and said, "Hi Tiffany, how are you?"

Tiffany looked at Tommy with a not-so-pleasant look, "I'm good, how are you?"

"I'm good, thank you. I had $38.75 on pump two and these two items."

Tiffany tapped on the register's keys and said, "That'll be $40.00 even."

Tommy pulled out his envelope filled with cash and removed a fifty-dollar bill and handed it to Tiffany. Her eyes lit up at the cash she saw in the envelope and she looked at the two men and nodded toward Tommy. They too were impressed with the wad of cash. Tiffany tapped again on the register keys and the drawer dinged open and she made change. Tommy took it, scooped up his purchase, and went for the door.

One of the men yelled out, "Hey man, where'd you get all that cash?"

Tommy kept walking.

The other man said, "Hey, we're talking to you!"

Tommy exited the station and headed to his truck. He heard the doorbells ring as the two men came from inside, but they said nothing. Tommy looked over his shoulder as the men waved him off and one pushed the other back inside, which told Tommy that Tiffany was a bit more important than the cash in Tommy's pocket.

The dark and cold temperature made Tommy's decision easy. He will find a room, eat a nice meal, take a hot shower, and get on the road come daybreak.

Chapter Twenty-Seven: December 26, 1986, Los Angeles, CA 07:27

Robert looked at Decker and again said, "What's going on?"

Decker looked at Robert and leaned into him. "I got a call this morning. Tina was killed by a drunk driver on her way to work this morning."

Robert leaned back, "Wait, what! No, I'm planning to go home this weekend. We were going to shop for an engagement ring. So, no, she can't be gone!" Robert began to weep and buried his face in his hands.

Decker placed his right hand on Robert's left shoulder, "I'm truly sorry, son. I know how much you loved her. Listen, go home, gather some things, and head up. Her family needs you."

Robert looked up at Decker and then into the bullpen area. He saw Miller staring at him with a look of "what's going on?"

Decker stood and looked over Robert, who turned and walked out the door, closing it behind him.

Robert wiped tears from his face. He stood and sat at his desk staring at the phone. He picked up the receiver and dialed a number. Within a few rings, a woman's voice answered, saying, "Hello, Franklin residence."

Robert was silent and again the voice said, "Hello, Franklin residence."

Robert leaned forward in his chair and cupped his right ear and said, "Hi Mom."

Marilynn Franklin replied, "Hello Robert. Merry Christmas! We missed a call from you yesterday."

"I know, I'm sorry, I had a lead—"

Marilynn interrupted, "Why do you sound so down? Is the CIA working you too hard?"

"Mom, Tina was killed by a drunk driver this morning on her way to work."

Marilynn was silent for a moment and said, "Oh Robert, I'm so sorry, oh my. John, please pick up the other phone!"

"Hello, Pastor John Franklin. May I help you?"

"John, it's Robert on with us. Tina's gone."

"Hello son, you mean you broke up?"

"No Dad, she was killed by a drunk driver this morning on her way to work."

There was a long silence and then John said, "Robert, I'm so very sorry. What can we do? Do you need us to come out?"

"No, I'm going up state to be with her parents and will call you tomorrow. Oh, by the way, my home phone is scheduled for hook up Monday next week, which was why I didn't know of her death until I got to the office. Again, I'll call tomorrow."

"Okay son. We love you. Be careful."

Robert hung up the phone and just sat staring at the top of his desk. He reached down with his right hand and moved the sleeve of his coat upward to look at his watch. It's now 07:54 and he needs to get on the road. He stood, grabbed his keys and his briefcase, and walked to the door. He stopped, turned to the credenza, and saw photos of Tina and him and tears build. He walked over and took the photo of their first date, which oddly enough was in front of Chin Lea's restaurant. Jake had taken the photo and then poked fun at the two. Robert knew he needed to call Jake, but thought he'd wait until he got to the Bay Area. The stairs to the parking garage seemed to go on forever and Robert felt the weight of the world on his shoulders.

"Agent Franklin!" a voice yelled out. Robert turned to see Randy Miller missing every third step to catch him. Robert stopped about four steps from ground level and leaned against the handrail.

Miller stopped just short and said, "Hey, I'm really sorry to hear about Tina. If there's anything I can do, please…"

Robert looked at Miller and said, "Thank you. Just keep an eye on things. Oh, and find out about the necklace. I'll be north and will return Monday, January 6. I probably won't be calling in, so whatever you come up with can wait until I'm back, okay?"

Miller looked at Robert, nodded his head, and motioned as if to hug Robert in his time of loss. Robert extended his right arm and the two men shook hands and parted ways, Robert to his car and Miller back to the office a few flights up.

Robert unlocked the Impala, opened the driver door, and hit a button to unlock all other doors. He threw his items into the back seat, removed his overcoat and suit coat, and laid them on the bench seat and closed the door. He slid into the front seat and started the car. He reached over his left shoulder and retrieved the seat belt and brought it across his chest and latched it at his right hip. He looked at his watch and it's now 08:02, and he knew that once he's on the 5 going north, he should be able to make it in less than eight hours, and since he was in a government vehicle, maybe seven hours. On a normal day just getting to the freeway and out of LA could take an hour, and traveling the speed limits could take nearly nine hours. Robert reached for the gear selector and it hit him—Tina was gone, and he began to weep. She was his first and only love. He began to shake the steering wheel and then pulled it together and put the car in reverse and then into drive, and he squealed off.

Chapter Twenty-Eight: April 1968, Petoskey, MI

Despite the cool air, the sun had decided to shine, and this made Lisa Marie smile as she walked east with no real place to go. She found Petoskey to be a charming little town with just enough going on, but not overwhelming. Of course, it's only April, and maybe during the summer months, the streets were filled with people and the lake was packed with boats. So many little shops to choose from, so she approached a Ben Franklin, a department store that has most of what a person needs and some of what you don't. The store windows were lined with all sorts of items from spring clothing to kites, and this made her smile. She thought of her bothers back in McCormick and then her mother. Just then she was nearly knocked off her feet by a few high school boys horsing around with a football.

"Oh, ma'am, I'm terribly sorry," a boy said as he helped stable himself and Lisa Marie. The other boy ran up and took Lisa Marie by the elbow and said, "Miss, I'm very sorry."

Lisa Marie smiled and replied, "It's okay. You've got some arm on you. And you, when you hit me it was like a truck backed into me."

All three laughed, and Lisa Marie asked, "Do you mind if I toss you a pass?" The boys looked at each other and smiled as if to say, sure, whatever lady.

Lisa Marie took the ball and gripped it the way her father had shown her years ago and told the boys to start running. The boys made a short stride and she kept waving them out. Finally, one boy made a mad dash and Lisa Marie hurled the ball skyward, which passed the first boy and the second boy turned just in time to receive the throw. The first boy stopped and stared at her and the second boy jogged back to his friend, shaking his head.

Lisa Marie smiled and said, "Have a great day!"

Both boys looked at each other and then reply, "You too, ma'am…" and then make small talk among themselves as they kept looking back at Lisa Marie.

Lisa Marie looked back once more and then smiled, followed by a slight laugh. Now she must decide her next move since Mack was no longer in Petoskey, but her thoughts soon change as the need overcomes her and she began to shake. Under her breath she said, "Not now, please, not now."

She decided to go into the Ben Franklin to buy a map of the United States. A ringing of a bell hanging just above the door that was triggered upon entering and exiting. An older man wearing a vest walked up to her and said, "Hello young lady, what can Bill do for you?"

Lisa Marie smiled and replied, "Hi Bill, I'm looking for a map of the United States."

"Well, you've come to the right place. Come with me."

Lisa Marie followed Bill across the store to the book section, and sure enough, there were maps: folded maps, maps in book form, etc. "So, do you need a big map or something to carry in your purse?"

"Well, Bill, I just need a map I can keep in my purse and use it only when I need to."

Bill reached down and picked up a Rand McNally folded map and handed it to her and replied, "Ok dear, this should suit you just fine. Is there anything else Bill can help you with?"

"No, Bill, that will be fine, thank you so much."

He motioned toward the registers and said, "Ok, if you're all set, Amy can take it from here. Have a wonderful day!"

Lisa Marie smiled and made her way to Amy. Lisa Marie laid the map on the counter along with her purse and fished for her pocketbook.

"Hello, did Bill take good care of you?"

"Oh, yes, he's very kind. Say, does he always refer to himself in the first person?"

Amy smiled, "Yes, he's been at this store for so long that some folks call him Ben, you know, as in Ben Franklin, so Bill wanted to remind people of his name. He's cute, isn't he?"

"Yes, he is. So, what do I owe you?"

Amy looked at the map's upper right corner and tapped the register and then said, "Okay, with tax that'll be $1.26 please."

Lisa Marie removed a dollar, a quarter, and a penny from her pocketbook and handed it to Amy.

"Would you like a bag?"

"No, thank you. I'll put it in my purse. Oh, do you happen to have the bus schedule?"

Amy looked to her right and said, "Yes, here it is. Where were you headed?"

"I'm not sure, maybe San Francisco, California."

Amy lit up and said, "Wow, I'd love to go to Hollywood. I've only been north of here to the Upper Peninsula and Flint."

"Well, up until a few weeks ago, I had never left South Carolina."

Amy's excitement resonated, and she asked, "Did you live on the ocean? I have dreams of seeing the ocean someday."

Lisa Marie looked at Amy with a smile and replied, "No, we lived inland, but I had been to the ocean, and let me tell you, it's overwhelming. The air has a salty taste and the waved coming in remind of you of just how small you really were, especially when they knock you around." The two women laughed, and Lisa Marie said, "Well, thank you again, I appreciate it. Oh, is it possible to get that bus schedule?"

"Oh, yeah, sorry. Here you go. Good luck to you!"

Chapter Twenty-Nine: Saturday, December 29, 1962, Brooklyn, NY

Tommy woke to a knock on his driver door. He scrambled to get dressed and said. "Hold on, I'm coming."

A voice from outside the truck replied, "No worries, sir, take your time."

Tommy shrugged his coat on after tying his boots and climbed into the driver seat and rolled down the window. There were two police officers who stood there looking up at him. Tommy said, "Hello officers, may I help you?"

The two cops looked at each other before one said, "Good evening, sir. I'm Corporal Mike Jameson and this is Officer Chris McCarthy of the NYPD and we received a complaint about a running semitruck keeping the residence awake in the building to my right." He pointed, and Tommy's eyes follow. "It's posted on that pole right there, no idling for more than thirty minutes, and you've been here a couple of hours now."

Tommy had a clear look of concern on his face and replied, "Yes sir, I'm terribly sorry. I didn't see the sign. Am I in trouble?"

Officer McCarthy replied, "No sir, but you may want to shut down the truck."

Tommy slapped himself on the forehead, "Yes, of course... sorry." He reached down and turned the key to the left and the truck shook, and the engine went silent.

Tommy asked, "Do you have the time please?"

McCarthy moved his bulky coat sleeve upward and replied, "It's 02:30."

"Great, thank you, again I apologize."

Corporal Jameson replied, "No worries, sir. You have a few hours before this place opens for delivery, so stay warm."

"Yeah, I'm here picking up. Thank you again."

"Well whatever, you have a few hours to go, and I hope I don't come out again to find you frozen in that bunk."

Tommy looked over his right shoulder and replied, "I should be okay; I have a military grade sleeping bag tucked away in here somewhere."

The two officers turned and walked to their patrol car. Tommy looked straight ahead and saw the sign, now clear as day. He stooped down and looked out the top of the windshield at the apartments and saw a light turning off. He waved and said, "I'm sorry, didn't know." He stood bent at his waist and digs through his gear stored at the side of the bunk and behind the passenger seat and brought out a tightly rolled sleeping bag. He began to untie the cords, holding the bag taut.

Suddenly a knock at the door startled him and he jumped. Under his breath he said, "I shut my truck down, now what?" He then said, "One second please." He threw the loosened bag into the bunk area and turned and flopped down on the driver seat and reached for the window crank. He saw a woman wearing barely enough to keep a child warm standing there puffing on a cigarette.

"Hi, can I help you?"

The woman dropped her smoke and with her shoe turned the burning cigarette into a pile of ash, paper, and tobacco. "No, the real question is, can I help you, honey?"

Tommy placed his right hand into his crotch and replied, "No thank you. I'm tired and have a long day tomorrow."

"Well, let me come in and help you sleep, handsome."

"No, thank you. I'm all set. Have a nice night," He rolled up the window.

The woman then smacked the door with her purse and walked away. Tommy rolled down the window again to see if it did any damage, but the streetlights weren't good enough and his angle was all wrong, so he cranked the window up. He stood again, removed his coat, and kick off his boots, and climbed into the bunk. He laid out the sleeping bag, unzipped it, and climbed in. It was already warm from the heat of the cabin, so it made it nice for falling asleep, which he did within a few minutes.

Tommy woke a few hours later to the sounds of people outside the truck. He rose up and rubbed his face with both hands and then crawled out of his manmade cocoon. It was clearly morning despite his windows being frosted over. He followed the same routine with putting on his boots and shrugging on his jacket from a slight bent over position and sat in the driver's seat. He reached down and turned the key to start and pressed the starter button a few seconds later. The truck coughed to life and he moved the heat selector to defrost and moved the fan speed to high. He then opened his door and climbed out and onto the ground. The ground was hard, and there wasn't nearly as much snow as Michigan, which made Tommy smile.

He retrieved his papers from behind the seat and walked to the back of the trailer. A few men walked by without a word as Tommy approached the door with "Office" hanging on a board above it. He turned the handle and it opened, and he walked in.

The room was small, but it seemed more like he was back in Chicago with all the Italians just sitting around. The smoky air was so thick you could barely see five feet out.

A man said, "Hey, you, can I help you or something?"

Tommy looked for where the voice came from and saw a short, stout, middle-aged man waving his right hand with his index finger wrapped around a cigar as big as a Coke can. Tommy walked over and said, "Yeah, hi, I'm here for a load. Giovani Brothers, going to Detroit."

The man sat back in his chair and replied, "Oh yeah, you were sent specifically for the load, right? You were well liked or something, right?"

Tommy looked around as all eyes were now on him and replied, "Sure, I guess. I just like to drive I suppose," and laughed.

The fat man responded with a puff of cigar smoke right into Tommy's face and Tommy fanned it away and coughed slightly. The man said, "Okay, here's the thing; pull your truck out and head east about two blocks and you'll see loading docks on the right-hand side. Back your trailer into dock five and they'll get you loaded, capiche?"

"I'm sorry?"

The fat man replied, "Do you understand!?"

Tommy leaned back, "Yes, I understand. What am I hauling, anyway?"

A few men began to laugh, and the fat man replied, "Hey, if they didn't tell you, then forget about it, okay? Now take this paper and go to dock five and get this load to Detroit by tomorrow 10:00 a.m., got it!?"

Chapter Thirty: Monday, April 26, 1999, 05:30

Robert Franklin's alarm went off, but he was wide awake several minutes before. It's now 1999 and his relationship with Jennifer Sanders was strained at times, and he couldn't seem to make heads or tails of this animal he's been chasing since 1986. Now as a Special Agent in Charge with nineteen years under his belt, he had put together a small task force to seek out and arrest the man deemed the "Pearl Necklace Killer" because, just like the necklace he found in the loft apartment in LA, the guy had left each victim the same necklace. So far, every woman had been found wrapped in a plastic drop and wearing the same necklace—same jeweler—a high-end jewelry company out of San Francisco that went out of business in the early 1980s. Oddly, none of the women were sexually assaulted. They had obvious marks around the wrists and ankles from being tied. The killer had taken twenty-six women thus far, and sadly, New York had seen seven within the past five years. The first known killing took place in the Bay Area of California more than twenty years ago.

Robert's BlackBerry rattled and rang on the kitchen table as he sipped his coffee and did his best to eat something before heading to the office. He walked over to the phone, picked it up, and saw the name "Jameson." He stared contemplating whether to answer. He pressed a button on the side and brought the phone to his ear and said, "Franklin."

"Hey kid, did I wake you?"

Robert rolled his eyes and replied, "No Lieutenant, what can I do for you?"

Lieutenant Mike Jameson, a near thirty-year veteran with the NYPD homicide division, had been working with Robert Franklin of the FBI for nearly four years regarding the serial murders in and around the area.

Mike replied, "I was hoping to have lunch today and introduce you to a new detective on my team. He's a bright kid, much like yourself."

"So, are you finally going to retire?"

Mike laughed, "Well, I'm coming up on thirty years and the missus has been leaving brochures around the house—you know, condos in Florida. So, I'd say I'm close, and June of this year will be thirty years on the force, and the kids are all grown and gone; so yeah, it's close."

"I'd say well deserved for sure; besides, your old bones could use the warm weather of Florida." Robert laughed and then said, "Look, I'll see you at Ray's. The good one we always go to, okay?"

"Okay, great. Oh, and you're buying this time, you cheap—"

Robert stopped the call and set the phone on the table near the door. He reached for his shoulder holster, slid into it, and then grabbed his suit coat from the coat hanger where his holster once hung. He snatched up his badge and clipped it to his belt, collected his phone and keys, and headed out into the hall and to the elevator. Being on the fifteenth floor had advantages, like the view and less street noise, but the elevator was slow, much like the elevator at the office in LA. He laughed and flashed back to the days of taking the stairs, which was okay since it was only three flights up, and he was a bit younger, too.

The elevator opened and Mr. and Mrs. Jameson (no relation to Lieutenant Jameson) stood there, holding hands. Mrs. Jameson held Trixie, a very small dog. They're a handsome couple with tons of money, so it seemed, and in their early fifties Robert guessed.

"Hello Robert!" Mr. Jameson said.

Robert extended his right hand and the two men exchanged handshakes. "Mr. and Mrs. Jameson, how are you this fine morning?" Robert reached out to pet Trixie and she snapped at him, which caused him to pull his hand back quickly.

"Sorry Robert, Trixie is a bit under the weather I'm afraid."

"So, where are you two off to so early?"

"We have a car waiting for us and a plane at JFK taking us to Miami for a couple of days."

Robert looked around them at the floor and replied, "Oh, no luggage?"

Mrs. Jameson replied, "We have a condo in Miami and plenty of clothing to sustain us."

Robert looked at her and smiled, but on the inside his thoughts are, oh, excuse me. He replied just as the door opened at the lobby, "Have a safe trip!" and stepped out. He waved at the doorman as he walked out onto the sidewalk and hailed a cab. The Yellow Checker pulled to the curb and Robert opened the rear door and slid in. He much liked the Checker cabs over the Impalas or the Crown Victoria because you sat higher and the car just felt safer, like riding in a tank.

Through the partition and into the rearview mirror, he saw a Middle Eastern man with bushy eyebrows and a scruffy beard.

Robert said, "Good morning, sir, 26 Fed please."

The driver looked at Robert in the mirror and replied, "Yes buddy."

The ride was noisy with honking horns and garbage trucks and people; a city that never sleeps was so true. The big car pulled up to the front of Robert's stop and the driver turned back and said, "Are you FBI?"

Robert nodded and asked, "What do I owe you?"

The man turned back to the meter and replied, "That will be $4.75 buddy."

Robert handed the man a five-dollar bill and said, "Keep the change!"

The man looked at his take, winced, and turned forward.

Agent Franklin entered the lobby of 26 Federal Plaza where he showed his credentials and headed to the elevators. A door opened in front of him and he thought today could be a good day, but that would be short lived because numerous others rushed to the door to catch the car up. Robert leaned forward and around a woman and pressed twenty-nine, his floor.

The woman turned to look at the owner of the hand and said, "Hello Robert, how are you?" Her name is Stacey and she worked on his floor, but on the opposite side of her and his team.

Robert cleared his throat and replied, "Good morning, Stacey. I'm well, and you?"

Stacey smiled, "I'm well, thank you." She turned back to the front and the door opened at floor twenty and most of the car emptied. Floor twenty was a newly established team that monitored internet traffic and sought out the bad in the world, those who preyed on unsuspecting elderly with scams using what's called a "pop-up," an annoying advertisement for products and or services offered by "clicking here."

The elevator stopped again, at floor twenty-nine, and Stacey, another woman, and Robert exited. Stacey called to Robert, "Have a great day, Robert."

09:00, NYPD Headquarters

Lieutenant Jameson walked into a conference room and closed the door. There were seven other officers seated as he walked around the tables to a podium. He set his papers down and looked over his glasses at the small group and said, "Good morning!"

"Good morning, sir."

Jameson then looked at his papers and replied, "Okay, we have a new team member. He's joining us from Los Angeles, CA." Jameson pointed to Sergeant Steven Stevens, a man 6'5" tall weighing easily 260, maybe 270 pounds of solid muscle.

A few of the officers laughed and one said to another, "His name is Steven Stevens, who does that?"

There was small laughter again and Stevens replied, "Yeah, I know. I get it all the time. What made it worse is my middle name is Steven too." The room went silent and Jameson again looked over his glasses and Stevens said, "Just kidding, it's Steven George Stevens, but you can call me Mick."

The room filled with laughter as Jameson said, "Okay, enough. To be clear, Stevens, or Mick, is in line for my job when I go, so you'd better watch yourselves."

Those that were laughing are now squirming a bit in their seats and the room went quiet.

Jameson said, "Okay, here's what we know. The man we call the 'Pearl Necklace Killer' is getting sloppy. We got a partial print from the last necklace taken from the victim; however, we haven't been able to identify him, because he obviously never did time, or served in the military, so we are at a stalemate until—heaven help us—he does this again."

The room was slightly busy and team members were moving in their chairs and looking at notes. Stevens stood and said, "Well, if that's it, I'd like to find my desk, get situated, and then have conversations with each of you regarding the case and to get to know you, okay?"

Jameson smiled knowing he's made the right choice with Stevens. He's had the temperament, his skin was thick, and he's was big as a house. He then said, "Okay gang, you heard the man. Stokes, show Sergeant Stevens to his office."

Stokes stood and replied, "Yes, sir. Right this way, Sergeant."

"Why would you leave the sunshine and women of LA to come here?"

"I'm originally from Maine, and I've been wanting to get closer to home for some time now, and when I heard about this opportunity naturally, I applied."

Stokes scratched his head and said, "I guess. We, the rest of the team, had no idea you were coming. Say, do you work out?"

Mick laughed. "Yeah, I like to throw the weights around a bit. I played ball at Stanford and caught the 'I want to be a cop' bug and ended up in LA and now here I'm here. I've slowed down a bit since I have a baby girl and a five-year-old boy that take up most of my free time."

"Well, you're definitely the biggest guy in the building, and I'm sure you'll get a lot of stares and some bullying."

"Bullying?"

"Yeah, there's a couple smaller guys here that have rank and a Napoleon complex, and if you're above six foot, they will be sure to mess with you, just saying. Oh, and they're brothers, a part of a long list of NYPD family. You won't miss them: short, squat, and bald."

Mick laughed and replied, "Well, thanks for the heads up."

Stokes put his hand up and said, "Okay Sarge, here's your office. The guy that was in here recently passed—"

"Wait, passed as in died, not in here!"

Stokes looked at Mick and with a straight face, "We just cleaned up the chalk outline yesterday." He then laughed and finished with, "No, he died at home on the toilet, just like the King. Sad really, he was a great man, but he smoked way too much and loved donuts."

Mick put his right hand on Stokes' shoulder and squeezed, which caused him to squirm with discomfort. Mick then said, "That was pretty funny," and then he let go and stepped into his office.

Stokes used his left hand to rub his right shoulder and replied, "Gosh, I hope I never really piss you off. You have some grip!" as he continued to massage the pain away.

"Thank you, Stokes. I'll take it from here."

Stokes extended his right hand and Mick took it and Stokes said, "Welcome aboard, Sarge. Gosh, your hand is like a bunch of bananas," and then he turned and walked out of the office.

Mick placed his briefcase on his desk and opened it, removing a photo of him, his wife, and their two children. He then removed a few articles suited for his desk and job: pens, pencils, and files pertaining to the Pearl Necklace Killer. He closed the case and set in on the floor next to his desk, pulled out his chair, sat, which scared him, and he jerked forward because the chair nearly gave way to his weight.

A woman's voice said, "Hi, yeah, sorry the office furniture in this building is older than Lieutenant Jameson, and he's old."

Mick stood and responded, "Hello, I'm Sergeant Stevens, and this is my first day."

He extended his right hand and she took it and replied, "Hi, nice to meet you. Listen, if you need anything, I'm next door. I'm with domestic crimes."

Mick nodded his head and replied, "Thank you, nice to meet you, Miss?"

"Oh, yes, sorry. I'm Sergeant Michelle Jameson."

Mick looked at her and responded with a question in his voice, "Jameson, as in Lieutenant Jameson?"

"Yes, he's my father." She pushed herself off the doorjamb and walked away. Mick looked down at his desk and laughed, shaking his head.

10:30, Jersey City, New Jersey

Despite the brightness of the day, the windows of the room where a woman lies, tied and gagged, do not let much light in. She was naked, and there was dried blood around her mouth and nose. She began to move, and her eyes flickered open. She began to cry but cannot speak, just moan because her mouth was filled with a cloth of some sort. She moved her tongue side to side hoping to work the gag free. She realized the cloth was held in place by another cloth tied around her face. She could feel the pressure from the cloth's knot on the back of her head. Her right shoulder and hip were sore and numb from lying in that position for God knows how long. She rolled to her back, which caused her bound hands to press into her lower back in an awkward way, so she rolled to her left side and then she drew her knees inward and rolled onto them, using her forehead as a means of pushing herself upward and into a kneeling position. She looked around the room, but the darkness was too much, and she had no idea where she was or how she got here, and she began to whimper.

Tears flowed down her cheeks and suddenly a door opened, letting in light, which caused her to bow her head and close her eyes. A man's voice said, "Well, hello sleepy head. I was beginning to think you'd never wake. How are you feeling?" He squatted in front of her and moved her hair away from her eyes. He's a well-built man in his late thirties or early forties. His glasses are of a vintage nature and his hair was professional looking.

She blinked her eyes completely open and looked at him, doing her best to focus. He moved to the gag and she pulled back and winced. He replied, "Hey, no need to worry. I'm just going to remove the handkerchief, so you and I can have a conversation, okay?"

She closed her eyes as he pulled down the cloth and slowly removed the wadded cloth from her mouth. She moved her tongue from side to side, licked her lips, and then screamed, "LET ME OUT OF HERE! PLEASE, LET ME GO! WHY ARE YOU DOING THIS TO ME?!!!"

The man stood and kicked the woman in the stomach, and she fell to the floor groaning in pain. Seconds later, blood came from her mouth. The man said, "I could do this all day because where I live, no one will hear a damn thing, so we're going to try this again, but this time, you won't scream at me, okay?"

He reached down and grabbed the woman under each arm and pulled her to her feet. The woman looked at her attacker and cried out, "Please let me use the bathroom. I feel sick!"

"Of course, dear. I was planning to have you clean up anyway. You're covered in blood. After you're clean, I'll clothe and feed you, and then we'll talk about why you're here."

He removed a knife from the front pocket of his corduroys, flipped it open, and bent down to cut the silk ropes that keep her feet together and then to her wrists to repeat. He then turned the woman and led her into a hallway and to a bathroom. A bathroom of white marble and nickel-plated fixtures. It was bright and sterile and very clean. He stood her in front of a mirror that started at the floor and stopped at the ceiling, a good nine feet tall and six feet wide. The man said, "Okay, let's see how well you listen to directions. I will start the shower and when I say go, you enter the shower and wash your hair with this shampoo and then clean your entire body with this bar of soap using this washcloth, okay?"

The woman reached for the items. He then from behind lifted her chin so that she can see his face and her body in the mirror. He said, "You are such a lovely woman, but you were so rude to me. I never asked for that. I even offered to buy you a drink, and you snubbed me. I hate being snubbed!"

The woman looked down and began to cry. She managed a response by saying, "I'm sorry. Please, I'm so sorry."

The man quickly became irate and screamed, "You should have thought about that before! I wasn't mean to you. You poked fun at me, you called me old, and your friends, they too laughed at me. I'm not old, I'm only forty-three!" He motioned as if to hit her and then stopped and in a soft voice said, "Okay, do you remember how I told you to clean yourself?"

The woman stared into the mirror at him and nodded her head yes.

He replied, "Good, let's get to it. I'll check back with you in twenty minutes." The man walked to the large open shower and twisted the handles and checked the water's temperature, adjusting until it's just right. He walked out of the room and closed the door behind him.

The woman began to cry again and turned toward the shower. It's a colossal sight—water was coming from the ceiling and from the walls—it reminded her of a drive-through car wash. She stepped into the shower and the pressure from the wall nozzles knocked the shampoo, soap, and washcloth from her hands.

11:28, 26 Federal Plaza

Robert stared at his computer screen and started to think of his sister, Lisa Marie. He recalled how motherly she was and how beautiful she was, yet there was a fear in her. She never wanted to be home. He thought about why she moved to the third floor of the house and shut everyone out for so long, about the drugs, and of course her untimely death.

He lifted his head to look at photos on his desk. There was Mom and Dad and John Jr. with his family; Jake, his college roommate; and of course Jennifer Sanders, his love of close to three years. She was smiling at him. He recalled the day the photo was taken. The weather was seasonably warm for March and the sun lit her up like a diamond. She was a stunning woman already, but something about that day really showed her true beauty.

He smiled and reached for his desk phone, lifted the receiver, and put it to his left ear and began dialing. Soon a few clicks and a ringing tone for five, maybe six rings and a voicemail greeting said, "Hi, you've reached Jennifer Sanders of Tharman, Metzger, and Sanders Associates. I'm unavailable currently. Please leave a detailed message, time of the call, and a return number. I'll call you as soon as I am able. To send a fax, please dial 347-555-2600. Thank you."

Robert spoke into the phone, "Hello Jennifer, it's me. I thought I'd check in, see how you're doing, and to confirm our dinner tonight. I have a lunch meeting with Jameson and a new guy from his team, and I'll probably cut out a bit early, hit the gym, and then see you. I love you." He hung up the phone and leaned back in his chair.

"Hey sunshine, you okay?" a man's voice said. Robert turned in his chair to see Agent Randy Miller, his shadow as he's called.

Robert stood and replied, "Hey, how was your weekend?"

"You know, it was all about a three-year-old and a newborn, so I'm going on negative eight hours of sleep. Are you okay? You look a bit troubled?"

"No, I'm good. It's been twenty-nine years today that my sister, you know."

Miller put his hand on his friend's shoulder and said, "I'm sorry, Robert, truly. Can I get you anything? Coffee, a hug?"

Robert smirked, "No, I'm good thank you. Oh, you and I are meeting Jameson at Ray's. He's got a new guy on the team and we need to meet him. How about we head out in fifteen? I need to make a phone call, okay?"

"You bet. I'll see you at the elevators in fifteen. Are you sure you don't want that hug?"

Robert drew back and punched Miller in the shoulder and waved him off. Miller laughed and headed toward his office. Robert walked to his phone, lifted the receiver, pressed speed dial number one, and brought the phone to his ear. The ringing continued and then a frail voice answered the phone, "Hello, Franklin residence."

Robert said, "Hello, Mother. How are you?"

Marilynn Franklin replied, "Just a second, Robert. I'll get your father."

"No, Mother, I called to speak to you."

Marilynn was silent for a moment and replied, "Well, this is a surprise. You know, today is twenty-nine years since your sister left us."

A clicking sound was followed by a lot of fumbling and a man's voice said, "Who is it, dear?"

"Hello Father, it's Robert."

"Hello son. Your mother and I are thinking of moving into a retirement home in Columbia. This old house has always been too much for us, and since I've been retired, it seems right to let the new pastor move in here."

"Well, that would make sense, but the church sure has been generous to our family over the years. Say, I only have a minute and thought I'd call and say hello, you know, check on you both. Do you need anything?"

Marilynn replied, "Thank you, son, but we're fine. Your brother comes by now and again, and sometimes Missy will check in on us. John Jr. thinks this will be his best year since taking over the hardware."

Robert closed his eyes and pictured his brother and the day he bought the town hardware. He smiled and said, "Okay, great. Well, Jennifer and I will be down to see you soon enough, okay?"

Robert hung up the phone, turned, and grabbed his coat from the back of his door. He made his way to the elevator. Miller was standing patiently, and when he saw Robert, he leaned forward and pressed the call button. Miller asked, "All good?"

Robert looked at the floor indicator, "Yes, all good."

The elevator door opened and out walked Stacey and another woman from her area. She looked at Robert and said, "Hello

Robert. Going out for lunch?"

"Yes, headed out, are you just coming back?"

"No, had some things to do downstairs. Grabbing my purse now, want some company?"

Robert looked at Miller who was looking at the floor smiling. He replied, "Sorry, lunch meeting." Robert moved toward the elevator opening and Miller meanders behind him.

"Maybe next time," and waved him off.

The door closed and Robert stared at Miller's reflection and said, "Shut up!"

Miller began to laugh and put his hands up, "Hey, I'm not saying a thing, but it's obvious somebody likes you, which kind of hurts because it was as if I were invisible. Like what am I, chopped liver?"

Robert punched Miller again on the should.

Noon, Jersey City

The man knocked on the bathroom door and asked, "Are you okay, my dear?"

The woman jumped and drew her knees into her chest. She's sitting on the floor of the shower wrapped in a towel. She had done everything asked of her and the corner made her feel safe. The man then said, "Well, since you won't answer, I'll come in and see for myself." The man put a key into the doorknob, made a slight turn, and pushed the door open. The room was damp, and the mirror and glass surrounds were still fogged over from the long shower.

The man saw his prey in the corner of the shower, motionless. He said, "Ahh, there you are, all better now?" The woman remained still, and he said, "My dear, why so rude? This is what got you in this predicament—BEING RUDE TO ME!" The woman looked at him and began to shake. He asked again, "All better now?" The woman nodded her head slowly and he said, "What's wrong, dear, cat got your tongue? I'M TALKING TO YOU!"

The woman screamed and began to cry. She looked at the man and her eyes became bigger and she said, "Yes, I'm better. Why are you doing this to me?"

The man was wearing what appeared to be a vinyl suit, which covered his entire body, and the gloves he had on were duct taped around his forearms. He was wearing goggles and had a covering over his face, like a surgeon would wear during an operation. The area around his mouth was now fogged over from his breathing. In his left hand she saw what could be a bracelet or even a necklace and, in his right hand, a knife. The blade was about nine inches long, and the handle was stainless steel. It glistened when he moved the knife side to side, as if taunting her.

The man said, "Please dear, stand for me. I have a gift for you. STAND NOW!" The woman jumped and then slowly rose to her feet, clutching the towel to her body. Over his shoulder she saw a folded drop cloth on the sink, but it appeared to be plastic, and this sends her mind racing and she began to shiver. The man said, "Dear, please let loose of the towel and put both hands at your sides. I need to look at you."

The woman looked around the room, and then to save her

attacker from becoming agitated, she slowly lowered the towel and let it fall to the floor in a small pile. He looked her over from head to toe and motioned for her to turn around, like a ballerina in a young girl's jewelry box. He hummed as she turned. Once she's made several rotations, he extended his left hand to her, and she slowly took his hand and he bows, saying, "My lady, please step out into the light. Your king must see you."

The woman slowly moved forward with his guidance and the large bathroom became a stage. It was in fact a necklace in his hand, a pearl necklace. He motioned for her to stop and to turn around. He set the knife on the plastic drop and then got very close to her from behind. He breathed into her ear and placed the necklace around her neck and let it lay as he fastened the clasp. He placed both hands on her shoulders and slowly turned her around. They were now face to face.

He said, "My dear, please don't move. I must lay out the ceremonial carpet for you to walk on." The woman was about to pass out from fear as the man moved the knife to the second sink, placing it very exacting. He reached for the plastic drop and began to unfold it, carefully laying it onto the tile floor. He retrieved a roll of duct tape from a pocket of the suit and ripped four pieces about six inches in length. He taped down each corner of the plastic drop and set the tape next to the knife. He extended his right hand and motioned her to him.

They were now centered on the drop and he stepped back to look at her in detail; every curve of her beautiful body, the long hair that barely covered her ample breasts. He turned her in front of the full-length mirror, and from behind, he said, "Look at you, lovely you are, and the way this necklace accentuates your skin.

You know, there is plenty more where that came from, but you will never know because you were rude to me."

The woman closed her eyes and recalled their encounter. He walked up to her and some friends and asked to buy her a drink. She laughed at him and then her friends joined in. His face soon showed anger, and when he walked away, they continued to laugh. She opened her eyes and said, "I am sorry for being rude. I had been drinking for several hours and you were one of many men that came to me. I'm so sorry. What can I do to make it up to you? Please sir, please don't kill me!"

The man replied, "My dear, sometimes life's destiny isn't determined by God, but by the actions we take. You and your friends like to make others feel less than, and it's wrong. It's painful, it's uncalled for, and that is why you're here with me. I've decided the rest of your life. Please close your eyes as you hear these words that I'm about to speak."

The woman stared at the man in the mirror as her eyes filled with tears. He said again, "Please my lady, close your eyes and listen to me." She closed her eyes as the man removed the blade from a side pocket of his suit and slowly brought it to her throat. In a fluid motion, he sliced her open. She grabbed for her throat in a panic, and he held her tightly around the waist as she struggled to stop the blood, but all her efforts were not enough, and she went limp. Soon, she lost consciousness and slumped forward. The man slowly lowered her to the tarp, being careful not to allow too much blood to reach the perimeter. He then laid her flat, putting her hands together on her chest. He adjusted the necklace so that it looked presentable despite being covered in blood.

He stood and went to each corner of the tarp to remove the tape and fold the tarp from top to bottom and then side to side, and then he rolled her until the tarp was taut and had essentially formed to her body. The roll of duct tape appeared again as he began to wrap around the body, starting at the head and working downward in an even spacing. Once finished, he threw the lifeless body over his right shoulder and made his way to the door. He headed into the hallway to the opposite end of his loft and to a door that led to a large unfinished space and a waste tunnel that had been placed in an opening to allow him to discard materials during the renovation process.

He must act quickly because the refuse truck will be on site at any moment to take away the dumpster several stories below. With his left arm, he moved the tarp covering the tube and shrugged the woman's lifeless body into the cylinder, and like a football player, he pushed forward until her body began to move down and into the waiting dumpster. He stared for a moment and then heard the ever-familiar beeping of a large truck backing in to take the dumpster to some unknown location.

Noon, Ray's Pizzeria

Robert and Miller entered the restaurant and were greeted by Geno, the owner of Ray's, which always seemed odd, but the food was great, and the atmosphere was always the same: cops, feds, and an occasional stockbroker. This spot hadn't been held up since the late sixties, which was why Geno was so attentive to his patrons.

Geno saw Robert and put his arms up and shook his knotted fingers. "Here they are, my favorite cops. Please come in; have a seat where you'd like!"

Robert waved and looked around and saw Jameson waving him over and said, "Thank you, Geno. Bring a couple of sodas over to the table."

Robert and Miller made their way through the crowd and stood at a small table in a back corner. Jameson and his partner stood. Jameson said, "Robert, I'd like you to meet Sergeant Steven Stevens."

"Or also known as Mick, right?" as he extended his right hand.

Jameson looked surprised as does Mick. Mick replied, "Have we met somewhere?"

Just then Miller said, "Is this the guy that took that door down?"

"Yes, Christmas 1986. I met you and a few other cops at a loft, and you took that door down with one swing of the sledge. I talked about it for weeks. People didn't believe me."

"Well, I believe you now; this man is huge!" as he extended his right hand to exchange greetings with Mick.

Mick replied, "Yes, I do remember now. I wasn't on the force that long. When did you come to New York, Agent Franklin?"

Robert looked at Miller and replied, "How long has it been, Randy, five years or so?"

Miller took the glass of water from his mouth, swallowed, and replied, "Yes, that's about right."

Mick leaned in to take a glass of water from the center of the table and said, "When you say we, you both came from LA?"

"Yes, that's correct. Agent Miller and I have been on the same team since he joined the FBI. Besides, he needs me to keep him in line so that his wife doesn't kill him."

Everyone laughed and Miller replied, "True, he does do that."

Jameson raised his hand and said, "Okay, now that we've gotten the introductions out of the way, let's get Geno to bring us a large pie. I'm starving!" Jameson waved at Geno and does a circular hand gesture, which means we need food and need it now.

Jameson had been coming to Ray's since the late sixties, and every Monday, Geno reserved this table for two hours if Jameson didn't come in. Geno waved back and headed toward the kitchen barking orders.

Robert said, "So, Mick, have you had a chance to look over the files?"

Jameson interrupted, "Hey, Franklin, give the guy a chance to get settled in. He's been on the job," he paused to look at his watch then continued, "like four hours!"

"Yes, I have looked at the file, Agent Franklin. Not in detail, but it seems this is our guy, same style, same necklace, and of course, no witnesses before, during, or after. Oh, I looked at the photos and compared them to his earlier work and he's slacking on the distance between the tape. In the beginning, the distance was exact, no deviation, but the last two were off by as much as a half inch."

Miller said, "You know, I thought the same thing and of course the word 'copycat' came to mind, but the necklace, an item that can't be had anywhere, and since the jeweler had closed all those years ago, we have no idea how many he bought. Will he stop once he runs out? Then we have nothing but a cold case."

The men stay silent and then Robert said, "You know, I just thought of something. The bodies have been found within garbage, but not real garbage, construction material, you know, from a site being renovated."

Jameson interjected, "I know where you're headed Bobby, and we would never find where the material comes from, I mean never. There are thousands of renovations going on daily all over the city."

"Bobby? I haven't been called Bobby since my college days. Anyway, you're right, Mikey, so I guess we hope for a lead among the trash."

Mick replied, "You know, sooner or later he will make an error, giving us exactly what we need. We stay vigilant."

Jameson said, "By the way, I'm officially retiring June 1. I will have my thirty, and besides, the missus has found us a place in Florida. A nice little community on a golf course not far from the beach. I'm going to work on my tan, gain some weight, grow my hair, and drink martinis daily!"

Miller replied, "Don't you think you're big enough now?"

Jameson reached into his ice water, removed an ice cube, and tossed it to Miller, striking him on the forehead. Miller replied, "Hey, that's assault on a federal agent!" The table began to laugh.

"Okay, here you go, made special for you guys." Geno set the large pizza on the table and a waiter passed out plates and utensils.

Jameson said to Mick, "Get ready to set your taste buds ablaze my friend; this is the best pizza in the city, hands down!"

Robert and Miller both nod in agreement as they reached for a slice. Robert said, "So, what brought you all the way to New York from sunny LA?"

Mick wiped his mouth of pizza sauce, "Well, I'm from Portland, Maine, and my wife wanted to be closer to home because our parents need time with our son and daughter, so when I saw the opening with the NYPD, I applied, and now here I am. We went from about fifty hours by car to just seven, and we'll either go home once a month or our parents will come see us a couple times a month. It's nice all around. How about you, why New York?"

Robert looked at Miller and replied, "Well, since this case has become so in-depth, we felt it best if I, we were at the mother ship; more resources, you know, and he seems to be here, at least now for a while. We'll get him."

Miller spoke up, "Yes, we have a greater chance here than we will anywhere else, despite the city size, we can close in on him using local PD, etc. So, we're happy to have you as part of the team, and if we need any doors opened, you'll be the guy."

Mick laughed and Robert replied, "Yes, that's for sure."

Jameson is eating quickly as he always does. He slammed his Coke to the table and said, "Okay, listen, we need to set up a meeting either at my office or at 26 Fed. We'd prefer the latter of course, and you feds have better coffee, and conference rooms with comfortable chairs, oh and the pastries."

Robert laughed and said, "Yes, I get it, old man. I'll set something up for later in the week or even next week. We can make it a pre-retirement meeting too!"

The men laughed and Geno joined in. Jameson said, "Geno, give the bill to Miller over there; he's got all the money!"

Miller pointed to himself and said, "Yeah, right; kids, a non-working wife, all the money in the world!"

Robert extended his hand and said, "Geno, give me that. I'll expense it as a working lunch."

Jameson replied loudly, "Oh, now we know who's got the deep pockets, care of Uncle Sam."

Geno handed it to Robert and Robert looked at it briefly, reached into his inner breast pocket to remove a slim credit card case, and removed his government AmEx and handed it back to Geno. Robert said, "Add twenty percent for the tip, okay?"

Jameson said, "WOW! Big tipper too," and rustled Robert's hair. Jameson stood as does Mick and the two men said their goodbyes.

Robert looked at Miller and said, "See, I told you that guy was huge. Now you have to believe me."

Miller looked over his shoulder and then at Mick's calves as they stretched his khaki pants with each step. He laughed and replied, "I'd hate to upset him during a traffic stop." He then acts as if he's being pulled from a car window. Both men laughed as Geno walked up with a small tray containing a receipt for Robert to sign and his AmEx card.

"Robert, Randy, thank you so much for coming in; it's always good to see you both. Take care out there, okay?"

Robert took the tray, lifted the items from it along with a pen, signed the check, and said, "You bet, Geno. The best pizza!"

Miller nodded his head as he took the last draw from his straw, which caused a slurping sound in his glass. Robert looked at him with a "what are you six?" look and Miller said, "Oops, sorry, having kids I sometimes forget; besides, they think it's funny."

Robert waved him off and stood. Miller stood, wiped his mouth one last time, and tossed the soiled napkin onto a plate. The two men waved at a few others and then to Geno and step out onto the sidewalk. Robert stretched and rubbed his belly indicating he's full. Both men looked up and down the street and made their way across to the government-issued black Crown Victoria.

05:30, McCormick, SC

John Franklin Jr. stepped onto the porch of his parents' home. He turned around and stared out, looking left and right down the street. He stretched backward and then put his left arm above his head to stretch even more. He can't lift his right arm because it was removed at the shoulder January 21, 1968. It was 05:30 and he and thirty-nine other fellow Marines were injured, and eighteen lost their lives at Khe Sanh, Vietnam. The showering mortars and rockets kept the Marines at bay for several days.

He looked to the heavens and mouthed, "Thank you, Smitty." Smitty, or Mike Smith, was the man that put himself in harm's way to save John Jr. Yes, John Jr. lost a part of himself, both mentally and physically, but he's also a man of unwavering faith in God, America, and his family. He came home from

152

Vietnam late spring of 1968 after spending time at Walter Reed for rehabilitation. McCormick welcomed him home with love, and he went to work right away at the McCormick Hardware Store, which he later acquired and renamed Franklin and Son's Hardware.

John Jr. wiped a tear from his face and walked to the front door and entered, calling out, "Father, Mother?"

John Sr. looked up from his paper and called back, "In here son."

John Jr. went to his father's study and stood in the doorway. He looked back at his father, a frail man with lively eyes, and despite his decaying physicality, his mind was as sharp as a tack. "Hey Pop, how are you?"

John Sr. looked up over his glasses, "I'm old and cranky, but at least I have your mother."

Just then Marilynn walked up behind John Jr. and hugged him and replied, "That's right; he's got me! How are you, son?"

John Jr. lifted his left arm, embraced his mother, kissed her on the top of the head, and said, "Hello Mother. I'm well, how are you?"

John Sr. spoke up, "Say, let's all go into the living room and sit a spell." He slowly stood and reached for his cane, and the three made their way into the large living room.

Marilynn asked, "Sweet tea?"

"How else would the tea be, but sweet?"

They laughed and she disappeared into the kitchen.

John Sr. sat in his favorite chair and John Jr. sat on the couch and said, "So, have you heard from Robert?"

John Sr. looked over his glasses, "Yes, he called this morning. He sounded tired as usual and made mention of coming down soon."

John Jr. looked to his left to see his mother entering the room with a tray of glasses and a pitcher of sweet tea. He stood and helped guide the tray to an end table. Marilynn said, "It's hard to believe it's been twenty-nine years. Not a day goes by I don't think of Lisa Marie. I think back on that night all those years ago, and it haunts me, seeing her bloodied and bruised and raped the way she was." She began to cry, and John Sr. looked over his glasses at his wife.

John Jr. poured three glasses of tea and distributed. He placed his hand on his mother's shoulder to comfort her, "Did Robert say when he'd be here?"

"No, just that it would be soon. Hopefully he'll bring Jennifer with him and surprise us with an official engagement. Your mother and I would like more grandchildren."

Marilynn looked at John Sr. and replied, "Yes, that's what we need. We can barely keep up with the five we have now."

John Jr. laughed, "I'm with them every day, and sometimes I need a break. Don't get me wrong. I love them dearly, but I wish we would have had them a bit closer together. Johnny is doing great at Clemson, and I can only hope and pray he comes home to take over the store, but I have a feeling it will be Jack."

John Sr. interrupted, "Why do you say that?"

"Well, he's nineteen and has no desire to attend college and he loves it. I mean he really understands the whole business side of the store, and he's great with customers. Marty's been coming to help a lot more after school, which seems odd that a fifteen-year-old boy would rather stock nuts and bolts instead of riding his bike with his buddies or chasing after girls, but I'll take all the help I can get. And it's cheap, just feed them for the most part."

All three began to laugh and John Sr. replied, "Son, enjoy it while it lasts. When we took Robert to school all those years ago, we never in a million years expected him to become an FBI agent. Sure, he seemed regimented, but we had assumed more of a business type or even a banker."

Marilynn replied, "Or a lawyer."

John Sr. raised his glass, "Yes, a lawyer."

John Jr. leaned back into the sofa and replied, "I worry about him sometimes. He hardly talks when he's around and I know he's consumed by that psychopath. It's got to be hard on him and Jennifer. I mean, they've been dating now, what, three years?"

Marilynn said, "No, close to four."

John Sr. removed his glasses, "We'll not live long enough for that boy to give us more grandchildren, so let's spoil the ones we have."

Marilynn laughed, "Not sure how much more spoiling we can do, but count me in."

The room was quiet for a while and John Jr. said, "I sure do miss her. She was a great big sister, so smart and caring." His voice began to crack, and Marilynn looked at John Sr. and he looked at her and his head went down.

Marilynn looked away and removed a framed photo of

Lisa Marie from the end table next to her. She smiled and then clenched the photo to her bosom and began to weep.

John Jr. looked at his mother and then his father. He looked away and did what he can to hold back the tears. He stood, stretched, and said, "Mother, Father, I'd better get back to the store. I love you both. See you tomorrow for lunch."

John Sr. stood and hugged his son and Marilynn remained seated, but she looked at John Jr. and then at where his right arm should be and said, "Yes, son, we'll see you tomorrow."

He walked to her, bent, and hugged her. He took his glass to the kitchen, rinsed it, and placed it in the sink. He walked out the front door and north on Oak back to the hardware.

15:30, Brooklyn

A woman sat at a desk reading a file handed to her moments ago. Jennifer Sanders was an up and comer when it came to real estate law, and her firm had taken notice. She's also the longtime girlfriend of Special Agent Robert Franklin.

One of Jennifer's biggest clients, a real estate mogul, wants to buy a building, tear it down, and put up townhouses. His hope was that once complete, Brooklyn will see a revitalization sending values up, and he can then capitalize, ut the zoning committee was against such a thing because the building he wanted was considered historical and had been used for industrial purposes, which would require rezoning, and a lot of preparations required by the EPA and other organizations, which could prompt a complete restructuring of that area at tax payers' expense. In other words, this project could open a giant can of worms, but Jennifer was confident she would be able to convince the city otherwise and that her client will accrue all expenses leaving the taxpayers alone.

A man stepped into the doorway of Jennifer's office, knocked on the door frame, and said, "Hey, how's it going?"

Jennifer turned to see Kevin, a new lawyer, barely out of school, and said, "Hi Kevin. What's up?"

Kevin's arm dropped as he entered Jennifer's office. He sat in the visitor's chair and then leaned onto her desk with his face about a foot from hers and said, "So, you know Katie, the new paralegal? What's her story? I mean, I'm just curious."

Jennifer looked at Kevin and can see it in his eyes. He was smitten with Katie, and maybe she can help make a love connection. She replied, "Well, she's twenty-three and has another year of school. She lives alone."

"Okay, that's all great, but is she single!?"

"Why don't you ask her yourself?" She leaned back and crossed her arms, as does Kevin. Jennifer held fast for a moment and began laughing as Kevin became somewhat agitated. She said, "Yes, Katie is single, and I have it on good authority that she likes a certain man that works here."

Kevin stood and said, "Great, Jeremy strikes again. Why do all the girls like him? Mr. Big Shot, son of a partner, nice clothes, nice car!"

Jennifer looked at Kevin, and in a serious face replied, "No, silly, she likes you."

Kevin slowly sat down and said, "Wait, what?"

"Yes, she likes you."

"How do you know all this? Seriously, how do you know?"

Jennifer toward her door to ensure no one is standing there and replied, "Well, she was first year at Columbia and you had given a perspective in American legal history, a class she was taking at the time."

"Wow, that was like three years ago, maybe."

"Whatever! Anyway, Katie was so awestruck by how well you knew the subject matter, and how well-spoken you were, and this part I don't understand, but she thought you were the most handsome man she had ever seen."

"Wait, what do you mean, you didn't get that part?"

Jennifer began to laugh and pushed his shoulder and replied,

Mann - McCormick

"I'm just kidding, you goof."

Suddenly there was a knock on the door and Jennifer sat back quickly and then Kevin turned to see Katie standing there. He gulped and looked at Jennifer, and his face became flush. Katie said, "Hi, excuse me, Jennifer, I have some forms for you to sign."

Jennifer motioned for Katie to come in. Kevin sat there, staring at Katie, and she smiled. Kevin unlocked his gaze and stood, saying, "Well, thank you, Jennifer. I'll look into that matter right away." He looked at Katie and stutters, "Hi, ummm, hi. Okay, ahhh, see you."

Katie smiled and replied, "Hi, I hope so." This comment caused Kevin to walk into the door frame after he stumbled, knocking over a trash can and spilling its contents. As he bent to pick up the trash, he bumped his head on the arm of the second visitor's chair.

Jennifer said, "Kevin, please stop. I'll take care of it; just be safe." The two women laughed as Kevin waved and walked away.

Katie looked at Jennifer and said, "Did you say something to him?"

"Say something about what?"

"Yeah, okay...whatever." Again, the women laughed.

Kevin sat at his desk staring at Jeremy and in his mind, he said, "I guess you're not as great as you think you are, Jeremy." He then laughed and clicked his mouse to wake his computer. He leaned toward the screen and put the cursor in the address bar of his browser and began to do a restaurant search, still laughing.

Kim, his cube mate, turned and said, "Hey, what's so funny? Do I have a fabric softener sheet stuck to me again?"

Kevin looked at her and replied, "No, I'm just happy is all, nothing to do with you. I mean, that's funny, not that you don't matter. I mean, you know. Gosh, I'm a wreck, sorry. You look fine."

Kim replied slowly, "Uhh, okay, I guess."

Kevin looked at his computer just as a pop-up appeared, letting him know he had a message. He clicked the icon to see that Jennifer had sent him an instant message and it read, *"Good going champ."*

Kevin moved the cursor to the reply section and typed, *"Yeah, I'm an idiot!"* and selected send. He stared at the screen and then another pop-up told him he had a new message, but this time it's from Katie. He looked around the office and then locked eyes with Katie. She smiled, and he smiled back.

He looked at her message, which read, *"Hi, would you like to have lunch, maybe dinner?"* Kevin's heart began to pound, and he looked back at her and nodded.

Then another message popped up and it's Jennifer again. *"Well, what did you say?"*

"I said yes, of course."

"You've got this."

"Thanks."

He then responded to Katie, *"We could leave from here and walk to Mario's or even Mick's. Have you been to either?"*

Katie wrote, *"Mario's. You can't go wrong, and yes, from*

here."

Kevin blurted, "Yes!" which prompted several coworkers to look toward him. He looked around and said, "Sorry," and put his head down. He looked up again at Katie and she was giggling and does the index finger to her lip to shush him. Kevin smiled, shook his head, and looked back at his screen.

19:40, Robert's Apartment

Jennifer and Robert were snuggled up watching a recorded episode of a popular sitcom and suddenly his BlackBerry vibrated and rang on the coffee table. Jennifer stopped Robert as he reached for the phone and said, "Don't you dare! I haven't seen you in days; we've eaten, and now we relax—got it!?"

Robert sat back and looked deep into her eyes. He smiled and kissed her forehead and replied, "Yes, love."

Seconds later that BlackBerry gave a quick ding and vibrate indicating a voicemail, but then it vibrated and rang again. Robert looked at Jennifer. She moved away from him and he leaned forward and reached for the device, tilted it, and looked at the screen and read, "Miller." He looked at Jennifer and said, "I'd better get this, sorry."

Jennifer folded her arms across her chest and stared at the television. Robert stood, pressed send, and said, "This had better be good!" as he looked at Jennifer.

Miller replied, "Hey boss, sorry to bother you, but we've got another body, and from what Mick told me, this body is very recent, within hours ago."

Robert brought his left hand to his forehead and rubbed it.

He looked at Jennifer and she too can see that the conversation is not good. She mouthed, "What is it?"

Robert covered the bottom of the phone and replied, "It's another body, same as before."

Jennifer reached for the TV remote and turned it off and stood. Robert said to Miller, "Where are you now?"

"I'm in the car headed toward you. I'll be out front in five minutes."

Robert clicked off the call and put the phone in his pocket. He looked at Jennifer and said, "There's another body, same MO, but he's early."

Jennifer replied, "Yes, I agree, maybe his desires are greater out of boredom or maybe he's getting out more than usual."

Robert took her hand and led her to the door. He slipped on his shoes, knelt to tie them, stood, buttoned his top collar, and drew up his tie. He took his holster from the coat hanger and put it on like a coat. He then reached for his jacket, draped it over his left arm, and pulled her to him. He kissed her, hugged her, and said, "I don't know what I'd do without you in my life. I love you so much."

Jennifer looked at him and said, "I know you do, and I love you too. I hope this is the break you've waited for. I'll be here if you need me."

Robert and Jennifer kissed, and he walked out the door and toward the elevator.

The night air caught Robert by surprise, but the black Crown Victoria sitting curbside was warm for sure. He rounded the front of the car and got into the passenger side. Miller said, "Hey, sorry to bother you."

Robert looked at Miller, "No worries, Randy, we need to get this guy and if you had called at 02:00 I would have been out here—groggy—but out here. So, where are we headed?"

Miller looked at his notepad and replied, "The body was found in a waste separator in Fairview."

Robert interrupted, "As in Fairview, New Jersey?"

"Yes, it was a large haul from all over the area, many different dumps. The trash was being sorted, you know, plastics, metals, etc. I was told the body flopped onto a belt, and then to the floor, and a few of the workers went to lift it back onto the belt and then realized it was a body. The whole place went into a panic and people just walked off the job, literally."

Robert looked out his window and said, "I don't blame them. It's probably not often a body comes down a conveyor to be sorted. Do we have an idea of where the trash came from?"

"No, it was an end of the month push to get as much sorted, so they accepted several trucks and most times they don't even record who dropped—too many and it moves too fast."

"How many trucks could have come in one day?"

"Let's see, seventy-nine and fifty-six of those were forty-yard dumpsters, seventeen were thirty-yard dumpsters."

"Damn, that's a lot of trash."

Miller leaned forward and flipped a switch that activated a red light on the dash and motorists began to move over. The Crown Victoria made the near eleven miles in about thirty minutes. They reached the site and made their way through a sea of people to a yellow caution tape that was lifted by two uniformed officers, so they could get to the hub of the scene. There were many people meandering around, which upset Robert because the more people, the more chance of contamination. Both he and Randy walked to Jameson and Mick.

A uniformed officer stopped them and just as both men reached for their credentials, Jameson said, "Hey, let them through!"

The officer stepped aside, and the four men exchanged greetings. Miller leaned down to assess as did Robert. They looked at each other and Miller removed a pen from his shirt pocket and used it to lift the pearl necklace from the dead woman's neck. Robert leaned in and with a flashlight to inspect the necklace, looked at Miller, and nodded his head.

Both men stood, and Robert said to Jameson, "Do you have gloves and an evidence bag?"

"Here you go."

"Thank you." He put on the gloves and slowly removed the necklace as Miller held the evidence bag open. He then dropped the bloodied necklace and Miller, using two fingers, sealed the bag and wrote "April 26 at 20:23—Fairview, NJ," and shoved the bag into his coat pocket.

The coroner's office had pulled up and want the body, so the men stepped away to discuss their findings. Miller asked, "Who found the body?"

Mick pointed east about ten yards and said, "The two men and the woman over there. Their English isn't that good, but the one guy was very expressive when explaining how the body fell from the top conveyor, then to the second conveyor, and then to the floor. The woman hit the emergency stop over there and all three went to put what they thought was a large roll of trash onto the belt, break it open, and then sort, but, well, and that's why we're all here."

Robert replied, "Understood. I guess we wait for the body to make it to the morgue and we get photos and check this poor woman over before they do what they do."

Jameson replied, "She reminds me of the woman that does my wife's hair. I've seen her through the window of the salon. In my head, I say to myself, 'So, you're the one that takes one hundred sixty dollars from me each month.'"

The men laughed, and Miller said, "Where were you earlier today, Lieutenant?"

"Yeah, not funny, kid."

Robert smacked Miller on the shoulder and shook his head in disapproval for the comment just made.

21:00, Mario's

Kevin reached for the water carafe and asked Katie, "Would you like more water?"

"Yes, thank you," and lifted her glass to aid in the pouring.

"When you finish school, do hope to stay at the firm?"

Katie took sip and replied, "Actually, I'm hoping to work family law in upstate New York."

Kevin felt his heart skip and with a somber voice asked, "Where about?"

"Saratoga Springs, where I'm originally from. My father and

his brother have a small office there and of course the office in Queens. For me, it's about the serenity and slower pace of Saratoga Springs. I hope to start a family there too." She took Kevin's hand and he looked at her, surprised.

"Well, maybe we could take a trip up, and you could show me around. I mean, if you want too, not that I'm inviting myself."

Katie laughed, "You are so cute when you're nervous."

Kevin blushed and looked at the table and began to play with the spoon. He looked at her and said, "So, how many children do you hope to have?"

Katie blushed. She leaned in and kissed Kevin on the check and said, "I've dreamed of this day, Kevin. I asked around and found out where you worked, and despite my father's wishes, I applied for a job with hopes of meeting you. I thought that if you were involved, I would work a few months and then go to work for my father."

Kevin looked at her, deep into her eyes, and replied, "The first time I saw you, I said to myself, 'There's my wife, right there. The woman I will spend the rest of my life with.' But I felt I wouldn't stand a chance, not with Jeremy in the office."

"Why Jeremy?"

"Well, for one, he's rich."

"No, his daddy's rich."

"Well, he's handsome, like a movie star handsome, and all the women seem to gravitate toward him, and I thought for sure you would too."

Katie laughed. "No way, I can't stand his type, all full of himself, always checking a mirror, spending his father's money to impress people. Oh, and that car he drives, a Diablo or something? Really? How do you put a family in such a car?"

"So, I guess my Plymouth Voyager my parents gave me is okay?"

They laughed, and the waiter came to the table and asked, "Will there be anything else?"

Katie and Kevin looked at each other and then to the waiter and the same time they replied, "We'll have a cannoli, please."

The waiter laughed and said, "Wow, have you two dated long?"

Kevin smiled, "No, this is our first date."

The waiter stepped back and replied, "Well, you're off to a great start if you already know what the other is thinking, wouldn't you agree?"

Katie smiled and took Kevin's face into her hands and said, "Yes, I believe we are."

"I'll be back with your desert."

Kevin turned to him and said, "Excuse me, what's your name?"

The waiter turned slightly left exposing his name tag that read: Michael. The waiter then said, "I'm Michael."

"Thank you for the great service, Michael."

Michael smiled and turned away toward the kitchen.

23:16, City Morgue

Mick and Robert were with the coroner and had begun

inspecting the woman's body. Jameson and Miller were in the hallway going over notes.

"Mick, what do you think?"

Mick looked at Robert and said, "It's our guy for sure. Same methodical cut, same wrapping of the body, same distance between the tape from head to toe, and same smell of shampoo and soap. I guess all these years I've wondered why he's never raped any of his victims. You can see where they've been bound and gagged based on bruising around the ankles, wrists, and mouth, but never does he touch them sexually. What are your thoughts?"

"Miller and I put together a theory some years ago that this man is impotent, and he's angry for that and the women upset him in some way, which led to this. How he got the women to come with him is another question—no signs of blunt force trauma, no chemicals in the system, nothing."

Jameson and Miller walked up, and Jameson said, "I have a feeling the necklace is the lure. I mean, maybe he tells them this necklace is just the beginning of what you can have."

Mick nodded his head, "Yeah, I guess it's plausible. The women have all been between nineteen and—"

Miller interrupted and said, "Nineteen and twenty-nine. No sign of initial struggle, no penetration, no external DNA, just dead, and a pearl necklace from a jeweler that is no more!"

Robert looked at Miller and said, "Hey, are you okay?"

"Sure, I just think about my daughter."

Mick placed his hand on Miller's shoulder and replied, "I get it, but it won't be long, my friend. This guy is going down!"

Miller exchanged a head nod with Mick.

"I have what I need, and I'll have Miller take me home and we'll reconvene in the morning."

The men stood and stared at the victim's face before Jameson covered her and the men left the room. Mick and Jameson headed toward their vehicle as Robert and Miller get into the Crown Vic and squealed off toward Robert's apartment.

Robert said, "This has been a day, right?"

Miller shrugged, "Yes, it sure has."

The car floated down city streets and came to a stop just outside Robert's apartment. Both men sit in silence staring out the front glass watching a street sweeper spray water, brush, and vacuum all at the same time. The machine was large and noisy, but did a wonderful job keeping the city clean.

Robert reached for the door handle, looked at Miller, and said, "Don't worry about your daughter, my friend. This guy is going down. He's getting bored and his cadence has increased, which means his quality will suffer, and he'll make a mistake."

Miller nodded as Robert exited the vehicle and slammed the door. The tires of the black car chirped as it disappeared into the night.

Robert didn't enter the building right away; instead he continued to watch the sweeper and his mind went back to Los Angeles and the diner where the girl was supposedly abducted from. Turned out it was an affair. Some high-profile athlete wasn't happy in his marriage, so the two snuck around. The attendant from the gas station was right; the man that the girls made fun of was never to be heard from again.

Just then a taxi pulled up and Mr. and Mrs. Jameson got out. The driver removed numerous suitcases from the trunk and set them curbside, and Mr. Jameson paid the fare and gave the man a fifty-dollar tip. Robert recalled them leaving early this morning with no luggage and they returned more than twelve hours later with a great deal of luggage, and the driver seemed to struggle with the weight of it.

Robert stepped forward and asked, "May I help you with that?"

Mr. Jameson looked at Robert with an almost surprised "what are you doing out here?" look. Mr. Jameson quickly responded, "NO! I mean no, we're fine, thank you Robert."

Robert put his hands at chest height palms out and replied, "Sure, just thought I'd ask."

Mrs. Jameson replied, "Thank you, dear, but we can get it from here."

Mr. and Mrs. Jameson produced the retractable handles from each suitcase and inside the building they went. They both stopped dead in their tracks when Robert called out, "I didn't see Trixie; is she okay?"

Mr. Jameson looked at his wife and over his shoulder replied, "Thanks for asking. Yes, she is fine. She is with friends in Miami. We're going back in a couple of days."

"Okay then, well, if you need anything, please let me know."

The couple continued inside and to the elevators.

Robert turned to the street again, looking both directions, and then he walked across and turned to look at the building in which he lived. He pondered his relationship with Jennifer, smiled, and thought of all the great times they've shared and how easy it would be to call her his wife. He thinks of Tina and the loss. Her death rocked him to the core, and he swore he'd never love again. But that one fateful day when several papers slapped against his face while walking through Thomas Paine Park during a lunch break, he knelt to pick up what were important court documents and then looked into the eyes of Jennifer Sanders, Attorney at Law. He knew that someone was looking out for him. He's been in love from that moment and eventually she came around. He laughed to himself and then jogged back to the building and inside to the elevators.

Chapter Thirty-One: 07:00, Tuesday, April 27, 1999

The building at 26 Federal Plaza is buzzing, especially the twenty-ninth floor. Robert and Miller were briefing the task force on their findings and Stacey was standing with several other women outside the conference room.

Stacey said, "Would you just look at him? He's so focused and in charge. I do feel his tight shirt gives a girl all she needs to know about what's under it."

The girls laughed, and Robert looked at them and they quickly scattered, but not Stacey. She stared a bit longer and bit her lower lip in a seductive way, which distracted Robert. Miller saw this and left the conference room.

"Stacey, right? Hi,"

"Yes, Randy?"

"Oh, you know my name."

"What was that?"

"Look, Stacey, we are in the middle of an investigation and you standing out here is distracting. I'm pretty sure it's against policy, you know, to stare at people, so please go back to your side and let us do our work; otherwise I may have to have a conversation with your superior."

Stacey looked at Miller and it's clear she is upset and replied, "Fine, I wasn't hurting anyone, and I can't help how I feel bout Agent Franklin."

Miller replied softly again, "Lucky man."

"What was that?"

"Maybe it's not my place to say this, but he's deeply involved."

Stacey looked right at him and in a low, but stern voice responded, "Well, if that's the case, he needs to tell me!" She turned and walked away. Miller did a half wave and went back into the conference room.

"As usual there are no prints on the necklace, and the prints we found on the plastic and duct tape were from those at the recycling site and we've cleared them already. We all know this guy is precise and we know he's not motivated sexually, so let's get out there. Talk to Rebecca Clark's family, coworkers, and find out where she was last, and talk to the staff, or a salesperson from where she shops, whomever we can to get something. Okay, that's it, get out there."

Miller walked up to Robert and said, "Have you talked to Jameson or Mick?"

"Yes, Mick and I spoke around 06:30 while I was driving in. He wants you and I to meet him at the site around 09:00 and look through surveillance tapes, maybe we can reach out to some of the truck drivers that came in and out."

Miller walked out of the room and to his desk, and Robert sat and picked up the phone and dialed. After several rings, a woman's voice answered, "Good morning, Franklin residence."

"Hello Mother."

"Hello again, Robert. Twice in a week, boy do I feel lucky."

"Well, I think it's time."

Suddenly John Sr. said, "Time for what, son?"

Robert sat up a little taller and replied, "Well, I'm going to propose to Jennifer."

Both his parents began talking so fast he can barely understand them.

He interrupted and said, "I'm planning to come down Friday and stay until Monday, or even Tuesday, provided Jennifer can get the time off. We'll land in Charleston and stay at a nice bed and breakfast. I will propose to her on the beach Saturday after breakfast. She and I will rent a car and drive up and spend Saturday evening and Sunday morning in McCormick to celebrate, and then we'll head home."

"That sounds wonderful, Robert. We'll have your room ready for you, and Jennifer can sleep in John Jr.'s room."

Robert rolled his eyes, but knew it's their home, and since he and Jennifer aren't married, he would respect their wishes. He replied, "That would be fine, so I'll call Thursday to let you know when we arrive, okay?"

John Sr. replied, "That will be fine, son. Oh, and we're both happy for you and look forward to more grand babies."

"Hold on, let us get married first. Besides, I don't even know if she'll say yes."

"Yes, I agree, no need putting the grandchild before the marriage."

Robert ended with, "Again, I'll call you Thursday with the travel information. Have a wonderful day."

He hung up the phone just as Miller opened the door to the conference room.

"Hey, are you ready?"

Robert took a last drink from his coffee cup and stood and walked toward the open door. "So, what was that gaggle doing outside the conference room?"

"Well, it's pretty obvious that..." He stopped as Stacey walked by.

"Good morning Robert," she said, flashing her big blue eyes.

"Good morning."

Miller continued, "She has a thing for you."

Robert brushed off the comment as he and Miller headed toward the elevators.

"Did Jameson already speak to the victim's family?"

Miller flipped through his notepad. He stopped at a page and replied, "Yes, they live in Manhattan."

Robert looked at Miller and then his watch. It's now 07:36, and in order to make the meeting with Mick, they need to get on the road now. He pressed the elevator call button numerous times and looked at the floor number indicator. His patience was running thin and he said, "Well, let's stop and see them on the way back, maybe the cops missed something."

"We can't just stop by."

"What do you mean, we can't just drop by? Manhattan isn't that far!"

Miller looked at Robert who is now looking at him and said, "They live in Manhattan, Kansas. Her parents are professors at Kansas State University."

The elevator ding took Robert out of his gaze and both men entered the car. Miller pressed G for garage and the doors closed and the elevator made a slight jerking motion. Miller and Robert looked at each other and Miller said, "Well, that didn't feel right, maybe this elevator will end up like LA."

Robert replied, "That wouldn't be good; there are many more floors."

08:00, McCormick

Marilynn Franklin was standing at the door that led to the stairs and to the third floor. She was frozen and couldn't hold back the tears. John Sr. placed his right hand on her left shoulder, and she looked to her left and put her cheek on his hand.

"John, it's time, I think."

John put his head down and moved to her side. "Dear, it's never time. Too many years have passed; she's gone and there's nothing we can do to change that."

Marilynn stepped forward and to her left and down the stairs. John Sr. watched her go and then he too is transfixed on the door. He recalled Lisa Marie the night she died. Her complexion was pale, and her head hung over the bed. The needle was still in her arm. She was naked. A journal she had kept for many years lay open on her stomach. He knelt before her and wept. Marilynn came to the room and she too went to her knees crying out, which brought John Jr. and Robert running up the stairs. Robert was just a few days over thirteen when his sister died. John Sr. turned away from the door and made his way to his study.

McCormick – Part Three

08:52, Fairview, New Jersey

The Crown Vic rolled to a stop and Miller just stared at the chaos in front of him. The recycle center was in full swing and there were trucks lined up for blocks. He maneuvered the car through, using the red light on the dash. Drivers outside their trucks slowly move aside with much resistance and the Crown Vic passes through the guard gate and to the silver NYPD Impala parked at a dock. Mick and a uniformed officer exit the vehicle.

Robert removed his seat belt and said, "That kid looked a lot like Jameson. Could that be Mickey?"

"Yeah, I'll bet you're right."

Mick walked up to Robert and they exchange greetings. He began to introduce the officer, and Miller interrupted, "Mickey, is that you?" as he hugged the officer.

Robert too is going to exchange greetings but followed Miller and hugged Mickey and said, "Wow! Look at you, all grown up. Now we can attest that you are definitely not your father's kid."

A loud laugh came from a few feet away as Lt. Jameson entered the scene. He replied to Robert's comment, "Yeah, you're probably right, but he did get his old man's way of being a cop. I have him for the day and thought I'd bring him along. He graduates from the academy in a few weeks, so I thought a day with the old man might do him some good."

Mickey replied, "Hey, it's really good to see you both. It's been too long."

Mick spoke up, "Okay, as you can see, this place doesn't shut down for anyone, so we can only hope the tapes will give us something. I spoke to the site manager and he's agreed to give us an hour or so to scan his archives."

The five men made their way to a door that read "OFFICE" and step inside. A woman greeted them and took them into what could be deemed a control room. There were switches, buttons, and computer screens everywhere, and several people at stations monitoring the activities shown through the large windows. The woman waved the men into a room and she closed the door behind them. A man of about sixty is asleep at a control console and the woman pushed through and tapped him on the shoulder.

"Wake up, we've got cops here!"

The man lunged forward and then to his feet, wiped saliva from his lower lip. He adjusted accordingly and said, "I'm sorry gentlemen. I dozed off there."

Robert looked at Jameson and rolled his eyes. The man then asked, "So, what exactly are we looking for?"

Mick stepped into the man, causing him to sit back down and lean away from the massive man before him. The man said, "Hey, listen, I haven't done anything, big guy, so no need to get rough."

Mick extended his hand to exchange greetings and said, "Hello, I'm Detective Stevens of the NYPD, and with me I have Lieutenant Jameson, Officer Jameson, Special Agent in Charge Franklin, and Agent Miller, both with the FBI. We'd like to look at the recordings of incoming and outgoing trucks from 06:00 to 19:00 yesterday."

The man replied, "Wait, NYPD? This is New Jersey."

Lt. Jameson replied, "Yes, we are NYPD, and we have complete cooperation of local law enforcement and we brought the heavy—you know, the federal government, to back us up, so let's see the tapes, okay!"

The man looked at Jameson and then back at Mick's legs and nodded his head. He turned toward the console. He ejected the current tape and pulled tapes from a box and inserted the first tape.

Miller said, "Wait, how do you know that's from yesterday? It's not marked."

"I know it's from yesterday because after the body was found, I ejected the tape and put in a fresh tape and set this tape aside, knowing someone will be coming to review it. Of course, I didn't expect so many. Is it getting warm in here?"

Robert looked over his shoulder and saw the door is closed and stepped over to open it, and hoped to circulate the air a little, but the noise was so overwhelming they wouldn't be able to hear each other, so he closed the door and stepped back to the console. The man pressed play and the screen came to life, but it's wavy and in black and white. There were trucks entering; however, the grainy video made it impossible to gather any information.

Mick asked, "How old is this tape?"

The man looked at Mick with a puzzled look and replied, "It's from yesterday."

Mickey replied, "No, he means how old is this tape, as in how many times has it been used over and over to record?"

Robert looked at Jameson and Jameson winked and nodded

approval of his son's question and said, "See, I told you, smart kid."

The man shook his head and replied, "Oh, yeah, sorry. We reuse these tapes for months on end, or until they break. Sorry, but this is the best I can do."

The door opened and the woman stepped in and asked, "Gentlemen, are you getting what you need?"

Robert turned to her and asked, "There are no logs kept at the gate? Truck names, truck numbers, nothing?"

The woman replied, "No, I'm sorry. It's so busy and the drivers get so irritated waiting that we just roll them through. But we've been sold to a large corporation, and there will be changes coming, but until then, I'm sorry we can't be of more assistance."

Jameson barked back, "Well, maybe the guy should have waited to kill the woman after the changeover!" He pushed through and slammed the door into the wall.

Robert looked at the woman and said, "I'm sorry, this has been an emotional two days for all of us." He followed Jameson.

"Hey, Mike! You got a second?"

Jameson stopped, turned, put both hands on his hips, looked to the floor and then to Robert, and replied, "You know, it's only going to get worse."

"What's going to get worse?"

"The whole infrastructure of American society, that's what."

Robert looked a bit puzzled and said, "I'm not sure what that means, exactly."

"They said computers would make life easier, right? But they really don't; they make the world go faster, but we humans can't keep up, and we get lazy, and greedy, hence trucks rolling in and out of this place as they damn well please. It's crazy that this place doesn't have records!"

Robert put his right hand on Mike's left shoulder and said, "You know, you're right, but it's what we have to look forward to, so right now, let's keep our wits, not let it distract us from the case, and find this animal. I have a lot of respect for you, Mike. You're one of my closest friends, and yes, sometimes I look up to you, so do what you do, and keep all of us on track, okay?"

Jameson looked at Robert and then the floor, "I'm retiring in a few months, and I will give you all I can until then, but after that, it's up to Mick. I'm tired, Robert, tired as hell. I need that beachfront condo and a golf course, so let's get out of here and get busy!"

Robert walked back to the room, poked his head in, and asked, "Anything?"

"No sir, nothing."

"Okay, let's get back, make a few phone calls."

The men shuffle out of the room and the lady closed the door and motioned forward as if to say, "the exits that way." Robert and Mick stopped to watch two workers sorting through mounds of trash, separating paper, plastic, and glass. The line was moving at a rapid pace and the room looked like an ant farm with people everywhere, pushing full carts away and bringing back empties. It's an orchestration of nothing the men have ever seen.

Mick looked to Robert and said, "The people out there can

do what they're doing, but the people in that room can't keep record of who comes in? Amazing, don't you think?"

Robert looked at Mick and nodded his head sideways as if to say, "let's get going." He looked back to see Miller staring into the large room through the big windows and said, "Randy, c'mon."

Randy looked at Robert and then back to the production and replied, "Yeah, I'm coming."

The five men were now outside the business office making their goodbyes. Robert and Miller got into the Crown Vic and back out, and again maneuver through the people and trucks to get onto the Bergen Turnpike toward 26 Federal Plaza. Robert retrieved his BlackBerry from a leather holster and scrolled through the screen using the thumbwheel on the side until he finds "Contacts." He selected "Jennifer Sanders" and pressed "Send Call." The phone rings five or six times before voicemail and Robert hung up without leaving a message.

He scrolled through the contacts again and selected "Vito" and the phone rand once. A man answered, "Hello Vito's! This is Vito, how can I help you with your jewelry purchase today?"

Robert laughed and replied, "What do you do, sleep with that phone? One ring, are you desperate for a call or what?"

"Yeah, it's slow today, can't put my finger on it. Who is this?"

"What, you don't recognize my voice? It's your old pal, Agent Franklin with the Federal Bureau of Investigation!"

Miller looked at his boss and smiled, because he knew that Vito will do anything to please Special Agent in Charge Robert Franklin of the FBI, especially after Robert found his daughter six hours after she went missing two years ago. It was a jealous boyfriend, and he thought he'd prove his love by staging a kidnapping and ransom, but what he didn't expect was Agent Franklin, a man that specialized in many things, and one of his specialties is finding missing people, knowing that nine times out of time the whole thing is bogus.

Vito screamed into the phone, "Oh man, Agent Franklin, how are you, my friend? How's that lovely girlfriend of yours? It's time, isn't it? I knew you'd call."

Robert looked at Miller and then replied to Vito by saying, "Yes, Vito, it's time. You know my budget and her style, so can you bring a few settings by my office around 14:00 today? I know it's short notice, but I'm on a schedule."

Vito replied again with great enthusiasm, "Are you kidding me? Of course, I can be there, but I only have one question, well, maybe two. What time is 14:00 and did you bring a credit card to work today?"

"You civilians; 14:00 is 2:00 p.m., and yes, I have my credit card with me. So, when you get to the lobby, have security call me and I'll come down. Sound good?"

"Yes, sure. See you at 14:00, Captain."

Robert moved the phone from his ear to look at the screen and ended the call. He scrolled again and dialed Jennifer and this time after just three rings she answered.

"Hello honey, is everything alright? I missed a call from you less than ten minutes ago."

"Yes, everything is fine. Can you get away starting Friday morning through Monday afternoon? I'd like to go home, to

McCormick, for a couple of days, and my parents would love to see you."

"Yes, of course. Kevin can handle things while I'm away. Is your family okay?"

"Yes, they're fine. I just need to go home is all, and I want you to come with me."

Robert pointed out the windshield and whispered, "Take the Lincoln Tunnel; it's probably quicker." Miller checked his mirrors and made an abrupt lane change and headed toward the tunnel.

"Okay, it's settled then; see you later tonight, okay?"

He ended the call and put the phone back in its holster and smiled from ear to ear. Miller can't help but notice and Robert pointed out the windshield and said, "Pay attention to the road." Both men laughed as the car floated along at a good clip.

9:15, Jennifer's Office

Jennifer hung up her phone just as the screen of her computer indicated an instant message. It's Kevin and it read, "Katie is AMAZING. We had a wonderful time, and yes, I see her as my wife!"

Jennifer stood and made her way around her desk and leaned out the door of her office and said, "Kevin, may I see you in my office, please?"

Kevin swiveled in his chair and noticed those around him were staring as if he may be in some sort of trouble. He stood, pushed his wool slacks down from being bunched up, walked toward Jennifer's office, and entered, closing the door behind him. He said, "Am I crazy for feeling like this? She feels as I do and has been hoping we'd meet for some time."

Jennifer motioned for him to sit in the visitor's chair next to her desk. She leaned back, intertwined her fingers, and put her hands to her mouth. She stared at Kevin for a bit, which made him squirm in the seat. She lowered her hands and said, "Wow, this is great! I'm so happy for you both. She and I spoke before you got here, which reminds me, why were you late? Anyway, it doesn't matter. Tell me all about the date. What did you talk about?"

Kevin leaned back, puzzled, and asked, "I thought you already spoke to her?"

Jennifer replied, "Yes, I did, but I want to hear your thoughts." She leaned in and looked right into Kevin's eyes and the two began to laugh.

"Well, even the waiter felt we were a good match, but I'm concerned."

Jennifer sat back in her chair and waited for Kevin to express his concern. He looked around and then back at Jennifer as if he's about to speak and then looked to the floor, and then back to Jennifer and said, "She wants to work for her father's law firm, not the office here, but in Saratoga Springs. Have you ever been? It seems so far away, and isolated, maybe, I don't know, but she wants to get there soon so that I can see where she's from and to meet her family."

Jennifer leaned forward and threw her hands in the air and said, "Wow, that is awesome. I knew this would happen. I mean really, you two were meant to be, and yes, it's sudden, but why

185

fight destiny? And yes, I have been to Saratoga Springs. It's lovely, and the lifestyle is very laidback, and it will be a great place to raise a family."

Kevin leaned back in his chair and put his hands up as if to say, "hold on, wait a minute here."

"Jennifer, she and I have gone out once, and yes, it was awesome, but please don't have us with children just yet. Her parents may not approve of me. By the way, when are you and this mystery man that none of us have met or even seen a picture of getting married, and why do you keep him a secret?"

Jennifer sat back in her chair and plopped her arms on each rest, looked out the window, and smiled. She had been keeping Robert a secret for so many years because she isn't sure where his heart is. She loved him deeply, but wanted him to lead the way, but until then, no one knew who he is or what he looked like.

She replied, "Well, it's complicated, and his career is even more complicated; however, this weekend we are flying to his hometown, and I have a feeling this will be the weekend he proposes." She smiled from ear to ear and brought interlocked fingers to her face as if she's praying.

"That would be great, Jennifer! You see, things are looking up for the both of us. I really enjoy Katie, and she's so lovely, in all aspects of who she is." Kevin stood and then said. "Well, I'd better get back to work. Wait, I forgot to ask." He sat again and leaned in toward Jennifer, "So, did she say anything about me?"

Jennifer looked at Kevin with a big smile and replied, "She's head over heels for you, kiddo." She tousled Kevin's hair and then laughed, "Be the gentleman I know you to be, and have

186

an open heart. Saratoga Springs is a great place, and a beautiful story could be written there."

Kevin leaned back in his chair, smiled, and looked out the window. He imagined his life with Katie and the children they will have. He was lost in his thoughts and then Jennifer said, "Hey, what about getting back to work?"

They both laughed, and Kevin stood and made his way to the door. He stopped before opening it, turned, and said, "Thank you, Jennifer, for giving me the courage to make the move. I would have never done it on my own."

Jennifer waved him on and tuned toward her computer screen. Kevin smiled and opened the door, and Jennifer said, "Kevin! You're welcome." She smiled and followed it with a wink. Kevin smiled and looked at the floor and then back to Jennifer and stepped out of her office.

Jennifer swiveled in her chair, dropping her posture to a relaxed state and stared at the people walking to and from just a few flights below. The weather was warmer than usual at sixty-four degrees Fahrenheit, which meant there will be people in long coats, people in jogging suits, and of course the die-hards in shorts milling around as if they're in Florida. Just then a knock at the door snapped her out of her daydream. She swiveled toward the door to see Katie.

Jennifer looked at Katie and they both break into a girlish laugh. Katie entered the office, closed the door behind her, and said, "So, what did he say?"

Jennifer smiled and replied, "You two will be fine. He doesn't want to ruin it by moving too quickly be he's smitten with you."

Katie's face showed puzzlement and she said, "What is smitten?"

Jennifer laughed, "Sorry, smitten is a southern word for crazy about you. Robert's mom told me that's how he is with me, smitten."

Katie's face lit up and she said, "Well, the smitten is mutual."

Both ladies leaned into each other and laughed. Katie then stood to make her way out of the office and said, "Hey, would it be okay if I took Friday off? I'd like to get home to Saratoga Springs Thursday night and prepare the house and to coach my father on how to act toward Kevin. He can be a bit intimidating, but he means well."

Jennifer looked at her calendar and replied, "Sure, I won't be here, either. Robert and I are headed to South Carolina to see his parents, and I believe this could be the weekend he proposes to me!"

Katie flopped back into the visitor's chair and looked at Jennifer in total silence.

"Katie, what's wrong?"

"Jennifer Sanders, you're just telling me this now?"

"Yes, because I just found out about the trip less than twenty minutes ago, and Kevin was in here, so I couldn't tell you just yet."

"Did you tell Kevin?"

"Yes, of course. Kevin came in just as I hung up with Robert."

Katie stood, walked over to embrace Jennifer, "I'm just giving you a hard time because you told Kevin first."

Jennifer stood and they embrace again, and Jennifer said, "This could be it. All these years and this could be the weekend where my dreams come true."

"You'd better take pictures this weekend, and hopefully we'll finally meet this mystery man!"

"Yes, I will have pictures and you will meet him."

Katie turned and left Jennifer's office, but not before turning to her and said, "Isn't life grand? I mean, we're both smitten." She headed back to her desk while staring and smiling at Kevin. She sat, opened her instant messenger, and typed, "Hi, I'll be leaving for Saratoga Springs Thursday around 8:00 p.m., which means I'll be off Friday, so here's the address: 222 Clement Avenue. Take 87 north to Broadway or 9 into Saratoga Springs then west on Clement. It's a yellow house with a big front porch. Call my cellphone if you get lost, but know the reception is spotty at best, so keep trying."

Kevin read and wrote the address on a piece of paper. He looked across his desk and saw Katie looking at him. They both smiled, and Kevin then folded the paper and placed it in his shirt pocket.

13:51, Robert's Office

Robert Franklin was staring at crime scene photos trying to come up with something that may lead to the arrest of the man, responsible for the recent murder of a young woman found dead at a recycling plant in New Jersey. His phone beeped once, and then twice, taking him out of thought.

He reached for the speaker button, pressed once, and said, "Franklin!"

A female voice on the other end said, "Yes, sir, there's a man named Vito in the lobby to see you."

"Great, tell him I'll be right there." He stood, took his suit jacket from the hook on the back of his office door, and verified his wallet was still in the left side inner pocket. He placed his right arm into the sleeve and repeated with his left and then shrugged his shoulders, allowing the jacket to rest as it should. He glanced at himself in a mirror and adjusted his tie. He opened the door and out he walked toward the elevator.

As he reached forward to press the down button, Stacey walked up and said, "Hello Robert, in a hurry?"

"Yes, I'm meeting a jeweler in the lobby."

"Oh, is this part of a case?"

Robert looked at her and then forward again and said, "No, it's a personal purchase. I'm going to ask Jennifer to marry me."

Stacey stepped back and it's as if life left her body, "Well, I guess congratulations are in order."

The elevator chimed and the door opened as Robert stepped in, saying, "Thank you, Stacey."

The door slowly closed, and Stacey turned walked back to her desk and under her breath said, "Sure, don't mention it." She slumped into her chair and stared into the monitor.

Robert began to sweat and became nervous. He recalled the same feeling more than thirteen years ago with his first love, Tina Kettering, and how he felt before proposing to her. The elevator stopped at the tenth floor and a couple of stuffed shirts enter talking about playing golf this coming weekend. Robert's thought was, golf, what a waste of time. Chasing a stupid ball from one hole to another.

One of the men turned to Robert and asked, "So, what's your handicap?"

Offended, Robert looked at the man and said, "Excuse me?"

"You know, how you are hitting?"

"Oh, you mean my golf game. Well, I scored three goals once and brought in two runners with a home run."

Both men looked at each other as the elevator chimed and the doors opened to the main lobby. Robert walked to the front counter and there's Vito, waving with excitement as he held a small box up. Robert waved back and made his way toward him.

They greet each other with a handshake and Robert motioned toward the doors leading to the sidewalk and said, "How about we get a coffee and discuss my options?"

"That would be wonderful. The Beanery is just a block up."

The two made their way up the street among a sea of people and entered a coffee shop filled with even more stuffed shirts and some executive-type women. Everyone was standing around either waiting to order or waiting for that cup of 14:00 energy.

Vito looked at Robert and said, "Are you okay? You look a bit nervous."

Robert glanced at Vito and then forward, "Yes, I am nervous. It's been a long time since I've done this."

"Oh, you were married before, yes?"

"No, I was engaged. Unfortunately, she was killed by a drunk driver on her way to work many years ago."

Vito put his hand on Robert's right shoulder, "I'm so sorry to hear of this, my friend, so sorry."

Robert looked at Vito and it's clear he meant it. "Thank you, Vito."

A small woman asked, "Hi, what can I get you?"

"Go ahead, it's on me."

"I'll have a large coffee with cream and sugar please."

Robert looked at the woman and said, "I'll have the same."

The woman repeated the order, allowing another employee to repeat the order, "That will be $2.50 please."

Robert was taken aback, "Wow, Vito, you're an expensive date!"

The woman laughed and Vito said, "I'm sorry, what did you say?"

Robert laughed as a man handed him the two coffees. The men made their way toward the door and a voice yelled out, "Pick a good one, Robert!" It was Miller grinning from ear to ear. Robert looked at him and smiled.

Robert handed Vito his coffee and suggested they head back to 26 Federal Plaza and sit in the lobby and discuss the acquisition. Robert held open the door to 26 Federal Plaza and motioned for Vito to go ahead. They moved to the far side of the lobby and found two open seats. The leather chairs squeaked as both men sit. Robert placed his coffee on an end table as does Vito. Vito then opened the small box and brought out the first ring and handed it to Robert. Robert leaned toward him and took the shiny ring. He looked at it and said; "How many karats is this?"

"That, my friend, is just over a half karat and is really good quality. I will sell it to you for $2,225!" Robert looked at Vito, who was grinning from ear to ear like a lion about to pounce a large T-bone steak. Robert then shook his head and Vito sensed discouragement and leaned back in his chair and said, "What's wrong, you don't like the ring?"

"No, it's fine, but I was hoping for something more of a karat or bigger?"

Vito leaped to his feet and yelled, "Oh man, do I have the ring for you!"

Others in the lobby look at Vito. Robert leaned forward, motioning Vito to sit, and said, "Sorry folks, my friend is a little excited."

Vito sat and reached into the box and brought out a small, red velvet pouch. He handled it like a prize and then with both hands he gave it to Robert and said, "This, my friend, is the ring for Jennifer. I just know it. Please, have a look."

Robert slowly opened the bag as to ensure the ring doesn't fall to the floor. With two fingers he reached into the bag and grasped the ring and removed it from the bag. The ring is stunning, and the shine is incredible. "Tell me about this ring, Vito."

Vito stood and moved to the seat directly next to Robert. He leaned in and said, "Well, that my friend, is 1.10 karat and as good as it's going to get. The band is white gold, and for you I will sell it for $6,500!" He leaned back away from Robert and watched for a reaction.

Robert was holding the ring to the light and moving it, allowing the sparkle to reflect off the marble walls. He then looked at Vito and said, "Vito, you've done well, and I will take it, but it will need to be a size five by Thursday, okay?"

Vito stood, "Agent Franklin that ring is ready for you now. When you introduced Jennifer to me all those months ago, I took note of her fingers!"

"Are you saying just by looking at her fingers you knew the size?"

"Are you kidding me? Yes, of course. I've been at this long enough to know many things, my friend. Just like I knew to check her fingers because I could see in your eyes, she was the one!"

Robert stood and removed his wallet from his inside pocket. He handed Vito the rings and asked for a box to put the second ring in. Vito took the first and second ring, placing the second ring on the tip of his left-hand pinky, and he put the first ring away. He pulled out a nice burgundy felt-covered ring box, opened it, and placed the second ring into the ring slot inside the box.

Robert opened his wallet and brought out cash and then a MasterCard. He said, "Okay, here's $5,000 in cash. Take down my credit card information and charge the balance, okay?"

Vito smiled, took the money and card, and handed Robert the small box. He then sat to write down some information. "Please send the receipt of purchase to my apartment."

Vito doesn't look up but acknowledged Robert by shaking his head yes.

"Great, I have to get back to work!"

Vito stood and hugged Robert, which made him feel uncomfortable because it happened so quickly. He just lightly patted Vito on the back. The men parted ways; Vito signed out and Robert went to the elevator. He pressed the button and looked at the ring again, smiled, and then heard a chime as the doors opened, allowing patrons out and him to step in. He pressed twenty-nine and stood against the back wall of the car. It was like a giant weight had been lifted. He now had everything he wanted: the woman of his dreams and a ring to show her just how much he loved and adored her.

16:15, Mario's

A man walked to the host station at Mario's and said, "Hi, how are you?"

The host behind the podium looked him, up and then down, and said, "I'm well, and you?"

"I'm doing well, thank you. I was in Monday around 6:30 or so and I couldn't help but notice a nice young couple sitting in that window seat. The young man was handsome and the woman he was with, well, she was stunning."

The host said, "What can I help you with?"

The man then looked back to the window and then back to the host and replied, 'Yes, I was wondering if you may know them? The young lady looked very familiar to me."

The host looked at the window and then turned to the back of the restaurant and said, "Michael, please come here."

A tall, slender-built man made his way to the podium and said, "Yes, how can I help you?"

"This man is asking about the young couple you waited on Monday afternoon?"

"Oh yes, Katie and Keith, or maybe it was Kevin. It was their first date."

"You seemed to remember her name quickly; does she come in here a lot?"

Michael looked at the host and then asked the man, "Why do you ask?"

"Oh, she looked familiar to me is all, maybe the daughter of a former colleague."

"I see; well, her father is a big-shot attorney here in Brooklyn and Katie works just down the street as an intern or something for an office that handles mainly real estate law."

The man raised his right hand and then said, "That's right, her father worked on a case for me some years ago, and I recall meeting her briefly. Thank you, you've put my mind at ease. I've been dwelling on her face since I saw her Monday."

The man nodded and then turned and walked out of Mario's onto the sidewalk. Michael turned to the host and said, "He was rather handsome, but he shouldn't wear such tight shirts. It made me feel bad about myself."

The host laughed and said, "Yes, me too!"

Both men laughed and Michael walked to the back of the narrow place and the host scanned the guest book just as the phone rang. "Mario's, may I help you?"

17:30, 26 Federal Plaza

Robert leaned back in his chair, brought his hands to his face, and slowly rubbed his eye and shook his head. There was nothing in the photos, nothing from the coroner's office, nothing leading his team closer to the monster that took another innocent life! He sat forward and shuffled the photos into a neat stack. He raised them and squared them by tapping the bottom edge of the pile to his desk and then placed the entire lot in a folder. He stood and stretched, and there was a sudden knock on the door.

"Dang, boss, you need to lay off the weights. You're about to tear out of that shirt!"

Robert quickly brought himself straight and said, "You could stand to spend a few hours a week in the gym too, you know?"

"Not when you have kids, no way. Mrs. Miller would kill me, and then what would you do?"

"I'd celebrate with her."

Miller laughed and walked in and sat in the visitors' chair. He laid a file on Robert's recently created folder and said, "I have looked at every angle of the scene and nothing stood out. I just can't get over it. This guy is really good."

"Yes, I agree, but sooner or later everyone makes a mistake, and his or her day is coming!"

Miller leaned back placing both arms on the chair and said, "So, on another note, did you buy the ring?"

Robert scrambled to his jacket and reached into a pocket and removed the felt-covered box. He opened it, dropped to one knee, and said, "What do you think?"

Just then, several people walk by and stop to stare. Robert brushed them off and Miller said in a high-pitched voice, "YES, of course I'll marry you!"

Robert stood and punched him in the shoulder.

Miller reached for the box and looked at the ring and then to Robert. "WOW!" he said.

"Yes, I know, but she's worth it. I've been saving since before we met. I knew one day I'd meet the woman I'm to spend the rest of my life with. I feel blessed knowing she put up with me for so long."

Miller laughed, "Yes, putting up with you is the key. I've been doing it more than a decade and some days..."

Robert snatched the box away and put it back in his jacket pocket, "Okay, get out of here. Go home to your family. Oh, by the way, Jennifer and I are going to South Carolina this weekend and will leave Friday, and painful as this sounds, you're in charge! I won't have my phone, so if anything comes up, it will have to wait until I return Monday. Got it?"

Miller stood and saluted Robert and replied, "Sir, yes sir!" Both men laughed as Miller left the office.

Robert sat again. He leaned toward his desk phone, raised the phone receiver, and dialed a number.

"Franklin residence, John Franklin speaking!"

"Hello Dad, how are you?"

John yelled without taking the phone away from his mouth, "Marilynn, pick up the other phone; it's Robert!"

Robert moved the receiver away from his ear and shook his

head and then he laughed. John said, "What's so funny, son?"

Marilynn said, "Hello Robert, how are you?"

"I'm well, Mother, and you?"

"I'm well. Your father is doing well too. We're all well."

"Well, that's great! Are we still okay for this weekend?"

John Sr. replied, "Yes, of course. Did you buy a ring?"

Robert looked at his jacket hanging on the back of the door, "Yes, I sure did, and it's beautiful!"

Marilynn chimed in and said, "Oh Robert, we are so happy and so proud of you. Have you told your brother?"

Robert leaned back, "No, I will call him next."

John said, "Okay son, we'll see you soon. This is a costly call, I'm sure."

"Sure, okay. We'll see you Friday!"

Robert opened a desk drawer and removed airline tickets, reading through them. JFK leaving at 08:05 arriving in ATL 10:50, Hertz rental car confirmed—midsize car. He slapped the documents on his left hand, stood, and then quickly sat down. He reached for the phone but stopped, stood, and walked to the door. He grabbed his jacket and headed toward the elevators. He looked at his Paneria watch and smiled, and then the doors close, but quickly they opened again as Stacey walked in. She looked at Robert and he smiled.

Stacey said, "You look happy."

"Yes, I'm very happy, thank you. How are you?"

She paused and then said, "I'm okay I guess…long day."

The elevator chimed and the doors opened, allowing four others to enter, moving Stacey next to Robert. The doors closed and there was total silence the rest of the descent. Another chime and the doors opened to the lobby floor and everyone exited but Robert.

"Have a nice night, Robert."

Robert doesn't even look her way and replied, "You too," as he pressed the button for the parking garage again. The door soon opened, and he walked to his Crown Victoria. He got in, started it, and backed out doing a "J" turn and onto the street.

20:02, Brooklyn

Katie looked at her watch and then around the office, which by now is empty. She stayed over to do some research for an upcoming assignment and lost track of time. She stood, turned off the computer monitor, and grabbed her jacket from a hook on the wall. She snatched her purse from her desktop and headed toward the door, but before leaving she began to turn off the lights. A small voice called out, "Hello, we are cleaning, please leave the lights on."

Katie had been so engrossed in her work that she didn't even know the night crew had come in. She replied, "I'm sorry, I didn't know you were here. Have a wonderful evening." Katie exited the building and headed out onto the sidewalk. She looked left and then right before crossing to where her car is parked.

A man sitting in a car waved to her and she ignored him by looking away. Just then a voice said, "Katie?"

She turned to see a well-built man standing next to a car. She stopped and replied, "Do I know you?"

Just then an ambulance went screaming by and Katie walked quickly to her car. The man followed, but as soon as she got into her car, he stopped, waved, and turned back. Katie locked her door, started the engine, and drove off into the night. She checked her mirrors to see if the man is following her; after all, she had no idea who the man was.

The man got into his car, started the engine, and squealed off into the night.

20:45, Robert's Apartment

Robert parked the Crown Victoria in his designated spot and made his way toward the elevator. He pressed the up button, and seconds later there's a chime and the doors opened. He entered and pressed fourteen, and there is another chime and the doors closed. The elevator barely moved and then a chime and the doors opened at the lobby.

Mr. and Mrs. Jameson are there along with Jennifer. They've been talking as everyone is laughing. Robert said, "What's so funny?"

Jennifer looked at him and smiled and said, "Hello love, how are you?"

Trixie, the Jameson's' dog, began barking. Mrs. Jameson said, "Trixie, stop that. Robert's a nice man. I'm sorry Robert; she's never like this with anyone else."

Robert looked at Jennifer and then back to Mrs. Jameson and replied, "It's okay, really. Maybe I'll start carrying dog treats with me."

The three and Trixie enter the elevator and Robert pressed fourteen again. There is a chime and the doors closed. Jennifer nestled in close to Robert and he smiled. Within a few seconds, the elevator chimed, and the doors opened, allowing everyone to exit. Mr. and Mrs. Jameson head out first followed by Jennifer and Robert. They exchange pleasantries and Robert opened the door to his apartment, motioning for Jennifer to go in first. He closed the door behind him and removed his suit jacket and hung it on a coat rack next to the door.

He then said, "Hello love, do you have a kiss for me?"

Jennifer swirled around, "Yes, of course I do, but tell me why you're just getting home."

Robert reached for her and replied, "Well, I went by your office to see if I could catch you before you left, and we could have dinner at—"

She interrupted and said, "You were willing to try Mario's, but all those carbs."

"Yes, all those carbs."

The two then embrace and kiss. Jennifer looked at Robert, "I'm looking forward to seeing your parents. Oh, and your brother and his family."

"Hey, don't get any ideas about trying to copy my brother by wanting five children!"

"Of course not, just four."

Robert's face went blank, "Really? You want four children?"

She bites her lower lip and replied, "Is that too many?"

He looked at her and shook his finger, "You almost had me

there."

She broke away and went into the kitchen. She opened the refrigerator and moved boxes around and said, "Well, I guess we're ordering Chinese tonight?"

Robert looked at his watch and replied, "Yes, and ten, nine, eight..." Just then, the doorbell rang. Robert went into his coat pocket and retrieved his wallet. He opened the door to greet a small Asian man from Hunan Palace, a local favorite of most everyone in the building, including Robert and Jennifer.

"Hello Rick, how are you?"

Rick lifted a bag to Robert, nodded, and replied, "Hello Mr. Franklin, how are you, sir?"

Robert opened his wallet and handed Rick a twenty-dollar bill and replied, "I'm well, Rick. Thank you for asking."

Jennifer came to the door, "Hello Rick!"

Rick looked to the floor and replied quietly, "Hello Ms. Jennifer."

Robert smiled and took the bag, "Thank you, Rick. Have a nice night." He closed the door and said, "I think Rick likes you."

Jennifer laughed at the comment and took the bag headed into the kitchen to remove its contents. The two eat, making small talk, and then head to the living room to watch *Friends*, a popular sitcom that Robert had set to record each time it is on. Soon they're both in the kitchen cleaning up and then off to bed.

Robert leaned over to the alarm clock, which read 11:06. He ensured the alarm is set for 05:45. Robert leaned toward Jennifer who was already on her side, and yes, she was snoring. He kissed her cheek, "Good night, love."

The MSG from the Chinese food always knocked her out shortly after eating. Robert's fingers were intertwined behind his head as he stared at the ceiling, and soon he too was sound asleep.

Chapter Thirty-Two: Wednesday, April 28, 1999

Robert stepped off the elevator and walked toward his office, but not before Miller stopped him and said, "Hey boss, how are you?"

"I'm well, and you?"

"I just received a call from Mick. He and Jameson want to meet us as soon as possible."

Robert looked at his watch and replied, "What's going on at 07:30?"

"Seems they may have another murder and there are some similarities to our guy."

Robert looked at Miller, "Okay, let me grab an umbrella from my office; looks like rain."

Robert walked briskly to his office, opened the door, reached to a canister just to the left, and grabbed an umbrella. He looked to his phone and noticed a flashing light, which indicated a message, but he knew it could wait. He closed the door and made his way to the elevator, where Miller had already pressed the button. The timing was perfect as the doors opened and the two men entered. Miller pressed P for parking. The elevator chimed at the lobby and the doors opened.

Miller said to those waiting, "Sorry, going down," and then pressed the button to close the doors.

Robert looked at Miller who was tense and said, "Randy, calm down. We'll get there."

Miller looked at Robert and nodded. The doors opened and the two men walked to the Crown Victoria and got in. Robert looked at Miller as the car backed out and squealed toward the exit and said, "Did Mick tell you where to meet them? Oh, and why didn't they call me on my cell phone?"

Miller opened his notepad and replied, "Liberty State Park, and they did call you, but no answer."

Robert leaned to the left and reached for his phone attached to his belt, but the phone isn't there. He scrambled into his suit coat pockets and replied, "Damn, I left cell phone on the kitchen counter! We'll go after it later."

Miller nodded agreeing as the car weaved in and out of traffic. Despite the red light flashing from the dash, the rush hour traffic didn't give way to police, or federal agents, or any first responders for that matter. Finally, a break, and the black car moved quickly to the Holland Tunnel and within minutes onto the Jersey Turnpike. After nearly forty minutes fighting traffic, the car rolled up to a sea of red flashing lights. A crowd had assembled, and the local police were doing what they could to keep everyone at bay. Robert and Miller exited the Crown Vic and made their way toward the scene. They're stopped by a local and Robert flashed his credentials and the crime scene tape is lifted for him and Miller to enter.

A voice yelled out, "Agent Franklin, over here!"

It was Mick and as usual he stood out among everyone around him. He was an intimidating sight for sure. Robert raised his hand as if to acknowledge Mick. He, Lt. Jameson, and a few locals are standing over a covered body. Robert said, "Why's the NYPD all the way over here?"

Jameson looked at him and replied, "We are here at the request of the local sheriff, and that is why you are here. This is another pearl necklace killing. We waited for you to get here before we started investigating. By the way, we've been calling you all morning!"

"Yeah, I know. I left my BlackBerry at home. I'm a bit preoccupied I guess."

Miller chuckled, which is followed by a smack to the shoulder from Robert. Mick looked at Jameson and then said, "What's so funny?"

Robert looked at Mick and replied, "My girlfriend and I are going to South Carolina this weekend and I plan to propose to her, and my colleague has a funny way of keeping things to himself!"

Jameson flicked a cigarette into the damp grass and replied, "That's great news, Franklin. Good for you. Marriage is a sacred institution. I know. I've been in that institution a few times!"

The men laughed and then the mood quickly changed as a local said, "Not sure what's so funny gentlemen, but we've got a dead girl here, and a crowd looking to lynch, so please are you going to help us here?"

Robert looked at the man, who appeared to be the local sheriff, a heavy-set man of about sixty, and extended his right hand and replied, "Hello Sheriff, I'm Special Agent in Charge Robert Franklin, and this is my colleague, Special Agent Randy Miller of the FBI."

The sheriff extended to accept the greeting and looked at Jameson and said, "Wow, you really brought the big guns with you! Nice to meet you both. I'm Sheriff Tony Moceri of the Plainsboro Township Police. I called Jameson because we go way back. I've read stories of the 'Pearl Necklace Killer' and this has his signature all over it."

Miller interjected, "Sheriff, tell me how you came to that conclusion."

Sheriff Moceri called over a deputy and said, "Son, remove that cover, but keep it so that people cannot see, okay?"

The deputy doing as instructed removed the tarp slowly, but a breeze came through, which took the tarp above everyone's head and exposed a naked dead woman. The crowd gasped in horror and a few children screamed and were quickly moved away by their parents. The sheriff wrestled with the tarp, brought it back to earth, and gave his deputy a look of disappointment. He then instructed other deputies to move the crowd back another twenty yards or so. The sheriff spread his legs, getting him a little closer to the body, but given his size there would be no getting him to kneel; that was certain.

Robert and Miller both stepped in and knelt next to the body. Miller removed an expandable pointer from the breast pocket of his suit coat, extended it, and began to lift the pearl necklace from the woman's neck, exposing the clasp. Both men looked at each other and stand.

Robert announces, "What we have here is a 'copycat kill' and—"

The sheriff interrupted, "What are you talking about? She's naked and was wrapped in burlap, and she's wearing a pearl necklace. Isn't that your man!?"

Robert stepped back and looked at the man and then at Miller, who then responded, "No Sheriff, this is not the guy. First off, the necklace is easily costume jewelry, probably bought at a local Kmart. The burlap is another mistake, so to speak. All the past victims have been wrapped in an industrial plastic used for sectioning an area during construction, you know, to keep dust down and so forth. And lastly and most certainly this woman was raped, judging by the dried blood on her inner thighs and vaginal area. Our guy has never raped any of the victims. I'm sorry, this is definitely someone trying to get attention and he's probably standing among the people in the crowd getting off on this scene!"

Robert placed his hand on Miller's shoulder and stopped him, "Yes, what Agent Miller is saying is true, and if it were me, I'd talk to as many of the people here today, and maybe a nervous bystander will give himself up. By the way, who found the body?"

The sheriff asked his deputy to find the man who called it in, but the deputy replied, "Sorry Sheriff, he's gone."

The sheriff looked at the deputy and the other men and said, "What do you mean he's gone!? Didn't you put him in the squad car?"

The deputy looked at the car and then the ground, and then back to the sheriff, "Yes, I did put him in the car, but I didn't close the door and asked him to sit tight and I'd be right with him."

Mick spoke up, "Deputy, is there a chance you checked his ID or got a name, something?"

"No sir, I did not. I'm sorry."

The sheriff looked up and said, "The coroner's office has

arrived."

All the men looked up to see a dark blue van stopped until the yellow tape is moved and then proceeds to the scene. Jameson walked toward the sheriff and extended his right hand, "Sheriff Moceri, I wish we could have caught up under different circumstances, but it's clear this is not our guy. Have a great day."

The other men followed suit and headed toward their vehicles. Jameson stopped at his unmarked vehicle and said, "Well, thanks for coming out. Sorry for wasting your time."

Robert put his arms on the roof of his black Crown Victoria, "No problem, it's better to be certain, right?"

"Hey, congratulations on your upcoming engagement. Let us know when you're back and we'll meet for lunch."

Robert waved at the two men and got into the car. Miller joined him and buckled in after tossing his notepad to the dash. The car moved forward toward the exit of the park and back onto I-78 toward the tunnel and back to 26 Federal Plaza's twenty-ninth floor. It was a very quiet ride as neither man said a word.

Robert pulled up to the front of the building, looked at Miller, and said, "Hey, I'll be back in a bit. I need to run by my apartment to get my phone, okay?"

Miller released his seat belt and reached for his notepad, "Okay, sounds good. I'll see you soon."

Robert grabbed Miller's left arm pulling him back into the seat, "Randy, I know this case is tough, but when you let anger in, you'll lose sight, so relax and keep your head in the game, okay?"

Miller looked out the windshield and then to Robert, "Yes sir, I know, but sometimes this work gets to me. I think about the loss, and for why? What is this guy getting from killing these women?"

Robert squeezed Miller's arm, "I get it. Like I said, he's going to make a mistake and then we'll have him."

Miller exited the vehicle and Robert signaled he's coming out into traffic. The tires made a chirping noise as he headed home to retrieve his phone.

10:15, Brooklyn

Katie made her way down the sidewalk toward her office. A man sitting in a dark car was watching her, but she is oblivious and stepped into her office building. The car started and the man pulled away and hears a woman's voice. "Robert!"

He kept moving and checked his rearview mirror to see a woman standing in the street with both arms in the air waving he held a steady clip leaving the street.

Robert arrived at his apartment building to find the front of the building blocked off by Chevrolet Suburban's and Crown Victoria's that matched his. He pulled up to an opened spot and parked, got out, and made his way to the building entrance. He's stopped by a man wearing a jacket reading "DEA."

A voice yelled out, "Let him through!"

Robert saw an old friend, DEA Agent Wayne Patrick, waving him in. Robert investigated the back seat of a car and saw Mrs. Jameson and then to another vehicle and saw Mr. Jameson. Mrs. Jameson raised cuffed hands and covers her face while Mr. Jameson looked away. Robert extended his right hand to Agent Patrick and said, "Hey Wayne, what's going on here?"

Agent Patrick exchanged greetings by shaking Robert's hand and replied, "Do you know Mr. and Mrs. Jameson?"

Robert looked back at the vehicles where his neighbors were confined and turned back to Wayne, "Yes, of course, we live on the same floor. What's going on?"

Wayne looked right at Robert and said, "Your neighbors have been bringing cocaine into New York for several years via

Miami, and they aren't even married. They're brother and sister and their real names are Hector and Rosa Martinez, and they're a part of one of the largest drug cartels since the death of Pablo Escobar."

Robert stepped back and said, "Are you serious? I would have never guessed in a million years. I thought he did real estate!"

"Yes, anyone would have thought that, but we've been following these two for more than two years and we had an insider do a lot of video and recordings, which gave us enough evidence to bring them to justice."

A young lady walked up and said, "Excuse me sir, we are ready to move out. Everything needed has been placed into evidence."

"Wait, what about Trixie?"

Wayne looked at Robert with a funny look and said, "Who's Trixie?"

"Trixie is their little devil dog."

The young woman replied, "We have her in custody too. Would you like to take care of her?"

"Oh, no thanks. I'll be fine."

Wayne extended his right hand, "Well, we must go, Special Agent in Charge Franklin."

Robert shook Agent Patrick's hand and walked into the building shaking his head.

He entered his apartment and went to the kitchen and retrieved his BlackBerry from the counter, but it's not there. He looked down to find it lying on the floor where it must have vibrated right off the counter. He picked it up and the screen showed twenty-six missed calls. Using the side wheel, he scrolled through and saw where Mick tried twice, Jameson once, Miller once, and Jennifer twenty-one times, which scared him, so he called her immediately, but got her voicemail.

"Hello, love. How are you? Sorry I've missed your twenty-one calls. I was in Jersey and I forgot my phone on the counter, well, the floor, and I'm now at the apartment getting it. You won't believe what's happened here today. Call when you can. All my love."

Robert ended the call and headed back out to his car. As he left the building, he noticed the doorman holding Trixie and he said, "Good luck with her, Richard. She's a mean one."

Richard looked over, "No sir, Mr. Franklin. She's fine."

Trixie saw Robert and began to growl, and Robert under his breath said, "What an evil monster she is."

He was at his car and his phone vibrated. He raised it to see Jennifer's name on the screen. He pressed send and said, "Hello love, how are you?"

Jennifer responded with a hint of frustration in her voice, "Why didn't you stop earlier when I saw you by my office? I yelled your name and waved at you as you drove away! I called out numerous times!"

Robert was now confused and said, "Yes, you called twenty-one times, but I haven't been anywhere near your office today. I got in, went right to Jersey, and then back to the apartment to get my phone. I'm here now, just outside getting ready to go back to my office."

Jennifer was silent for a while, "You were not outside my office this morning?"

"Jennifer, I'm telling you I was in Jersey at a crime scene."

"I'm sorry. I swear this guy looked just like you and was in a dark car just like the one you drive. A BMW 7 something."

Robert laughed, "Love, there is no way the Bureau will spend that kind of money on a car like that. I drive a Ford Crown Victoria that's five years old with nearly 150,000 miles on it and it buzzes and rattles. It's horrible, but it's fast."

Robert then said, "Oh, you know the Jameson's down the hall? Turned out they're really brother and sister and have been bringing drugs into New York for a long time. When I got here to get my phone, my friend Wayne from the DEA was outside and had them in separate cars. Here all this time I thought he was some big-shot real estate tycoon!"

Jennifer replied, "Robert, do you promise you were not by my office today?"

"Honey, I swear, I was in Jersey. Do you want me to have Randy call you to confirm my alibi?"

Jennifer exhaled into the phone, "No, I believe you. It was amazing how much this man looked like you. I mean, exactly like you."

Robert looked out to the street and replied, "Honey, there can only be one Robert Franklin. Look, I must get back to the office. I'll see you tomorrow, right? Don't forget to pack tonight. I have a car coming for us at 06:00 Friday morning."

"Yes love, I'll be ready. I love you,"

Robert put the key into the door lock and opened the door of the Ford. He climbed in and sat back in the seat with both hands on the steering wheel. He looked around and said, "Yeah, I wish you were a BMW." He patted the dash and then said, "You've been a good car, Vic. Keep it up!"

The car roared to life and the tires chirped onto the street. Robert looked at his BlackBerry and scrolled through his contacts and pressed send. A chipper voice answered, "Franklin Hardware. Sally speaking, how may I help you?"

Robert smiled, "Hello Sally, it's your uncle Robert. Is your dad available?"

"Hello Uncle Robert, let me get Dad."

She was a lot like her grandpa and didn't move the receiver from her mouth and yelled, "Dad, Uncle Robert is on the phone!"

Robert moved the phone away from his ear and listened. The sound of another receiver being lifted brought a voice saying, "Hello little brother, how are you?"

Sally slammed the receiver down and John said, "Sorry about that. She got that from her grandpa, not me. So, what's new, Robbie?"

"Well, I'm bringing Jennifer home to McCormick and I'm planning to propose. I'm hopeful that you'll be my best man when we do get married?"

John's voice cracked, "Yes, of course. I'd be honored. Wow, thank you!"

Robert smiled, "Hey, suck it up. See you Friday. Have a great day!"

Robert ended the call and wiped a tear from his right eye and

217

continued onward to 26 Federal Plaza. He entered the parking garage and whipped into his designated spot. He slammed the car into park, got out, and jogged toward the elevator. Seconds later, a chime and the doors opened. He entered, pressed twenty-nine, and moved to the back wall. He rested his palms on the rail behind him. The elevator chimed and the doors opened at lobby level.

Stacey looked at Robert and walked up to him, turned, and leaned against the same rail just inches away. She looked at him, and he looked at her. Robert said, "Hello Stacey, how are you?"

Stacey turned to Robert and placed her right hand on his left shoulder, which caused him to stand straight and move to the right. Stacey replied, "Hello Robert. I'm fine but I'm sad at the same time. I mean, don't get me wrong. I'm happy for you and Jane—"

Robert interrupted her and said, "Jennifer, her name is Jennifer, and thank you."

Stacey stepped away from Robert and then said, "Robert, it's no secret that I have feelings for you, and I guess I'm saying that if it doesn't work out with Jennifer, my hope is that you and I could go on a date."

Robert looked at Stacey, "Stacey, I truly love Jennifer. I'm flattered, but I plan to spend the rest of my life with her, so I wish you the best. He's out there, but it's not me."

The elevator chimed and Robert thought, saved by the bell. The doors opened, and they exited. Stacey went to her desk and Robert to his office. Robert entered his office and looked at his phone. A flashing light indicated messages, but he decided to remove his jacket and walked out to chat with Miller.

12:45, Brooklyn

Kevin and Katie were flirting back and forth with instant messenger. Jennifer is or seemed to be distracted as she's doing all she can to concentrate on an upcoming deposition where a superintendent neglected to fix a decaying stoop, which led to a tenant falling and breaking her ankle. She ran her fingers through her hair and then stood, stretched, and walked out into the common area of the office. She went to Katie's desk and said, "Hey, let's go for some lunch, my treat."

Katie looked up at Jennifer and replied, "Sure, is everything okay?"

Jennifer looked at Kevin who appeared to be eavesdropping, "Yes, I'm fine. And this is a ladies' lunch only, Kevin."

Kevin quickly looked back at his monitor and pretended to be reading something important while pointing at the screen.

Jennifer smiled and Katie stood. Jennifer went back to her office and retrieved her jacket and made her way to the lobby. Katie was waiting and the ladies took the stairs to the main floor and out onto the sidewalk. It was overcast and may rain, but it felt good for Jennifer to get out of the office to clear her mind. Just then a male voice said, "Hello Katie, how are you?"

Jennifer and Katie turned to see a tall, slender man arm and arm with a shorter, bulkier man, and Katie replied, "Hello Michael! How are you, and who's this?"

Michael looked down at his companion and replied, "Katie, this is Reggie, my dearest friend in the world. He's in from Atlanta for a few days." Michael looked at Jennifer and said, "Katie, who is this lovely woman?"

Jennifer stepped forward and extended her right arm and said, "Hello, Jennifer Sanders. Nice to meet you. My boyfriend and I are flying into Atlanta Friday and then driving into South Carolina to see his family."

Reggie looked Jennifer up and down and said, "Honey, be sure to bring shorts. It's already hot and getting hotter."

Jennifer smiled and nodded. The four looked at each other and then Michael in an excited voice said, "So, how are things with you and Keith?"

Katie laughed and replied, "You mean Kevin. He's wonderful, thank you!"

Michael then said, "I guess you have a fan. A very muscular built handsome man came in the other day asking about you two, well, you mainly. He said you looked familiar, like maybe he met you some years ago through your father's firm."

Katie looked at Jennifer and then said, "Did this man happen to drive a black BMW, and his shirt looked a bit too tight?"

Jennifer was now confused because Katie was essentially describing the man from this morning, the man that looked just like Robert.

Michael laughed, "Sugar, I'm not sure of the car he drove, but yes, his shirt did fit quite well."

Reggie pulled on Michael's arm and said, "I'm right here you know!"

Michael laughed, "Anyway, he asked about you and that was about it. He mentioned seeing you and Kevin sitting in the window, and again, he thought he knew you. Well, you two have a great afternoon."

The two men made their way down the sidewalk and Michael whispered to Reggie, "You know I only have eyes for you."

Jennifer looked at Katie and then at the two men and said, "It's funny. I saw a man that looked like Robert in a black BMW this morning. I called out to him and he sped off. Maybe you have a stalker?"

Katie looked up to a window where Kevin is standing and smiled and then replied, "I'm sure it's nothing. A mistaken identity for sure. This guy was old, you know, like your age."

"Excuse me, old like my age? I'm not that old. I'll have you know!"

Both ladies laughed as they intertwine walking toward a local deli. Kevin looked up and down the street from above and then turned toward to his desk.

The door to the deli opened followed by a ringing bell and an older man came from behind a curtain and said, "Jennifer, Katie, my favorite girls. How are you today? Please have a seat and I'll bring you a surprise!"

The deli was on a street corner and the ladies took a window seat away from the main street and sat while Mr. Cotler prepared the best bagel sandwich within a fifty-block radius.

Katie took Jennifer's hands and said, "So, are you excited, scared, nervous? I mean, what are you feeling right now knowing this weekend is all about you?"

Jennifer smiled and looked out the window as an elderly couple slowly walked past. She said, "See that? That's what I'm hoping for. Robert and I growing old and taking leisurely walks. You know, but I'm worried. I'm worried he may not feel that way, and maybe this weekend he'll propose, but not for the right reasons."

Katie sat back, "I don't get it. What other reasons could there be for proposing?"

Jennifer was now twisting a napkin, "I just hope he's doing this out of love and not convenience or considering me the best he can get. I know it seems silly, but he's successful, he's incredibly handsome, and I know that other women would love to be with him. So yes, I get a bit jealous, and of course I worry that he's settling."

Jennifer's eyes began to water, and Katie leaned in, "Jennifer, you have no idea how incredible you are, and gorgeous. Robert's lucky to have you and I know he knows that too. So, stop worrying, enjoy the weekend, and keep thinking about the elderly couple that just passed by. That will be you both."

Jennifer looked at Katie and used the wadded napkin to dry her eyes, being careful not to smear her mascara. Just then Mr. Cotler walked up with half sandwiches and lentil soup. He said, "Here you are ladies, lox on a poppy seed bagel and Momma's homemade soup for a chilly day! I'll be right back with tea."

Katie looked at Mr. Cotler, "Thank you, Mr. Cotler. This is wonderful."

Jennifer smiled and then nodded as if to approve of the meal, and Mr. Cotler walked away. Jennifer looked at Katie and said, "It's funny, you have a man that asked about you that could be Robert, and I saw, well, thought I saw, Robert this morning, which has been bothering me all day. But he swears he was in Jersey this morning and then back to the apartment to get his phone that he conveniently left on the counter. I've never been insecure when it comes to him being faithful, but again, this morning really scared me, so to speak."

Katie took a bite of her sandwich nodding her head and then gave the one-second gesture with her index finger. She swallowed, "Again, you have nothing to worry about. I have a feeling you suffer from pre-engagement jitters."

Jennifer smiled and used a spoon to move the soup around in the bowl.

18:00, 26 Federal Plaza

Robert looked at his desk phone and the message light still blinked, but he ignored it. He knew if it were truly important, whomever it was would call again or call his cell phone. He stood, looked out into the office area, and saw the normal sea of people getting up to leave for the day.

Miller was leaning back in his chair staring at the ceiling before leaning forward to stand. He stretched and turned slightly to remove his jacket from the coat hanger next to his desk. He then looked at Robert, waved, and made his way toward the elevator.

Robert looked to the left to see Stacey had left, so he grabbed his jacket from the back of the door and took the elevator to the second floor where the FBI had recently sectioned off part of that floor to accommodate a larger cafeteria and a state-of-the-art workout facility. Robert entered the men's locker room, found his locker, and turned the face of the lock right to thirteen, left around to twenty-five, and then right again to seven, followed by a tug and the lock opened. He removed his jacket and hung it on the hook inside the locker. He then reached for a mesh bag where his workout clothes are neatly folded inside—another perk of using this facility was that each night, the bags were removed, and if the clothing had been used, they will be washed and returned before 05:00 the next day, but the sneakers he's had since 1978 are truly a sight to be seen, and not smelled, but Robert had only used them for working out, so it didn't make sense to replace them. He changed and then grabbed a provided towel and made his way into the weight room. He added thirty-five pounds to each side of a waiting Olympic bar on a flat bench. He sat at the end staring into a mirror and then laid back on the bench and reached for the bar, lifted it from a stationary position. He pressed the weight twenty times before re-racking. His workout went on for about an hour consisting of weights, a stationary bike, and then a long, hot shower, then home for the night.

08:35, Brooklyn

Katie was still at her desk continuing her research as Kevin walked up and said, "Hi, studying hard?"

Katie jumped, "Kevin, you scared me. I thought I was alone, well, me and the cleaning crew."

Kevin stepped back bending forward, "Katie, I'm so sorry, I didn't mean to scare you." He kissed her forehead and then said, "Are you going to be okay? I'm going to head out. It's my mother's birthday and my father had promised an epic meal followed by cake and ice cream."

Katie stood and hugged Kevin, "Yes, thank you. I'll be fine. Go be with your mother and wish her happy birthday from me."

The two kissed and Kevin walked back to his desk, powered off the monitor, grabbed his jacket, and headed out the door to the stairs. Katie rubbed her eyes and continued to read articles she found on a site called Yahoo. After another forty-five minutes, she decided it's time to go home. She stood, stretched, and then reached forward and turned off her monitor. She turned and grabbed her jacket from her seatback and said, "Good night!"

A small voice said, "Good night."

Katie left the office and walked down the stairs. She stopped at the exit door and looked out to see that the rain had come early, and it was darker than normal, but she knew her car is just a few yards away. She removed her jacket and opened it above her head and out onto the sidewalk she went. She walked quickly to her car, put the key in the door lock, and opened the driver's door. She flopped inside tossing her jacket to the passenger seat. She put the key into the ignition and the small four-cylinder engine came to life at a high idle, but she waited for the idle to drop, something her dad taught her. She flipped the wipers to high and turned on the headlights. After a few wipes she looked forward and saw the black BMW parked in front of her, and the car was running. The taillamps were bright and magnified by the raindrops hitting the windshield. She wiped the glass in front of her and peered into the back window of the BMW, but the car is empty. She looked left and then right and checked her rearview mirror before pulling out. She moved the transmission's gear selector to D and steered slightly right. Just then a man appeared, the same man from before. He stopped, put his hands up, and said, "Whoa, slow down there Katie!"

Katie clutched the steering wheel and leaned inward and

Mann - McCormick

screeched, "Oh my God! I'm so sorry!"

The man smiled and waved her on. Katie proceeded, checking her mirrors to ensure she's not being followed. The drive was slow due to the rain and she sat back and turned on the radio. A recent hit song called "No Scrubs" began to play. She increased the volume and began to sing along with the group TLC.

22:30, Robert's Apartment

His cell phone began to vibrate and ring. He looked to see that it's Jennifer. He pressed send and said, "Hello love, how are you?"

Jennifer replied, "I'm okay, and you?"

"I'm well. Just got home a few minutes ago. Are you packing for the trip?"

Jennifer paused and then said, "Robert, do you really love me, and do you hope we grow old together? I mean till death do us part old?"

Robert pulled a chair away from the table and sat. "Jennifer, of course I do. Why do you ask? Are you worried or are you having second thoughts about us?"

Jennifer rolled from her stomach to her back, "Not having second thoughts. I guess sometimes I need reassurance is all. By the way, I've called you several times this evening."

Robert sighed, "Is this about me not answering earlier today, and then supposedly I was near your office and then tonight I didn't answer your call until now, which is giving you anxiety? I can assure you I did leave my phone home, I was in Jersey, and I was nowhere near your office today. I only have a heart and eyes for you, my love."

Robert waited and then said, "Are you there?"

"Yes, I'm here. Just taking in what you just said. I love you more than you know and I'm so looking forward to this weekend. I'd better get back at it. I'll see you tomorrow afternoon. Answer your phone when I call please."

Robert moved the phone from his ear and ended the call. He walked into the bedroom and removed his clothes, leaving them in a heap on the floor. He flopped onto the bed and rolled to his left side and reached for the charging cord. He plugged in his BlackBerry for a nightly charge. He rolled back and to his left side to ensure his alarm was set, he rolled back and pulled a sheet and blanket over himself and interlocked his fingers behind his head and drifted off.

Jennifer placed her packed suitcase near the door, walked into the bathroom, put her hair in a rubber band, and began to remove her makeup, brushed her teeth, and then her hair. She took her phone from the countertop and plugged it in next to the bed. She lifted the sheet and comforter combination and slowly crawled into bed, rolling to her left side to ensure her alarm was set. She rolled to her right side and then fell asleep within minutes.

Chapter Thirty-Three: Thursday, April 29, 1999, 13:45, 26 Federal Plaza

Miller stepped out of a conference room where Robert just gave assignments for the rest of the week and to remind everyone that Miller was in charge and that he was not to be disturbed this weekend. Stacey walked out in front of Robert, turned to him, and said, "Have a great weekend, boss, and congratulations."

Robert smiled and then made a hard-right run toward his office. He entered, looked at the blinking light on his phone, and decided it's time to check the messages. But before he even sat, his desk phone rang. He reached over the desk and picked up the receiver and said, "Franklin, FBI!"

A gruffy voice said, "Hey, kid! Got a minute? You're on speaker with myself and Mick."

Robert covered the lower receiver and yelled for Miller. "Miller get in here! Yeah, give me a second. I want Miller in here for this."

Miller walked to the door and said, "What's up?"

Robert motioned for him to come in and close the door. Miller closed the door, removed a small notepad from his shirt pocket, and sat in the visitor's chair. Robert went around his desk, sat, and then pressed the speaker button and said, "Okay, go ahead."

Miller and Robert leaned into the speaker and Mick said, "Okay, so the man that the officer put in his squad car—the man who found the dead woman in Jersey—well, it turned out he was the man who killed the woman. He had been released from psychiatric care a day earlier and went into Kmart and grabbed numerous pearl necklaces of varying sizes and lengths, ran out the door, and then went into a fabric store and stole a roll of burlap. While running from the store, he ran into a woman on the sidewalk, yes, the woman he killed. Witnesses say he hit her, knocking her down, and she called him an idiot or something like that. He just froze, staring at her, and then yelled something back at her like 'you're dead' or 'you're getting it now'—unclear. The woman, a Samantha Green aged twenty-two, worked at the fabric store until closing that night and he waited for her. She got into her car and he pushed her to the passenger side, and well, we know the rest."

Robert looked at Miller and then Miller fell back into his chair and said, "Hey Mick, it's Randy. What's this guy's name, and why?"

The sound of paper ruffling came through Robert's speaker phone and Jameson said, "His name is Herbert James McEntire of Hamilton Park and the abduction took place in Marion, about five miles from where the body was found. Herbert turned himself in thirty minutes ago. He said he regrets what he did, he was sorry, and he wanted to be known as the 'Pearl Necklace Killer.' He said if the girl had not screamed at him, he wouldn't have given her a thought because he had another woman in mind from earlier in the day. I guess the first woman, who we cannot locate, waited on him and she brushed off his advances and called him a pervert. He was then asked to leave the diner, but not without telling her he'd be back. Of course, the incident wasn't taken seriously because men like him come into that diner all the time and nothing has ever happened."

Miller interjected, "Well, lucky for her, but not so lucky for Samantha Green."

"Yes, not so all lucky at. A typical wrong place at the wrong time."

"I can't help but wonder if our guy has the same reaction when rejected by women and the reason he doesn't rape them is he's impotent."

Miller said, "You know, that Herbert may help us better understand the motive behind the killings we've been investigating for so long. A man that's wound a bit tight, and when a woman said something to anger him, he snaps."

"When we spoke to the last victim's parents, we learned that their daughter could be a bit conceited, or even downright cruel, to men especially."

"Yes, we were told the same things when interviewing the families of past victims. The girls were gorgeous but stuck on themselves. I recall a case back in 1986 where the father of…let me think here…"

Miller reminded Robert, "Linda Kaminski, the girl with auburn hair, short, but very well built."

Robert gave Miller a strange look and replied, "Yes, Linda Kaminski was according to her father very flirtatious, and it would drive the boys crazy. Some would even call her names like 'whore' or 'slut.' But it turned out she had real low self-esteem brought on by her mother, which drove a wedge between them, and soon her parents divorced due to alcoholism, leaving the father to raise Linda."

Jameson replied, "Well, sounds like we have a man with an

inferiority complex, and women bring out the worst in him."

"Yeah, maybe, but I'm not sure why we never thought about this before, so I guess thank you Hebert McEntire? Oh, don't forget, I'll be out after today until Monday, so Randy's in charge. Don't give him a hard time!"

Jameson laughed, "Sure thing, Mr. Franklin. Have a safe trip and give Jennifer my best. Oh, and let's all get together at my place for a nice BBQ in a few weeks, capiche?"

Miller responded, "*Capisco!*"

"Hey, I knew you had some Italian in you, kid!"

Robert pressed the speaker button and the phone went silent. He looked at his phone and the message indicator was still blinking, but he ignored it and stood, motioning Miller to do the same. Both men leave the office and Robert waved Miller his way, back into the conference room. They entered, and Robert closed the door and said, "Randy, have a seat. I need some advice from a married man."

"Sure, but why in here? I mean, your office is soundproof, right?"

Robert responded, "Yes, I know, but I need a big whiteboard because I have questions and want to lay it all out."

"Wow Chief, I've never seen you so worked up before, worked up and yet, so vulnerable."

Robert looked at Miller and quickly responded, "Yeah, well don't get any ideas during my time of weakness."

Several hours later the two men left the conference room. Robert rolled his sleeves down and Miller walked back into the room to erase the notes Robert took. Robert gave him a thumbs up and walked to his office. He grabbed his coat and headed toward the elevator. Miller yelled out, "Good luck, Boss. You'll be fine!"

Robert waved at him and entered the elevator. Miller looked at the wall clock that read 20:30. He looked at his watch and shook his wrist to ensure his watch isn't broken. He then ran to his desk and grabbed his jacket and cell phone. He looked at the screen and saw four missed calls from his wife. He knew he was in trouble, so while putting his jacket on, he dialed home. After just one ring, a female voice rather loudly said, "Randall John Miller, where are you?"

Miller felt like calling Robert and telling him to call the whole thing off. He had no idea what he's getting into. But instead he said, "Honey, I'm so sorry. Robert and I were in a late meeting, and we lost track of time. I'll be home shortly. Oh, do we need anything?"

"No, I just need a bath, a break, please."

Miller signed off and ran to the elevator. He pressed the down button in a frantic manner and said, "C'mon, c'mon," as he watched the floor indicator. Then the chime and the doors opened, but not fast enough, so he pushed his way in causing a disturbance with the doors and they seemed confused.

Katie spent another late night at the office. She doesn't want to work on her paper this very important weekend and figured she'll get up early and leave for Saratoga Springs, getting home by 09:30, maybe 10:00, which still gave her plenty of time to prep her father before Kevin arrived. She looked at the clock and it's 7:20. She hit save and then print. A menu came up asking her to select a printer. She did and pressed enter. A few seconds later, she heard the printer in the mail room come to life and soon it produced page after page of a paper she'd spent nearly two weeks writing.

She stood, reached forward to turn off the monitor, and headed to collect her work. A few minutes later she was using an industrial paper clip to hold the twenty-five pages together. She wrestled on her coat and walked to the door. A little man nearly ran into her and startled her, which caused the clip holding the assignment to fall off. She is unaware and apologized; she walked to the door and down the stairs and to the sidewalk.

When outside, she started walking toward her car, but then stopped and crossed the street to go a block up since she couldn't park close today. Of course, the street she parked on was more like a dark alley, the place where garbage trucks and delivery trucks came every day. She reached into her purse and found her keys. She brought them out and to the door lock, all while trying not to lose the paper, but now she knew she no longer had the clip. She let out a frustrated sound as a man said, "Miss, may I help you?"

23:15, Robert's Apartment

Robert was doing his best as he juggled bags while putting a key into the deadbolt of his apartment door, but there's no need as the door opened and Jennifer is standing there. He smiled and entered. She said, "Hello love, and how are you?"

Robert walked to the kitchen and placed the two bags on the counter. He turned to Jennifer and said, "I'm well, and you?"

Jennifer stepped up and kissed Robert, "I'm better now. Where were you?"

Robert turned back to the bags and began to remove t-shirts, showing Jennifer a varying display of screen prints in multiple sizes. She looked confused and said, "Those are cute, but why, and for who?"

Robert laughed and said, "I stopped off at a few shops on the way home and picked up souvenirs for John's kids and my parents."

Jennifer lifted and tossed the shirts while reading them, and said, "You were in Brooklyn?"

She lifted a shirt holding it open, which read, "Brooklyn – Forget About It!"

Robert looked at the shirt and then back to Jennifer and replied, "That shop had all sorts of shirts to choose from."

Jennifer laid the shirt on the table with the rest and grabbed Robert's right upper arm and drew him close. She whispered, "I love you Robert James Franklin."

Robert turned, embraced Jennifer, "I love you too, Jennifer Sanders."

Robert looked over Jennifer's shoulder at the t-shirts and then to the clock on the wall and said, "Honey, we'd better get some rest. We have an early flight."

The two turned and make their way to the bedroom. Robert ensured the alarm was set, and Jennifer did her usual makeup removal and brushed her teeth and hair. Robert was already in bed and this time he was fast asleep, so she slowly and quietly crawled into bed with him. She couldn't help but notice a small abrasion on the left side of his neck; she assumed maybe razor burn. She covered herself and rolled toward Robert. She kissed him and then rolled the other direction and fell asleep.

Chapter Thirty-Four: Friday, April 30, 1999

Jennifer leaned down and kissed Robert on the cheek and again noticed the abrasion on his neck and another on his left upper arm. She slowly shook Robert awake and said, "Good morning sleepy head. It's time to get up."

Robert rolled to his back and grabbed Jennifer by the wrists and pulled her down to him. He looked into her eyes and said, "Wow, this is a first. You up before me?"

He went in for a kiss, but she turned her head and then stood up and said, "You may want to kiss a toothbrush first."

Robert held his right palm to his face and breathed out, "Wow, I guess so. No more late coffees for me."

Jennifer then asked, "What did you do to your neck and arm?"

Robert brought his right hand to the abrasion on his neck, "Oh that, I was working out and while doing an exercise my hands slipped from the bar and it came back and got me. The lat-pull-down bar that is. Luckily, I was the only one working out. It would have been embarrassing."

"Maybe someone should have been in there to help you workout."

Robert laughed and jumped out of bed and into the shower, saying, "Give me ten minutes and we'll be on the road. I have a car picking us up out front!"

Jennifer moved her bag to the front door, went into the kitchen, and started the coffee pot. She went to the shirts Robert purchased and thumbed through them but can't help but cling to the Brooklyn shirt. After all, the other shirts made a reference to New York.

She then neatly folded each shirt and placed them in a paper sack and then folded the bag over and took tape from the junk drawer and secured the bag. She heard Robert gargling and laughed.

Robert yelled out, "Love, please fold the t-shirts and put them back in the paper sack. Oh, and there's tape in the junk drawer, if you will please tape the bag closed."

Jennifer smiled while bringing a hot cup of coffee to her lips. She sipped and then replied, "Yes love, no problem."

A few minutes went by and Robert entered the living area with a suitcase in tow. He placed his bag next to Jennifer's and came into the kitchen and went in for a kiss. Jennifer responded by kissing him back and then handed him a coffee in a to-go cup. They both turned toward the door, but then Robert stopped, turned back toward the kitchen, and grabbed the bag full of t-shirts and said, "Can't forget these."

They left the apartment and headed to the elevator. In under a minute, they were both getting into a waiting car.

11:18, Brooklyn

Kevin had been at work since 5:30 with a goal of leaving no later than 2:00 for the drive to Saratoga Springs. He was also a bit worried for two reasons: one, he hadn't heard from Katie since yesterday, and two, meeting her father. His legs were going a hundred miles an hour under his desk, like lifters in a high-performance cylinder head.

He was interrupted by a male voice. "Dude, what's going on with you, too much caffeine? I mean, you're making the floor tremble. Calm down!"

Kevin snapped out of his self-induced nervousness and looked over to see Jeremy looking right at him. He replied, "Oh, sorry. Yeah, too much coffee I guess."

"Don't worry about meeting Katie's parents, especially her dad. You'll be fine."

Kevin looked puzzled, "How do you know about that?"

Jeremy looked around the office and leaned forward to Kevin, "We all know about you and Katie."

Kevin leaned back in his chair and he too looked around and noticed the office admin smiling at him. She waved and mouthed the words, "You'll be fine."

Kevin turned back to his monitor, embarrassed. He started scrolling through the deposition on his screen with no real purpose, maybe to look as though he's busy. He prayed the day would be over soon by mouthing, "Please be 2 p.m. so I can leave."

The day crawled and Kevin's stomach told him it was time

to eat. He looked over at Jeremy and saw he's nodding off and said, "Hey, Jeremy, do you want to head over to Mario's for lunch?"

Kevin's voice startled Jeremy and he inadvertently tossed his ink pen upward and onto another desk next to him, which caused Kevin to laugh.

Jeremy looked to ensure his pen didn't kill anyone and he too laughed, "Yeah, I could eat and get some coffee in me. Mario's it is."

The two men stood, grabbed jackets, and headed to the stairs and then to Mario's. The weather was a bit warmer today, and the sun was trying to poke through the clouds. Mario's was nearly empty because most patrons took lunch around noon, or even later, but Kevin needed food, and since Jeremy was willing to go, 11:30 seemed a good a time as any.

The host greeted the two men and asked, "Smoking or nonsmoking?"

Kevin looked at Jeremy who then said, "Nonsmoking please."

The host took the two men to a table at the window, "Michael will be right with you."

Jeremy looked at the host as he walked away, "Great, thank you."

Moments later, Michael appeared with a carafe of water and a basket of bread. He sat the items down and said, "Hello Jeremy, and Keith, right?"

Kevin looked at Jeremy and then back to Michael and replied, "No, Kevin."

Michael made an "I'm sorry" gesture and then put his hand on Jeremy's shoulder and said, "Where have you been, handsome?"

Jeremy squirmed in his seat and replied, "I've been busy. Sorry for not calling you back."

"It's okay, I'm not upset. Oh, by the way, Reggie gave his best."

Jeremy looked at Michael, "Well, you give Reggie my regards."

Michael then winked at Jeremy and turned his attention to Kevin, "So, where's that lovely girlfriend of yours?

Kevin again looked at Jeremy for a bit and then replied, "She went home last night, and I'll be leaving shortly to meet with her and her family."

Michael brought his right hand to his heart, leaned in, and said, "Oh, be careful. Her father can be a bit difficult to talk to. He doesn't like it when I'm his server. God knows why?" Michael laughed and then said, "I'll be back with some coffee. Look over the menus and decide while I'm gone." Michael turned and walked away, leaving a very awkward energy in the air.

Kevin looked to the menu and then to Jeremy and then back to the menu, and Jeremy said, "Listen, I'm, you know…"

"It's cool, no worries."

Kevin then looked back at his menu and to himself he said, "And here I was worried about nothing." He smiled and closed the menu.

"So, how long before you take the State Bar?"

Kevin looked out the window, "I'm hoping for December, maybe January. I have two more classes and then I thought I'd spend a few months studying."

"It's hard, but you'll do fine. I got it the first try and I did the same thing—finished school, studied for a few months, and then took it. Oh, do me a favor and keep my personal life to yourself, please."

Kevin looked at Jeremy and then Michael interrupted and said, "Okay gentlemen, here we go. Nice hot coffee. I brought cream and sugar in the event you need it. So, have you made a lunch choice?"

Kevin looked at Jeremy and then said, "Yes, I'll have the chicken basil tortellini, please."

Jeremy, still looking at the menu, "You know, that sounds good. I'll have the same, thank you."

Michael reached for the menus and thanked the men and walked away. Kevin poured a coffee, added a little sugar, and Jeremy followed, but with a bit of cream. It was silent for a bit and then Kevin said, "You know, Jeremy, I'll admit to not liking you, actually I was jealous of you, and I was worried that you would have gotten to Katie and ruined my chances with her."

Jeremy laughed while stirring his coffee. He removed the spoon from the cup and placed it on a saucer. He looked at Kevin, "Well, now you know. I put up a big front as being a ladies' man, but I'm not. Katie is a lucky girl, Kevin. I mean, you're smart, articulate in speaking, and very handsome. You two will have beautiful children for sure. How do you see the future with her?"

Kevin looked out the window, "Well, as you know, I'm

meeting her parents today, and it may seem odd doing so just after one date, but Katie and I have a connection that can't be explained. I mean, I knew I loved her the first time I saw her, and when she came to work at the firm, I was such a wreck, and yes, I was worried. She's so honest, and pure, and smart, and funny—"

Jeremy interrupted, "Yes, and she's absolutely stunning!"

Kevin sat back, "Yes, and she is stunning!!! She wanted to move back home after school and work in her father's office, doing local law. She desires a peaceful life, and to be honest, I didn't expect that, but when I drive these streets, and I fight the crowds going to and from, I now understand her desire and I want it too. But my family is here, you know?"

Jeremy smiled, "I get it, but it's a short drive, and when you two are married and her father buys you a house, you could have your family up for long weekends."

Kevin looked at Jeremy, "Her father will buy us a house, what made you say that?"

Jeremy leaned in, "Because that's her father. Despite his tough exterior, he loves Katie very much and wants the best for her no matter what. The apartment building she lives in is owned by his firm; her cars are never more than two years old before they're replaced."

Kevin leaned back as Michael approached the table. "Here we go gentlemen. Chicken tortellini for you and chicken tortellini for you. Wait, you had the chicken tortellini and you had the chicken tortellini," Michael said as he jokingly moved the plates around poking fun. The men laughed and removed utensils from a rolled cloth napkin and began to eat.

16:12, McCormick, SC

The Chrysler LHS rolled to a stop outside the Franklin home and Robert looked at Jennifer and smiled. He turned the car off, took her hand, and said, "Jennifer, again, I love you with all I am. I cannot tell you how happy I am that we are here."

Jennifer smiled and leaned in for a kiss.

A woman's voice yelled out, "Johnathan, they're here!" Mrs. Franklin came off the porch and walked slowly to the car. Soon John Franklin made his way out of the house and limped toward the car too. Robert opened his door and got out to hug his mother. John had Jennifer's door opened and she too stepped out to receive a hug and kiss from her future father-in-law. The two made their way around the car to Robert and Marilynn and the two men hug along with the two women.

John Franklin took a bag from the trunk and Robert said, "Dad, it's okay, I'll get the bags, you head on in with the ladies. I'm going to walk down to the hardware to see Johnny. I'll be right back."

Jennifer looked at Robert and said, "Robert, do you want me to come with you?"

Robert shook his head, "No, love. I need to talk to my brother, privately."

Jennifer smiled and then Marilynn said, "Come on dear, let's get out of this heat. You must be exhausted. I just made some lemonade."

Robert leaned in and kissed Jennifer on the cheek and then kissed his mother on the forehead and walked away, waving his right hand. The air was humid and chilly as he walked down the sidewalk toward Franklin Hardware. As he approached the front of the store, he recalled being a small boy going into the store and looking at all the toys, and sometimes he'd play Jacks with a boy named Lump. He was a twin, but only in looks and not in capacity.

Robert smiled as he entered the store when the bell above the door jingled. He stood in the doorway and looked around the store, which was immaculate as always, far better than when the Joseph family owned it some years ago.

A man walked up to the front of the store and said, "Sir, is there something I can help you find?"

Robert looked at the man and said, "Yes, I'm looking for a short man, rather ugly and old."

John pushed Robert and said, "Well, I'm him."

The two men hug, and John yelled out, "Sarah, come up here. Your uncle Robert is here."

The patter of a toe runner carried through the store as a young lady ran from aisle five and jumped up to receive a hug. Robert stumbled back and hugged his niece with great love. He sat her down and said, "Wow Sarah, you're turning into quite the lady. What are you now, thirteen?"

Sarah laughed and said, "No Uncle Robert, I'm fifteen going on sixteen."

John replied while side hugging his daughter, "That's right, my baby is going to be a woman soon, and then what will we do? I guess her mother and I will grow old together."

Sarah quickly kissed her father's cheek and said, "No Dada,

I'm staying home with you and Momma, and one day all of this will be mine." She opened her arms and swung from side to side.

John looked at Sarah, smiled, "You say that now pumpkin, but one day a boy will come into your life and you'll quickly forget about the store and your mother and me."

Sarah shook her head no and walked back to her tasks.

Robert watched her walk away and then looked at John and said, "So, I'd like to take Jennifer to McCormick Lake and propose to her, but I need a boat, a radio, and some flowers, and judging by the weather, I'll need a blanket too. Can you help me out?"

John looked at the floor and then said, "Of course, I can provide the boat. As a matter of fact, I'll take the boat out an hour before you take her there and set it up with everything; you'll need to make this a great day. Of course, I'll ask Tina to arrange the flowers; after all, we bought the florist shop about six months ago, so you'll get the family discount." He then laughed and punched Robert in the shoulder.

Robert rubbed where John connected and said, "You bought the florist, you have the hardware, and the car wash, before too long you'll own the whole town. Good for you, John!"

"Yes, thank you, just trying to create a legacy and a future for the kids. Maggie and Tina take care of the flower shop, Johnny has the car wash, and when Christopher's home from school he helps his brother. Steven is still in Colorado trying to find himself, but he's got him a girlfriend now, so maybe she'll settle him down. And of course, Sarah's here with me."

"Wow, you're doing well. I'm proud of you, but don't count

on Steven's girlfriend settling him down; she's probably a ski bum too and they're feeding off each other."

John changed the subject when two men walked in. The first man said, "Hello John, how are you, and is that you Robert?"

John stepped back and said, "Well, I'll be. Mike and Steven Joseph, how are you?"

Robert stepped forward to exchange handshakes with Mike but Lump just stood there staying quiet until Sarah came to the front of the store. John took Sarah to his side and said, "Sarah, honey, this is Mike and Steven Joseph. Your daddy bought the hardware from their father a long time ago."

Mike leaned forward and said, "Hello Sarah. You sure are a pretty young lady. Nice to meet you."

Lump put his hands in his pockets and became restless. Sarah watched him and said, "Sir, what's the matter with you?"

John covered her mouth, "Sarah, that'll be all, dear. Go back to what you were doing."

Sarah waved at the men and disappeared into the store, but not without Lump following her every step.

John said, "I apologize. Please, she meant no harm."

Mike rested his right hand on John's left shoulder and said, "No apologies necessary. Lump and I are headed to Charlotte to see our parents and thought we'd come through McCormick and reminisce. I see you've done well. Good for you!" He then turned to Robert, "So, Robert, let's see; last time I saw you was when you were just starting with the FBI. Are you still with them?"

Robert replied, "Yes, sir, I'm at the Federal Building in New

York—Special Agent in Charge."

Mike's face went to more of a wow, I'm impressed, look, "That's pretty respectable. What is your field of expertise for the FBI, if you don't mind?"

"Oh, not a problem. I am at the early stages of profiling, determining the types of people that commit certain crimes, for example, serial killers. My team uses technology to create—"

John interrupted, "He's also here this weekend to propose to his longtime girlfriend Jennifer, a lovely young woman who is an attorney in Brooklyn, right Robert?"

Robert took the hint, "Yes, that's correct. Jennifer does real estate law."

Mike looked at Lump and then said, "Well boys, we'd better get on the road. I don't much care for driving in the dark. I'm happy to see all of you, and Robert, best wishes to you and your soon-to-be fiancée. Come on Lump, say goodbye."

Lump removed his hands from his pockets and said, "Bye-bye, Sarah, bye-bye."

Robert looked at John and the two men leave the store. John said, "Hey, sorry I cut you off. I just didn't want Sarah to hear what you do is all."

Robert replied with a slight slap to John's shoulder, "No worries. So, back to the boat and such, let's say tomorrow around 19:30 I'll have Jennifer at the dock?"

John laughed, "Sure. I haven't used 24-hour time since Vietnam. So that said, I'll have it already by 21:15, SIR!"

Robert looked at his brother and the two men laughed. Robert left the store and made his way toward the house when a car pulled up. It's Mike Joseph. The driver's window went down and Mike said, "Robert, I wanted you to know that McCormick is a great southern town, but she's got her secrets. You'll catch that animal soon, I know it. It may be sooner than you think. Give my best to your parents, especially your father. Make sure you tell him Mike said hello, okay?"

The window went up and the Buick slowly pulled away. Robert just stood there watching the car disappear. Then he heard Jennifer say, "Hey, who was that?"

Robert turned to see Jennifer standing there, wearing one of his FBI sweatshirts and her hair was in a ponytail. He walked to her and picked her up and hugged her.

"That was Mike Joseph and his twin brother. His father once owned the hardware store. He stopped to say hello. Anyway, have my parents driven you crazy yet?"

"No, I just missed you is all, so I thought I'd come looking for you, and here you are, looking all handsome. Your mother has made dinner and I'm starving, so let's go eat."

Robert wrapped his arm around Jennifer's shoulder, drew her close, and the two make the short walk back to the house. It felt ten degrees cooler as the sun hid behind the clouds. The two make their way up to the steps, and once on the porch, Robert turned to look out at the street and said, "A lot of good memories in this town and this house. I guess I miss it sometimes."

Jennifer came from behind him, wrapping her arms around his waist, and said, "Well, maybe we could move here someday and raise some children. You could work at the hardware with your brother and I could open a small office on main street and practice family law."

Robert turned while in her grip and looked at her and said, "I don't know if there is enough here to keep us busy, but then again, maybe that's what we need. I guess for now let's take each day as it comes, sound good?"

Jennifer looked at Robert, nodded her head, and put her face to his chest. The two eventually turned and entered the house. The smell of fried chicken filled the air as they make their way to the dining room where John and Marilynn were waiting.

Robert looked at the feast before him and said, "Wow, this is what I've been dreaming of!"

Marilynn said, "Jennifer, you don't cook?"

Robert looked at Jennifer, who had begun to blush, "Yeah, Jennifer, do you cook?"

Jennifer tossed a biscuit at Robert, "No Mrs. Franklin, I do not, unless using the microwave counts. We get so busy and we don't spend a lot of evenings together, well, not until we're married, and Robert moves into my place."

Robert put up his hand, "Why am I moving in with you? I thought we'd live at my place."

Jennifer smiled at Robert, "Well, my place is bigger and closer to all the great restaurants and shopping, honey."

Robert laughed, "Oh yeah, the shopping, something I live for."

John Franklin interrupted and said, "How about we bless this meal and eat before it gets cold." He bowed his head as did everyone else. "Dear Lord, thank you for this meal, let it nourish our bodies so that we may continue to do great works in your name, amen."

Everyone said amen and the plates were passed from person to person. There was small talk during the meal as Jennifer talked about an upcoming deposition and having made partner a few months ago. Robert just stared at her as she talked, smiling and occasionally winking at her, which made her blush.

John Franklin asked, "Robert, you should be close to retirement from the Bureau, right? I mean, you have close to twenty years."

Robert looked at Jennifer and replied, "I'm planning to do twenty-five, maybe thirty years before I retire. I really love my job and my goal is to make deputy director soon, and then maybe director. I have a pretty big staff now and the organization is well disciplined, and things are going accordingly."

Marilynn interrupted, "Robert, if things are going so well, why haven't you caught that monster?"

Robert looked at his mother, cleared his throat, "Well Mother, we have just started a new strategy and have been compiling data."

"What is data?" Marilynn asked.

Robert looked at Jennifer and replied, "Data is information that allows us to narrow our search."

John stopped him and said, "Son, it's okay. Mother is frustrated for you, not at you."

Marilynn placed her fork down, "I'm sorry Robert, your father is right. I'm frustrated for you, that's all."

Robert looked to the table, "Thank you, Mother. It has been very frustrating to say the least, but we will catch a break soon. After all, this guy will make a mistake soon."

The rest of the meal was eaten in silence. When everyone had finished dessert, Robert and Jennifer began clearing the table and doing the dishes. Robert washed and Jennifer dried while Marilynn put them away. John went to the porch to watch nothing happening in the sleepy little town of McCormick, SC. John Jr. and Sarah drove by, honked, and waved.

Robert asked his mother, "Mom, is Dad okay? He seems very distant."

Marilynn looked at Robert, "He's getting older, he's bored, and he has a lot on his heart."

Robert rinsed the last plate and handed it to Jennifer, "On his heart, like what?"

Marilynn walked up to Robert and placed her right hand on his left forearm. She replied, "Son, he's been feeling guilty about many things, like, was he a good father? Could he have done something to help your sister? That's all."

"Well, for what it's worth, I'd say he did pretty good as a father. I mean, I turned out okay, but John Jr., well, the jury is still out. Lisa Marie had many demons of her own, and I'd say she did her best to fend them off, but they became too many to handle, and well..."

"Yes, Lisa Marie had her demons, but her biggest was always right in front of her!"

Robert knew she meant drugs and left it at that. He continued to dry his hands, folded the towel into thirds, and hung it from the oven door handle like he had always done as a boy. Robert kissed Jennifer on the cheek and then said, "Love, I'm going to sit with Dad for a bit."

"That's a good idea. Jennifer and I can have some coffee and catch up."

"Yes, that would be wonderful."

Robert walked to the screen door and looked out to see his father just staring into space. The rocker he sat in was not moving, just as still as can be, almost majestic, he thought. He pushed open the door as it made all sorts of noises, the return spring stretching, the hinges grinding. Instead of letting the door slam, he held it and let it slowly close. He walked up, kissed his father on the top of his head, and said, "What are you thinking about?"

John looked at Robert and said, "I was thinking that I'm eighty, and have I done enough in my life to make things right with God? I served Him and the people of this town for a very long time. The church needed a different approach, but luckily your mother and I were able to stay in this house when the new pastor took over. My heart is heavy with regret, son."

Robert walked to the porch rail and leaned on it. He looked from side to side and then at his father and said, "Is there anything you want to tell me, anything I can do to help?"

John looked at his hands and then at Robert, "Did I do okay as your father? Was this home good enough for you and John Jr. and Lisa Marie?"

Robert leaned forward, "Dad, you did fine. We all knew we were loved; we all knew you cared for us, and Mom was wonderful too."

John Sr. began to tear up, "I know, son. I just think about Lisa Marie at times and I know I could have done more, but I failed her."

Robert stood and sat next to John, "You did the best you could. Sometimes we must accept what we have no control of. Remember you would say that from time to time in a sermon?"

John put his left hand on Robert's thigh, patted it, and said, "I know, son, I know. I'm happy you're here, and Jennifer too."

Robert leaned back in his chair and took his father's hand, "I love you, Dad."

"I love you too, son."

Soon the screen door repeated the earlier noises and then slammed shut, making a dribbling sound. Jennifer stood frozen and brought her hands to her face and said, "Oh my gosh, I'm so sorry."

John and Robert looked at her and began to laugh. Soon after Marilynn came out and then a Chrysler minivan pulled up and John Jr., Tina, and Sarah exited the vehicle. Sarah was carrying what looked to be a fresh baked apple pie. A few seconds later a Jeep Cherokee pulled up and a country song was coming from the sound system. Two men exited the vehicle, John the third and Christopher, John Jr.'s. boys.

Tina made her way to Christopher and gave him a big hug and kissed his cheek and said, "Wow, what a pleasant surprise. When will you go back to school?"

Christopher hugged his mother tightly while looking at Jennifer and said, "Wow, Uncle Rob, are you sure you're good enough for this woman?"

Robert walked to Jennifer and put his arm around her and said, "Don't get any bright ideas, kid. I'm not too old to whoop your butt!"

Robert came down the steps and hugged his family, but hugged Christopher more as if he were a son. He and Robert had always had a special bond. As a matter of fact, Christopher was at Clemson studying criminal justice and in another year wanted to join the FBI.

Robert pushed him back to get a better look and said, "I see you're hitting the weights. How's school going?"

Christopher looked at the ground and then back to Robert, "Well, I made the Dean's List again, and I will graduate summa cum laude and then hopefully from there right to Quantico!"

Robert smiled and shook his hand. He then went to Tina and gave her a hug. Finally, he went to John, his brother's eldest, and shook his hand and said, "Nice Jeep! How's the wash doing?"

John looked at the Jeep and then said, "Thank you, Uncle Robert. The wash is doing very well. We now offer full details and I've added a few bays for self-washing."

Robert smiled and then walked to the porch and extended his hand to Jennifer. He guided her down the steps and said, "I'm sure you all remember Jennifer?"

The family all came to Jennifer and they exchange pleasantries. There was pure joy in the air as the women went into the house to make coffee and to prepare another dessert. John Jr. went back to the van and grabbed another pie, which smelled like cherry, and took it into the house.

Christopher, Johnny, and John Sr. are standing on the porch making small talk as John Jr. came back to join them. He said, "So, I've told the boys the plan and we'll have everything ready for tomorrow."

Robert looked around, "Great, I really appreciate it, fellas. Jennifer means the world to me and I want this to go well."

Christopher looked around and then said, "Well, you'd better be careful; she may just fall in love with me over the next couple days, and then what will you do?"

Robert side slapped Christopher in the stomach, taking the wind out of him. Soon laughter filled the air and the men all head into the house.

18:56, Saratoga Springs

Kevin Nickels came to a stop in front of Katie McCann's home on Clement Street, Saratoga Springs, New York. He looked at his watch and then the clock on the Voyager's radio. A four-hour and fifteen-minute trip took him nearly five hours due to traffic and a flat tire about thirty miles back. Thank goodness the owner's manual was in the glove box; otherwise, he would have been really late. He looked in the rearview mirror to groom himself and then to straighten his tie before exiting the vehicle. He breathed in opened the door and stepped onto the street shook both legs forcing his pant legs to drop from bunching up during the drive. He used his hands to press them downward, pushed his shirt into his pants, and then adjusted his belt. He walked to the sidewalk, going to the front door of the massive home.

The front porch was bigger than his family's home he thought. He looked around, stood at the front door, and twisted the handle in the middle of the door, which made a ringing noise. Seconds later, a well-dressed woman of about fifty-five opened the door, and soon she was joined by a man of the same age. He was tall with broad shoulders and his hair was gray and slicked back. They're both tan as if they just returned from Florida.

The woman extended her hand and said, "Hello, Deborah McCann and this is my husband Richard or RT."

Richard McCann extended his right hand and said, "Not so fast Deb, he has to earn the right to call me RT."

"Hello Mr. and Mrs. McCann, it's a pleasure to meet you."

Richard looked over Kevin's shoulder and replied, "Of course, it is. So, where's Katie?"

Kevin looked behind him and then back to the McCann's, "What do you mean sir, she came up last night."

Richard looked at Kevin and then his wife and replied, "Son, I hope she didn't put you up to this. Katie is not here; we assumed she came up with you!"

Kevin's life left his body and he began to sweat. He replied, "No sir, I came up alone. Katie said she would be here when I arrived. She said she wanted to prepare you for my arrival."

Richard looked at Kevin and with a stern voice, "What does that mean, prepare me for your arrival?"

Kevon's voice cracked, "Yes sir, she said you would probably be a bit scary, which you are, and she wanted to—"

Deborah interrupted, "Kevin, dear, Katie is not here, and we have not heard from her since yesterday around, oh I don't know, maybe 7:30 p.m."

Kevin looked to the floor of the porch and started to recount his steps and replied, "Yes, that sounds about right. I left the office about that time. She said she would be leaving soon too and was going to call you. She had been working late each night to finish a big paper and the internet at the office is much faster than what she has in the apartment."

Richard McCann was now angry, "Faster in her office, well, I'll be sure to change that!"

"RT, the internet is the least of our concerns right now. Where is Katie?"

Mrs. McCann motioned for Kevin to come in. The three walked to what could be considered a parlor and sat, RT next to Debbie and Kevin across from them. A small woman entered the room and asked, "Excuse me sir, may I bring beverages?"

Debbie looked at RT and then Kevin and said, "Kevin, what would you like to drink?"

Kevin looked at the woman and then back to Debbie, "I'm fine, thank you."

RT replied, "Please bring coffee and three cups, thank you, dear."

The woman left the room and RT went for a phone on the table next to the sofa. He lifted the receiver and pressed buttons and seconds later, he said, "Jimmy, RT here. Listen, Katie's gone missing. I'm here with Kevin, her boyfriend, and he hasn't seen her since last night around 7:30. Please go by her apartment and have a look around and call me back, thank you!"

He returned the phone to the table and then stood, walked to a window, and then back to the others. He said, "Maybe she took sick and doesn't have the strength to call us."

Kevin stood, "Sir, that could be true, but when I saw her

last, she looked and seemed fine, maybe a little stressed with her paper, but nothing more."

RT walked to Kevin and stood before him, "Son, I have some pretty powerful friends, and if you're hiding something..."

Debbie stood up in front of her husband and said, "Kevin, what RT is saying is that he has connections and they will find Katie."

RT turned and walked away, but not without giving Kevin a stern look. The woman returned with a pot of coffee, three cups, a small pitcher of cream, and some sugar. She poured two cups and added the required number of extras for the McCann's, and then said, "Sir, may I add to your cup?"

"Yes, both, thank you."

The woman did as requested and handed the cup and saucer to Kevin. He sat and then placed the items on the table in front of him. The room was silent except for the spoon against the brim of Mrs. McCann's cup as she stirred her coffee, staring concernedly into space.

The phone rang. RT lunged for it and answered, "Jimmy, what did you find?"

A voice on the other end was not Jimmy, but it was a friend confirming dinner tomorrow night. RT hung up and the phone rang again, and he answered, saying, "RT McCann! Yes, Jimmy, what did you find?"

He pressed his right hand over the mouthpiece and said, "It's Jimmy, he's at Katie's apartment."

RT did a great deal of nodding and saying words like "okay" and "are you sure?" before hanging up. He looked at Debbie and said, "Jimmy went into her apartment and nothing looked out of place. It was obvious she packed a smaller suitcase because the larger suitcase was open and on the floor of the bedroom. You know that Gucci set we bought her for Christmas last year? Jimmy's going to her office and then he'll canvas the area. Kevin, have you tried her cellular phone?"

Kevin leaned to his left side extended his right leg and removed his cell phone from the right front pocket of his pants and flipped it open. He dialed, pressed send, and no answer. He replied, "Sir, no answer."

Debbie sat her cup down and stood. She left the room and began to sob. RT excused himself to care for his wife. In the hallway, the tender side of RT came out and he said, "Dear, don't worry, she's fine and Jimmy will find her. Please don't cry. He called out, "Kelly, please take Mrs. McCann to her room."

RT came back into the parlor and paced. He looked at the phone as if to will it to ring. He looked at Kevin and said, "Son, are you certain about the time you saw her last?"

"Yes sir, I'm 100 percent. I had to leave right at that time to be home for a family commitment. This had been an unusually busy week at our home, and I needed to accomplish a lot before coming here to Saratoga Springs."

"Well, that would make sense, I suppose. Did she mention anything that may make you assume a change in her plans?"

Kevin was silent for a moment and then said, "I know she had a long conversation with our boss, Jennifer Sanders, yesterday. They actually went for a walk."

RT looked at Kevin and said, "Do you have Jennifer's

number? Maybe she knows something we don't."

Kevin flipped open his phone and dialed, but the call went right to voicemail.

"Sorry sir, voicemail. She's in South Carolina with her soon-to-be fiancé and did say she would not have her phone on."

RT paced and asked, "Do you happen to know the boyfriend's name or have his number?"

"No, none of us have met him yet. He's got a job that can't be talked about. I do know his name is Robert, but that's it."

RT asked, "Did she say where in South Carolina they'd be?"

"I'm sorry sir, she did not."

The phone rang and RT stepped quickly to answer. "Jimmy! What is it?"

Jimmy replied, "Sir, I found Katie's car parked near the office, but on more of a service street, and well, sir—"

Debbie interrupted and yelled, "And what, Jimmy?" Mrs. McCann had picked up the phone from the bedroom.

Jimmy cleared his throat and replied, "Yes ma'am, I found what appeared to be a school paper scattered about and as I was collecting them up, I noticed a page that read, 'Tenant Rights By Katie McCann.' I'm sorry, sir, ma'am."

Debbie screamed out and RT dropped lifeless to a chair. He set the receiver down and slowly turned to Kevin and said, "Katie's been abducted."

Kevin stood, bringing his right hand to his mouth with a gasped, "Sir, this can't be. What are you saying? Please sir, this can't be!"

RT looked at Kevin, "Her car was found, keys in the door, suitcase inside, and her term paper was scattered about the area around her car."

Kevin fell to the couch and his eyes filled with tears. He started to think about their first date, and the cute instant messages back and forth, and his conversations with Jennifer prior to asking Katie out. He's frozen, and the room sounded like a war zone, but no one was saying a thing.

The phone rang and startled him and Mr. McCann. RT brought the phone to his ear and said, "Yes?"

It's Jimmy and he began to explain a plan to find Katie, which brought RT back to life and he stood and began to bark orders. It was like he was in a courtroom defending a man on trial for his life. Kevin sat in awe of how quickly he transformed from a scared father to a man on a mission. He ended with, "Jimmy, Kevin and I will be there in a few hours. We'll meet you at Lieutenant Jameson's office!"

RT slammed the phone down on the table and said, "Kelly, prepare me a bag that will last a couple of days! Kevin, we'll take my car. Please get your bags from your car and meet me in front of the garage!"

Kevin scrambled to his feet and made haste out the front door. He opened the Plymouth and grabbed his bag and looked right and then left for the garage. He darted left and looked down the side of the house, nothing. He ran right and looked down the side of the house and saw about a quarter of a garage door. He ran around to the back and found four garage doors and waited patiently for one to open. Seconds later the third door from the right opened and the giant car black Mercedes S-class squealed out onto the driveway. Its headlights were almost blinding as the car came to a stop. The trunk popped open and Kevin tossed his bag in closed the trunk, and then he got in the passenger's seat. The door closed like a bank vault, nothing like the rattle trap he drove.

He looked at Mr. McCann who is now laser focused. RT reached to a radar detector affixed to the windshield and turned it on. The device made several odd noises and the car raced off and onto the highway within seconds. RT reached down near Kevin's left thigh where a phone is fixed to the center console. He dialed and hit send. Seconds later a man with a hard voice came through the vehicles sound system and said, "Lieutenant Jameson!"

RT put both hands on the steering wheel and gripped tight and said, "Mike, it's RT, how are you?"

Jameson cleared his throat and replied, "RT listen, Jimmy called me, and I've got the team in route. When was the last time you spoke to Katie or physically saw her?"

RT looked at Kevin, "Mike, Deb spoke to Kate around 7:30 last night. Her boyfriend, Kevin, he's with me now, he saw her around the same time. She was working on some paper at the office. He left just before she called her mother."

Jameson said, "Kevin, I'm Lieutenant Mike Jameson with the NYPD, a longtime friend of Mr. and Mrs. McCann. Katie is like a daughter to my wife and me. Tell me anything that may help us find her, anything at all."

Kevin looked at RT and then at the phone and replied, "Yes, sir, Katie was so ingrained in her paper that despite her and I being the only two in the office, we hardly spoke. She was focused, and despite my trying to converse with her, it was impossible. I had to get home, so just before she called home, just like Mr. McCann said, I left. She barely looked at me when I said goodbye. Oh wait, the cleaning crew was still in the office. It's two Latina women that come in at 7:00 p.m. every night, but occasionally they bring a Latin gentleman with them. They're all related somehow."

Jameson cupped the phone and they heard him say, "The car's here? Okay, we'll be down shortly, thank you. RT, we have Katie's car and Jimmy was able to round up as many pages from Katie's paper. We'll put them in order and check for prints."

RT relaxed a bit at the wheel, looked down to the phone, and said, "Make sure you have Sergeant Stevens on site, that way when we find her and the man that took her, he can then rip the guy in half!"

RT disconnected the call and dialed another number.

An Unknown Location

Katie woke and slowly opened her eyes. Her hands were tied behind her; her feet brought together and bound. Her mouth was taped over with a slit just big enough to breathe from, but her cries for help were a mere whisper. The room was dark and cold. She was naked and the floor felt like marble, but she can't be sure. She had no idea of the time or the day, but she was hungry and thirsty. She rolled to her back and then to her left side and saw a glimmer of light about three feet wide at the floor. She assumed it's a door and she rolled to her back and used her legs to push herself to the light. It hurt. The marble floor was gripping her cold skin. She winced with each push until her head knocked

263

on the door. She raised her head from the floor and banged the door once, twice, three times before she could no longer. She spun a quarter turn and waited.

The light under the door was interrupted and then she heard what sounded like a key enter a lock. The door opened, allowing in blinding light so intense she moved her head from side to side, which caused saliva to build up and she began to choke. A man knelt and raised her exhausted body and pulled her to the wall, allowing her to lean her torso against it.

The man said, "Hello Katie, how are you? He then said, I'm well, thank you."

Katie blinked, allowing her eyes to focus, and there he was, the man from the car, the BMW. She pressed hard against the wall and he said, "I'm going to remove the tape, but you need to be quiet, okay? I need you to agree with me by nodding yes."

Katie nodded accordingly and the man slowly removed the tape. He took special care as to not rip the skin. Katie breathed in and out, gasping for air and licking the spit from around her mouth. She began to cry, and the man stood and reached into his pocket for a handkerchief. He wiped her mouth and tears.

The man said, "In a few minutes I will bring you food, but before I do, I'll need you to wash your hair and shower. Can you do that? I have clothes for you as well."

Katie nodded and the man lifted her to her feet and slowly removed the silk cloth used to bind her. She rubbed her wrists, but there wasn't scarring, not even fabric burns. The same with her ankles.

The man said, "I use the finest materials to ensure the greatest comfort to you. I don't want to damage your beautiful skin."

Katie looked at the man and said, "Why are you doing this to me? Please, what have I done to you?"

The man looked at his watch and said, "You have twenty minutes to clean up, so I'd get started if I were you!"

The man turned, opened the door, and walked out. He closed the door and then locked it from the outside.

Katie observed and noticed there is no door handle, but a double-sided deadbolt. She went to the large shower stall, reached in, and turned the shower on. She then went to the toilet to pee. Steam had filled the room and she entered the shower. The hot water felt good against her cold skin. She washed her hair and then her body, scrubbing every inch of herself. She spent a few minutes basking under the water and began to cry. She thought of her parents and of course, Kevin.

She stopped the shower and removed a large towel from a hook outside the shower door and began to dry herself. The towel was large and thick, very luxurious and warm. She went to the mirror and found a brush, toothpaste, and a toothbrush. She brushed her hair and then her teeth. The quietness worried her, and it felt like an eternity since the man left the room.

She heard a key enter the lock and then a slight knock at the door before it opened. The man stepped in with a black velvet-covered box atop folded white material. He said, "I hope that shower felt nice. You looked cold, Katie. I've brought you pajamas and a gift, but the gift will be for later, depending how good you are, so I'll put that right here."

He placed the box on the counter and then handed her the

pajamas. She reached for them, which caused her towel to fall.

The man stared at her and replied, "You are an incredible beauty, and Keith is lucky to have you."

"His name is Kevin."

The man smacked his forehead and replied, "Yes, Kevin, I'm sorry."

He motioned for her to dress as he watched her. His eyes are fixed on her every move and every curve of her delicate frame. He then extended his left hand and said, "Please, come with me. I have something to show you."

Katie reached for his hand and he gripped hers, leading her out of the room and into a large open area, a sterile area with a large leather couch facing a window high above the city. At the other side of the room was a kitchen with numerous cabinets and he took her there and said, "I don't come to this apartment often, so the provisions are minimal, but there's enough food to last a few days."

He then struck her on the right cheek, and she fell to the floor crying. He knelt and said, "I need to leave for a few days, so while I'm gone you will need to know that I'm not playing here. You deserve all that's coming to you. Oh, and don't try to escape or to scream. No one will hear you. I had this apartment built to be 100 percent soundproof and there's only one way in and one way out."

The man extended his right hand to help Katie to her feet. She stood and he then said, "I almost forgot to introduce myself. My name is Robert. You and I met by chance a few months ago. You were incredibly rude to me, and frankly, I just couldn't let it go!"

Katie looked at Robert, "Mister, I have never met you before. Please, you have me confused with another woman."

Robert raised his left-hand and struck Katie again. She fell to the floor and he knelt down, "Katie my dear, I never forget a rude stuck-up self-centered woman. You are no better than me; you are no better than anyone. I could buy you and your daddy a thousand times over and still live a comfortable lifestyle. I want you to go back into your memory and recall a day when you were with friends at Nikko's."

Robert stood and looked at his watch again and said, "I'm going to be late. I must go, big weekend plans!"

He walked away leaving Katie on the floor. He came out of the bathroom with the black box and said, "Until we meet again my dear, until we meet again!"

He exited the apartment and powered window shades made of some form of metal closed. They stop any light from the city coming in. Katie ran from the kitchen and back to the bathroom and then she found a bedroom with a king-sized bed in the center of the room, nothing else, just a bed. She went back to the kitchen and began to scream until she can no longer stand and fell to the floor. She laid on her back and then curled into the fetal position and began to weep.

McCormick – Part Four

22:16, NYPD Headquarters

The desk sergeant stood and said, "Are you Richard McCann?"

RT placed both hands on the desk and replied, "I'm here to see, Lieutenant Jameson."

The desk sergeant spun a clipboard toward RT and replied, "I'll need you both to sign in."

A voice a few feet away said, "Sergeant, let them in now. I'll sign them in later!"

RT tossed the pen on the desk and walked to a door. A buzzing sound filled the space and the door popped open and he and Kevin walked through. Jameson extended both arms and hugged RT and then extended his right hand toward Kevin and they shook.

"RT it's good to see you, my friend. I just wish it were under different circumstances. Come with me, I have us in a conference room."

The men snaked through desks and entered a room where there are another four officers. Jameson placed his hand on RT's right shoulder and said, "RT, this is the team that will find Katie. That said, Keith, tell us what you know."

Kevin moved forward and said, "My name is Kevin, sir, and yesterday at around 7:30 p.m. I told Katie I was going to head home, and like I told Mr. McCann, she barely said a word to me, but mentioned that she needed to call her mother and that she would see me tomorrow, well, today. She was so consumed with a paper."

Mick walked toward Kevin and said, "So, you just felt she'd be okay in that office alone, and instead of waiting with her you went where?"

Kevin looked at Mick and began to sweat and cleared his throat, "Sir, Katie knew my week was very busy with family commitments and I would have stayed with her as long as I could, but she wasn't alone. The cleaning crew had only been there thirty minutes before I left."

Jameson interrupted, "What do you know about this cleaning crew? Anything that might stand out? Did the men pay close attention to Katie or any of the other women in the office?"

RT replied, "What would the cleaning crew have to do with Katie's disappearance?"

An officer moved forward and replied, "If I may, we've been monitoring specific groups that come from places like Russia or the Middle East. They learn the lay of the land and the females in the area, and then they take the women and before too long these women are out of the country and sold into prostitution."

RT lost his balance and Kevin steadied him. Kevin then said, "This cleaning crew consists of the same two women and once a month a male will join them. He's there to ensure quality control. Never has anyone from the crew said anything to Katie or anyone in the office for that matter. They've been cleaning the office for twelve, maybe thirteen years, and nothing."

Jameson looked at Mick and then Mick looked at another officer who then left the room, but not without Kevin. Jameson then said, "RT have a seat. What do we know about this kid that Katie's dating? Do you know anything about his family?"

RT sat and then looked at Jameson, "Well, from what I know, Katie's only had one date with Kevin, but she's known him for some time now. He occasionally gave lectures. And she's smitten, I guess that's the word she used."

Mick looked at Jameson and then dropped a file on the table in front of RT and said, "Well, I did some digging and it turns out Kevin Nickels is actually Kevin Nikonechnaia, which means he's Russian. His parents came here when he was just two years old to escape the Russian Mafia. It appeared Kevin's father is, or was, a very bad man. He was into moving people, guns, money, etc. One day he found God and tried to walk away from his lifestyle, but the Russian Mafia wouldn't let him, so he turned over a great deal of information along with people in exchange for safe passage to the USA."

RT glanced through Kevin's file and the photos of Kevin's' family and then said, "Mike, you gathered all of this information tonight? This looks like it took days, even months."

Jameson replied, "RT, when Katie started talking about this kid last year, I started doing some of my own digging to ensure he's on the up and up. I went as far as watching him and his family and from what I gathered, they seemed to be legit. Dad works as a mechanic, Mom works at a grocery store as a cashier, and Kevin, well, he's a pretty boring kid: work, school, and dedicated to his family."

RT looked at Jameson, "You always did care for Katie, thank you. But now what?"

Mick looked at Jameson and then RT and replied, "We have

Kevin in an interrogation room, and he's being settled with small talk. I want him to be relaxed and laughing a bit before I go in as a bad cop. It's a tactic I developed some years ago and it works very well. Make the guy your friend and then you go for the juggler, and they always mess up!"

Mick removed his jacket and laid it on the table. RT looked at his hulking physique and swallowed hard. RT grabbed Mick's right wrist and said, "Mick, find my Katie, please!"

Mick nodded his head and left the room.

Chapter Thirty-Five: Saturday, May 1, 1999, 08:00
McCormick, SC

Robert woke and rolled to a seated position. He stood and put on a sweatshirt and sweatpants, slid into his slippers, and walked out of the room and to where Jennifer was sleeping. The door was open, and Jennifer's bed was made. He heard laughter from downstairs but decided to go to the third level to his sister's room. The stairs creaked under his weight. The door to the room is slightly open and he entered. Not an item out of place, the room was just as it was twenty-nine years ago. Faded blacklight posters, a lava lamp on a nightstand, and at the foot of the bed were Lisa Marie's platform shoes. On the closet door handle hung a leather fringed jacket. He lifted the jacket and brought it to his chest. He smelled the collar and then began to cry.

A voice said, "Robert, are you okay?"

He quickly wiped his eyes and then put the jacket back. He turned to see Jennifer standing there in a robe holding a cup of coffee. He turned to her and said, "Hello love. Yes, I'm fine. It's been a long time since I've been in here. Seeing all of this untouched for nearly thirty years is a bit surreal I guess."

Jennifer kissed him on the cheek, handed him the coffee, and replied, "I wish I could have met her. She seemed to have had quite an influence on your life."

Robert nodded and they left the room and took the stairs to the main level. His mother and father were sitting at the table and the bounty of hot cakes, scrambled eggs, ham, and orange juice brought Robert's senses to life. He said, "Good morning everyone. The food smells delicious, thank you Mother!"

"Don't thank me, son. This was all Jennifer!"

Robert sat back in his chair and looked at Jennifer with a surprised look, "Wait, all this time you've never made me breakfast and I learn today that you've got a bit of southern in you?"

The room was filled with laughter and plates were passed from person to person.

John said, "So, what are you two doing today?"

Robert wiped his mouth, "Well, I thought Jennifer and I would take a nice walk through town, and then later, who knows?"

Jennifer looked at Robert and smiled.

Marilynn responded, "Your father and I have a few things to do this morning, and then we'll have dinner here around 5:00. Your brother and his family will be here."

John Sr. said, "So, Robert, Jennifer, how'd you sleep?"

Jennifer looked at Robert and replied, "I had a hard time falling asleep. It's too quiet here. But once I did, my dreams were vivid."

Robert smiled, "I agree, love. Once I was out, I didn't move until fifteen minutes ago."

Marilynn reached across each side of the table and took the hands of Robert and Jennifer and said, "We are so happy you're here. We love you both."

"Yes, we love you both."

08:15, An Unknown Location

Katie was awakened by a stream of sunlight coming through the floor-to-ceiling windows. She quickly jumped and made her way to the windows, but the shades closed before she can catch a glimpse of where she might be. The microwave clock read 08:15 and she made a mental note. She went to the refrigerator and opened the massive doors. There wasn't much to choose from, so she took a yogurt and a bottle of mineral water. She opened drawer after drawer to find rolled of paper towel and plasticware. She removed a spoon and tore a towel from a roll and sat on the floor by the entrance. The room is so quiet it's almost deafening.

She scooped the very last of the yogurt and took a final drink of the water, stood, and found a trash can. She walked around the open space looking for anything that may help her escape, but the apartment was so well built, even the duct work was well hidden. She went to the stove and turned on a burner, nothing. So, starting a fire would not work. She opened the refrigerator again, looking for anything made of metal to start a fire in the microwave, nothing. She made her way to the bedroom and then to the bathroom; there was nothing in this apartment that can be used to aid in her escape. She fell to the floor and began to cry.

09:00, Katie's Apartment

RT was looking through Katie's photos so neatly framed and on tables throughout. He smiled at a recent picture of the three of them at Hilton Head where the family would spend two weeks every winter at a condo he purchased when Katie was born. He thought back to that trip and recalled telling Katie, "One day Katie, this will be yours and the office in the Springs, that will be too." He recalled Katie hugging him as he brought the photo to his chest and closed his eyes. Suddenly his phone rang. He scrambled to remove the phone from his pocket. He flipped it open and said, "Richard McCann here!"

"Mr. McCann, Sergeant Stevens here, how are you, sir?"

RT set the framed photo back in its place and went to a window and replied, "Good morning Mick. I'm well, and you?"

"I'm good, sir, thank you. So, I spent hours with Kevin and in all my years I have never met a more sincere young man. That said, there is zero chance he knew anything about Katie's whereabouts. To be honest sir, if Katie were my daughter, I'd be honored to have him as a son-in-law. I mean, if it ever comes to that."

RT moved a curtain to catch a glimpse of a young lady walking toward the building, hoping it may be Katie, but his expectation is for naught. He replied, "Sergeant, I appreciate the call, thank you."

RT closed the phone and opened it again and dialed. After a few rings a woman's voice said, "Hello."

RT paused and then said, "Hello dear. I just spoke to the police and Kevin is not a suspect in Katie's disappearance.

Jimmy is on his way to discuss a strategy. I'll call in a while. I love you."

RT closed the phone again and then there was a knock at the door. He opened to see a squat man, thick in the neck, resembling a linebacker. RT extended his right hand and said, "Come in, Jimmy."

Jimmy entered the apartment and looked around. He said, "I went to the cleaning company's office and spoke to the owner. I showed Katie's picture and he said he hadn't been to the building in a few days, but the last time he was there, Katie was working and left sometime around 8:30 or so. His crew finished at 9:15 and that was it, rinse and repeat, except the next night it was just the same two women that have always cleaned the office."

RT looked at Jimmy and replied, "Okay, great work, but what about Kevin's family?"

Jimmy removed his cap and placed it on a counter, "I've gone to the father's work; he was there and had been there every night until 7:00 p.m. and then home to be with his family. I spoke to a few of his neighbors and they confirmed. This family is very close. I don't see a thing that would raise a red flag."

Mr. McCann looked out the window again, turned to Jimmy, "I've been told when a young woman went missing and is not found within three days, she will be gone forever. Gone, Jimmy! Did you hear me, GONE!"

Jimmy crossed his arms, "Well sir, I've got some guys looking. We will find Katie, and when we do, the man or men who have her, well, you know, it will be taken care of!"

09:15, An Unknown Location

Katie flicked her eyes open as a bright light entered the room. She jumped to her feet and noticed the blinds have opened again. She ran to the window and tried to keep them open but cannot. She looked at the clock on the microwave and it read 9:15, another mental note. She did an estimate of timing and it seemed the blinds open for no more than ten, maybe fifteen seconds. She went to the refrigerator and counted fifteen yogurts, twenty bottles of water, and what appeared to be stew in a plastic container. She found another ten plastic containers with some sort of food in them. She removed all the containers and put them in the sink.

Noon, McCormick, SC

Robert and Jennifer had been walking for some time talking about how peaceful it was and how nice it would be to retire here someday. They walked into the Franklin Florist to see Tina and Maggie prepping flowers.

Jennifer said, "Wow, orchids, my favorite." She bent to smell them.

Tina replied, "Hello, you two. Enjoying the weather?"

Robert winked, "Yes, it's so nice that I may take Jennifer for a boat ride later this afternoon!"

Tina and Maggie exchanged glances and continued working. Jennifer was walking around the shop looking at trinkets and cards. She saw a photo behind the register of two women, one is clearly Tina, and she asked, "Who's in the photo with you?"

Tina looked up and then to Robert and said, "That would be Lisa Marie, Robert's sister."

"Yes, my sister and Tina were really close some years ago, like sisters, right?"

Tina finished a knot, "Yes, like sisters we were. I miss her every day."

"Me too."

The store was quiet and then Robert said, "Well, we'd better get going. I'd like to grab some lunch down at Lucile's. Nothing like a hamburger, fries, and a milkshake the way they did it fifty years ago!"

Jennifer took Robert's hand and they said goodbye, but not before Robert gave Maggie a wink. They walked hand in hand down Oak Street and Robert said, "So, are you serious about me moving in with you? I mean, I don't have a problem, but I honestly hoped we'd buy a house in the suburbs or maybe we find an apartment that would suit us both."

"I'd like to buy a house too, but the commute would be horrendous, so maybe we look for an apartment that allows us easy access to things we need and allowing enough room in the event we have a baby."

Robert laughed, "Okay, deal. We'll find an apartment that makes sense."

Jennifer interrupted, "Wait, are you proposing to me, Mr. Franklin?"

Robert gave a confused look, "What, no, I'm just making conversation is all."

Jennifer's mood soon turned somber and Robert pulled her close and said, "I love you."

The door of Lucile's has the same bell as the hardware and

the seven patrons all turned and looked at Robert and Jennifer. An older woman walked to the couple and said, "Well, bless this day, it's Robert Franklin!"

Robert hugged the woman and said, "Hello Mrs. Jones, this is my girlfriend, Jennifer Sanders."

Mrs. Jones took Jennifer's hands and replied, "It is so nice to meet you, Jennifer. I've known Robert since he was in diapers, and you, my dear, are lovely. Isn't she lovely everyone?"

The fellow patrons agreed, causing Jennifer to blush, and she said, "Thank you, Mrs. Jones, you're too kind."

Mrs. Jones motioned the two toward a booth and they sat. Robert nodded and then said, "Thank you, give us a few minutes, please."

Mrs. Jones waved as she walked away, and then Robert said, "I'm sorry about that. Mrs. Jones has been here a very long time and she's been showing signs of getting older and will forget and make outward comments without thinking."

Jennifer smiled while watching her walk away and said, "It's okay, she's cute. So, who is Lucile?"

Robert turned the menu over and pointed to a photo and said, "This is Lucile, Mrs. Jones' mother. Yes, when I said she's been here a long time, I wasn't kidding."

Jennifer read a short bio: "Lucile Jones, born in the deep South in the year of our Lord 1868 and with just $255 dollars, opened Lucile's in 1916 and worked here until her death in 1975."

Jennifer looked at Robert and said, "Wow, she lived a long time. A very long time!"

Robert replied, "Yes, and Mrs. Jones was born in 1906 and started working here at age five. She took over in 1975 when her mother passed."

Jennifer looked at Mrs. Jones and smiled.

16:00, NYPD Garage

Mick stood over Katie's car as a man from forensics dusted for prints. Jameson walked up and asked, "Well Mick, anything?"

Mick looked at his boss and replied, "We'll have prints to check shortly but other than that, nothing. She keeps this car immaculate."

"Actually, RT has it cleaned once a week despite the weather, so luckily for us we got to it before he did."

Mick replied, "Seriously, once a week?"

Jameson shrugged his shoulders and walked away, "Let me know when you have something!"

Mick leaned into the back seat of the car and looked around hoping to see something that doesn't belong. He stood straight and then the officer inside the car announced, "Well, I've got enough I think; let me get this upstairs and scan for matches."

Mick patted the officer on the back and walked back to the car to have another look now that there is no one around. He canvassed every inch of the interior and again, nothing, so he decided to stop and head back to his office and wait for forensics. In his office he thought about his wife and picked up the phone. After a couple of rings, he said, "Hello honey, how are you? I thought I'd call to say hello and to let you know that I won't be leaving today, maybe tomorrow or Monday. I'm sorry."

After a few nods of his head he hung up the phone and it rang. He answered, "Mick!"

A voice on the other end said, "Hello Sarge, we scanned prints and we have Katie's for sure, a man named Michael Sparks, and an unidentified palm print on the top of the driver's door."

Mick leaned forward and said, "Okay, Michael Sparks. Got it, thank you!"

Mick tapped his keyboard and hit enter. Seconds later the hard drive stopped chattering, and he read, "Michael David Sparks, Brooklyn."

He wrote down some information, stood, grabbed his jacket, and went to Jameson's office. He knocked on the door and said, "We have fingerprints from a Michael Sparks, Brooklyn, and palm prints from the top of the door and next to the B-pillar. I'm going to pay Mr. Sparks a visit."

Jameson stood, grabbed his jacket, and said, "I'll go with you!"

The men leave the station and get into the dark blue Chevy Impala. Jameson flipped his phone open and dialed a number.

"Hello RT, Mick and I are headed to Brooklyn to speak to a Michael…"

Jameson looked at Mick and Mick replied, "Michael Sparks."

Jameson finished the name and closed his phone. Mick looked at Jameson and asked, "Do you think letting Mr. McCann know where we are going is wise?"

Jameson looked straight and replied, "Mick, sometimes you

have to pick your battles, and frankly, I don't want to battle Mr. McCann."

Mick looked forward and drove the Impala steady and quickly through the streets and soon they're on the Brooklyn Bridge. Moments later, the Impala rolled to a stop outside an apartment building just blocks from Katie's office. Before the men exit the vehicle, Mr. McCann was standing outside Lt. Jameson's door. RT reached for the door handle and opened the door for Jameson to exit. The two men shook hands and stepped to the side to talk. Jameson and RT looked to the left at Jimmy, a shorter version of Mick, but probably a lot tougher.

Jameson waved Jimmy over, and Mick followed, and he said, "Mick, this is Jimmy and he works for Mr. McCann. He'll be with us during the interview of Mr. Sparks."

Jameson looked at the building and then up and said, "Great, he lives on the sixth floor. Just what my knees need right about now!"

Mick replied, "No elevator?"

"Yes, but I'm betting it's out of order just by looking at the building's exterior."

Mick looked at the building and shook his head. The four men entered the building and make the climb to the sixth floor. They soon found apartment 6E, and Jameson made a "hold on a minute" gesture and said in a labored voice, "Let me catch my breath first."

Jameson stood straight up and knocked on the door. A few seconds passed and he knocked again. There were footsteps from inside, but no one was answering, so Jimmy knocked on the door and a voice said, "Oh, my goodness, give me a second!"

The door of apartment 6E opened and a short man said, "What do you want! My God!"

Jameson stepped forward and flipped open his wallet to show his credentials and said, "Hello, I'm Lieutenant Jameson of the NYPD and we're here to speak to a Michael Sparks. Is he available, please?"

The man adjusted his robe, "What's this about?"

Mick replied, "Sir, is Mr. Sparks available, please?"

Reggie looked at Mick and replied, "Good God man, you're a cop? Anyway, Michael is working tonight and won't be home until 2:00 a.m.

Jimmy then asked, "Where does he work?"

Reggie looked at Jimmy, a man of roughly the same height as himself but twice the size, and replied, "He works at Mario's."

Before he can say anything more, Jimmy grabbed RT's arm and said, "I know the place."

The men left the apartment and headed down the six flights and to the sidewalk. Again, Jameson is bent forward with both hands on his knees. RT looked at him and said, "I hope that when you retire you find time to get in shape, Jameson. I've got a couple of years on you and could run circles around you."

Jameson looked up at RT and waved him off. The men make their way just two blocks up, turned right, and the door to Mario's is in front of them. Mick looked up at the address to make a mental note and Jimmy opened the door and stepped in, followed by RT, Mick, and then Jameson.

The host stepped to the podium and said, "Hello gentlemen, smoking or nonsmoking?"

The three men turned and looked at Jameson and then back to the host, and Mick said, "Yes, sir, actually we need to speak to Michael Sparks please."

The host seemed irritated and said, "I'm sorry, but Michael is working, may I help you?"

Jimmy stepped forward and RT placed his right hand on his shoulder, which made Jimmy stop. Mick opened his wallet to show credentials and the host changed his tone and said, "I'm sorry, let me get him."

He walked away quickly and then stopped to talk to a tall, slender man. They both looked to the front of the restaurant to see Mick, and mostly Mick. They chatted briefly, and Michael walked away and to the podium and said, "Hello. I'm Michael Sparks, how can I help?"

"Hello Michael, I'm Lieutenant Jameson, NYPD. Is there somewhere we can talk?"

Michael looked around, "Well, to be honest, maybe we should step outside, or we could go to my apartment a few steps away?"

Mick, RT, and Jimmy looked at Jameson again and he said, "No, we can talk outside."

The men left the restaurant and created a semicircle around Michael. RT is the first to speak and said, "Son, I want you to be very honest with your answers. My daughter, Katie McCann, is missing, and your prints are in her car."

Michael brought his hands to his face and his voice almost

came lady-like as he said, "What do you mean Katie's missing?"

RT said, "Yes, she was to be in Saratoga Springs Friday and never made it."

Michael looked down the street to Katie's office and replied, "Have you talked to Keith, her boyfriend?"

Jameson said, "We spoke to Kevin last night. He actually went to Saratoga Springs assuming Katie would be there, and her father, Mr. McCann, thought she came with him."

Michael started looking around, side to side, and then said, "Let's see, Tuesday Katie and I went shopping. She wanted new shoes, and I needed shoes."

Michael lifted his right foot to show a patent leather loafer and said, "I bought these and a pair of jeans and—"

Jameson interrupted and said, "Okay, son, why were your fingerprints on the shifter, steering wheel, and rearview mirror of Katie's car?"

Michael looked at Jameson and then RT, "Well, I don't own a car and I really like Katie's car, so she lets me drive it occasionally, and Tuesday was one of those days. Wait, I have the receipt to prove we shopped Tuesday."

He reached for his wallet and Mick waved him to stop. RT placed his right hand on Michael's left shoulder and said, "Michael, please tell me when you saw my daughter last."

Michael paused and then said, "Reggie and I were walking Wednesday late afternoon and we ran into Katie and Jennifer, her boss. They were going to lunch, lunch at Cotler's Deli, right over there. Let's see, what else? Oh yes, I told Katie that a man came into the restaurant asking about her. He drove a black BMW, a big car. I remember Jennifer saying the man reminded her of Robert, her boyfriend. Anyway, Reggie and I said goodbye and that was it."

Mick asked, "You said a man asked about Katie, had you seen him before? Can you describe him, please?"

Michael looked at Mick, "He was very handsome and built, but not like you. He was lean, maybe six feet tall, his hair was professional, like a federal agent would wear his hair."

Jameson extended his right hand toward Michael and said, "Young man, you've been helpful. Here's my card; if you think of anything else, please call me, day or night."

The four men turned and walked away, leaving Michael dumbfounded.

Jameson looked at RT and then at Jimmy, "I know old man Cotler, so let me do the talking. I don't want to upset him, okay Jimmy?"

Jimmy looked at Jameson and winked. Jameson looked forward as they walked the few blocks, but the walk would be for naught. On the door was a note, "Closed due to illness."

RT looked down the street and said, "Where was Katie's car?"

Jimmy motioned for the men to walk to the side of the building and up a service alley. They stopped at the very spot Katie's car was found and Mick knelt and scanned the area. RT put his hand on a wall and does what he can to hold back the tears. Jameson placed his hand on RT's back and said, "Richard, you need to sleep. You look exhausted."

RT turned and looked at Jameson, "You're right. I can't be

on my game like this. I'll go back to Katie's."

Jimmy replied, "Boss, do you want me to come with you? Maybe the actual intent was for you and not Katie. You have enemies."

RT looked at Jimmy and then back to Jameson. Mick replied, "I guess Jimmy brings up a good point. Have you had any recent threats against you? A case from the past that's been a thorn in your side? Something?"

Mr. McCann looked at Jameson and replied, "Well, there was a Thomas Angello from a few years back. You remember, Mike? I defended the man who Angello beat into the ground nearly killing him. Angello swore revenge on me. As a matter of fact, he said on my kids he'd get me back. He received fifteen years with possibility of parole after ten, and I recall a letter recently stating he was released."

RT went flush and steadied himself on Jimmy. Mick replied, "Let me make a call."

Mick stepped away and Jameson said, "I can't imagine what you must be feeling, RT, but I can assure you this will end soon, and in our favor. Katie will be back."

Mick came back and said, "Mr. McCann, I don't know that this Angello will be a problem. He was found in Trenton two days ago sitting in the front seat of a car with an ice pick in the back of his head."

RT looked at Jimmy and Jimmy turned away. Mick looked at Jameson and then at Jimmy. The men decided to call it a day and RT walked to Katie's with Jimmy about twenty yards back until Mr. McCann entered the building. Jimmy stepped into a coffee shop just across the street from the apartment and sat in a window seat and placed an order.

Mick and Jameson headed back to NYPD. The ride was quiet and the whirring sound of the Impala's tires on the Brooklyn Bridge was almost mesmerizing. The big car dipped down a ramp and into the precinct garage and came to a stop. Mick looked at Jameson and said, "Do you think that Jimmy guy had something to do with Angello's death?"

Jameson reached into his jacket pocket and brought out an empty cigarette pack, crumpled it, and replied, "To be honest, I don't know, and I don't really care. It's one last scumbag on the streets of New York!"

Jameson then said, "Listen, Mick, why don't you head home and spend time with your family. I've got a few things to take care of here and then we'll reconnect in the morning. As a matter of fact, I'll call you."

Jameson opened the door, twisted, brought his legs to the concrete floor, and used the A-pillar and B-pillar to lift himself from the car. He turned back and said, "This will not be how I go out. We will find Katie!" He slammed the door and walked away. Mick sat there looking at the steering wheel and then brought the car to reverse, throwing his bulking right arm over the seatback, turned, and backed out. He pulled out of the garage and onto the street.

15:45, McCormick, SC

The Franklin home was filled with laughter and the clinging sound of forks, spoons, and knives on dishes. Marilynn Franklin stood and said, "I'm so grateful that we are all here. I'm grateful for Jennifer. She's brought Robert joy and we hope that soon enough she will be Mrs. Robert Franklin."

The family raised their glasses and the words "here, here" were said.

John Jr. looked at his watch and said, "Oh, would you look at the time? Honey, boys, we've got to go."

John Sr. looked at John Jr. and said, "What do you mean you have to go? It's early yet."

Tina replied, "I'm sorry Dad, but we had a commitment this afternoon and we must get going, sorry."

Marilynn watched as the room emptied quickly, leaving just Robert, Jennifer, Mr. Franklin, and herself. She looked at Robert and said, "Do you know what's going on?"

Robert put his glass down, looked at Jennifer, and said, "I have no idea, but it must be important."

Jennifer looked at him with an equally puzzled look and drank from her glass. They stand and repeat the night before. Robert washed, Jennifer dried, and Marilynn put away, but there were many more dishes and after about twenty minutes or so, Robert said as he handed the last dish to Jennifer, "I need to use the restroom."

He kissed her and headed to the stairs, taking two steps at a time. He entered his room, went to a small bag, reached in, and brought out the ring box. He opened it and admired the ring and its beautiful shine and clarity as he held it toward the window allowing the sun to bring out the prism of impeccable lighting. He closed the box and put it in the front pocket of his khaki pants.

In the kitchen, Jennifer was leaned against the counter and said, "Mrs. Franklin, did you mean what you said before, about Robert and me?"

Marilynn walked to Jennifer, hugged her, and replied, "Yes dear, of course. He's happy, you're happy, and that makes us happy. Robert can be complex, but he's a good man, and I see the way he looks at you."

Johns Sr. interrupted from his study, "Yes, I know my boy and he's smitten, young lady."

Jennifer blushed and Robert entered the kitchen and said, "Hey, what's going on?"

Jennifer looked at Marilynn and laughed. Robert looked at John Sr., "Did I miss something?"

Jennifer walked to Robert, kissed him, "No, love, we were just chatting."

Robert stood there puzzled as Jennifer went upstairs. Marilynn took Robert by the hand and said, "Son, is it going to happen soon?"

Robert looked at his mother and asked, "Is what going to happen?"

Marilynn playfully slapped Robert's forearm and replied, "You know, are you going to propose soon?"

Robert winked, "Yeah, someday."

Robert looked at his watch, which read 16:22, and then checked his pocket to ensure the ring is still there. He walked into his father's study and found him napping in a lounge chair, so he then decided to go to the front porch to practice what he will say to Jennifer in about an hour. He began to whisper his lines.

"Jennifer Marie Sanders, I knew the moment I walked into you at Gino's Market and saw you, I'd spend the rest of my life with you. When you looked at me it was like a lightning strike to the heart; I felt more alive than ever before. You've put up with my goofiness for more than four years now, and today I feel it's time to…"

The screen door opened with its usual creaking noises and a spring being stretched and then slammed shut, fwapp, fwapp. Robert turned to see Jennifer again with both hands at her face with that "I'm so sorry" look. "You'd think I'd remember after the hundredth time."

"No worries, love. When I was a small boy, I'd let that door slam all the time without a second thought."

Jennifer looked back at the door and then to Robert, "So, who are you talking to?"

Robert looked at her puzzled, "I wasn't talking to anyone."

Jennifer laughed, "Sure, okay, so what are we doing this evening?"

Robert looked out into the chilled air and said, "Well, I thought we'd go for a drive out to the lake and go for a nice boat ride. It's been a long time since I've been on the water and being with you would make it extra special. What do you think?"

Jennifer stepped up and kissed Robert, "I think I love you, Robert Franklin, and that sounds wonderful!"

Robert leaned back, "You think you love me?"

Jennifer laughed and buried her face in his chest, "I know that I love you. I love you with all my heart!"

The two embraced on the front porch when a car went by honking its horn. Robert turned to see Johnny with his left arm out the window giving a thumbs up. He waved and the car continued. Jennifer said, "What was that all about?"

Robert looked back out to the street and replied, "I guess he's happy to see us. I don't know; he's always been an odd kid. Anyway, why don't you grab a sweater and I'll find a nice blanket to take with us just in case."

Jennifer and Robert entered the house, but Robert slowly closed the screen door to avoid the noise and the two head upstairs. A couple minutes later they were in the car and down the road. About twenty minutes later they pull up to a boat landing.

Robert parked the car, shut it down, and got out with Jennifer waiting. Robert went to her door and opened it. He said, "My lady."

Jennifer extended her right arm and slowly exited the vehicle with Robert's aid. The boat launch was beautifully lit with soft white lights, and there were a few tiki torches lit to add to the ambiance. Jennifer looked at Robert and then Tina, Maggie, and the rest of John Jr.'s family come from behind the amazing palmetto trees that line the lake's shore. Tina had a basket showing breads and cheeses and a bottle of champagne with two crystal glasses. Maggie was holding a small radio with romantic music filling the air. Sarah walked to Jennifer and presented her with a dozen roses and bows. Jennifer looked to Robert and began to cry.

After a few minutes she said, "Love, what is this?"

Robert turned as a Buick pulled up and his mother and father exited the vehicle. The entire family is standing in a semicircle around Robert and Jennifer. Moments later a large, black Chevrolet Suburban pulled up and a man and woman exit. Jennifer nearly fell when she realized it was her parents. She broke away, ran and hugged them both at the same time, almost knocking her mother down in the process. Mr. Sanders walked to Robert and they shook hands and then hugged. Mrs. Sanders did the same minus the hand shake of course and the parents exchange hellos.

Jennifer said, "Everyone, these are my parents, Scott and Heidi Sanders. Wow! I can't believe you're here."

The group replied in stereo, "Hello, Scott and Heidi!"

19:00, An Unknown Location

Katie had monitored the blinds since this morning and found cycle happening three times in the morning starting at 8:15 AM and then again at 1:15 PM three more times, and nothing since the last cycle at 5:15 PM. She had removed all the food from the containers and piled it in the large sink. The stew and sauces and so forth make an almost dark brown color, especially since she removed the potatoes, the pastas, and other nonliquid ingredients. She went into the bathroom and removed a hand towel from the linen closet and soaked them in the sink with the mixture she created and waited patiently.

19:06, McCormick

Robert looked at Sarah and nodded his head. Sarah looked

293

down and pressed play, which started a CD spinning. She then increased the volume and the voice of Céline Dion and her song "The Power of Love" was playing.

Jennifer looked at Sarah, smiled, and then said, "That song played on our first date, many times that night. You remembered?"

Robert smiled, "Yes, how could I forget? It must have played a dozen times. It was the biggest hint a man could take."

Robert knelt before Jennifer and produced the ring box and slowly opened it to ensure the ring didn't become dislodged and fall onto the ground. He then took her hand and said, "Jennifer Marie Sanders, I have dreamt of this day since the day we met. You have captured my heart unlike anyone before. I know I live a crazy life and you've been with me through it all, and I cannot see my future without you in it. I love you and was hoping you too feel the same. That said, make me the happiest man on the planet and be my wife?"

Jennifer was barely able to contain herself and fell onto Robert and replied, "Yes, yes, it would be an honor, yes! I love you too!"

The group of people began clapping and then gathered around the newly engaged couple to show their love. A voice called out and said, "Mr. and soon-to-be Mrs. Franklin, please join me for a romantic getaway on the *SS McCormick!*"

Robert and Jennifer looked to see Christopher standing at the helm of a pontoon boat and wearing a captain's hat. Standing next to him was Maggie and she was holding two glasses of champagne. Robert and Jennifer looked at each other, she looked at her ring, and they made their way to the awaiting boat.

They climbed aboard and Robert turned to the crowd and said, "Come on everyone, enjoy this night with us."

John Sr. asked in a worried voice, "How many can this boat hold?"

Robert stood atop a seat and began counting, "Dad, it can hold eleven!"

Marilynn took John's hand, "Come on dear, don't be a worry wart."

The boat now had its passengers and slowly backed away from the dock. The sun had set and off in the near distance fireworks filled the night sky. Robert looked to John Jr. and mouthed, "Who's doing that?"

John Jr. replied, "I have no idea."

The sky is filled with beautiful colors and shapes. Sarah pointed and expressed her joy. After about ten minutes the display stopped, but the boat continued at a slow speed as everyone laughed and talked about the old days, the future, and of course Robert received a bit of teasing.

Christopher commented, "Sorry folks, we need to make a quick pitstop," as he closed in on a dock. There were two figures that stood in wait as the boat came to a stop. The two entered the boat and it became clear that Steven and his girlfriend made the trip from Colorado to share in the celebration. Robert hugged his nephew and his girlfriend and then made introductions to Jennifer's parents. Steven was unkept, smelled, and hadn't shaved in a very long time, but it didn't matter. He's home and now the boat has thirteen passengers.

Chapter Thirty-Six: 04:30, Sunday, May 2, McCormick

Robert gently touched Jennifer and said, "Love, I'm sorry to wake you, but we need to leave soon. Our flight leaves at 10:00."

Jennifer slowly opened her eyes and replied, "What time is it?"

Robert looked at the clock on the nightstand next to the bed and said, "It's 04:30."

Jennifer rolled up and then stood. She stretched, yawned, and said, "Why are we flying out so early?"

Robert replied, "Well, I have to meet with Jameson at 16:00, I mean 17:00, I mean 5:00 p.m. I'm sorry, I should have told you."

Jennifer frowned and said, "Look what I got!" She held up her left hand to show the engagement ring. Robert smiled and then kissed her. She replied, "Okay, give me ten minutes."

Robert left her room and headed back to his and grabbed his suitcase. His bed was nicely made, and he opened the shade, which flew up and flipped around itself numerous times before stopping. Robert laughed and left the room with the door about six inches from being closed. He took the stairs slowly to not wake his parents, but when he got to the front door his mother was standing there staring out into the darkness. The only light was coming from the porchlight and a corner streetlight.

He was cautious to avoid scaring her, but she said, "Good morning, son."

Robert stood next to his mother, "Hello Mother, why are you up?"

Marilynn turned and smiled. She reached for Robert's hand, "Robert, your father and I are so very proud of you. You've accomplished so much. I just wish Lisa Marie could be here to see the man you are today."

Robert hugged his mother and said, "Thank you, I too wish she were here. It's hard to believe she's been gone twenty-nine years. She had such a kind soul. A loving woman she was."

The two stand in silence and the stairs began to creek as Jennifer made her way down. She stood at the bottom and said, "Good morning. I hope we didn't wake you."

Marilynn looked at Jennifer and then at Robert, "No dear, I've been awake. I wanted to see you off. Last night sure was a lot of fun, and we couldn't be happier for you both."

Jennifer hugged Marilynn and then kissed Robert on the cheek. She extended her left hand and said, "Can you believe it? I'm engaged!"

Robert smiled and kissed her and then his mother, "Well, we'd better get going. I want to avoid as much of the Atlanta traffic as we can."

Robert took Jennifer's bag and the two made their way out the door, but this time Jennifer held the screen door from closing to avoid the noise, and down the steps and to the car they went. The Chrysler's large trunk popped open and Robert placed the two bags inside. He pressed another button and the dome lights illuminate the car's interior. He opened Jennifer's door and she slid in. As he walked around the front of the car, he looked back to see his mother standing on the porch. He waved at her and she at him. He slid into the driver's seat and seconds later the car came to life.

08:15, An Unknown Location

Katie waited patiently for the blinds to cycle. She noted the time and went to the refrigerator and took out a yogurt and water. After she finished, she went to the shower. Minutes later she was walking around the apartment in the fluffy white robe while using a towel to dry her hair. The clock on the microwave read 9:15 and the blinds opened, going the opposite direction, and then they closed. She sat on the floor facing the windows and began to cry.

She recounted the last months of her life and the night in question when the man reminded her of how rude she was. She now recalled the man named Robert. He had asked her friend Marcie if he could buy her a drink and Katie told him to get lost, and that Marcie was happily married. She scolded Robert for not observing Marcie's wedding ring. She really made a scene and she knew it was an alcohol-induced tirade, or was she upset that he didn't pay attention to her? Regardless, her actions don't deserve a kidnapping and anything else that he planned for her. Katie fell to her right-side weeping and then fell asleep.

09:20, Katie's Apartment

RT sipped coffee from a cup that read "Brooklyn – Forget About It!" He finished calls with his secretary, and she had moved his appointments to an associate at the firm. He took the phone receiver from the wall, pressed redial, and moments later a woman's voice said, "McCann residence."

RT responded, "Good morning, Deb. How are you holding up?"

Deborah McCann paused, "Hello Richard. How much longer before Katie is back with us?"

Richard knew the clock had essentially run out, but does his best at being positive, "Honey, we've had some really good leads, talked to many people that saw Katie before she went missing, and Jimmy is leaving no stone unturned. I'll be home with Katie soon."

RT hung up the phone and took another drink of his coffee and then heard a knock at the door. He looked at his watch and then walked to the door. To his surprise, Kevin was standing before him. RT smiled and said, "Good morning, son. Please come in."

Kevin entered and closed the door behind him. He said, "How are you, sir?"

RT looked at Kevin, "I'm doing my best to hold it together, but I have my moments. By the way, how did you know Katie lived here?"

Kevin looked to the floor and then to RT, "I called Lieutenant Jameson and he gave me the address. I hope you don't mind me coming by unannounced."

RT removed a cup from an upper cupboard and replied, "Actually, I'm happy to see you. Mick, the big guy, told me you checked out fine and Jimmy did his homework and we've moved away from you."

Kevin took the coffee cup from Mr. McCann, "Sir, I'm sorry this is happening. I care for Katie very much, and I'm hopeful for the future—"

RT interrupted, "When Katie was a little girl, she had her whole life planned out. She would be married by twenty-five, starting a family by twenty-seven, and of course obtaining a law degree like her old man. But what made me happiest is that she wants to continue a family tradition that my grandparents started so long ago. Are you familiar with Skidmore College?"

Kevin shook his head no and RT continued, "My great-grandmother was a teacher at Skidmore when it was first known as 'The Young Women's Industrial Club.' If memory serves, 1922 is when it became Skidmore College. My point is that every member of my family started their academic career at Skidmore, and when my great-grandfather opened McCann and Son's, it had been a great dream that the firm would continue for generations. Saturday, November 3, 1990, our son, Katie's brother Richard Thomas McCann the fourth, was killed in the Gulf War. He was a second lieutenant in the US Army and his Bradley was taken out by friendly fire. We didn't know for nearly a week that he and his crew were dead."

Kevin can see the pain in RT's eyes and said, "Sir, I had no idea Katie had a brother."

RT looked at the counter and then to Kevin, "She was
300

fourteen maybe fifteen, and he was coming up on twenty-two. He was way smarter than all of us. The name McCann will go on, but we will be known as 'McCann and Family – Attorneys at Law.' So be prepared, young man. When Katie has her mind set, you will not sway her."

Kevin smiled, "I have seen that mind at work, and yes, I agree."

RT placed his used coffee cup in the sink as does Kevin. RT said, "I could use some breakfast, are you hungry?"

"Yes sir, that would be great."

The two men left the apartment and down the six flights of stairs. RT looked back at Kevin and said, "Did you know that I own this building? I bought in 1975 Deborah was pregnant with Katie. I reckon now it might be worth several million. It brings in about one hundred thousand a month. Don't tell Katie, but I plan to give it to her as a graduation present."

Kevin looked around the narrow staircase and replied, "Sir, that's an incredible windfall for sure."

They stepped out onto the sidewalk and Jimmy pushed off the hood of the Mercedes and said, "Good morning, boss! Good morning, young man!"

RT nodded and Kevin replied, "Good morning, Jimmy. How are you?"

Jimmy didn't reply and the three men made their way down the sidewalk to a small breakfast place called Toasted and Fried. They're known for having the best fried egg sandwich anywhere. It's the mayonnaise that made it so good.

12:20 Arrival, JFK International Airport

Robert nudged Jennifer awake and said, "Hey sleepy head, we are about to land, and you need to bring your seatback up and put your tray in the stowed position."

Jennifer sat straight, stretched her arms above her head, and pressed a button on the inner front of her armrest bringing the seat forward. She then leaned forward and closed the tray and locked it. She looked at Robert, smiled, and then put her left hand inches from his face and said, "Yep, I'm engaged!"

Robert smiled, "Are you happy, love?"

Jennifer kissed his cheek, "So, tell me, how long did you plan this, and how did you get my parents in on it? My mother can't keep a secret to save her life."

"I started the planning about a month ago, and everyone gladly went along. I had the long conversation with your father three weeks ago and his words to me were, 'Robert, I've been waiting close to four years for this day.' I replied, 'Oh, really?'"

Jennifer took Robert's right hand into her lap and said, "I can tell you this much, my parents really love you and yes, they are surprised it took this long."

Robert squeezed Jennifer's hands and smiled. The plane touched down with a loud screech and minutes later the passengers stood in the aisles waiting for the cabin door to open. Robert stood above Jennifer with his right forearm resting against the overhead compartment and said, "How about I drop you off? I'll go see Mike, check in with Randy, and then call you later. We should start to plan the big day and where we will live, right?"

Jennifer pouted and replied, "Fine, I guess, but don't be out too late."

Robert smiled and then moved back so that Jennifer could stand. She's in front of him now and he leaned forward and said, "I love you."

The taxi stopped in front of Jennifer's building and Robert helped her out, removed her bag from the trunk, and walked her to the door motioning reminding the driver to wait. The driver nodded and pointed at the meter. They hug and Robert kissed her forehead and then walked back to the cab. He gave an address and the cab took off. Robert entered his apartment and went to the counter where his BlackBerry sat all weekend on the charger. He unplugged it and turned it on. There are five messages: two from Friday, two from Saturday, and one from minutes ago. He dialed a number and pressed send.

13:49, An Unknown Location

Katie was still at the windows staring at the aluminum blinds when she hears a ringing noise, like a phone. She stood and ran toward the sound. It was coming from a painting on the wall near the bed. She said, "Hello, can you help me, please? I've been kidnapped. My name is Katie McCann. Hello, can you hear me? Please can you hear me?"

A man's voice replied, "Hello Katie, this is Robert. This is will be a one-way conversation, so listen carefully. I will see you in about forty-five minutes. I have a gift for you, so I expect you to be cleaned and waiting for me!"

Katie placed her mouth onto the mesh and said, "Please, if you can hear me, let me go, please! I'm sorry I offended you. Please!"

Robert then said, "I hope you found food and were able to stay busy while I was away. See you soon."

Katie ran to the kitchen and investigated the sink and began to panic. He will certainly not like what she has done; she started putting the contents of the sink back into containers and into the refrigerator. She wiped down the counter, hurried to each room, and cleaned: the bathroom, the bedroom, and the floor where she had been sitting. She looked around again and decided it should be okay. The clock on the microwave read 2:15, which means she had about fifteen, maybe twenty minutes. She began to pace, and then cry, and then pace.

14:36

Robert looked again at his phone but decided to wait on

checking messages. The streets are nearly empty as he made his way, block after block. He entered the building and headed to the elevator. There was a chime and the doors opened, he entered.

14:39

Katie began to shake as she heard a key enter the lock and then the door handle moved downward, and Robert entered. He saw her and smiled then said, "Hello love, how have you been? Miss me?"

Katie walked toward him and then struck him on the right cheek. He flinched, gained his composure, and set items on the counter. He said, "Katie dear, why would you do that? This is essentially why you are here. I don't like women like you that feel they are better than everyone else, women that think it's okay to hurt others. Well guess what, your daddy isn't here to help you. Oh, and Kevin, he had his chance months ago, but he took too long!"

Katie looked at the items he placed on the counter. She saw a roll of duct tape, what looked to be a clear plastic drop cloth, and a black velvet-covered box about six inches square and maybe an inch tall. Robert noticed her staring and said, "Oh yes, the gift I promised. Please go into the bathroom, go now!"

He backhanded her and she fell to the floor. He then kicked her in the stomach and screamed, "You should have never touched me! Go into the bathroom now!"

Katie began to crawl, and Robert kicked her again, and again. Her breathing is labored as she entered the bathroom. He extended his right hand to provide aid and she stood. He placed the box on the vanity and turned her toward the mirror. He's behind her and said, "You know, this clothing doesn't do you justice."

He pushed her into the mirror and began to tear the clothing from her body. She's now on the floor nearly naked and he kicked her again and screamed, "Stand up! Don't make me say it twice!"

Katie stood—naked, bruised, and crying. Robert turned her again to the mirror and from behind he pulled her hair back away from her face and then cupped her breasts. She's crying harder as he dropped his pants and boxers. She felt him and began to shiver. He suddenly stopped and pulled his underwear and pants up and zipped them followed by the ever-important button. He smiled and said, "Where are my manners? I almost forgot your gift."

He reached for the velvet box and stood in front of her and then opened it. She barely looked and he said, "What's the matter, you don't like it? They're real, I promise that. I have several boxes with the same style, length, and size."

Katie's eyes were wide open, and she now knew who this man was. She's read about him and she recalled seeing the necklace in the papers. She nearly fainted and he said, "Please allow me to put this on you."

Robert moved behind her and brought the necklace over her head and then rested it on her neck just above the clavicle. He brought the two ends together and secures the necklace. He put his hands on her shoulders and said, "You, my dear, look lovely. I'm sorry for causing you to bleed, please forgive me, but before too long it won't really matter."

Katie fainted and Robert carried her to the bed where he laid her out and then covered her naked body.

16:45, NYPD

Robert stood at a desk and a squat black woman of about thirty-five said, "Hello Agent Franklin, they're waiting for you."

Robert nodded and walked to a door waiting for that dreaded buzzing sound just before entering. The desk sergeant then said, "Have a nice night, sir!"

She winked and Robert smiled. He found his way to Jameson's office, knocked on the door, and Jameson, Mick, and two men he's never seen before are leaning over Mike's desk. Mick said, "Special Agent Robert Franklin, this is Richard McCann and his associate Jimmy."

Robert exchanged handshakes with the men and Jameson said, "Why don't we take this to the conference room. I can barely breathe in here." The four men exit the room with Robert following.

Mick said, "Special Agent Franklin has been in South Carolina and should now be an engaged man, if I'm not mistaken?"

Robert replied, "Yes, Mick, that is true. I'm officially engaged."

The men gave their congratulations as Jameson closed the door. He looked at Robert and said, "Hey, did Jennifer do that to your face?"

Robert reached to his right cheek and said, "No, I stopped at 26 Fed and got in a quick workout, and of course a cable on a machine broke and well, this is what happened."

Mick replied, "I can attest. I've had that happen as well. That's how I chipped my front teeth!"

Robert looked at Mick's arms and his only thought is, yeah, and the machine probably went out a window.

Jameson said, "Again, congratulations kid, but our initial meeting was to talk strategy and that has changed 180 degrees."

RT interrupted and said, "It's our understanding that your fiancée Jennifer Sanders is an attorney, and my daughter Katie has been working for her."

Jimmy slid a photo to Robert. He looked at the photo and then back to Jimmy, "What's this about, Mr. McCann?"

RT sat back and replied, "My Katie went missing Thursday night. She should have been to Saratoga Springs where we live the next morning. Her boyfriend Kevin confirmed she was still at her office around 7:30 and she did speak to her mother around the same time."

Jameson said, "Her car was found door open and pages from a term paper were blown throughout the alley. We took prints from the car, everyone checked out, but the palm prints left on the exterior of the car were not a match for obvious reasons."

Robert stared at the photo of Katie and Jameson said, "Robert, are you okay?"

This snapped Robert back to the conversation, and he replied, "Yes, I'm just a bit tired."

Robert's BlackBerry began to ring and vibrate, and Mick said, "Do you need to get that?"

"It's Jennifer, excuse me."

Robert left the room and answered, "Hello love."

Jennifer is frantic. Her words are hard to make out and Robert said, "Yes, I know about Katie. I'm with her father, Jameson, Mick, and some guy. Let me call you back."

He canceled the call and went back into the meeting. "Sorry about that, Jennifer just found out about Katie."

Jameson replied, "Robert, I've known his family since before Katie was born. She's like a daughter to me and we need to make this top priority."

Robert looked at Jameson and then RT and said, "No disrespect, but all cases are top priority. I am sorry this has happened, but I need to be clear on a few things."

Jimmy stood and RT motioned him to sit. Robert said, "Sir, I certainly hope you weren't trying to intimidate a federal agent, because your body language is telling me a lot right now. I said all cases take a top priority. Tell me about the scene; tell me all that you know. That's what I need right now!"

The room went quiet and then the men began giving Robert all that he needs to know. They bring him up to the present and it's now 21:30. Robert stood as do the others. They shook hands and left the room.

Jameson called out, "Robert, a moment of your time please."

Mick stopped too and pointed to his chest, a way of asking, me too? Jameson waved him on.

Mike asked, "So, what happened in there? You seemed—"

Robert interrupted, "I'm sorry, I just take this so personal sometimes, and when people essentially tell me how to do my job, it gets old."

Jameson placed his hand on Robert's right shoulder, "Hey, I get it. It's a job we love to hate, right?"

Robert extended his right hand and Jameson accepted, "Mike, I'm sorry. I guess that hit close to home. I mean, it's where Jennifer works too. It could have been her."

"I understand, pal. We are so close; it's almost like he's right here."

Robert smiled and walked out of the precinct. He looked at his phone and dialed.

Chapter Thirty-Seven: Monday, May 3, 1999

Katie woke early and removed the storage containers from the refrigerator and plugged the sink and began to pour container after container into it. She took small towels from the bathroom and soaked the white towels until they became a reddish-brown color and went to the blinds.

07:30, 26 Federal Plaza

Robert was in his office and looked at his office phone. The message light was still blinking, but he ignored it and looked at his BlackBerry and dialed. A voice answered and he said, "Good morning, love. How are you?"

There's a brief pause and Jennifer replied, "I'm sitting in my office. I think about so many things and I think it could have been me. Don't get me wrong, I'm upset that Katie's gone, but I recall that man in the black BMW and how he—"

Robert interrupted, "Jennifer, my team is coming together in about five minutes to discuss Katie. We are going to do whatever it takes to find her and to find her alive. I have to go."

Robert ended the call and dialed another number.

Katie was eating a yogurt and stared at the blinds, waiting for them to rotate. A voice filled the apartment and said, "Good morning Katie, I hope all is well? I've decided you and I will have a date tonight. That said, please ensure you've showered. I have it all planned out, and oh, I'll have another surprise for you."

Katie ran to the speaker and cried out, "Robert please let me go. I want my mother. I'm certain my family misses me. Please just let me go!"

Katie placed her face to the wall and began to weep. She knew what this man has done. She had read the horrific way he kills his victims. She soon gained composure and went back to the window blinds, and she waited.

11:45, Jennifer's Office

Kevin leaned against the wall outside. He wanted so badly to speak to her, to congratulate her, but he was struggling with words to say and with little energy to knock. He was a defeated man, and the office is essentially at a standstill; no one was working. It was so quiet the if a pin dropped, it would be heard for sure.

Jennifer leaned back in her chair and said, "Kevin, please, just come in. I can hear you breathing."

Kevin turned and entered Jennifer's office. He walked to Jennifer and hugged her. He stepped back and tears began to well up. She stood and they hug again. Kevin said, "I'm scared. I'm so scared right now. I'm worried that it's him."

Jennifer leaned back still in an embrace and said, "Who, Kevin?"

Kevin looked to the floor, "The Pearl Necklace Killer. I just feel that it's him."

Jennifer cupped Kevin's face with her hands and said, "Kevin, my fiancé is working very hard to find Katie. He will not rest until he does, trust me."

Kevin looked at Jennifer and responded, "Congratulations by the way, but what does your fiancé have to do with this?"

Jennifer replied, "Robert is an agent with the FBI. As a matter of fact, he's the Special Agent in Charge of cases like this."

Kevin's face dropped, "So, he's in charge of the team that's been looking for this animal? Why haven't they caught him yet!?"

Jennifer stepped back and then went to the window and motioned Kevin to join her. She then replied, "See that man right there?"

Kevin replied, "The man in the three-thousand-dollar suit?"

"Do you see that homeless man over there?"

"Yes, I see them both. What's the point?"

Jennifer said, "That's the issue. Every man, despite how they're dressed, or what their living situation could be, is a suspect. The point is it's been a struggle because this guy is meticulous—no foreign fibers, no fingerprints, nothing—he doesn't even rape the women; he just kills them, but his means of doing so are always the same and no one is that perfect. Eventually, he will make a mistake."

Noon, City Skyscraper

A group of people have gathered at a window twenty stories above the street below. A man said, "I wonder what the point of putting your name on a window like that means?"

A young woman read, "Katie McCann."

The group decided it's probably nothing and they walked

away, and most head out for lunch not giving the name another thought.

14:55, 26 Federal Plaza

The conference room on the twenty-ninth floor was packed, standing room only. Among the agents were Lieutenant Jameson, Mick, officers from the NYPD, Mr. McCann, and of course Jimmy. The west wall was covered with paper, photos, string going from thumbtack to thumbtack, and the most recent addition is a picture of Katie McCann. Miller was standing next to Robert and the room was watching a slideshow being narrated by another agent of the special task force.

The lights came on and Robert said, "Mr. McCann, I have a very pointed question, and please don't take offense, and Jimmy, you stay seated. We have come to an idea that the women he's taken in the past were known for, let's just say, being not so nice. For example, we talked with our latest victim's family and we were told their daughter suffered from low self-esteem and she would treat men like doormats. So, my question is this—"

Mr. McCann interrupted and replied, "Agent Franklin, if you're asking whether my daughter was a bitch, I'm going to stop you right there and tell you no! Katie is the kindest young lady you'll ever meet. She gives so much to others; she's loving…"

Miller spoke up, "Mr. McCann, with all due respect, we've heard that before, but we've learned that when most of the women drank, they weren't so nice. Did Katie drink, sir?"

RT looked at Jimmy and then said, "I understand what you're saying, Agent Miller, but I only know of a few times where Katie had too much and she was what one might call a happy drunk. She was never mean."

Robert lifted a piece of paper from the table in front of him and said, "Mr. McCann, is it true that on November 3, 1992, Katie was stopped by New York State Troopers? And is it true she was not yet licensed, there were open wine coolers throughout the vehicle, and she was incredibly combative with the trooper, which led to an arrest for DUI, driving without a license, and assault on a police officer?"

Mr. McCann stood as does Jimmy. He put the index finger of his right hand in Robert's face and screamed, "What does that have to do with Katie's disappearance?!"

Robert placed both hands up motioning for RT to back down. He then said, "Sir, that's the point, it may have a lot to do with her disappearance. This man is fueled by treatment of women, most likely brought on by his own home life."

Jameson looked at RT and gave a reassuring look that it's okay and that the FBI is only doing what they're trained to do. Mr. McCann then said, "Agent Franklin, I guess I'm more upset that her arrest was even known. It was to be dissolved, locked away, and never to return."

Robert looked at Miller and Miller, "Yes, sir, and it still is, but we sometimes go to places most don't know about to gather as much information to improve our chances."

RT sat and Jimmy followed.

The room was quiet and then Jameson and Mick both reached for their phones. They ignore the calls, and seconds later again, both reached for their phones. Mick looked at Jameson and let him know he'll step out to take the call. After all, the calls are from the NYPD.

Moments later Mick blasts into the room excited and said, "We may have found her!"

Robert looked at Jameson and then Mick. Jameson replied, "Tell us what you have."

Mick took the phone from his ear and said, "We need to get to 126 Water Street. An office across from the building in question noticed the name 'Katie McCann' spelled out on blinds earlier this morning and thought nothing of it, but just a few minutes ago they said the blinds now read 'HELP ME.' The apartment seems to be on the twentieth floor."

Everyone in the room stood and shuffled out. Jameson yelled, "Mick, get a team there now. We are at least thirty minutes out!"

Mick gave the thumbs up and made the call. Robert took Miller aside and said, "Get the car ready. I need to go to my office."

Miller nodded and headed out with the group. Jameson said, "Randy, where's Robert?"

"He's on his way."

Jimmy looked at RT and then back to Miller. The elevator opened and the team rushed for the sidewalk and into their vehicles. Mick tossed a red flashing light onto the dash and Jameson turned it to ensure motorists see it. The streets were crowded; most people are going home, or maybe a late lunch. Robert looked at his desk phone and saw the flashing light. He ran from his office and pressed the down arrow and waited for the elevator car to return. He entered and pressed L for lobby since Miller should already be out front waiting for him.

Nearly twenty minutes had passed, and Jameson took a call. He then said, "The boys in blue got her, and she's in an ambulance headed to Mass General."

Mick looked at Jameson and said, "Tell me how to get there."

Jameson looked out the windshield, "Turn right here!"

The car made a quick turn and other motorists show disapproval by honking their horns for being cut off. Jameson dialed a number and a man's voice said, "Mike, what is it!?"

Jameson looked at Mick and said, "RT, Katie's on her way to Mass General. She's beaten but alive!"

Mr. McCann hung up, told Jimmy where to go, and then he then called his wife.

Another twenty minutes later and the men were rushing into the hospital's emergency room doors and asking for Katie. A nurse pointed to a door and pressed an access button allowing them to enter.

A doctor greeted them and said, "Gentlemen, please slow down. She's stable, a bit bruised and battered, but she'll be fine. We have her on an IV and I've administered some pain medication, so she may be a bit out of it."

RT looked at the doctor and said, "I'm her father, where is she?"

The doctor responded, "Sir, I'll take you and only you to see her for now, okay?"

The others looked at RT and nodded. They watched as RT and the doctor walked away, and they began to hug and high-five. All of them but Jimmy headed to the waiting room, but Jameson noticed that neither Robert nor Miller are with them and said, "Oh man, I didn't call Robert to tell him we're here. He's probably at the apartment building."

He reached for his phone, which is in the car, and Mick said, "I'll call him."

Another half hour passed, and Robert with Miller joined the group. Robert said, "How is she?"

Jameson replied, "RT's in with her now. She's been beaten pretty good, but stable. She's on some good stuff for pain."

RT called out, "Mike, come in, you too Agent Franklin."

The men follow RT into Katie's room where it appeared she was sleeping. RT said, "She knows I'm here and doesn't feel a whole lot with all the morphine they've given her. There's no internal bleeding and she was a bit dehydrated."

Jameson walked up to Katie and kissed her forehead and said, "It's okay, kid. You're safe now."

Katie's eyes flickered open and she groaned and tears fell from her eyes. She's pointing at Robert and everyone looked at him, but she was out once again. RT reached for a plastic property bag given by the hospital. He reached in and removed the pearl necklace. He handed the necklace to Miller who inspected it and nodded to Robert.

Miller said, "This is our guy for sure. We'll head back to the apartment where our team is and get back to you later."

Robert extended his hand to RT as Katie slowly woke again and pointed at Robert and then she's out. The men look at Robert, but this time with a more curious look.

Robert said, "Great work everyone. Now let's find this guy."

He and Miller left the room and headed out to the Crown Vic. Miller looked at Robert and said, "Do you know that girl?"

Robert looking forward, "I've never seen her before in my life."

Soon the car squealed off headed for the apartment. Robert called Jennifer letting her know Katie was found and was doing well. Jennifer expressed her joy by screaming into the phone, causing Robert to move it from his ear. He ended the call and Jennifer ran out of her office and grabbed Kevin and cried, "They found her, they found—oh my God, they found her!!!"

Kevin and the office gather around Jennifer and everyone is hugging. Kevin said, "Where is she!?"

"She's at Mass General, stable and sleeping."

Kevin grabbed his coat and said, "Jennifer, we must go now!"

Jennifer ran to her office and took her coat from the back of her door and grabbed her purse. The two were on the sidewalk and hailed a cab.

The Yellow Checker pulled up and they entered the vehicle. Jennifer said, "Mass General, please!"

The cab driver nodded, and the tires of the giant car chirped on the concrete as it made its way down the busy street.

21:25, The Apartment

The NYPD had done its job and they've taped off the apartment entrance. Robert presented his credentials and the officer at the door let he and Miller enter. Miller walked to the window and stared at the blinds. The words "HELP ME" were written in what looked to be blood, but after further investigation it was clear that Katie used the broth from all the meals and with hand towels wrote her message.

Robert came from the bathroom and said, "This apartment is very familiar to me. It's like I've been here before."

A voice then said, "It's a lot like the loft where I knocked down the entrance door of the main lobby with a sledgehammer."

Miller and Robert looked to see Mick standing there. Robert nodded and said, "Yes, that's it. So, we were close in 1986, but he was a few steps ahead. However, I knew eventually this day would come. I wonder why he waited with Katie. I mean, what was it about her that she survived with the necklace on?"

Mick looked at Miller and then at Robert and replied, "Maybe he's getting old? Say, Robert, tell me again how you got the mark on your face?"

Robert looked at Mick then touched his face, "Like I said, cable failed on the machine I was using, and the bar came back and caught my cheek."

"How does a bar do what looked like a fingernail scratch?"

Robert looked at Mick and said, "What is this, Mick? Why do I feel you are interrogating me? The bar came back, I turned my face to avoid being hit in the nose, and I guess my thumbnail scratched me. I don't know, but it is from working out."

Jameson entered the room and said, "I guess what's more troubling is that you worked out before coming to my office."

Robert looked at Miller who shrugged his shoulders, "Again,

what's this about?"

Mick walked to Robert and placed his right hand on Robert's left shoulder and Jameson said,

"Robert, Katie identified you as the kidnapper. She told us how she scratched your face and that you took her there Thursday and then came back yesterday, just before you came to see us."

Robert stepped back and replied, "Come on, are you kidding me? I was in South Carolina with Jennifer all weekend!"

Moments later Jennifer entered the apartment. She was crying and said, "Robert, please tell me you didn't do this. Tell me you're not the man you've been searching for. Please tell me who you are!"

Miller stepped in front of Robert, "Wait a second here! I've known this man more than a decade. This is ridiculous! What is going on here?"

Mick slowly brought Robert's left arm behind his back and then the right arm and said, "Robert Franklin, you are under arrest for the kidnapping of Katie McCann. You have the right to remain silent…"

Robert screamed, "I'm a FEDERAL AGENT! You can't be serious!!!"

Mick continued, "Anything you say can be used against you in a court of law. You have the right to an attorney; however, if you cannot afford an attorney, the court will appoint an attorney to you. Do you understand your rights as I've read them to you?"

Robert looked at Jennifer as she removed her engagement ring. She walked to Robert and put the ring into the right front pocket of his jeans. She turned and walked out.

Jameson motioned for Mick to take Robert out. Miller walked to Jameson and said, "Mike, come on, man. You know this is crazy. There is no way Robert is the Pearl Necklace Killer. No way!"

Jameson looked at Miller and said, "Randy, we have to follow procedure, and right now, Robert is innocent until proven guilty. If Katie is wrong, we'll find out soon enough. I'm sorry, son, but we have to follow the book, and Robert is a suspect in the kidnapping of Katie McCann."

Chapter Thirty-Eight, Tuesday, May 4, 1999

06:00, NYPD

Robert Franklin laid in a cell staring at the ceiling, trying to piece together the charges and the allegations brought against him. A key entered the lock and the steel door opened. Jameson and Mick are standing there. Jameson said, "Robert, come on, get up. We need to talk."

Robert stood and grabbed his jacket and shook it out. He looked at Mick and said, "Do you need to handcuff me, Sergeant?"

"I'm not worried about you, Agent Franklin."

The men entered a conference room where Agent Miller and Robert's boss were waiting. Robert smiled at Miller and then noticed Director Tom Hall of the FBI. Robert said, "Good morning, sir."

Director Hall replied, "Robert, I trust you're doing well under the circumstances?"

Robert looked at Jameson and then to Miller, "Yes sir, considering."

Jameson started with, "Robert, it seems that I owe you an apology. Agent Miller went back to 26 Federal Plaza after we arrested you."

A woman entered the room and set a clear plastic bag in front of Robert, which contained his personal effects, including the engagement ring.

Robert looked around and Jameson continued, "The workout

facility where you claimed you were before we met Sunday afternoon has cameras and Miller showed us the video of the cable breaking and the bar hitting you in the face. So, that said, your alibi was all thanks to the FBI putting cameras in that room to ensure agents wouldn't deliberately hurt themselves and go out on some form of medical leave. At least that's what your boss told us."

Tom Hall looked at Robert and nodded. Robert looked at Jameson, "Mike, be honest, do you really think I would do something like this or that I could be that animal?"

"Robert, we have to go on all leads. I'm sorry for what you went through, but I'm just doing my job!"

Robert stood and said, "Well, if we're done here, I need to hope and pray that Jennifer will talk to me!"

Director Hall stood and said, "Agent Franklin, I'm putting you on administrative leave for two days. Get this behind you and let's catch this man!"

Robert sat and said, "Hold on, what's going on at the apartment? We need to get to the apartment now!"

Miller looked at Robert nodding in agreement. Mick asked, "What do you mean?"

Robert looked at Mick and said, "Well, this time the door was opened gently, right? So, we go back, put the apartment as it should be, deep clean, etc., and we wait!"

Jameson looked at Miller and then at Robert, "What made you think he's not onto us?"

Robert looked at Jameson, "Because I know you've got that place staked out, but not obvious, right?"

Jameson nodded and Director Hall then replied, "Agent Franklin, do you believe he may come back?"

Robert stood, "Miller, let's go!"

The men left the room and headed out to the sidewalk. Robert reached into the bag and retrieved his Paneria wristwatch and it read 06:48. He and Miller got into the waiting Crown Vic and the car moved quickly to the corner and did an abrupt U-turn and headed down the street.

Miller looked at Robert, "Hey boss, I knew it wasn't you. No way."

"Thanks Randy. I'm more worried about Jennifer."

"Don't worry about her. I called her first and told her about the video. She asked about another bruise she saw, and I went even further back and was able to find where you nearly took your head off. I told her we were going to stop you from working out. You're too much of a risk. Oh, by the way, why did you work out before meeting with Jameson?"

Robert looked at Miller, "Do you have any idea what this past weekend did to me mentally? I was wound tight as a drum and needed to let off some steam."

Miller laughed, "Yeah, I remember when I proposed. I let off steam by eating a half-gallon of Ben and Jerry's ice cream."

"So, are you still letting off steam?"

Miller looked at his stomach.

The men reconvene in the lobby of the building. Mick said, "I spoke to the night shift and our man hasn't been here."

The men entered the elevator with a cleaning team and Miller pressed twenty. Moments later there was a ding, and the doors opened. An officer seated at a window away from the door stood to attention and Jameson said, "Son, go home. There will be no need to come back."

The officer nodded and left the area. The team entered the apartment and Mick directed the cleaning crew. Robert noticed the blind read "Katie McCann" now. He then tried to open the blinds, but they're fixed and a heavy gauge aluminum. He said, "These blinds were not cheap! They must be on some form of timer."

Mick walked over and looked up and down the blinds, trying to assess the mechanicals. He said, "Do you want me to make them work?"

Robert replied, "No, Sergeant. We'll wait."

Robert looked at his watch as the cleaning crew wrapped up. It's now 08:12. Mick ushered the crew out and then inspected the space. The smell of bleach and other chemicals fill the air.

Robert stated, "I hope before they came through, this place was gone over with a fine-tooth comb."

Miller replied, "Yes, it was. We found only prints belonging to Katie McCann, and a match on the palm print taken from her car was found on the door jamb of the bathroom."

Suddenly the space is filled with light as the shades opened, and then seconds later they close again showing the words "HELP ME." Robert looked at Mick and said, "Should we call them back? The cleaning crew?"

Mick nodded and flipped open his phone and called. Suddenly a voice came from the bedroom. The men moved quickly, and the voice said, "Hello Katie, it's Robert."

Miller pointed to the wall and placed his index finger to his lips, indicating to be silent.

The voice continued, "How are you, my dear? I trust you slept well. Oh, do you enjoy the necklace I gave you? It looked especially nice on you, which is why I broke protocol and waited TO KILL YOU!"

The men moved away from the speaker and the voice continued, "I've decided that this morning is when you'll die, so please, be a good girl and clean yourself extra well today. I'll see you soon."

The men are now looking at Robert and they slowly moved out of the room and into the kitchen area. Miller looked at Jameson and said, "I'm sorry, but that voice was a lot like yours, and what are the chances this man calls himself Robert?"

Robert was blank. He stared at Jameson. Mick replied, "Robert, are you okay?"

Robert snapped to, "Yeah, that was a bit creepy."

There was a slight knock at the door and the men jump, drawing their service weapons. Mick slowly walked to the door, but since there's no peephole, he motioned for Miller to open and he will grab whoever is on the other side. Miller opened the door and Mick brought a small Asian man above his head.

The man screamed and said, "I here to clean! I here to clean!"

Mick sat the man down and straightened his polo shirt and apologized. Mick motioned for the man to clean the blinds. Within minutes the man was done, and Jameson thanked him and handed him a twenty-dollar bill. The man nodded and left the apartment. The men decided to wait in the bathroom. Before too long, the three of them are seated on the floor resting against the wall as Robert paced.

Jameson said, "Robert, you're going to wear a path into the tile; have a seat."

Robert thought about Jennifer. He thought about his family and he visualized the message light on his phone. Moments later the area was filled with light and Robert stepped out of the bathroom and watched the blinds rotate the opposite direction. He looked at his watch and it's 09:15. He turned and said, "The blinds rotated."

There was total silence and then Jameson snorted himself awake. The sound of a door handle turning filled the space and the men slowly rose to their feet. The door closed and a man said, "Hello love. I hope you're ready?"

Robert's heart was now pounding out of his chest as the man entered the room and is rushed to the ground. All four men were on top of him now, feet and hands flailing and the commands, "GET ON YOUR STOMACH" and "DON'T MOVE" were said. Mick wrestled the man to his feet and the room went silent; the only sound heard are of the men breathing heavy from adrenaline. Robert fell back to a wall and put his right hand to his mouth. The man tilted his head and he too was at a loss. It was as if Robert was staring into a mirror.

Jameson replied, "What the hell is going on here, Robert?"

Miller stared at the perpetrator with his mouth open; he couldn't speak.

Mick pushed the man out into the open space and pushed

him against a wall, where he too stepped back. He looked at Robert and then at the man and replied, "Yeah Robert, what the hell is going on?"

Robert looked at Mick and then walked up to the man and said, "Who are you? WHO THE HELL ARE YOU!?"

The man cannot speak. Mick flipped him around and shoved his face into the wall, reached in his back pocket, and pulled out a wallet and handed it to Jameson. Jameson opened it, retrieved a New York driver's license, and read, "Robert James...Carroll, born April 1, 1957."

Jameson looked up at Robert and said, "Isn't your full name Robert James Franklin, born April 1, 1957?"

Robert looked at the man that is was twin and replied, "Yes Mike, how did you know that?"

Mick turned the man around and slammed him against the wall and said, "Didn't we just arrest you not long ago?"

"Yes, I suppose that you did."

Miller is still dumbfounded, "So, who in the hell are you, mister?"

Robert Carroll replied, "I have nothing to say."

Agent Franklin replied, "Mick, put him in our car. We'll take him to 26 Fed."

Jameson replied, "Sure, we can do that," and motioned Mick to take the prisoner out the door with Miller followed close behind.

Robert leaned on the marble kitchen counter and Jameson placed his hand on his right shoulder and said, "Hey kid, we'll figure this out. Keep it together."

Robert turned, "I was never told about him, and this is how we meet. My supposed twin brother is a serial killer. This is way too much."

He put his hand up, bent at the waist, and threw up. Jameson stepped back and went to the bathroom for a towel and returned to hand it to Robert. Robert took the towel and wiped his face.

26 Federal Plaza

The four men and the prisoner entered the lobby at 26 Federal Plaza, and everyone stood and stared. The only people moving were Mick, who was holding Robert Carroll, Miller, Jameson, and Robert Franklin. Miller pressed the up button and they waited. Robert and Robert are fixed on each other and it's clear they were both at a loss for words. A chime and the doors opened. People exited and stopped to stare and then the men entered. Another person not part of the group tried to board, and Miller stopped her and said, "Sorry miss, you'll have to wait."

The woman stepped back, looked at the two Roberts, and saw that one is in handcuffs. She nodded and backed away.

Not a word was spoken as the elevator traveled upward. A chime was again heard, and the doors opened. Mick pushed Robert Carroll out and the rest followed. Fellow agents stood to see what the commotion was about. Stacey stood and with her mouth open was frozen. Director Hall hadn't returned to Washington just yet and came out of his office. He stopped and stared as the men went into the conference room.

Robert stopped Miller and said, "I need to call Jennifer. I'll be right there."

Miller nodded and Robert redirected to his office and all eyes were now on him. He looked around and then entered the room, closed the door, and went to his desk phone. The message light is still blinking, but he pressed the speaker button, then nine and Jennifer's office number.

Moments later she answered, "Jennifer Sanders." Her voice is sad and distant.

Robert paused and said, "Good morning, love."

Jennifer began to cry as does Robert. She told him of how sorry she is for doubting him and that she wanted to be Mrs. Franklin so badly it hurt.

Robert then said, "Jennifer, we caught him this morning."

Jennifer stood and walked to the door and whistled, which caused everyone in the bullpen to turn toward her. She motioned for Kevin to come into her office. Kevin pushed away from his desk, which sent his chair into the watercooler nearly knocking it over. Kevin entered the room, closed the door, and sat in the visitor's chair.

Jennifer replied, "When and how? I mean what happened?"

"We put the apartment back to how it was, and since no one had come or gone, we decided to wait. He showed, and we got him!"

Jennifer and Kevin high-fived and Kevin said, "So, does he look like you?"

Robert replied, "I'm sorry, who is this please?"

"I'm sorry honey, that was Kevin. He's Katie's boyfriend."

"Hello Kevin. I'm so sorry for what you and everyone else that cares for Katie has been through. Speaking of which, how is Ms. McCann?"

Kevin looked at his watch, "Right about now she's being released and headed to Saratoga Springs. At her request I will go up Friday."

"Well Kevin, Jennifer and I may have to join you. I have some questions."

"Robert, don't you feel it may be too soon?"

"No, love, the sooner the better, while it's still fresh. Listen, I need to go. I'll see you later tonight. Oh, I have a ring for you."

Jennifer leaned back in her chair as the phone disconnected and said, "He never did answer the question whether or not the man looked like him."

Kevin stood, "I'm just relieved the man is off the streets."

Jennifer nodded, "What time do you plan to leave Friday?"

"I thought I'd work until noon and then get out of the city before rush hour."

"Good plan, and since you will be staying at the McCann's, I'm going to find a nice B&B for Robert and me."

Kevin turned to leave and said, "You have no idea how happy I am right now!"

Jennifer smiled and nodded. Kevin walked out of her office and she began to do a search for a place to stay in Saratoga Springs.

10:00 AM

Robert Franklin entered the conference room and all eyes are now on him. He silently sat across from Robert Carroll. Mick said, "I have a question. Christmas 1986 we knocked the door down at your building, but you had already gone. How did you know we were coming?"

Robert Carroll looked at Agent Franklin and replied, "Were you there on that night, Christmas 1986?"

Agent Franklin looked up, "Yes, I was."

Jameson said, "You two never knew of each other?"

The men looked at Jameson and Agent Franklin replied, "I had no idea." He then said, "Is there a chance you attended San Francisco State University, in late seventy-five?"

Robert Carroll looked up at him and replied, "How did you know that?"

Agent Franklin stood and began to pace and said, "I went there from seventy-six to eighty." Robert paused a moment and then asked, "Did you date a girl named Sara?"

Robert Carroll looked up at Robert, "Ah yes, Sara without an H. She almost became my first, but she was nice to me, so I spared her."

Robert looked at him and said, "Why? What was so bad in your life that you killed all these women?"

Robert Carroll replied, "I'm done talking until I speak to my lawyer."

Miller said, "That's your prerogative, Mr. Carroll."

Agent Franklin replied, "Randy, put this…animal in a holding cell. Mr. Carroll, is there anything we can get you to make your stay more comfortable?"

Mick stood and said, "Robert, do you really want to make this man's life comfortable?"

Mick lunged at Robert Carroll who barely escaped sudden death because Jameson and Miller deflect him. Jameson said, "Mick, damn it, calm down."

Jameson stood between Mick and Robert with his hand on his chest and said, "Come on buddy, let's go."

Miller waited until Mick and Jameson were on the elevator and stood Robert Carroll up and said, "Man, you got lucky. He's been known to do a great deal of damage very easily."

Robert Franklin said, "Robert, who is your mother?"

Carroll turned away not answering, and Miller took him out of the room.

Robert sat both forearms on the table and stared at the water ring left by the glass Robert Carroll drank from. He noticed that Robert lifted the glass easily twenty times, yet he placed the glass in the exact spot each time. This tells Agent Franklin this was a disciplined man. What was his family life like? Robert began to look back on his own childhood and how loving his family was, and how they encouraged him to follow his dreams and move across the country. He recalled when his mother's last drank alcohol. It was the day his sister Lisa Marie died nearly thirty years ago. He thought about his older brother, John Jr., who despite his disability had a family and owned numerous businesses in McCormick. He then imagined his life with a family, maybe retiring in McCormick with Jennifer. There was a knock on the door that interrupted Robert's thoughts.

Robert turned to see Stacey and she said, "I'm sorry sir, Director Hall would like to see you."

Robert waved and said, "Thank you, Stacey. I'll be right there."

Robert stood, pushed in his chair, and walked out of the room and toward his office. He stepped in, took his jacket from the hook on the door, glanced at the flashing message light, and walked to Director Hall's office. He knocked and was motioned in. Tom Hall was a very quiet man, but effective. He said, "Robert, I've tasked Agents Abraham and Davis with digging up whatever we can on this guy, but I've got to ask, did you know of him?"

Robert looked at Tom and replied, "No sir, but I will soon enough. My parents have a great deal of explaining to do. I'd like to take a week's vacation starting Thursday. I need to go to South Carolina, please."

Tom Hall responded, "Yes, of course."

Robert stood and said, "Will that be all, sir?"

Hall looked at Robert, "Son, in my forty-three years as an agent, this is a first."

Robert nodded and left the room. He entered his office and sat in the visitor's chair, scrolled through the screen of his BlackBerry, selected a name, and pressed send.

Moments later Jennifer answered, "Hello Robert, how are you?"

"These past few days have been a roller coaster that I'm

done riding, that's for sure. Listen, I'm going to pass on going to Saratoga Springs. I need to go home to McCormick."

Jennifer paused, "Sure, is everything okay?"

"I think so. I'm going home for the day; let's touch base tomorrow, okay?"

"Yeah, I guess. Are you okay?"

Robert replied, "All my love."

He ended the call and moved to his desk. He took a framed family photo from his desk and imagined Robert in the picture. He thought about how it would have been growing up a twin and the tricks they could have played on their parents and teachers. He laughed to himself and then placed the picture back in its place. He looked at his phone and lifted the receiver, pressed message, and is prompted to enter a four-digit code. A moment later a voice said, "You have four new messages. To listen to your messages, press the star key."

Robert does so.

The voice said, "Message one, received April 28 at 10:20… Robert, why didn't you st—"

Robert deleted the message because he and Jennifer already spoke about him not being in Brooklyn that day.

The voice said, "Message two, received April 28 at 16:18… Robert, it's your mother. Your father and I are looking forward to seeing you Friday."

He skipped to the next message and the voice said, "Message three, received May 1 at 09:00…Agent Franklin…"

The message ended and then the voice said, "Message four,

received May 1 at 09:03…Agent Franklin, this is Mike Joseph. When time allows, I'd really like to talk to you. Please call me at area code 904-555-4217. I'm in Jacksonville, Florida."

Robert replayed the message and wrote the number down. He stood and walked out of his office and to the elevator. Within a few minutes Robert was standing with Miller and the two were looking at Robert Carroll.

Miller said, "He hasn't moved since he called his attorney. No movement, not a word."

"When will his attorney be here?"

Miller shrugged, "Again, not a word from this guy."

Robert patted Miller on the back and said, "I'm going home for the day. Call me if needed, but only if needed."

Miller waved him off and Robert took the elevator to the garage and within minutes the Crown Victoria's tires were chirping.

Chapter Thirty-Nine: Wednesday, May 5, 1999

Robert woke before his alarm. He rolled to his left side, tilted the clock to him, and read 03:48. He then rolled back to his back and stared at the ceiling. He began to recall Lisa Marie and how loving she was toward him, and then he wondered if Robert had ever felt that kind of love, what would make him do what he's done? He flipped the blanket from the bed, swung his legs allowing his feet to touch the floor, and he stood. He stretched and put on a sweatshirt before going to the kitchen. He lifted the BlackBerry from the counter; no messages and it's fully charged. He added water to the coffee maker and began it brewing. He thumbed through a stack of mail—mostly junk— and took a cup from the cupboard, poured his coffee, and sat at the table.

The reality of the past few days hit him, and he began to weep. He recalled Jennifer telling him that she swore she saw him in Brooklyn, and he realized that Jennifer could have been the victim, and she could be gone. He swiped all the items from the table to the floor, even the cup of coffee. He put his hands around his face and then opened his eyes and saw the note he wrote, "Call Mike Joseph" and the number written below. He laid the paper down, reached for his phone, and set it down. He stood, walked to the bathroom, and started the shower.

Nearly thirty minutes had passed, and he stopped the shower, stepped out, grabbed a towel, and wrapped his waist. He patted across the tile floor, onto the carpet of the hallway, and into the bedroom, where he opened the closet. He selected his clothes for the day by laying them on the unmade bed, which wasn't like him; his bed was always the first thing he did each morning.

He dried off and dressed. It's now 04:36 and he made his way back to the kitchen to clean up the earlier mess. He grabbed his phone, the note, and at the door he hung his holster around him, shoulder to shoulder, put on a suit coat, and walked out the door.

05:30 26 Federal Plaza

Robert Carroll sat up and twisted, allowing his feet to touch the floor. He stood, stretched, and then folded the blanket, placing it on the head of the cot. He then did the same with the pillow. He sat and waited. A distant door opened and closed and then footsteps filled the empty hallway. There is a soft knock on his cell door followed by, "Good morning, Mr. Carroll."

Robert replied, "Good morning, Agent Miller."

"Agent Franklin will be here soon, I'm sure of it, and I feel it would do him and you some good to discuss what the hell is going on. What do you say?"

Robert faced forward and replied, "Given the circumstances, I'd agree. Despite all that I've done in my life, I cannot help but wonder how it is that he and I are twins."

Miller replied, "Robert, thank you. As soon as your attorney arrives, I'll bring him back, that is, if he's coming."

Miller walked away and Robert sat motionless. Minutes later the same distant door opened and closed and this time the footsteps are farther apart, which told him that Robert was coming.

The cell door opened, and Agent Franklin said, "Stand up please."

Robert stood and was handcuffed and then pushed back to the bunk where he sat. Agent Franklin said, "I'm a bit freaked out by all of this, but I need answers, but not about the murders you've committed. We'll save those for the jury. I want to know about you and where you're from!"

Robert leaned forward from his chair waiting for Carroll to talk. Robert leaned back and took a paper from his suit jacket inner pocket. He read:

"Robert James Carroll, born April 1, 1957, Ann Arbor, Michigan. Your birth mother isn't listed, but Dr. Carroll and Mrs. Carroll happily adopted you. Said here you were top of your classes all through elementary school and you graduated with highest honors at seventeen from Cranbrook, an all-boys school in Bloomfield Hills, Michigan. You were being scouted by numerous engineering schools and yes, Dr. Carroll had hopes of you attending the University of Michigan, but you chose San Francisco State University. Why?"

Carroll looked at Robert and replied, "Why did you select San Francisco State?"

Robert leaned back and said, "Well, I didn't have fancy schools seeking me, but I wanted to get out of South Carolina, spread my wings a bit. I knew I wanted to work in law enforcement, and nineteen years later I'm Special Agent in Charge of the FBI's serial task force."

Carroll breathed in and said, "I had read about how easy it was to get a woman in San Francisco, especially after Vietnam, and while there I caught the computer bug. Did you know that people with incredible math abilities were once called computers, mainly at NASA during the late fifties and early sixties? I became fascinated by the computer's abilities and soon I was writing code. By 1981 I was a multi-millionaire, and by 1995 I became a billionaire, just twice though."

Robert sat up straight and asked, "When did you know you were adopted?"

Carroll looked at Robert and replied, "I knew at seven, maybe eight. It was obvious to me because I was already taller than Dr. Carroll and there was no resemblance, but at thirteen they decided to tell me. I acted surprised, shocked really, but I knew. They professed their love for me and reminded me all the time that despite everything I was their son. I suppose I loved them too, but Mrs. Carroll was different when Mr. Carroll wasn't around. She would say such hurtful things to me."

"Things like what?"

Carroll continued, "She would tell me that no woman would ever want me, and obviously it was true. After all, I was adopted. She'd make fun of me constantly. She called me names like loser, garbage, and so on. It turned out she wanted a daughter, but Mr. Carroll wanted a son, and he won out. He had big dreams for me. I had Michigan spirit all over my room, and my school uniform jacket always had a U of M pin in the lapel. It was too much, and that's more the reason I wanted to go west.

Robert then said, "Did you ever wonder who your real mother was?"

Carroll put his head to the wall and said, "No, not really. I assumed she was loose or maybe a prostitute. Who knew, and I didn't care."

Robert looked at Carroll and said, "I can assure you; she was none of those things."

Robert put the paper back into his pocket and asked, "Why the necklace?"

Carroll looked at him, "The women I killed deserved it. The necklace signified my wealth over their peasant bodies."

Robert asked, "You viewed them as less than you because?"

"Because of the way they treated me. I was nice to them, Robert, and they would talk down on me, just like Mrs. Carroll did!"

Robert leaned back and said, "Robert, please calm down. I'm sorry I've upset you."

Carroll sat back and calmed his breathing. Robert then asked, "I noticed that none of the women appeared to be sexually assaulted, yet you killed them. Usually the women are raped and then killed, but you would just kill them."

Before Carroll could answer, there was a knock at the door. Robert stood and opened it to see Miller and a squat older man wearing the finest suit he'd ever seen. The man said, "What in the hell is going on!"

Robert opened the door fully and the man saw Robert Carroll handcuffed sitting on a bunk. The man then said, "Who are you?"

Robert replied, "I'm Special Agent in Charge Robert Franklin. And you are?"

The man looked at Robert and then at Carroll and said, "I'm his attorney, and I'm confused!"

He looked at Carroll and said, "Don't say another word! He then looked at Miller, "I need a moment with my client!"

Robert stepped out and Miller closed the door. He and Robert moved down the hall to converse. Miller said, "That's Al Fontan."

Robert looked toward the cell and said, "As in Big Al Fontan? I thought he'd be taller. I mean, he looks taller on television."

Miller said, "I did some digging on your brother and I found that his net worth is two point one billion—with a b—dollars. He made his money developing software in the early eighties. He sold his ideas and now collects royalties for each program sold. According to his bank statements, he brought in roughly three hundred grand a month, and that amount doubled from last year when there was a software update released."

Robert looked down the hall again and said, "Listen, I need to make a call. Can you handle this?"

Miller said, "Yes, of course."

Robert hurried down the hall and into the elevator and then to his office. He closed the door and sat at his desk. He reached into his shirt pocket and brought out a note, dialed a number, and after four rings a man with a sleepy voice answered and said, "Hello, Mike Joseph here."

Robert sat back and said, "Mr. Joseph, this is Robert Franklin. I'm sorry for calling so early, but you left me a message. You have something to tell me?"

Robert sat and listened to Mr. Joseph and as each minute ticked on, Robert became more physically and mentally drained. Tears built in his eyes and the call ended. Minutes later the phone began to beep and continued until he hung up. He stood, went to his office windows, and closed the blinds. He fell to the floor and began to weep, which then turned to all-out crying. The office area began to fill, but no one went to the office where Special Agent in Charge Robert Franklin was now wailing. Stacey stood ten feet away wanting to console Robert, but she cannot.

After several hours Robert opened his door and made his way to the elevator. The chime sounded and the doors opened. Again, no one said a word. He pressed G for garage. He slid into the driver's seat, started the engine, but sat there. Minutes later he backed out and onto the street. He removed his pistol from the holster and placed it on the seat next to him. He removed his badge from his belt and placed it on the seat next to his pistol. He removed his wallet, opened the money slot, and fanned out two hundred and eighty-three dollars. His BlackBerry rang, so he removed it from his jacket pocket. He read "Jennifer Sanders" on the screen and he laid the phone on the seat. He reached below the center of the dash and brought up a light, placed it on the dash, and turned it on. The red light caused traffic to part as he made his way out of the city. Within an hour and a half, he's on Interstate 95 headed toward Philadelphia.

Chapter Forty: Thursday, May 6, 1999

Robert startled awake. His dreams were vivid as if he were living them in the moment. He wiped his face, leaned forward to turn on the dome light, and blinked numerous times while he focused and then looked at his watch. It is 04:36. He sat completely up and looked around. It appeared he's at a highway rest stop, but where?

He exited the vehicle and walked to the building, but before entering to use the facilities there's a map behind glass. He saw the "You Are Here" arrow and he smiled. Spartanburg, South Carolina, now he knew that in roughly two hours he will be in McCormick.

06:00, Brooklyn, New York

Jennifer Sanders woke and rolled to her right to look at the clock. She slowly got out of bed and walked to the kitchen, started the coffee pot, and then headed to the shower. It's now 6:30 and she set the hairdryer down and then ran her fingers through her hair. She went to the kitchen and poured a cup of coffee. She lifted her phone from the counter and flipped it open. No missed calls. She selected menu, recent calls, and pressed send. After four rings Robert answered and she said, "Good morning, love. How are you?"

"Hello love. To be honest, I'm numb. I've been driving all night and I should be in McCormick real soon."

Jennifer sat her coffee down and turned to the counter, placing her left hand down. She said, "Robert, are your parents

345

okay?"

Robert took the phone away from his ear for a moment and then replied, "Yes, I guess. I have to talk to them is all."

Jennifer replied, "You couldn't call them? That's a long drive just to talk."

"No, this is a conversation that requires a face to face."

"Honey tell me what's going on, please. You seem so withdrawn since capturing that man."

"When I get back, I need to put that ring back on your finger."

Jennifer looked at her left hand, "Robert, talk to me, please."

Robert closed his eyes briefly and said, "Love, I'll tell you everything when I'm back. I love you."

Robert ended the call. Jennifer looked at her phone and then closed it; she said, "I love you too."

06:30, Saratoga Springs, New York

Katie McCann slowly woke and saw a tall figure standing near her. She screamed, "NO! Get away from me!!!"

Richard McCann knelt beside her and said, "Katie, honey, it's me, Dad. It's okay."

Katie embraced her father and began to weep. RT stroked her hair and repeated over and over that it's okay. Deborah McCann entered the room with coffee and placed the tray on the dresser. She went to her daughter's side and she too hugged her and said, "Katie, it's okay dear, you're home now."

Katie slowly pushed away and looked at her parents. Both

are crying but smiling. Katie said, "Did they catch him?"

RT nodded and then stood to pour coffee. He turned and said, "The FBI agent that you pointed to, I guess the man is a dead ringer. He's in a cell now. Katie, we are so happy you are safe. I've been told it was a matter of minutes."

Deborah interrupted and said, "Katie dear, why don't you rest. Your father and I will be downstairs if needed."

Katie laid back into her pillow, looked out the window, and said, "Have you heard from Kevin?"

RT smiled and said, "Yes, and what a fine young man he is. He and your boss Jennifer and her fiancée will be here tomorrow to check on you, and if you're up for it, the FBI Agent would like to ask you a few questions."

Katie looked at her father and said, "I cannot wait to finish school and move here full time. I don't want to be in the city any longer than I have to be."

Deborah looked at RT and said, "Your father and I couldn't agree more. As a matter of fact, for your last year of school, Jimmy will be in the shadows to ensure your safety."

Katie sat up, "When you say shadows, will Kevin and I have some privacy?"

RT laughed, "Yes, of course dear." He then winked at his wife.

RT and Deb left Katie's room closing the door within two inches of closed.

06:45, Jennifer's Office

Jennifer sat at her desk, raised both arms shoulder height, and shook them. She then reached forward and turned on her computer monitor. She opened the deposition and began to read. Moments later Kevin stood in the doorway and he said, "Good morning, boss."

Jennifer is startled, "Kevin! Good morning."

The two laughed and Kevin replied, "I'm looking forward to seeing Katie tomorrow. Oh, and we'll finally meet that mystery man of yours."

"Yes, seeing Katie will be nice, that poor girl, but Robert won't be joining us. He's tied up, so maybe next week sometime?"

"Well, did you find a place to stay?"

"Yes, but I changed to a hotel. After all, I don't want to stay at a quant B&B without Robert."

"Oh, that's too bad he won't be joining us. What time are you leaving?"

Jennifer looked at Kevin and said, "I hope to be on the road around 5:00, maybe 6:00 p.m. This case I'm, we're working on, has heated up. It turned out the super is the owner of the building, a Robert Carroll, and he feels our client did break her ankle, but not at his building because the steps are fine. He's countersuing, yes, countersuing for defamation of character. He also feels the woman has been incredibly rude to him, which has caused him emotional stress. The nerve of some people."

"The world we live in." He walked out and back to his desk.

Jennifer's desk phone rings and she answered, "Jennifer Sanders."

A man's voice said, "Yeah, Ms. Sanders, this is Al Fontan.

I represent Robert Carroll, and he will be tied up for a bit and we've decided to settle, to avoid going to trial, so what's a broken ankle worth today?"

Jennifer is awestruck and stood. She replied, "Hello Mr. Fontan, thank you for the call. You weren't listed as counsel on this case."

Al Fontan replied, "Yeah, I know, I usually handle much bigger cases for my client, but like I said, we'd like to settle. If we agree on the settlement, I'll have the money brought by carrier this afternoon. So, again, what's a broken ankle worth today?"

Jennifer wrote a number on a piece of paper, stared at it to ensure it made sense, and said in a very confident tone, "Well, sir, I feel a broken ankle is worth three hundred and twenty-five thousand dollars."

Jennifer bit her lip and Al Fontan said, "Done! I'll have the money brought to your office by 2:30 p.m.!"

He hung up, and Jennifer was briefly frozen. She sat in her chair and then snapped out of it and called her client. She paused and started to second guess the amount. Was it too much? Most cases were half of that. Then she shook her head and dialed.

08:45 Lucile's, McCormick, SC

Robert took a final drink from his cup, laid a ten-dollar bill on the table, stood, and walked out. He stood on the sidewalk and looked both ways up and down the street. He stepped forward and within a few minutes he was standing at the steps of his parents' home. As tears built, he wiped them. The front door opened followed by the screen door. His mother stepped out and said, "Robert, it was always a matter of time before you learned the truth. It's been haunting me for forty-three years, which led to more drinking, but when Lisa Marie died, I celebrated."

Robert climbed the stairs and then knelt. He's now weeping and said, "How could you celebrate the death of your daughter?"

Marilynn placed her hand on his head and said:

"I never loved Lisa Marie. I always felt she was more of a burden to us all. When she died it was a like a house had been lifted from me."

Robert looked to Marilynn and said, "Why couldn't you tell me she was my mother?"

Marilynn sat on a chair and began to cry, "We knew that Lisa Marie would never be a good mother to you, Robert."

Robert then said, "Did you know I have a brother!? Yes, he looked just like me, same hair, same eyes, same everything, Marilynn!"

Marilynn looked out to the street and said, "Robert, in those days if a woman had children out of wedlock it was frowned upon, and with your father being the pastor, we had to keep it hidden, so we took Lisa Marie out of school and told everyone she was staying with relatives up state to help raise children. I recalled my growth during my first pregnancy and did my best to look as though I was with child. Before too long, I essentially stayed in the house until Lisa Marie had you—and your brother—but we had not planned on twins, so we arranged an adoption to a nice family from Michigan."

"Yes, Dr. Robert Carroll."

"We never knew their names, but we were told he was going to a good home and that's all that mattered."

Robert replied in anger, "Well, Marilynn, he didn't go to a good home. Turned out his mother, much like you with Lisa Marie, never wanted the boy! He was treated like garbage, and he became angry against women!"

Marilynn looked at Robert with a puzzled look and replied, "Robert, why are you telling me this?"

Robert began to weep and said, "Because the boy that you abandoned, my brother, is the man that I've been chasing for all these years. Yes, my brother the serial killer. My twin brother, he's a murdering animal because you and dad, or grandpa, I don't know, decided he wasn't wanted. He's sitting in a cell right now. Do you have any idea what I'm feeling right now? Do you have a clue how emotionally draining this is? I've had a brother, but not a brother that became a doctor, a lawyer, a Wall Street executive. My brother kills women that are mean to him!"

Robert fell to the porch floor and was sobbing uncontrollably. He felt a hand on his shoulder and opened his eyes to see John Jr. standing above him. John Jr. said, "Hey little brother."

Robert stood and John Jr. hugged him. They cry, and then Robert said, "I need to know the truth about who my father is. All these years I've called him Dad, and he's not. I need to know!"

The door opened and John Sr. stepped out, letting the screen door slap closed. Robert turned to him and said, "Tell me the truth; tell me now!"

John Sr. replied, "I'm your father."

Marilynn stood, "No, John, don't."

John Sr. looked at her and replied, "It's okay, Marilynn."

John Jr. replied, "Mom, Dad, what is going on here?"

John Sr. sat in a rocking chair and stared at the side street.

Robert said, again, "Tell the truth! What really happened!?"

John Sr. wiped tears from his face and said, "A woman from the church came to your mother and me saying she was pregnant and that her husband had left her. She would not be able to keep the baby. We longed for another child, and God brought this woman to us, so we gladly accepted. On June 4, 1941, Lisa Marie was born. She was a lovely baby. She smiled all the time, never made a fuss, just a pleasant baby. But as she grew older, she became a handful and a temptation for many boys in McCormick. The summer she turned fifteen was the hardest summer I will ever recall."

Marilynn screamed, "John, please stop this!!!"

"No, you will not stop. Tell me the truth!"

John Sr. continued, "Lisa Marie became a woman overnight. Her long auburn hair, her body became more lady like, and she met a boy from Oklahoma. She gave herself to him."

Robert replied, "Keep going, and tell the truth!"

John Sr. looked at Robert and then John Jr., who was frozen as his father went on, "It was a hot August night and the Joseph boys had been coming around all day. They'd leave to tend to the hardware and then came back that night. Their car parked right there."

John Sr. pointed to the curb and then said, "Lisa Marie stood right there. She had on short pants and a shirt tied up exposing her midsection. She flirted with those boys and eventually she

352

left with them, Tom, Mike and Lump…they just left."

"Keep going, tell us the truth!"

John Sr. looked at Marilynn, "I brought Marilynn into the house and John Jr. and I went looking for Lisa Marie."

John Jr. said, "I remember we drove around, and I had fallen asleep in the back seat. We came home and a few minutes later Lisa Marie came home, nearly naked, muddied, and bleeding."

Robert looked at John Jr. and then back to John Sr. and said, "Keep going!"

John Sr. looked at the porch floor and said, "I found her; she was at McCormick Lake. It appeared the Joseph boys had taken advantage of her. She was naked, standing on the lake shore."

Robert then screamed, "But they didn't take advantage of her, did they? DID THEY!"

John Sr. looked at Robert, "No son, they did not."

John Jr. replied, "Who did then, Father? Please God, no!"

Marilynn began to weep, and John Sr. replied, "I've never been a perfect man. I have my weaknesses just like any other man, and when I saw her standing alone and vulnerable, I took advantage of her. She had no idea it was me at first. I found a log and hit her on the back of the head. She spun around and said, 'Daddy, why?'

"She went out and I removed my pants, laid them on the hood of the car, and I…"

Robert again screamed, "You what? You did what?!"

John Sr. started to blubber and said, "I raped her, not once, but twice."

Marilynn began to weep uncontrollably, and John Jr. fell to the porch. Robert then said, "But that's not all. What did you do next?"

John Sr. stayed silent, and Robert said, "I'll tell you what you didn't know. When you were raping Lisa Marie, the Joseph boys were watching you and doing all they could to keep Lump quiet. You finished, put your pants back on, put Lisa Marie on the hood of the car, and drove off! You drove a while and found a dirt road. You turned very fast onto that road and Lisa Marie fell off. You stopped the car, got out, checked her, and you thought she was dead, which is what you wanted, right?"

John Sr. is motionless as he stared at Robert. Robert continued, "You backed onto the asphalt and left her there to die, but what you didn't know is that Tom Joseph was following you. He turned to where Lisa Marie lay, and he and Mike picked her up and laid her in the back seat with Lump. Mike told how Lump cried the entire time. He was holding Lisa Marie and asking her to wake up. She finally did and then Tom Joseph drove Lisa Marie to that corner."

Robert pointed to where John Jr. was looking moments ago.

"Lisa Marie then walked to the front porch and crawled into the house...surprise! She didn't die, so now what? You tried convincing her that it was Lump Joseph and that's when you hit her. You meant to hit Lump...another lie! Lisa Marie became pregnant and then you finally confess your sin to Marilynn, but she loves you, till death do you part. The two of you come up with a plan to keep this home wholesome, to avoid tarnishing the pastor of McCormick Baptist Church. The small town with a big secret!"

Suddenly there are South Carolina State Troopers parked in front of the house. Marilynn stood and said, "No Robert, you can't do this! Robert please, no!!!"

Robert then said, "John Franklin, you are under the arrest for the rape and attempted murder of Lisa Marie Franklin. You have the right to remain silent; anything you say can and will be used against you in a court of law. Do you understand your rights as I've read them to you?"

John Sr. looked at Robert and in a split second he produced a small handgun. He put the handgun in his mouth and pulled the trigger. John Sr.'s head fell back, and his arms dropped; he was now motionless. Marilynn ran to his side, screaming.

She looked at Robert, who was crying, and said, "Look what you've done! Look what you've done!"

State troopers swarmed the porch and cleared the weapon. They pulled Marilynn from her husband. Robert turned to John Jr. and said, "I'm sorry."

John Jr. just stared at him as he walked down the stairs. Soon Robert is leaning against his Crown Victoria. The sounds of sirens filled the air. It's total chaos, but Robert is motionless.

Chapter Forty-One: Friday, December 22, 2000

Special Agent in Charge Robert Franklin placed a framed photo back on his desk. He's with Jennifer and their new baby girl, affectionately named after his mother, Lisa Marie. He then lifted an envelope from his desk with "White House" as the return address. He removed a letter opener from his top desk drawer. A knock on the door interrupted him and he said, "Come in."

The door opened and it's Stacey. She said, "Hello, sir, sorry to bother you, but you have a letter that requires a signature."

Stacey handed Robert the clipboard and letter and he signed, *Robert Franklin.*

He waved to the carrier and then said, "Thank you, Stacey."

Robert opened the cardboard envelope and inside that is a manila envelope addressed to Robert James Franklin. It's from Robert James Carroll. Robert opened the envelope and removed its contents, a one-page letter and a cashier's check. He laid the check on the desk and began to read the letter.

Dear Robert,

It seems strange to start a letter with my first name, especially since the letter will go to the better twin. I wanted to first say I'm happy for you and Jennifer. I received the photo of you and her with Lisa Marie. I've also wanted to thank you for the photos of our mother; she was a beautiful woman. Maybe one day we'll learn of who our father is, but for now it's important for me to stay on point.

I had never imagined my life would turn out like this. I

guess it's true what they say, "Money can't buy happiness." That reminds me, the enclosed check is my way of saying congratulations on your wedding and the baby, and I hope the amount given will only add to your happiness.

Robert looked at the check again, but this time his eyes widened, and he stood smacking his forehead. He then sat to continue reading.

My whole life I wanted to be loved; I wanted acceptance. My adopted mother showed displeasure toward me when Dr. Carroll wasn't around. Dr. Carroll was a great man, but died when I was sixteen, and Mrs. Carroll moved us to San Francisco where she did her best to manage a jewelry store. I saw how excited she became when those pearl necklaces arrived. All I could think of was hurting her, so I stole them, as well as high-end time pieces and gold. Later, the necklaces became my calling card, if you will. She was devastated, but I didn't care, and to add to her pain, the jewelry store owner had let the insurance lapse, and eventually the store went out of business. I sold the jewelry items I didn't want and well, the rest is, for lack of better wording, history.

Again, I am truly sorry for what I've done, and I wish that we had been together growing up in McCormick, South Carolina.

Yours truly,
Robert James Carroll

The End

"McCormick"

A Small Southern Town with a Big Secret

By

Raymond R. Mann

McCormick Synopsis

Robert Franklin knew early on in his life that he was destined for more than McCormick, South Carolina had to offer. 1976 Was the year He entered San Francisco State University to study Criminal Law. After graduation and the academy, he began his career with the Federal Bureau of Investigations – Los Angeles, California.

By 1986 Robert Franklin became supervisory special agent. He and his team spent countless man hours looking for the serial killer known as the Pearl Necklace Killer – his victims were brutally murdered, and his calling card was always the same, a pearl necklace he would place on his victims necks.

1999 became the turning point for Robert Franklin not only his career, but his personal life too. Working out of 26 Federal Plaza as special agent in charge, planning the engagement to his longtime girlfriend Jennifer Sanders and a family secret that would shake him to the core.

BIO - Raymond R. Mann

 Raymond (Ray) R. Mann is Veteran of the United States Army and has spent more than 28 years in the automotive industry. He holds a Master of Science from Kettering University, Flint, MI. Ray has always had a creative side but chasing corporate success took priority over most of his life and he set aside all else. The past few years Ray began writing as a means of escaping the corporate grind and started numerous books of varying genres, but he soon found his desire for suspense became priority and McCormick is his first published work.

.

Made in the USA
Monee, IL
12 March 2023

29725409R00215